FALLING FROM THE NEST

FALLING FROM THE NEST

THE SISTERS OF GREEN TREE

BOBBIE CANDAS

CONTENTS

AN EXCERPT FROM THE LOST AND FOUND OF GREEN TREE
Bobbie Candas

Falling From the Nest

The Sisters of Green Tree

Book cover design by Betty Martinez

ISBN 9798336035735

For Mehmet Candas
My Johnny Appleseed

CHAPTER 1

GOING UP?

JO-JO ANDERSON

Spring, 1946, Manhattan, NY

She walked away, high-heeling down 45th. Once she turned her back, I watched her go. Head held high and confident, shiny auburn hair topped by a stylish, angled hat, shoulder pads emphasizing strong shoulders, a slim waistline, and a most decided stride. A woman who knew where she was going and was out to get it. There was little doubt in my frightened mind. Out of the seven-and-a-half-million people living in New York City, I'd just run into the only person I could have possibly known...my former kidnapper, a lady I had once called Mother. She appeared not to have recognized me, but somehow, even after twelve years, I knew it was Nanette Jorgenson.

~

THE LAST OF the audition line moved forward and I was suddenly thrust up on the stage of the Imperial Theater. There were three lines of ten on stage, filled with nervous male and female hopefuls auditioning for chorus line spots for a new Irving Berlin musical,

Annie Get Your Gun. I could smell my fear as it branched out within me in tingling connections from my frozen face down to my feet. Feet that now felt like dead weights attached to heeled dance shoes whose soles were glued to the floor. I'd arrived late and was in the last group of an open-call audition and purposely nudged myself into the center of the middle line, hoping for a hiding spot. But hiding is hard when you're a leggy, five-foot-nine, pale blonde female in a string of short, muscular dancers. Kinda like a spotted giraffe among the lions.

After lining up, our executioner and choreographer took about sixty seconds to show us a dozen linking steps to an opening dance sequence. His arrogant face, slim body, and searching eyes leaned back appraising the lines. "OK, boys and girls, this one's simple. Think you got it?" Everyone around me anxiously nodded yes.

No, I wanted to shout. Repeat please!

The orchestra in the pit began cranking out a tune, as the choreographer yelled out…"And a one, and a two--knee up, kick left, circle back, hop, hop, knee up, kick right…" Then he motioned for the music to stop.

An exasperated expression covered his face. "Ladies and gentlemen, these are the basics, the *easy* connections. Let's start again on three. And a one, and a two--knee up, kick left, circle back, hop, hop…" He stuck his arm out, motioning again for the music to stop.

"Alright, first cuts." His long arm and dismissive finger pointed to the guilty dancers. "Tall blonde, center middle row, thank you. You…guy on the end, first row, that will be all. Back row, green sweater, left side, you may leave."

He sighed deeply, clapped his hands, and said. "Let's go again, cue music…repeat."

So that was it. Like a river, relief flowed through me as I did the walk of shame, clicking my way off the stage, tunneling through the dark halls to the back door of the theater. Within a few quick minutes, I'd suffered through my first Broadway audition and failed miserably. But what had I expected? I was tight, hadn't stretched or exercised in days, was nervous as hell, and on top of all that, I'd experienced the shock of my life seeing Nanette Jorgenson standing near me, as she yelled at her male client who happened to be in the audition line next to me.

The humiliated guy had called her Fran. Her blond hair was now an auburn, and her beauty was in some way touched with a harder edge, but I was pretty convinced it was Nanette. I arrived in Manhattan only eighteen hours ago. It could only go up from here.

I thought.

Wearing my shroud of humiliation, I scurried back to my simple room at the massive Dixie Hotel near Times Square. For twenty dollars a week, I had a bed, my own bathroom, and a radio. I pulled out *The Times* classifieds, purchased last night after arriving at Penn Station. Because a top choreographer had just informed me that I was *not* a prime candidate for Broadway, I decided to zero in on more easily attainable positions.

After days of interviewing, I tried marching up and down 8th Avenue and 49th Street wearing a heavy sandwich-board promoting the latest sporting events and performances at Madison Square Gardens. I stopped pedestrians, handed out flyers, and offered details about events. I had no idea why this job was listed in the classified's entertainers section, but I managed to do it for six weeks before my shoulders gave out. During my weeks of trudging up and down the busy sidewalks, I learned a few things: how to pick out the rubes and tourists from the regulars, perfect my ability to chat up strangers to a fine art, and how to take rejection.

Moving on, I attempted an eight-hour stint as an exotic dancer. When I applied, I envisioned exotic dancing as performing in veils and pantaloons with music provided by a colorful Arabian band, but I became less enamored when I learned the job involved wearing a skimpy costume with faceted beading sewn on in a few vital places, which became almost no costume at all after midnight. At two AM, I left the exotic dancer profession with ten dollars in my pocket. I liked the money but not the grasping hands.

An usher's position at Radio City Music Hall was next. But the lure of watching free performances while directing people to their seats with a flashlight, didn't pay enough to cover my weekly tab at The Dixie. After several more audition attempts, I recalled the words of the guy manning the Penn Station newsstand right after arriving from Green Tree. Just by glancing at me, he guessed I was new in town, hoping to make my mark on Broadway.

He warned me, saying, "Kid, it's a rough business. Take my advice, Iowa. Go see a few shows, ride the ferry, visit the Statue of Liberty, then go home. Save yourself the heartbreak."

SIX MONTHS LATER...

WHILE STARING through raindrops racing down the smudged windows of the Stage Deli, I was startled by impatient, snapping fingers begging for my attention. I'd been looking at the long line of well-dressed patrons curling around the block of Carnegie Hall. They were patiently waiting, with umbrellas open, to buy tickets to some amazing performance I'd never see.

"Hey you...doll-face." I looked over in Snappy Finger's direction. "Two grilled sky-highs on rye and two black coffees. We're in a hurry."

Ok, you grumpy, fat bastards. I pulled out a pad and pencil from my apron pocket and looked down at two burly men wearing pinstriped, double breasted suits with tacky wide ties. I flashed a smile, held back my real thoughts, and asked, "Mustard, mayonnaise, or both?" And added sweetly, "And how about a dill pickle on the side?"

"Yeah, all the above, doll. Just get it ordered, *quick*. Oh, and bring us a couple black-n-whites too."

"You got it handsome."

I turned, walking quickly down the tight row of wooden tables at the busy deli and called out my order to the cook behind the grill. "Hey, Chuckles! Two sky-highs, m-and- m, with a dill...and no rush, take your time with those."

The short-order cook, a balding, older man with a low tolerance for fools and a sucker for a friendly smile, called out, "No problem, Jo-Jo."

4

I poured the two cups of coffee and slid two large round cookies with chocolate and vanilla icing onto small plates. Six months ago, I would have been intimidated by those two men and their fancy suits. But now I knew they were only low-level number runners who wore the same cheap suit every day, except maybe on Sunday when, hopefully, they got them cleaned. I'd seen and learned a lot in the last six months.

Back at Snappy Finger's table, I purposely leaned over, balancing my tray. "Gentlemen, your coffee and black-n-whites." I set their cups and cookies down and said, "I told the cook to put a rush on those sandwiches. Seems to be a little backed up at the grill though." I then turned around and bussed the table beside them, stretching over to wipe it down, giving them a full view of my back side. I lived off tips. I'd learned what I had to do.

Tips were nice, but none of the hustling had allowed me to grab a toehold into some aspect of the entertainment business. After the war ended and the world began regaining a sense of normalcy, I naively thought I could easily show up on the sidewalks of midtown Manhattan's theater district and high-kick and tap my way into the limelight.

Before leaving home, I'd cobbled together about two month's worth of survival money, gingerly spending it while I tried to find my golden ticket. When the money ran out, the waitress job at the Stage Deli seemed an obvious choice. As much as I hated to admit defeat, my options were sleeping on the street, going home to Green Tree, or start waitressing.

The Stage Deli was strategically located on Seventh Avenue, which at least put me within spitting distance of movers and shakers in show biz. Initially, I foolishly hoped some stage director would glance up from his menu and declare, 'You have just the look we've been searching for. I don't suppose you sing and dance too?'

I'd had no takers. This part of Manhattan was littered with unemployed actors, entertainers, and musicians--all waiting for their next gig or big break. Looks didn't hurt, but casting directors wanted the whole package. And I now realized my training from the Green Tree High School drama department, with some dance classes on the side, had sorely prepared me for my highly anticipated debut.

While bussing tables and refilling cups, I heard the ding of Chuckle's bell. "Order up, Jo-Jo!" Unbuttoning the top two buttons of my uniform, I scurried over to pick up the two pastrami sandwiches and brought them to my thuggy-suited customers.

"So sorry for that wait, guys, but so worth it. Best sandwiches in town! You boys enjoy." I leaned down again, pushing the meaty sandwiches across the table. "Can I get you a warm-up on those coffees?" They both just nodded their heads, staring at my slightly exposed cleavage. "Well, alright then. I'll be right back."

I didn't feel bad using what little resources I had. It was all acting for me. I was simply playing a part, auditioning for my big break, and they ended up leaving me a buck tip on a three dollar tab. For now, I could live with that.

I generally worked the lunch to early evening shift so I could still get to some morning auditions, but as the months ticked away, I was becoming disheartened and my only cheerleader was my twin sister attending school back in Iowa. Her weekly letters of encouragement had kept me from buying a return ticket to Green Tree more than a few times.

The only stage I'd performed on was the Ebb Tide, a bar located within The Dixie Hotel. Most nights there was a five-piece band, featuring a female singer, crowded in on a corner stage. I was drawn downstairs by their music often, nursing a single drink while watching the band perform. One night, their singer, Dottie, was down with a cough and I nervously offered the band leader my singing services for free. I'd already memorized most of their standards.

He shrugged, looked out at the sparse audience of fifteen, and said, "Sure kid, we'll give it a go. Wha-daya-say, we start with one song and *I* decide if there'll be a second number."

My nervous rendition of *Chattanooga Choo-Choo* was decent enough to get me to the second tune, *In The Mood*. I began to calm down and relax enough to flow with the band's loose rhythm, easing my way into singing slightly behind the beat. When the band packed it up around one AM, the band leader, Slim, gave me five bucks, and added, "Kid, you done real good. Check back tomorrow and step in if Dottie don't make it." I was thrilled.

The next night, I put on my only decent dress, something my grandmother made me before I left home. I was sitting at the bar drinking water, when Dottie walked up to the band. When she found out I'd replaced her the previous evening, she came over to the bar, ordered a gin and tonic, and said, "Forget it, Blondie. This is my gig and no young gun's taking it from me."

Now, each time I stepped into the Ebb Tide to watch, Dottie gave me the cold shoulder. Even jobs like this were highly sought after.

~

A FEW WEEKS LATER, I was counting down the minutes for my shift to end. It was Wednesday, and it felt like every person working in Midtown had dropped in that day and every damn one had been in a hurry. My feet were throbbing. Growing up on a farm, I was used to hard work, but today felt especially brutal.

My replacement had still not shown up, as three young guys grabbed a table in my section. They looked too young to be decent tippers, but I knew I couldn't leave until Shirley clocked in. I handed them each a menu and asked for their drink selections. I noticed that one of the guys kept staring at me. He was nice looking, with big brown eyes, and a wavy, thick head of dark hair.

As I returned with water glasses, the guy said, "Hey, I remember you. I never forget a face. Especially that face."

I smiled at the compliment and gave him a long, questioning look.

"You're from Iowa, right?" I nodded. "Remember, months ago? We were both waiting at the end of the audition line...*Annie Get Your Gun*? Man, I was decimated that morning...so hung over. My agent, Fran, almost killed me for arriving so late."

Once he mentioned his agent, the memory came flooding back. "Yes...of course! I remember now. That was my second day in town. Fresh off the farm." I laughed recalling my actual audition. "I had no idea what I was doing. The choreographer cut me about a minute into my try-out. How'd you end up doing?"

"Believe it or not, I got a part. All three of us," he said pointing to the two other guys. We're all in the chorus line, but I'm an understudy too."

"Impressive. Congrats!" Just then Shirley, my sub, walked up to me looking frazzled, her mousey-brown hair pulled back in a messy ponytail.

"Hey Jo-Jo. Sorry I'm running late. I'll take over from here if you like."

"Gladly. My dogs are barking today." I looked back at the three guys at the table. "Hey, you guys mind if I join you for a minute? I'd love to hear more about the show and any advice you could share."

One of the other guys pushed out the fourth chair from the table with his foot. "Sure babe. Join us."

CHAPTER 2
BARS AND BOYS
SARAH ANDERSON

University of Iowa, Iowa City 1946

*M*y roommate, Barbara, and three other girls from our floor, had talked me into joining them for a Saturday evening out. The girls had curled their shoulder-length hair, smeared their mouths with bold red lipstick, added touches of mascara, all doing their best to imitate the style of popular Hollywood favorites like Lauren Bacall or Veronica Lake. Beyond washing my face, I did no additional muss or fuss. I wasn't going there to impress anybody.

We'd walked over together to the Hawkeye Hut--a campus favorite. It was a long, dank, dark bar on Clinton Street near the campus. The five of us crowded into our wooden booth, nursing our mugs of beer. It wasn't long before the girls' relentless chatter began driving me crazy. They were currently discussing the physical merits of a few guys standing out of earshot, leaning against the bar.

Barbara, our ring leader, said, "Now that tall drink of water in the letter jacket...he's just my type. I wonder if he lettered in necking? That would be something to cheer about."

They giggled, they cooed, they joked. Even Emily, a small, quiet girl from our hall joined in. "Yeah Barb, I agree. I'd go parking with him and wouldn't mind getting a ticket or two." Again, her comment was followed by howls of laughter.

They were well into their second round of drinks and all I could think about were things I'd rather be doing. Why go out and spend what little money I had on beer and listen to conversations with girls who didn't have a thought in their heads beyond finding a boyfriend? I'd listened to enough of their silly banter.

Barbara leaned over. "Sarah, the guy on the end, the one with glasses, he's gotta be your type. Cute but studious... and he looks like he's all by himself. Go introduce yourself." She nudged me as the other girls laughed. "Have some fun for a change."

I shook my head and glanced his way. "What's the point? You know Tommy's my boyfriend." This outing was an annoying waste of time and the one beer I'd allowed myself had gone flat and warm. Glancing down at my watch, I said, "In fact, I really need to get back to the room. You girls have a good evening."

Barbara looked exasperated. "Already, Sarah? We've been here less than an hour."

Scooting out one of the other girls, I stood up from the booth, and left my twenty-cent contribution to the tab. "I'm heading back... I have a career to study for."

Barbara and the others rolled their eyes. "So do we. That's why we're here." This was followed by more giggles.

Passing the boys, I leaned over to the tall guy they'd been sighing over and said, "Hey, the gal in that booth over there, in the tight purple sweater, she's got the hots for you. You should go over and make her night." Then I turned, flouncing my long dark braid and left the smelly old bar. I liked being direct. Why waste time?

Once back at Currier Hall, I checked my mailbox. Two letters! I was excited. Receiving mail from friends and family was one of the few highlights of my week. I dropped them into my cardigan pocket and noticed the silent lobby and stillness of the dorm hallways, so often full of noisy shrieks, chatter, and music. But Saturday nights were often like this ... quiet. Most of the girls had either gone out or went home for the weekend. Unfortunately, Green Tree was a costly five-hour bus ride away, so I usually spent my weekends here or at the library studying. Tonight would be a perfect time to relish my two letters in privacy.

I entered room 221. Two beds, two desks, and one window. Barbara and I each had a small space and two shelves for hanging and folding our limited wardrobes. Over Barbara's bed, the wall was filled with Hawkeye pennants, a large family portrait, her diploma from a Des Moines high school, and photos of friends. Several months in, my wall had yet to be adorned. I hadn't thought to bring any decorations and hadn't collected any while I was here.

In Green Tree, attending college was considered a big accomplishment. I was now a sophomore on scholarship and never took that honor for granted. I'd crafted my future with a deliberate plan and refused to allow for any derailments or deviations. The plan included earning a teaching certificate in secondary education, followed by getting my masters in educational administration. Upon returning to Green Tree, I would get a job at the high school and probably marry Tommy Martin. He was my oldest and best friend in the world, with the exception of my sister, Jo.

Actually, I was worried about her. In Jo's last letter, she'd seemed quite discouraged. Not like herself at all. I hoped my motivational response had helped buoy her spirits. She was so talented. Since her move to Manhattan months ago, I was really surprised she hadn't landed at least a small part on a radio program, joined a chorus line, or even a part on off-off-Broadway. I was positive something would break her way soon. I opened her new letter with anticipation.

Darling Sarah,

Still on the dean's list! I'm so proud of you. Congratulations! I should have studied more in high school cause this crazy job choice I'm chasing is kicking me sideways. Thankfully, tips at the deli are getting better each week. I'm starting to get a lot of regulars at my tables and learned a few tricks, turning their dimes into dollars. So, I'm still keeping a roof over my head at The Dixie and have a little extra for incidentals, but Manhattan isn't cheap!

I did have a bit of a breakthrough the other day, running into a handsome hunk named Damien Jones. He's a hoofer and understudy on Annie Get Your

Gun--a big musical! It's been open a few months now and getting lots of press. Anyway, Damien and I have gone out twice and he knows lots of people in the biz. So hopefully, I'll make a few connections through him, and if not, he's pretty fun to kiss! Don't blush, Sarah. We're grown women now and allowed to do those things.

Speaking of kissing, how's Tommy and life on the Martin farm? I bet you miss him so much. You haven't mentioned him in your last few letters. Is everything still good between you two? I was always envious. You two were so close. Anyway, update me in your next letter. Hopefully, I can take some time off during one of your breaks. I need some sister time!

Much love always, your big sister,

Jo-Jo

Big sister--that always made me giggle. She was six minutes older than me and always loved claiming the title. I was glad though; this letter sounded a little more optimistic than her last one. And now also my letter from Tommy! It had probably been three weeks since I'd heard from him, but since attending college, I'd discovered that boys were not great letter writers. My stepfather, David, and little brother, Sam, rarely wrote to me, and when they did, David's letters offered up crop margins, news of seed trials, and additional acreage purchases. Sammy, who was still writing with crayons, loved telling me about calves being birthed, or sent me drawings of him on his dad's tractor.

I looked over the simple white envelope containing Tommy's letter, extending the pleasurable anticipation, admiring his bold print of my address. Tommy Martin…we'd been childhood friends since my mother and I had lived on his father's farm years ago. After my dad died in a terrible accident, Mom was hired on as cook, housekeeper, and caretaker of Tommy and his two older brothers. Their mother had eventually passed away, due to TB. He was six and I was five, and he became my closest friend and protector for years.

Our family eventually moved on, but I was heartbroken leaving the Martin farm and Tommy behind. So, Mother made a promise to me and stuck to it, driving me over to the Martin farm for weekly visits which continued from early grade school through high school.

Now, away at college, I often thought of him and our future together. I'd teach, and he'd continue farming. But there was time to decide all those details when I graduated and moved back.

I tore open Tommy's letter with excitement, knowing I'd read it several times over before the next one arrived.

> *Dearest Sarah,*
>
> *This letter will perhaps take you by surprise. It kind of surprises me even while I'm writing it. I think you know I wasn't absolutely sure about sticking with farming. Well, once Ely returned from the army, Dad offered to rent him the northern section of our acreage, and that got me to thinking. Sarah, it's time for me to try something new. I've signed up with the U.S. Navy for a three-year stint. Who knows how I'll feel about things after that? Maybe it could be a career for me. Just not sure. But I figure it's the best way for me to learn new skills and see the world at the same time. Dad seems to think it's a fine idea. I know a lot about farming, but not much else.*
>
> *You inspired me, Sarah, to look beyond Green Tree and challenge myself. You were always looking forward and knew what you wanted. I've never really known. Perhaps the navy will help me make those decisions. Remember how we joked about marrying some day? I certainly never expected you to wait for me. I'm sure there are lots of college boys clamoring for your attention! But let's always remain friends and pen pals.*
>
> *I'm taking a train to San Francisco for basic training for six weeks and will ship out to the islands of Hawaii and possibly Japan. Can you imagine that? A farmer in the middle of the Pacific Ocean. Ha Ha! Anyway, I'll be thinking of you fondly.*
>
> *Your friend,*
>
> *Tom*

Pen-pals?... Don't wait for me?... Your fond friend?... I turned off my light. My eyes were burning as the tears began. Thankfully, Barbara was still out and no one would need to know. How could this have happened? The US Navy had never been part of our plan. We'd talked about it, hadn't we? I would teach and then join the school's administration and work my way up. Tommy would be there for me, cheering me on. And I would do the same for him. Stable, helpful, loving Tommy. If not farming, why couldn't he work at a store, maybe the post office, try a career in banking? There were so many other professions out there. Why the darn navy? And why thousands of miles from me?

I curled up in a ball and pulled the covers over my head muffling animal sounds of despair I'd never heard before. The howls upset me so much that they were followed by an overwhelming urge to vomit as I made a run down the hall to the communal bathroom. I raced into a stall and threw up. None of this was part of the plan.

CHAPTER 3
FAMILIAR STRANGERS
JO-JO

*W*hile leaning against the counter of the Stage Deli, I scanned the entertainment section of the classifieds while taking quick bites of my favorite sandwich. I was munching down on all four inches of a crunchy sesame roll, filled with delicious tuna, creamy mayonnaise, tomato, tart pickles and chopped walnuts--so good. After each bite, I'd wipe the excess off my mouth with a thick napkin, knowing Damien was swinging by to pick me up shortly. It was five o'clock, another waitress had just taken over my section, and I was busy taking full advantage of my one free sandwich a day.

Between bites of sandwich, I took sips of grape soda, while Chuckles, our cook, glanced across the counter at me. "That just ain't right Jo-Jo; good tuna washed down with grape soda? Crimes against humanity, that's what that is. Hey, anything happening with auditions lately?"

I looked up from the Times. "Chucky, trust me. You'd be the first to hear about it." After circling a few classified ads, I added, "I do have two that I'll try to make. A Roger's and Hammerstein production, *Allegro*, and the other is *Finian's Rainbow*. Fingers crossed," I said without enthusiasm.

"A looker like you; something's gonna happen. You wait and see."

"Thanks, but it's been a lot more waiting than seeing since I got here. But…I'm not giving up. I probably need a good agent. You know anybody?"

"Nah, never have time to mix with the public back here, but I'll ask around. I got a few contacts. So you're a singer, right?"

I took my last bite of sandwich and nodded, then wiped my mouth again. "I dance too. Tap, jazz, contemporary. But I probably need more lessons. Competition is stiff here."

"Heart of the world, babe. Best of the best."

Then our boss, Max Asnas, who always lorded over the register and telephone at the end of the counter, yelled down to us. "Jo-Jo, quit distracting Chuckles. He's got orders up."

We both grimaced while I folded my newspaper and grabbed a few peppermints from the bowl by the register. "Thanks, Chuckles. Hey, if a guy comes in asking for me, I'm in the back changing."

"New boyfriend?"

"Early days yet. We'll see."

Then he hit his bell. "One grilled liverwurst on rye…order up."

I squeezed into a corner of the storeroom in the back, stepping over bags of onions and potatoes. I yanked off my soiled uniform and pulled on my street clothes; a pair of wide-legged, high-waisted denim dungarees with side buttons, and a fitted striped knit top. I entered the tiny employees' bathroom and brushed my wavy, blond hair back behind my ears and adjusted a white sailor's cap at a jaunty angle. I'd picked up the pants and hat at the Army-Navy Surplus for a buck-fifty and pulled together what I considered the perfect chic, nautical outfit. After washing up, I popped the peppermint candy in my mouth, checked my lipstick, and walked back to the dining room.

As I stepped up to the counter, I saw Damien wolfing down a Danish. He looked up at me, dropped his fork, and whistled. "You look good enough to eat."

I blushed and then gave him a wide grin. "Just keep your mouth on that pastry. You about ready to get out of here?"

Damien scarfed up the remains, and grabbed my hand, kissed it, and continued to hold it as we joined the crowds on the packed sidewalk of 7th Avenue. "Quitting time," he said. "Feels like the whole world just got off."

It looked to be a perfect fall evening, with a crisp chill in the air and a clear sky. As we were jostled together, I pulled his arm over my shoulder, bringing us closer and I asked, "So, what do you feel like doing? By the way, I just ate a big sandwich. Not hungry at all."

Damien pulled out his wallet and looked inside. "I got five clams. How's about this? We take a horse and buggy ride around Central Park and then grab a spot of grass and watch the moon come up."

"Love that idea. It'll be my first buggy ride here. You know, back in Green Tree, I actually drove our buckboard and horses by myself before my stepdad finally sold them. I love horses."

"Then horse and buggy it is." Damien kissed my cheek while we waited at the crosswalk. "We should walk it; we're pretty close. By the way, I need to make a quick pit stop on West 59th. My agent's apartment; I owe her some payback."

I tensed up when he mentioned his agent. "Is it the lady that was so rude to you that morning we first met?"

"Yeah, Fran's got a tough mouth on her but she keeps managing to find me jobs, so I put up with it."

"I don't know. Seems like she should be the one working for you. Not bossing you around."

"Yeah, it's kind of a two-way street. It's complicated. Anyway... come in and I'll introduce you. Maybe she'll consider taking you on as a client."

Remembering the Nanette I knew as a kid, the thought of working with Fran made me shiver. "No thanks. I'll wait outside."

"Trust me Jo-Jo, you really need a leg up to get started in this business. I've had steady work since I signed with her."

"Oh, I believe you. Just think I'll keep looking for someone else though."

We walked down a couple long blocks heading west and stopped at an apartment building with a uniformed doorman and a green awning. Once in the lobby, I sat down on a silk striped settee across from a man behind a desk.

Damien told him, "Need to go up and pay Fran Jordan a quick visit. It's Damien Jones."

The lobby clerk called her apartment, nodded a few times and hung up. "Mr. Jones, she's coming down now for dinner. She asks that you wait here."

I needed to leave. I jumped up as Damien sat down next to me. "Uh, Damien, I noticed a drugstore on the corner. While you're waiting, I'm going to run over there."

He grabbed my hand. "Hey, it's just gonna take a minute. I'll go to the drugstore with you, after."

"It's something personal I need to get. I'll be right back."

Still holding my hand, he said, "But I'd really like…"

Just then, the elevator doors opened with a ding, as I stared at Nanette Jorganson walking out. Head held high, silky hair perfectly coiffed, with tan and white leather spectator heels clipping against the glossy marble floor, while my head took a spin twelve years back.

I would always remember her waving to me from Chicago's massive Union Station platform, while I stared at her through my dust splattered train window, both of us crying, with her blonde hair blowing in the wind. She waved a final time, wiped her eyes and turned away. She was moving on and sending me back home on the train by myself. She was fleeing the scene after promising to take care of me. Nanette had been the one lying, telling me my mother no longer wanted me and couldn't take care of me. But in the end, she left *me* with a note stuck on my coat saying: *Green Tree, Iowa*. And then walked away.

I was six years old at the time and spent a year yearning for her to return and bring back the life we'd strung together in Hollywood. But slowly I learned from my mother the twisted lies she'd told to keep me with her. And now I was about to face the monster who my sweet mother, Mariah, still hated to this day.

I looked down at the floor as Damien jumped up to greet his agent. "Fran, glad I caught you. I have your money." She nodded, ignored both of us, and moved quickly through the door out of earshot of the lobby clerk.

Damien and I looked at each other and followed her out. Maybe she wouldn't even recognize me. Surely, I'd changed so much. It had been almost thirteen years ago when she left. While walking behind her, I whispered to Damien, "Do *not* introduce me."

She briskly walked a few paces away from the awning. She was wearing a smart chocolate tweed suit jacket, nipped in at the waist with a fitted straight skirt. She glanced at me and turned to Damien, quickly taking his offered roll of cash and dropping it in her leather handbag, while admonishing him. "Why can't you get a bank account and mail me a check like a normal client? This is a high-class building. I don't want men just showing up here and dropping off cash. It doesn't look professional."

"Sorry Fran, never thought about that. Yeah…sure, now that I have steady paychecks rolling in, I'll try to do that."

I was looking around at the surrounding buildings, attempting to stay out of the conversation, but then she asked, pointing at me, "You look familiar. Who's this, Damien?"

I jumped in, not wanting to reveal my name. "I've hit a lot of auditions lately. Maybe you've seen me at some of those. You have a lovely dinner, ma'am." I grabbed Damien's arm and said with a smile, "We need to get going if we're meeting your friends." I gave his hand a yank and walked in the opposite direction of Fran.

We covered the block quickly and breezed through the crosswalk in silence, then Damien finally asked, "So what the hell was all that about?"

I stopped walking and looked at him. "Why do you let her talk to you like that? She's not your boss. She should be an advisor, a helping hand. Remember, you're making *her* money. Not the other way around. And what's this payback business about?"

We were entering the park now, and the tall canopy of trees overhead and less crowded sidewalks helped slow my nervous heart a bit. Damien shrugged his shoulders, explaining, "When I first came back from the service, I was desperate for work. My parents were on the road performing, all my old contacts had dried up, and someone told me about Fran. I was down to my last few bucks of military pay. She signed me, offered me a loan to get cleaned up, get a shared apartment, and buy some decent clothes. Unfortunately, it's a loan at twenty percent interest which never seems to get much lower. It's not quite extortion, but pretty darn close."

"See... she's not only rude, she's a predator too." I pointed to a line of carriages waiting down the road. "Hey, the buggies are all lined up to the left. Let's go pick a good one."

"I'm a city kid. You choose."

The sun was about to set and a chill was setting in from all the shade. We walked down the line until I spotted a large, shiny black mare decorated with red roses. "She's the one; a real beauty."

Damien negotiated the price and we climbed into the open carriage, also painted black and decorated with roses. "It's beautiful up here, Damien." Following me, he climbed in, pulled me close, and put a blanket over our legs. Our driver maneuvered his horse out of the line and kept a steady pace clopping down the paved trails of Central Park.

I looked up into Damien's face and said, "So, regarding Fran? If you really want to know... let's just say there's some history between us. It's kind of a crazy story, but if you want to hear it, let me start by saying Fran Jordan is *not* who she says she is."

CHAPTER 4

DEER IN THE HEADLIGHTS

SARAH

I could hardly breathe. I woke up with a sudden start, realizing I'd burrowed my head deeply below my blanket and pillow. I guess it was my way of disappearing from last night's tears and heartache, eventually falling into an exhausted sleep. My last lucid recollection was reading Tommy's letter.

Glancing out my window, I noticed the morning sun had yet to break the horizon. It was early, a new day, and I needed to take action. Instead of crying about Tommy leaving, maybe there was a possibility of me turning the situation around.

Close to six AM, I knew Mom would be up and just finishing breakfast dishes. Life on a farm was nothing but predictable and always began early. I decided to use the payphone outside the library. There was one downstairs in the dorm lobby, but I never liked any of the girls overhearing my private conversations. There were some terrible gossips living at Currier Hall and I happened to share a room with one.

Barbara appeared to be sleeping deeply. I tiptoed around our room, discarding yesterday's slept-in clothing, and grabbed a simple print dress to wear. Unbraiding my plait, I brushed through my long, wavy dark hair and threw some water on my face, noticing my still swollen eyes from last night's cry. I took a few text books off my desk and threw them in my satchel, along with a toothbrush, a change of underwear, and a nightgown. At the back of my drawer, inside a pair of striped socks, I pulled out a small roll of cash, stuffing it down the inside pocket of the satchel.

Briskly walking to the campus library, I pulled my long cardigan close. It was a cloudy, cool, fall morning. I dropped my nickel into the payphone, noticing there was nobody roaming the campus this early Sunday morning. I dialed the operator who connected me to the Green Tree switchboard for a collect call. Before long, I heard Mom promptly picking up.

"Anderson-Jackson Realty, Mariah speaking."

"Mom, It's Sarah." As a cost saving measure, I didn't call often so her tone immediately was on high alert.

"Sarah, what's wrong? What are you doing up so early?"

"It's already six-fifteen. Had something important to ask you."

"What is it darling; you sure you're alright?"

My voice sounded horse and wobbly after last night's crying binge. "Honestly, no. Have you heard Tommy's news…about the navy? I got a letter from him yesterday."

Her tone immediately sounded more sympathetic. She knew how I felt about him. "Yes, I heard, sweetie. I was in town yesterday and ran into your Aunt Elizabeth at the Coffee Cup." Elizabeth was Tommy's stepmother. "She told me about his big decision. It seems to have caught the whole family by surprise. How do you feel?"

Her steady calmness about this made me feel the opposite. "What do you think? Mom, it's Tommy!" I responded shrilly. "I love him and he's leaving. I feel sick about it. But I need to talk to him before he leaves. Maybe he'll stay if he knows how I really feel. When does his train leave for California?"

"Gosh, I'm not positive. Maybe tomorrow?"

"I'm coming home, Mom. Today. There's a seven AM bus I can catch if I leave now. Can you pick me up around noon in Green Tree and then take me to the Martin farm?"

"Honestly Sarah, I have a client meeting in Blue Earth today. I'm trying to sell another of Billy-Boy's houses." My Uncle Billy was one of Mom's real estate partners. He built the homes and she sold them.

I was twisting the phone's fabric cord around my wrist, as I became more agitated. "Mom, please! Can you reschedule? This is really important. I rarely ask you for anything."

"Alright, I'll reschedule." She asked sympathetically, "Sarah, are you sure you want to do this? I believe he's pretty committed to leaving. Elizabeth mentioned all the arrangements had been made. I doubt your visit will change anything."

"I have to try, and if I can't, at least he'll know how I really feel and I can tell him goodbye in person."

"Should I check and make sure he's there? The Martins have a phone now. I can call and find out."

"No time, Mom. I've gotta leave now if I'm going to catch that bus. And I want to surprise him. I should be there around noon. Thanks!"

I sprinted across campus and down several blocks of Clinton Street, turning the corner at the bus station. The Greyhound bus was still in the terminal with the engine rumbling. I ran up and banged on the doors of the bus and asked the driver to wait while I bought a ticket inside. The round trip charge was five dollars. The price had gone up fifty cents since I'd last taken the bus. I felt guilty spending so much on a seemingly frivolous visit, but this was important.

During the long ride home, I tried to concentrate while reading chapters from my text books, but my mind kept wandering. Three years in the navy? I still had a little over two and a half years until I finished school. I guess three years wouldn't be so bad. We could still get married. Tommy could come back to Green Tree and find work using new skills he'd picked up. In the light of day, thinking it through, maybe this wasn't the total catastrophe I'd felt last night.

I stared through my window, looking out at the rolling acres of tall green field corn, with the sunlight reflecting on the light frost below. This would be harvested soon. My stepfather, David, had taught me a lot about crops while growing up. Jo and I hit the jackpot when he and my mother married. Although very quiet, he was the kind of man you could always trust and look up to. He was kind, hard working, and clever, having greatly expanded his farm acreage over the last ten years. Apparently, David had a totally different personality than that of my late father, Samuel, who I really no longer remembered. But they both had one thing in common. They loved my mother fiercely.

That's what I wanted; a busy, meaningful life with someone I loved and who loved me back. Someone I could always count on. That's the boy and man Tommy was for me.

I dozed off and on between chapters of World History and Biology before the bus eventually pulled into the Green Tree station. I guess you couldn't really call it a bus station. It was a converted black smith shop which now sold gasoline, bus tickets, soda pop, candy, and homemade sandwiches. From my window, I saw Mother standing on the wooden platform, leaning against a Standard Oil gas pump, talking to the station owner, Mr. Gottlieb.

As my rubber legs came down the steps of the bus, they each greeted me with a hug. Mr. Gottlieb was still sporting his signature silver handlebar mustache and a faded pair of denim overalls. "So Miss Sarah, you still keeping those professors in check down in Iowa City?"

"I'm trying, Mr. Gottlieb."

My mother grinned, saying, "Yes, David and I are both so proud of our little scholar." Then she looked at her watch and hurried me along. "We really need to get moving, Sarah. I put off my meeting in Blue Earth until two-thirty. See you soon, Mr. Gottlieb."

I waved and we climbed inside Mother's dusty black Ford Deluxe parked in front of Gottlieb's pumps. "So, Sarah, you said you wanted to surprise Tommy, but remember… he may not be home, or the family may be having some sort of party for him. I have no idea. So David told me he'd be on call whenever you're ready for him to pick you up."

"Thanks. After that long bus ride, I sure hope Tommy's still there."

"Well, we'll soon find out."

Ten minutes later we pulled up into the familiar gravel drive of the Martin farm. Mom drove around to the back. She and Elizabeth were old friends and Mom always used the Martin's back door. I looked up and saw the window open in the attic bedroom where Mother and I used to stay. We had dubbed it the sky room when she worked there as the housekeeper because of its high, large window.

"Window's wide open in the sky room. I bet Tommy's home."

"Good. I'm glad he's here. I'll come in with you for just a minute then."

"It's OK, Mom. I can go in alone. You should go on to your appointment. I'll be fine."

"You sure?"

"Yes, I'll see you tonight at the house. Good luck with your client."

She reached over and embraced me, while patting my head. "You're so grown up now. Seems like only yesterday when you'd hide behind my skirts, so shy to speak."

I quickly got out and said through the open window, "Mom, that was a million years ago."

She laughed as she pulled out of the drive, while I waved, walking up the steps to the back door. I didn't want to admit it to my mother, but I was actually nervous about what I was going to say. After knowing Tommy so well for all these years, I shouldn't have felt that way, but I did.

I knocked and waited a while, and then knocked again. Mr. Martin opened the door with a surprised look. He had never been my favorite person. There had been issues between my mother and Tommy's father when she worked for him and he was often short tempered and sullen.

"Well, Sarah Anderson, we weren't expecting you. Guess you've heard about Tom, then? Coming to see our little swabbie off?"

"Yes sir. Is Tommy home?"

"Yeah, should be upstairs packing. Uh, let me tell him you're here." Then he closed the door while I waited on the doorstep. Yup, he was still rude as could be.

But thank the Lord, Tommy was home! There was so much I wanted to say. After a few minutes, he came downstairs looking a little disheveled, finger combing his light hair and tucking in a white dress shirt. "Sarah? My God, what are you doing here? Thought you were in Iowa City."

I laughed nervously. "Well, I was until this morning. I got your letter last night and wanted to rush back to see you."

Tommy nodded his head and guided me down the stairs. "Sarah, it's kind of you to come. Let's walk a little by the back garden. Do you mind?"

"Not at all. I was on that bus for hours. I need a walk. So... you're really going to do this? The navy? You're sure?"

He sighed and nodded. "Yup, I'm really going. Honestly, Sarah, I'm excited to go. I feel like the whole world just opened up to me, even if I only get to see it from a porthole or off the deck of some giant warship."

"Last night, reading your letter, I have to say, I was shocked. You really caught me off guard. But I think I understand. You're ready to do something on your own. Get out from under your father's shadow."

I noticed he kept his hands in his front pockets as we walked along. In high school, he always held my hand as we walked. "Yeah, something like that, I guess. Fresh start and all."

I was biting my bottom lip, not knowing how to start this conversation. "It's just that... I... uh... wanted to tell you something. Maybe you don't really know how I feel about all this. I have to say...last night...I was so upset. It's just that we've been friends for so long. And I always hoped and thought--"

"I know, Sarah."

I stopped and looked at him, surprised. "You know what?"

He looked off, away from me, across the garden. "I know that you think you're in love with me. And me with you. I've known for a while. But, maybe it's not like that anymore. We've grown up. You know...nothing stays the same as it used to be."

Then he turned and looked down into my eyes, his fists still shoved into his pockets. "Even when you were really young, I remember. Change was hard for you. Look, Sarah, we'll always be friends, someone we can both turn to. I'll stay in touch, but I don't want you to think that our futures are forever linked. I don't mean to hurt you, but that's just not the way I feel about things anymore."

My eyes were open wide, as I tried my darndest not to cry. I was tired of crying. "Tommy, it's not that I *think* I love you. I know I do. It's you and me, through thick and thin. Remember? And I can wait. Three years…it's not so long."

He shook his head, "It's a long time, Sarah. Who knows where I'll be then. Maybe back here, maybe California. I have no idea. But things *have changed* for me."

As he was explaining himself, a girl called out to us from the porch. "Tom, everybody's almost ready to go." She began walking toward us, as a chill crossed my body. She looked about my age, with a pretty face, and light brown hair tied back with a red scarf. "You about ready?" She waved as she approached us with a smile. "Hi, you must be Sarah. Tommy's told me all about you."

"Yes, that's right."

Then Tommy took a deep breath and said, "Sarah, this is my girlfriend, Lynette. She lives in Clear Lake. We met this past summer."

My face went stiff. I couldn't smile. I didn't speak. I just stared forward.

"Yeah, so sorry to cut this visit short, but Lynette and her family are meeting with my family in town for a special going-away dinner. Uh… Why don't you join us if you like? I hate that you came all this way…"

I shook my head back and forth. "No. No, you go on. Please though--I need to use your phone. Need to call my stepfather." I could hardly speak, feeling like I'd been punched in the gut. Of all things, I *never* anticipated this. But why hadn't I? Was I so wrapped up in my own life, that I couldn't see the needs of others? I turned quickly and walked ahead of them, attempting to hide my tears, certain I was dropping pieces of my broken heart trailing behind me.

CHAPTER 5

SCAMPERING DOWN
MEMORY LANE

JO-JO

*O*nce seated in the carriage, Damien wrapped his arm around me, pulling me close against him for warmth, while his face looked down at me in disbelief. "So, let me get this straight...my agent, Fran Jordan, is really not Fran Jordan? She's Nanette Jor-gen-son from no-where Iowa and... *she kidnapped you*?"

"I know this all sounds bonkers, but yes. She and my Aunt Elizabeth were best friends in Green Tree. That's how my mother met Nanette, through Elizabeth."

Damien brushed his dark hair back with his hand as the evening breeze picked up. "OK? Keep going."

"All this came about when my dad died suddenly in a barn fire on our farm. My twin, Sarah and I were only four, and my Mom was forced off our rented farm. It was really hard for her to find a job. The only thing she found was as a live-in housekeeper for a farmer who would not allow her kids to live with her. Sarah and I were devastated, but it was just as well. The farmer's wife was dying of TB. Highly contagious."

"Whoa, grim times. I thought I had it rough as a kid."

I nodded and continued. "So initially, Nannette really helped my mother out by offering to take care of me. She'd moved to Mankato, Minnisota for a job as a photographer's assistant and had room for me in her little apartment, while my sister, Sarah, stayed with my Aunt Elizabeth near Green Tree."

Just then, I was distracted as our carriage made a turn at the bend in the road. I noticed an arched stone bridge and just over it, the sun was setting between two thin bands of orange-tinted clouds. "Damien, look at that sky! It's gorgeous. Are you sure you want me to keep going with this?"

"Sure, if it doesn't bother you. Getting the inside scoop on Fran is fascinating."

I took a deep breath and continued. "So, while I was staying with Nanette, she recognized a young raw talent in me and put me in tap and voice classes. She bought me new clothes and started dolling me up to look like Shirley Temple. I had the blond pipe curls and cute little face, and I gotta say, I was a real ham. I loved all the attention and was not shy about performing."

Damien nodded. "Sounds about right."

"I found out some of these details later from my mom; my memories from that time are pretty fuzzy. But anyway, after the farmer's wife died, Mom sent Nanette a letter saying that he was going to let Sarah and I move in with her there. So, Nanette decided to secretly leave the area with me before my mother could bring me back to stay with her."

Damien shook his head in surprise. "Damn! You can't be serious."

"I remember Nanette was always obsessed with the movie business. So, she finds an agent for me in Hollywood from the back of a magazine, breaks all ties with her friends and boss in Mankato, and she and I skip town and move to California."

"Honestly, Fran can be kind of ruthless, but I never imagined her doing something like that."

"Yes! And while she and I were on that train ride out to California, Nanette told me that my mother no longer wanted me and had asked Nanette to take care of me. I'll always remember that because I was devastated...heart broken, really. Nanette explained that my mother only wanted to keep Sarah. And from that point on, Nanette asked me to call her, *Mother.*"

Damien whistled and said, "Holy smokes, Jo-Jo. That's not strange, that's diabolical."

"Yeah," I sighed, "So, long story short, the two of us moved out to Hollywood, lived in a hotel for a time, and she finagles me into some bit parts in the Our Gang reels, a couple of small roles in movies, and an ad for a doll campaign. Meanwhile, my real mom was going crazy back in Iowa, wondering where Nanette and I had gone. No one had a clue! For over a year, my mother heard nothing until a Mankato police captain helped her out. He got the Los Angeles FBI on the case, but when Nanette got wind of the FBI on her tail, she disappeared and sent me back to Green Tree, alone on a train."

Damien continued to stare at me. "Wow! Unbelievable. You're sure Fran is the same person as Nanette? People can change a lot in thirteen years. Like you said, you were just a young kid."

I nodded. "You're right. I hadn't thought of her in years, but when I saw her walking towards you, the day we met at the audition, I was pretty convinced, especially listening to her voice as she spoke to you. But after seeing her today, I'm absolutely sure."

Damien shook his head. "Fran comes off as so worldly and speaks of all her theater and movie connections, as if she's a real mover and shaker in the business."

"She may be that now, but during our time together she worked as a photographer's assistant in both Minnesota and Hollywood, but was always intrigued with the movie business. I think she was trying to give me the life she had always wanted."

Damien ran his hand through his hair, as the wind picked up. "You running into her now...in this huge city...that's *really* an amazing coincidence. Kind of like fate...you know?"

I stretched and sighed. "I agree. But it's true and that's all I'm gonna say about her for now. Let's just enjoy this evening." I shivered thinking about Nanette's face and haughty attitude. I wanted to spend time with Damien and not have to think about her. From the buggy, I watched passing couples walking hand in hand, and kids shrieking as they romped through piles of fallen leaves.

"Jo, sorry, just one more question. Did you ever meet her

daughter who died? A little blond girl? Nanette keeps a photo of her on the desk at her office. She told me one time that the kid in the photo was her daughter who passed away. Real cute, wearing a top hat."

I slowly turned my head and looked at him with unease. "Black top hat, cane, a spangly leotard, wearing tap shoes?"

"Hmm…Maybe?"

I laughed in amazement. "Never heard of any daughter, but I know that photo. It's me. She bought me that outfit for a recital and took that photo at the studio in Mankato. That was my headshot photo. She used it to send out to agents. I have a copy of the same photo. It's one of the few pictures I ever had taken of me as a little kid."

"OK, this is getting strange. So, she's still telling people that you're her daughter, but now you're *dead*?" We were both quiet for a minute. "You're right; let's change the subject. How about some hot chocolate? They sell it near the pond."

We said goodbye to our driver and walked over a hill to a small concession stand and got steaming cups of the sweet brew.

"Jo, now I get why you don't want anything to do with Fran, but I have to say, she has been an asset for me."

"I wouldn't care if she was the head of MGM studios. My mother would kill me if I got tangled up with her again." I took a sip of hot chocolate and then blew on it to cool it down. "Mom… she's pretty even-tempered with most people, but when it comes to Nanette Jorgenson…let's just say her name is *never* mentioned in our house."

We sat down on a bench and watched the kids playing by the pond. Damien asked, "Do you think she recognized you today?"

I shook my head. "Hopefully not. I'm certain I've changed a lot more than she has. I was her little cherub-face doll back then and now I'm this full-grown gangly giraffe."

Damien laughed and hugged me. "But you're a beautiful gangly giraffe."

"Thanks, but please, don't mention my name around her."

"Absolutely."

CHAPTER 6
PARENTAL POINTERS
SARAH

*R*elief flooded through me when my stepfather picked up on the second ring. "David, can you pick me up soon at Tommy's?" I'm sure my near-to-tears, high-pitched, wavering voice alerted him to come quickly.

After I hung the mouthpiece up, Tommy continued to stand near me in the kitchen, with Lynette looking on. I knew him so well and recognized the guilty look on his face. "So, David's coming for you soon? Guess I'll be saying my goodbyes now, Sarah."

I nodded and said. "Yeah, you guys should go on. I'll wait on the front porch. Good luck to you, Tommy. Uh, drop me a line some time."

I was trying to sound nonchalant as I held back my tears. If only *she* hadn't been there, we could have had at least a real hug. After fourteen years of friendship and more, it had come down to these few trite phrases, not much different than words used by two strangers meeting on a train. This brief visit felt like a bad dream. I reminded myself to listen to my wise mother more often. I never should have come.

I walked onto their front porch, sitting down on one of three white wooden rockers. Tommy and the rest of the Martin crew waved to me and piled into his father's truck, parked in the front.

Tommy, Lynette, and his brother, Eli, sat in the back of the pickup. As they drove out, I couldn't help but notice the three of them turning their heads to glance at the fields, rather than having to stare back at my tear-streaked face. The truck rolled down the long drive leaving spits of dust in its wake.

About twenty minutes later, David's reliable old green Dodge pulled up. I felt comforted seeing him as he got out of the cab and stepped over to hug me. My stepfather was not one to show much emotion and had *never* discovered the gift of gab, but when he said or did something, I knew he always meant it. I stepped up on the running board and slid onto the high bench seat.

As we drove out, David asked, "The Martins gone somewhere?"

"Yes. Tommy, his *new girlfriend*, and their families are all meeting in town for a going-away dinner. Seems I arrived just as they were getting ready to leave." I pulled out a handkerchief from my satchel and dabbed my eyes and wiped my running nose. "David...I felt like such a fool showing up like that. I had no idea Tommy had another girl. I never expected that!"

David patted my knee and nodded. "I'm so sorry, Sarah." I was sure that was about all he would be willing to offer me for a while. I knew my stepfather... he'd be contemplating his response for the entire drive home.

Passing a field of recently harvested soybeans, I began thinking about what else I could have said to Tommy and decided that although it had been excruciatingly painful and embarrassing, I had come to tell Tommy how I felt, and tell him goodbye. I'd accomplished those two things. But I certainly hadn't expected my entire visit with him to last only ten minutes, or have the shock of meeting a new woman in his life. My replacement.

As we bumped down the rutted back roads, I realized that Tommy had made a life-changing decision and, if I was truly a friend, I should hope the best for him and be proud of him for having the courage to try something so challenging. But I didn't have to be happy about it. I knew myself; today would linger in my heart and head for a long time. I wasn't the type that could just snap my fingers and move on. I wasn't Jo-Jo. The sister who could pick up and move into a city without knowing anyone; a city so large that it was unimaginable to me.

By the time we neared the turn-off to home, David broke his thoughtful silence. "You know, Sarah, don't think I ever told you this before, but never in my wildest dreams did I *ever* think I had a chance with your mother. Besides being beautiful, Mariah was so competent, curious, and sure of herself. She amazed me and I was just in awe of her strength. Sarah, you're so much like Mariah. Trust me… someday, somebody special will see those same traits in you. You just gotta be open to it. Things can't always stay the same."

"Yeah, Tommy kind of mentioned something similar." David parked by the back door and I reached over across the seat and hugged his wide shoulders and bulky frame. "Thank you, Dad." I touched the hanky to my eyes again. "I'll try to remember that."

He patted my shoulder gently again and smiled through his full cheeks and light green eyes. "How about a big, fat chicken sandwich? Whaddya say?"

My voice was still emotional as I attempted to appear more upbeat. "I say swell. I'm starving. Do you think it's a good cure for heartache?"

"Yup; highly recommended."

Around six in the evening, Mother returned with a grin on her face as David, Sammy, and I were sitting at the kitchen table dipping into big bowls of homemade vanilla ice cream. "If you three are already having dessert, I guess I missed dinner."

In mid-bite, I said, "Look in the Frigidaire. David made you the perfect chicken sandwich. You look happy, Mom."

She was already peeking into the cold box as she explained. "I am. Especially, walking in and seeing all of you here to greet me. But, besides that, I closed the deal on another one of Billy's houses. Our fourth in the last twelve months!" Mother stepped out of her heeled shoes and slipped on a pair of well-worn slippers waiting at the back door. "Sold it to another veteran and his wife, with a baby on the way. I'm telling you, the low interest housing loans from that

GI Bill have been terrific for business. If it keeps going like this, it'll be our best year ever."

I was so proud of my mother. A dozen years ago, she'd started a fledgling rental business with almost nothing, when she, her sister, and Uncle Billy bought a ramshackle old home at auction and converted it into a successful boarding house. From that point on, the three of them kept expanding the business with my mother always taking the lead. Like David said, she was pretty amazing.

Throughout the evening, Mom and I gossiped about the people of Green Tree, without bringing up the subject of Tommy. I said my good nights early, feeling tired from the stress of the day. Besides, I had another early bus to catch tomorrow morning. I changed into my soft flannel nightgown, feeling comforted by my old familiar bed and a raggedy teddy bear I still kept hidden under my pillow. I was way too old to sleep with such a childish thing, but tonight it eased my anguish.

A soft knock on the door immediately woke me. Mom opened the door a crack and whispered, "Still awake?"

"Pretty much--just started to doze off."

"OK if I come in for a minute? Sorry, I know it's late but Sammy still adores having me read to him." Mom sat down across from me on Jo's bed. "We didn't really get a chance to talk about Tommy tonight. If you still want to, I'm available."

"Yeah, I'd like that."

She turned on the small lamp between the twin beds. "Sarah, I know you're taking this hard and even though you and Tommy are both young, I don't want to trivialize how you're feeling. Just think, when I was your age, I was married with twins on the way. Your dad, Samuel, was *everything* to me. And just like you, we had enjoyed a long relationship, meeting in our early teens. The hurt may almost feel like a part of you has been amputated in some way. That's how I felt when Samuel suddenly died. A part of me died in that fire." My tears sprouted again, hearing my mom's feelings for my dad. Probably in loyalty to David, she rarely spoke emotionally to me about my father.

She moved across to my bedside, sitting next to me and noticed my bear, Jingles, clutched under my arm and smiled. "No need to hide old Jingles. We're all comforted by the familiar in tough times. I'm sure today wasn't easy for you…David told me what you said to him. Between the navy, another woman, and Tommy's abrupt departure, I know you're distraught."

"Mom, I do understand what you're saying about amputation. I always saw Tommy as my partner, companion, my best friend. And now all that has been chopped away with no discussion. There's just this empty shadow left."

"I know it's so hard…but, Sarah, you will get through this. Those wounds slowly heal. And honestly, Tommy will go through some dark and lonely times in the navy. He didn't choose an easy journey. I'd be surprised if he didn't want that strong friendship from you again at some point, probably just when you no longer feel you need him so badly. But, if you're smart, you'll be there for him anyway because that's what friendship is about. It can't be a one way street."

"Yeah… I think I may have needed Tommy more than he needed me. That was probably exhausting for him. And now that I think about it, I was way more interested in my own future than his. I rarely asked him about his plans or dreams. Maybe I'm just selfish?"

Mom smoothed my long, loose hair back and kissed my cheek. "Don't be too hard on yourself. These are your years to be focused on self development. Tommy was only lagging behind a little. Now he's stepping out to find himself." I nodded, staring into her beautiful large brown eyes as she continued. "But there is one more thing I need you to remember. College is not only about preparing for a career. I admire your focus on goals and grades, but please Sarah, take some time to enjoy and prepare for life in general. There's hundreds of interesting, like-minded people there at the university and you'll *never* get this opportunity again. Immerse yourself in all the options available; join a club, go to a dance, see a play, go to a party. And in time… go on a date, for goodness sakes!"

I shook my head and said, "You must think you're talking to Jo."

"No, I *never* had to encourage her in those pursuits. I'd be having the opposite discussion, begging her to start showing up for classes. Anyway, think about it?" She patted my hand still clutching the bear and kissed my cheek. "OK, darling, sweet dreams. I'll be seeing you and Jingles before sunrise; you're catching that first bus out."

I pulled the sheet over my head. "Ugh! Thanks Mom. I love you."

CHAPTER 7
JACKPOT JEOPARDY
JO-JO

I made it to two more auditions for chorus line spots for musicals, both ready to go to rehearsal, but once again, no luck. I knew I needed to attend some rigorous dance classes to get me up to snuff with my competition. But dance and voice lessons were high dollar and I was downright poor.

While totaling up my meager tips for the day, I considered trying to move to a cheaper place than The Dixie, or perhaps even look for a roommate. Pocketing my change, Chuckles called me over next to his grill. "Hey Legs, got a little tip. You interested?"

"Always. What is it?"

I waited as the edge of his spatula banged against the grill, quickly chopping and mixing sizzling hash browns with two bright yellow eggs. "Well, I been asking around for you. Like I said, I been here awhile. I know some of the back-end guys in the theater district." He looked up to make sure our boss, Max, wasn't listening. "I pass them a dinner or two; they occasionally slip me some tickets. Stuff like that."

"OK?" I was leaning against the counter, curious where this was going.

"So, there's a radio show. Real popular--The Talent Jackpot. Heard of it?"

"No. Maybe we didn't get that one in Green Tree."

Chuckles shook his head. "Jo, you gotta get out more. It's on WOR, part of the Mutual Broadcast Network. They're airing it all over the place. Anyway kid, my pal works security at the backdoor of the studio and he's got a thing for our cream cheese Danish. Just bring him a bag and you're in. But *you* gotta do the rest. They line up the talent on Wednesdays. You try out; practice with the band… then they narrow it down to about six contestants. *If* you're selected for Thursday, you perform on the Mutual network and you're heard in cities and towns nationwide."

"Wowza! Imagine that."

"You'd be in front of a live studio audience and they vote for the winning act. Best part is--the winner gets five-hundred smackeroos!"

My mouth opened wide; I was dumbfounded. "Five-hundred-dollars! I could use that money for lessons." Just then, Mr. Asnes got off the phone, noticing me still leaning against the grill. "Jo-Jo, table five looks ready to order."

I nodded as Chuckles leaned over and whispered, "Here's the thing. You gotta be there by eight AM. Make sure you go to the back door. Ask for Sammy Shine. He'll get you in as far as the lineup, but you gotta make the cut. You need to go in there looking really good and singing like a star, and be sure to pick a popular song. He says that helps."

I was excited. This sounded like something I'd be good at. "So… next Wednesday morning at eight? Chuckles, I can't thank you enough!" I smiled brightly and walked to table five.

That night I started practicing, singing in my room. I rehearsed several numbers but decided on a new jump-blues record by Louis Jordan called, *Choo Choo Ch'boogie*. It was up-tempo and I'd heard the band downstairs at the Ebb Tide play it several times. I even worked up my courage to ask Slim if I could rehearse the number with the band before the normal crowds came in. Their grouchy female singer, Dottie, still eyed me suspiciously, but when I explained I was rehearsing for a contest, she grudgingly let me to step in for a few run-throughs.

The possibility of winning energized me all week. Because the whole process was such a long shot, I didn't tell anybody else I was trying out. I was afraid I wouldn't make it. But I had to keep telling myself, anything was possible, right? I envisioned myself standing in front of a big black radio microphone, with a studio audience clapping along. And, if I did make it onto the show, whether I won or lost the competition, being heard by people all over the country was a wonderful prize in itself. There was no downside, except for the cost of a bag of half-price cream cheese Danish.

On Monday, I spent half of my week's tip money on a new dress from Macy's bargain basement at their gigantic store at Herald's Square on 34th. The new dress made me feel so elegant. It was black, slim cut and calf-length, with white satin cuffs, collar, and lapels, with sparkling buttons from the waist to the hem.

Thursday morning, I got up early. Took time with my hair and makeup, and slipped into my new lucky dress. I heated up a cup of coffee on my hot plate, walked to the Stage Deli and picked up a fresh out-of-the-oven bag of Danish. Checking the time, I walked briskly down to 1440 Broadway, home to radio WOR. I arrived out of breath with fifteen minutes to spare and noticed a big crowd of people by the front door, still hoping to audition. I rushed down the alley and knocked on a side door. With no response, I anxiously knocked again, louder this time. Finally, an older guy with black, slicked-back hair and a prominent nose, opened up.

He looked at me expectantly, "Yeah?"

"Hi there, I'm looking for Sammy Shine?"

"Sorry miss, he never showed today." Then he quickly closed the metal door in my face.

I stared blankly as the rusty door slammed shut. Stunned, I turned and walked down the few steps. I was so disappointed. It was as if the closing door had pressed all the gumption out of me. I sat on the steps and put my chin in my hand as I contemplated my next move. Was I giving up because some security guy didn't show for work today? Could I be that easily defeated? I took a deep breath and stepped up to the door again, pounding on it with determination.

The same guy opened the door, looking exasperated. "Hey, I got about twenty other things I could be doing besides opening this door."

I stood up tall, shoulders back and offered him my toothiest smile and a little laugh. "I bet you're right about that. It's just that I brought Sammy these fresh Danish rolls with gooey cream cheese straight from the Stage Deli." I opened the bag and swirled the scent of baked goods in front of his nose. "And now they're going to be wasted. I don't suppose you would want them? Best to eat them while they're still warm from the oven."

"Aw geez, the wife would kill me if she knew. Supposed to be watching the waistline." He sighed, put his hands in his pockets and looked out the door quickly, checking both sides. "I suppose I could share them with some of the crew. So, tell me… Whatcha' need from me, kid?"

"Well, Chuckles from the deli said Sammy might sneak me into the audition line today. I'm a singer, new in town, and could *really* use the break, mister."

He opened the door a tad wider and rubbed his chin. "Yeah, I know Chuckles. When it comes to cooking up omelets, that guy is cookin' with gas! Tell you what, if you sing as good as you look, you might make the cut. I'll sneak you through, but if you make it to the Thursday show, you're bringing me the full breakfast. We got a deal?"

I pulled my hand out for a firm shake and said, "I'm Jo-Jo Anderson. So pleased to meet you. What's your name?"

He shrugged his shoulders. "Sammy Shine. Hey…sorry about slamming that door earlier, but it was just a little test. I can't go vouching for every wobbly-kneed young thing that comes knocking. You gotta prove yourself a little." He opened the door wide enough for me to enter and cautiously checked outside again. "So, you got a number picked out?"

"Absolutely! I'm ready."

"OK, follow me." He pulled a Danish out of the pastry bag and consumed it in three wolf-sized bites. We wandered down a back-stage corridor lit by the occasional bare bulb. Sammy stopped in front of a door, pushed it open and told me to go in as he followed behind. It looked like an employee's bathroom, with two stalls, a urinal, a sink and mirror.

"You can freshen up in here. Just wait while I go twist the arm of the talent coordinator. He and I go way back and he likes the Danish too. Shouldn't be long, but first, I need a real good kiss from you."

Danish, a breakfast, and now a kiss? This Sammy guy was really pushing it. I wanted this so bad, but I knew I had to draw the line. I bashfully smiled and said, "Sammy, I bet that omelet's not going to be tasting too good after I tell Chuckles about a kiss you forced on me. Now... I'm waiting right here while you go and check in with the audition guy."

Sammy lifted one of his black leather lace-ups to the edge of the trash can and began to shine it with a cloth from his back pocket. Then he looked at me, as he headed out the door, and said, "Hey, can't blame a guy for trying. You better be great on stage with me vouching for you."

After he left, I felt like I'd just dodged a bullet and I hadn't even made it to the try-outs yet. I splashed cold water on my face and, noticing there were no towels available, I patted it dry with the skirt of my dress. I shook my hands out, trying to calm my nerves and reapplied my bright red lipstick and ran a comb through my wavy hair.

While waiting, I began practicing my song, initially in a low voice, and then on the chorus, I began belting it out loudly, liking the sound of the acoustics in the tiled bathroom. I'd just started practicing my hand and foot moves to go along with the perfor-mance when the door swung open and a different guy stared at me for a few seconds.

Wearing a bowtie and smoking a cigarette, he whispered loudly, "Hey, pipe down! You're not even supposed to be here. I take it you're the Deli Girl?"

"Sorry. I got carried away. Yes, Jo-Jo Anderson." I reached out to shake the hand not holding the cigarette.

"Danny Tucker, talent wrangler. OK, Deli-Girl, so far, I liked what I heard outside the door. But you gotta understand, there were forty other people waiting in line to audition, which I'll be letting you leapfrog over."

I nodded, as I hoped for a positive response. "Mr. Tucker, I'll be eternally grateful for anything you can do. I promise; I won't disappoint you."

You been on the radio before?"

"Never. But I'm a quick study."

He looked me up and down and said, "I bet you are. First off, you gotta remember; you're playing to two audiences. The live one, but more importantly, to the radio audience. So, as good as your little dance moves looked just now, they'll interfere with the sound of the broadcast. So move your hands and use your facial expressions, but not the feet. You gotta keep the mouth close to that mic. Got it?"

"Yes sir, thanks for the tip."

"There's eleven other people lined up on stage ready for auditions." Danny opened the door and pointed outside the restroom. "You follow this hallway around going the opposite direction and come in on stage left. Merge with the group as if you just got added. Don't say nothin' about this little exchange, OK?"

I nodded, listening intently.

"Hey Jo-Jo, before you go, where's *my* bag of Danish?"

"Oh…sorry, I handed everything to Sammy. But I *promise* I'll bring Danish *and* an omelet breakfast to you tomorrow morning if I happen to get picked for the live show."

He shook his head, with a partial grin. "So, now *you're* the deal maker? You better knock 'em dead out there. I select the talent, but the General Mills sponsor guy and the host make the final cuts. Good luck!"

CHAPTER 8
SEAT MATES
SARAH

*T*he following morning at daybreak, I waved goodbye to Mom and climbed the stairs of the silver and blue Greyhound bus. The bus had originated in Minneapolis and once I looked down the aisle, I noticed most seats were taken. My choices were sitting next to a smoking lady with a squirming toddler on her lap, or a man reading his open newspaper. I opted for the newspaper, but as I walked toward him and began to sit down, I was smacked in the face by body odor. I'd walked plenty of manure-filled fields in my day, but newspaper guy was worse.

I swerved back up and saw my final option, second to last row, a seat next to a reserved looking man wearing glasses, fussing with his briefcase. I took option three.

As I approached, I noticed he had papers strewn across my seat. "Excuse me, sir, but I need to sit here. Mind moving your paperwork, please?"

He looked over his glasses at me and then back down at his files. "I've noted there are two more available seats. Kindly take one of those. I've got important work to complete here and need the space."

I leaned down and whispered, "Yes, one of those seats is next to a baby about to explode, and the other is next to someone smelling

44

highly disagreeable. I'm choosing to sit here." I continued to stare him down, although this man looked like someone who was used to getting his way.

Continuing to organize his paperwork, he said, "Being a young woman, it might be kind of you to offer that mother an extra hand with her disgruntled baby."

His audacity was really getting my goat. Placing my hands on my hips, I attempted an authoritative tone. "Sorry sir, I'm not really the mothering type, and just like you, I have work to do. Now, unless you paid for two seats, kindly take your paperwork off of *mine*."

The bus' engine rumbled to life, as I lost my balance a bit and looked up front. The driver stood up, putting on his uniform's blue jacket and hat. He glanced down the aisle and called out, "Miss, I need you to take a seat. You're not allowed to stand as we start moving."

I waved back at the driver. Then I grabbed all the paperwork on the fabric seat and dumped it in the man's lap and quickly sat down.

He seemed visibly upset, his hands shaking with anger, while he wiped the lenses of his glasses. "I just spent the last thirty minutes collating these. Now they're all mixed up. Thanks to you!"

"I'm sorry, but if you'd picked everything up when I politely asked, they wouldn't be in that mess." I paused for a minute, taking a few deep breaths, trying to control my anger. There were five long hours of possible togetherness ahead of us. I decided to be the bigger person and apologize. "I think we got off on the wrong foot. I'm Sarah Anderson and I'm actually quite good at organizing. Maybe I can help you get that sorted again."

He shook his head and offered up a contemptuous laugh. "This is complex stuff. I'll manage without your help."

What an arrogant ass! I smoothed back the stray hairs escaping from my braid and waved away the blue cigarette smoke that was floating to the back, clouding our space. I jumped up again, leaning toward the window. "Excuse me, sir. Do you mind if I slide this window open? That smoke really bothers me." While asking, I gripped the narrow window pull next to him to slide it back.

He abruptly reached up and knocked my hand away. "Don't touch that window. Are you mad? I just told you…I'm *working* here. I'd suggest you try not to inhale."

"Breathing is something I'm rather fond of." I decided to ignore the noxious cloud of smoke and the unpleasant man. I pulled out my heavy world history and biology texts with a loud thump, tossed my satchel in the overhead rack, and tried to dive into the history of the original seven hills of Rome. At least my seething anger was temporarily displacing my heartbreak. While studying though, thoughts of Tommy, sitting alone on a train heading west, kept invading my history lesson. Would he be lonely, feeling overwhelmed when he arrived in San Francisco? I knew I would have a tough time making that trip by myself. I so wished we could have had a proper goodbye.

After a few hours, we stopped at a large terminal in the state capitol of Des Moines. Inside, travelers were transferring to other buses, using restroom facilities and buying snack options. I took down my satchel from the rack above, visited the restroom, and stretched my legs.

When I returned to the bus, I noticed there were now several empty seats and my former sour seatmate had decided to take one closer to the front. I was thrilled, retaking my aisle *and* unclaimed window seat at the back. Mother had packed me a lunch, but I hadn't dared open it earlier, afraid of disturbing Mr. Arrogant. I opened up the narrow window slightly and pulled out my bagged lunch. As we rolled out, I took my time enjoying a bologna and mustard sandwich, a ripe red apple, a tangy rhubarb hand pie, and chased it down with a soda pop.

I thought about my parents and considered my mother's advice about making time for other pursuits, rather than *only* focusing on classwork. I'd been flying solo at school for too long. No wonder Tommy felt the need to find his own path. Maybe all my dependence on him as my primary social outlet helped drive him away. I needed to be more independent, like Jo. She had already met a guy and had several friends.

I arrived in Iowa City a little past one o'clock and realized that even though I'd missed my first two classes, I could easily make it to my final class, biology. It didn't start until two, so I went to the dorm to freshen up. The weather had cooled so I put on a warmer pleated, plaid skirt and pull-over sweater. Approaching the classroom door, I heard the professor already droning on about cell division. Checking my watch, I realized I was five minutes late.

I entered and, eyeing the full classroom, grabbed an empty desk in the second row. I settled in, opened my text, searched for the correct chapter, hunted for my pen, and pulled a notepad from my bag. I suddenly realized the professor's voice had gone quiet. When I looked up, Mr. Arrogant was standing directly in front of me and said, "Take your time, Miss Anderson. We're all happy to wait while you get comfortable."

Stunned to be staring again at the horrible man from the bus, I asked, "What happened to Professor Jenkins?"

"If you had arrived on time, you would have heard my opening explanation. But now you can get the information later from a classmate." He pulled out an old fashioned gold watch on a chain and then announced, "Miss Anderson has caused us to lose another two minutes of lecture time. Let's get back to business, shall we?"

After keeping my head down in embarrassment for a few minutes, I eventually tuned in and found the lecture fairly interesting, which surprised me. During Jenkins' lectures, I'd often struggled to stay awake. After class, Professor Arrogant, once again, called me out, asking me to stay behind for a minute. My classmates looked at me, shaking their heads, probably wondering what the studious book mouse, Sarah, had done to garner this new professor's ire.

He continued to sit at his desk while scribbling something down on a notepad, ignoring me while I stood next to his desk, waiting as commanded. What a typical, deliberate professorial move, acting as if he ruled the scholastic universe. As the seconds ticked by, I couldn't contain my frustration with this fuddy-duddy any longer. I guess that description was a misnomer if fuddy-duddy meant somebody old. This man appeared to be in his thirties, but he was acting like someone who was positively ancient.

"Excuse me, sir, can we just drop the animosity please. I ruffled your papers and came in a few minutes late. I apologize... again. Does that about cover it?"

He continued writing and said without looking up, "You may address me by my name, Miss Anderson. I'm Professor Beckham Carter. I only wanted to emphasize how much I value punctuality. Time is a valuable commodity. You can wait for me, just as we waited for you to settle down in class. And by the way, I was able to make it to this class with several minutes to spare, even though we shared the same bus. Why couldn't you?"

I had to put this man in his place, professor or not. I decided to pull out a reliable line. "Professor Carter, I had some emergency female issues to attend to and got here as quickly as I could. By the way... good lecture today. I find the five phases of mitosis quite intriguing, especially the final cytokinesis phase. Which is your favorite?"

He dropped his pen, wiped his glasses, and stared back at me with...could that be a remote twinkle in one of his hazel eyes? He followed up, saying, "I find the telophase amazing as well, but I have to agree with you. Cytokinesis is also my favorite. Don't be late again. That will be all."

CHAPTER 9

THE CANARY SINGS

JO-JO

I wound my way around the backstage and peeked through an opening in the side curtains and saw the cluster of auditioners. I wandered up to the group and attempted to blend in. There was a tall, thin man holding a violin standing directly in front of me. I decided to engage.

"So, what is it we're doing now?"

He turned and looked down at me and asked suspiciously, "Where did you come from?"

"I was in the ladies room for a while…nerves, you know? So maybe I missed some directions?"

"The orchestra is tuning up in the pit and we're waiting for the judges. Should be any minute." Looking down at my empty hands, he asked, "You didn't bring any sheet music?"

"No. Didn't consider that. But hopefully the band knows my song."

He raised his eyebrows and turned back around. The chatter surrounding our group quieted as three men came down the theater aisle, stopped in front of the pit, and looked up at us. An older gentleman in a gray suit with gray hair explained that he was the chief marketing vice president for radio for General Mills. He mentioned his name but all I remembered was that our sponsor's product was Cheerios. He then introduced Talent Jackpot's host, a handsome man, Mr. John Reed King. Several in the group seemed excited, recognizing his name and golden voice. The third man, standing behind the other two, was talent wrangler, Danny Tucker, who I'd met in the bathroom. All the auditioners had already met him too, and he didn't seem to warrant an introduction from Mr. Cheerios.

John King spoke next, flashing his white teeth, cleft chin, dark wavy hair and his deeply resonating voice. "We're pleased as punch to have the dozen of you here this morning and I just wish we had space for each and everyone of you on the live broadcast. Unfortunately, it's a thirty-minute show, folks, so we can only present six acts on Thursday evening. So, our objective right now is to let each of you run through at least a portion of your performance and the three of us will determine who continues on in the competition and who also best represents the Cheerios brand. And then of course, on Thursday, the vote will be in the hands of our live audience. But I can tell you this; these audiences seem to have an excellent eye for talent. Everybody will be given one shot at this today and an equal amount of time. So, good luck to all of you!"

Mr. King, Mr. Cheerios, and Danny all sat down in center seats about ten rows back, while the stage manager handed us each a number and directed us off the stage to wait in the wings. I pulled number six, middle of the pack. Not great. To my mind, the most memorable performances would be the first and last. I'd just have to find a way to make myself less forgettable. I prayed my nerves wouldn't get the best of me and that my new lucky dress would prove worthy of my hard-earned tips.

The stage manager collected everybody's sheet music who needed accompaniment. I told him I was singing *Choo Choo Ch'boogie*, but hadn't brought any music. He shrugged and said, "Hopefully not a problem; we'll see what we can do." I was so glad I'd had a chance to practice this song a few times with the Ebb Tide band.

Within five minutes, number one was called to perform. Darn! It was a kid act. A little boy who reminded me of myself at his age, he was very small, full of spunk, smiles, and childish flirtation. Probably only four or five, he managed to belt out the title song to Oklahoma, a popular musical, in a high, squeaky but endearing voice. It also didn't hurt that he was dolled up in a cute little cowboy outfit, with rouged cheeks and long blond bangs under a straw cowboy hat. The kid was a shoe-in and I was sure Mr. Cheerios was eating up this cornball act.

I became nervous watching a few of the other contestants and ran to the bathroom again to practice my song, utilizing the built-in tile acoustics. After singing it a few times, I felt slightly more confident and came out to watch the rest of the competition from the side stage. The violinist went before me and, to my ear, played a classical piece quite well, but I thought it might be too high brow for this type of audience.

The stage manager called my number and I walked out on the empty, echoing stage and was immediately swamped with stage fright. I had to wonder, how would I do in front of a live audience? Mr. Reed, the announcer, called out, "So, number six, what do you have for us today?"

"I'd love to sing you a bit of "Choo Choo Ch'boogie, Mr. KIng. It's one of my favorites."

"Fantastic. I like that song too. Let's hear it, lovely."

The orchestra director below nodded up at me, tapped his baton on his music stand, held up his arms, and the band began playing, but the tempo was all wrong…too slow, not what I was used to at all. I stumbled on my opening lyrics missing the lead in. At the band leader's direction, the music stopped. I timidly looked down and asked, "Excuse me, but can we speed it up a bit. I'm used to singing a more up-tempo version." The director nodded, gave some instructions to the musicians and started again. The pace was quicker and I slid in with my vocals. While singing, I smiled, I was animated, and I think I sounded pretty good. I wasn't the Andrews sisters, but hey, there were three of them. When I finished, I thought I had a chance but I couldn't really see the judges reaction from where they sat.

After each act completed their audition, the stage director sent us to sit down in the first row and wait. I sat and watched tap dancing twin sisters, a young guy in his army uniform singing

Danny Boy--a tear jerker for sure, a clogger who danced, sang, and played accordion, and a ventriloquist with a sarcastic dummy. The more I watched the array of hopefuls, the more worried I became. Eventually, we were a front row of fourteen, counting the twins and the talking dummy who insisted on his own seat.

Mr. King told us the triumvirate was leaving to debate our fate and then he'd return shortly with the results. Our front row had turned into death row. Everyone was quiet, their eyes on the ceiling, or busy chewing their nails. I thought back on my performance and knew, if given a second chance, I could do it better and be more animated.

King returned and stood in front of us. "Well gang, I want to thank all of you for getting over here so early this morning. We had a real tough time deciding Thursday's roster and each of you should be proud of yourself. If you don't make it today, please feel free to try again in six months. OK, here we go…if I call your name, just remain seated so Mr. Tucker can give you further instructions for Thursday's show, and the rest of you can leave out the front door of the lobby."

I held my breath as he announced the names of the winning acts, using my fingers to count them down. When I got to my sixth finger, I exhaled, stood up, and walked up the aisle. Rejected again.

On my way to the lobby, the talent guy, Danny, was heading toward the front and stopped, touching my shoulder and said, "Hey, sorry. It was *real* close. You almost made it. Just gotta project more. Exude more conviction. You had my vote."

I gave him a shaky smile, holding back tears, and thanked him for the opportunity. I hated going back to tell Chuckles I hadn't made it, but I was relieved no one else knew.

That evening, after working the late afternoon shift, I tried calling Damien, knowing Wednesday was his one night off from *Annie, Get Your Gun*. I sat down inside one of a dozen wooden phone booths down the hall from The Dixie's lobby. After dropping my nickel, I got the expected busy signal. Damien lived in a small apartment he shared with three other guys. There was one phone down the hall and every apartment on that floor shared the one phone. I tried three more times and eventually some guy picked up.

"Hidey Ho, who's this?"

"I'm Jo-Jo Anderson, looking for Damien Jones. Lives in 204. Do you mind checking to see if he's available?"

"Sure thing. Hang on."

I heard some door banging, muffled words, and eventually Damien's sleepy voice. "Jo-Jo, sorry. Did I forget we were doing something?"

"No, nothing like that. Sorry to wake you. Sounds like you're tired."

"Yeah, I spent all afternoon of my one day off rehearsing the role I've been the understudy for. They asked me to replace Ray Middleton for two weeks. Apparently, he's got some big emergency back home."

"Actually, that's fantastic for you!"

"Definitely. Even if it's only for two weeks, I can claim I've had major billing on Broadway. The role of Frank Butler--that should carry a little weight on my stage credits. But the stress of rehearsal really wore me out today. Anyway, how about you?"

"Well, I tried out for the radio show, Talent Jackpot. The talent coordinator told me I *almost* made it into the final six for Thursday's show, but I needed to *exude more commitment*. It's frustrating; how can I build my confidence if I never get a chance to perform?"

"Yeah, Jo. It's a crazy business. All I can tell you is if you want to act or entertain, then act like an entertainer. Imitate the confidence you see in other singers and actors until people believe it. Never let them see your nerves."

"You're right. I shouldn't be sulking about it."

"And hey, remember. You *almost* made it. That's saying something. A lot of my pals have tried out for that show and never got that far. Try again later or audition for another radio show. I bet you'll get on."

"Thanks, Damien. That makes me feel better. I'll let you get back to sleep. If you're up for it, maybe we can get together this week."

"Actually, my parents are in town Thursday night. Why don't we meet up after my show at the Imperial and I'll introduce you."

"Terrific. I'd love to meet them."

The following day, I'd just finished working a busy lunch rush. It was two in the afternoon and I was wiping down the table tops and filling condiments. Mr. Asnas, standing at his post at the register, picked up the ringing phone and told the caller, "No, employees can't take personal calls. This is a business phone." Then he slammed the phone down, and it rang again almost immediately. This time he listened a bit longer. "Yeah…yeah. OK, she's here, but make it quick." The boss leaned over to me, dangling the receiver, "Some Romeo on the line wanting to talk to you. Says it's real important." He sneered while wiggling his fuzzy eyebrows.

I immediately assumed it was Damien. "Hi, this is Jo-Jo."

"Jo, it's Danny Tucker. Sounds like you work for a real asshole. I'll be brief. During rehearsals today, the accordian player twisted her ankle while clogging. We got an open spot if you can make it down here within the hour."

I couldn't believe it. "Is this a joke?"

"Don't flip your wig, Jo-Jo. I'm dead serious."

"I'd love to! But let me check. Hold please." I set the receiver down and touched the owner's arm. "Mr. Asnas, please, please, please! I have the opportunity to appear on a radio show, Talent Jackpot, tonight. It would be a huge deal for me if Bennie could cover my remaining shift. I'll work all the doubles you need for a month."

"Talent Jackpot? The wife and I listen to that every Thursday evening. So you gotta leave now?"

"Yes sir. Right now or I won't make it for rehearsals."

"Bennie does dishes, he's not so good with customers. Tell you what. You try to mention the Stage Deli on the air and I won't make you work the doubles. We gotta deal?"

Yes! I'll throw your bagels into the audience, just let me leave! I nodded at him and saluted. "Thanks, I'll do my best." I picked the receiver up. "Danny, I can make it if I run, but I'll be wearing my waitress uniform."

"Hmm. Just get here… and don't forget the Danish."

CHAPTER 10

A VOTE OF CONFIDENCE

SARAH

*A*fter receiving a glimmer of redemption from Professor Arrogant, I left and took a leisurely stroll through the center of campus, instead of my normal dash to the library carrels to study. While walking, my mother's advice recycled through my mind. According to her, I had a two-and-a half year shot left of making the most of my college years. She cautioned me about not spending all my time studying, wanting me to take advantage of my campus surroundings. I recalled her final words before this morning's Greyhound rolled in. "Sarah, use this precious time to gather skills, but also forge bonds and deep friendships. Life is about so much more. Learn to embrace it, darling."

I glanced at the clusters of students passing by me on the sidewalk. A couple walked past with hands touching. A circle of girls were sitting under a shade tree chatting, while several guys were tossing a football over other people's heads. I had to admit, I was lonely. Since arriving, I'd met only a few people from my dorm and, honestly, they didn't seem to like me much. Maybe I was too closed off. I never thought I needed anybody but my family and Tommy. I'd created this perfect plan and a big part of that plan had just fallen apart. It was a jarring realization that life was not going to follow my straight-forward plotting. Apparently, I needed to learn how to zig and zag.

I reminded myself to consider Jo-Jo's world. She was hanging on by her fingernails in the most competitive city in the world and still hadn't given up. She was meeting new people, working in unexpected places. I needed to open myself up to new possibilities. Passing through the quadrangle, I noticed the usual numerous student organization tables set up along the perimeter. I'd always ignored the friendly faces at the tables, thinking I had no time for extra stuff. I passed one with the sign: *Have You Registered to Vote Yet?* I thought about it and slowly circled back. Maybe that was something I could do? Minimal effort. I was eligible to vote but had never considered doing it. Women had fought hard for the right to vote twenty-six years ago. What was I waiting for?

There were two guys sitting behind the table, with trimmed haircuts, wearing gold University of Iowa monogrammed sweaters. As I slowly approached, one called out to me. "Don't worry, we don't bite." He offered a big smile and reached out his hand. "Hi, I'm Jacob. Interested in registering?"

I timidly shook his hand. "I think so. It'll be my first time."

"Yes, as students, it's important that elected officials know the younger voters' perspectives and needs. We need to be a formidable voting group. So, are you affiliated with any certain party?"

"No, I don't attend many parties."

"No, what I..."

I laughed, saying, "I'm kidding. I know what you mean. But the answer's still no. Guess I'm not sure which party I prefer, honestly. The republicans or democrats. I think my mother voted for FDR and Truman. But I'm open."

He handed me a printed form. "Well here's a voter registration form. If you have a little time to spare, I'd be happy to speak with you about the two parties and go into a few details. Don't worry, no pressure. Mark, here was just taking over my spot at the table."

Just do it, Sarah. Mother said to join in. This was signing up to vote, not a beer-drinking contest. "Sure. I'd be happy to have more information."

He stood up from his chair. "Great. I don't know about you, but

I could use an afternoon pick-me-up. How about a cup of coffee? Sorry, I didn't catch your name."

"I'm Sarah. Sure, coffee sounds great."

"Let's head over to Memorial Union. Coffee's always hot and the price is right."

We walked over to the large central campus building. I was curious about this person who was willing to spend his free time encouraging others to vote. "So Jacob, why are you so interested in doing this?"

"Well, voting is the cornerstone of our democracy. If people don't believe it's important, then the whole system stops working. Imagine that."

"Hmm, never thought about it like that before."

After we walked into the lounge area, Jacob showed me to a round table with two chairs. "I'll grab your coffee. How do you like it?"

I laughed and said, "I'm easy in that regard. Black, no sugar."

"Ah-ha, a true coffee drinker. I'll be back."

Well this was interesting. I decided to sign up to vote and I'm getting a free coffee and a lesson on democracy. I felt like shouting, *Look Mom, first day back and I'm joining in!*

After we exchanged hometowns and discussed our majors, Jacob got down to it, crossing his legs and leaning back in his chair. "Now, I'm not trying to sway anybody, Sarah, but I will tell you I'm interested in politics too. Might even run for office one of these days. I'm a little unsettled about the way our nation has been leaning so far left. All these democratic socialist ideas that Roosevelt and now Truman keep proposing, that's after spending millions fighting the war. And now they're giving all the money away on unnecessary programs and forgetting us middle class guys, the backbone of the country. I think it's time to move a little more to the right with some fiscal restraint. So, no big surprise here... I'm the head of the Young Republicans on campus."

I took a deep gulp of coffee, sat back, and said, "Hmm, just curious, do you spend this much time trying to win over every gullible convert?"

He shrugged and smiled. "Sometimes. Hey, the main thing is that you vote, Sarah. But it's important to stay on top of things going on in our country."

"Well, it seems the reenactment of the GI bill was really important for all the returning soldiers. Wasn't that a Truman-Roosevelt plan? My mother was just telling me about all the vets coming home and getting help with low-interest home loans and free college plans. All that seems like a good idea."

"Only if it's fiscally sound. I agree, a lot of good men will benefit."

"And the women who fought in the different services."

"Yes, I suppose that's true. But all those women that took on factory jobs while the men were away…that stuff has to stop, and all these pushy pro-union types; I disagree with them."

I gave him a noncommittal nod. "Hmm. Guess I'll need to study up on that." I took my pen out and filled in the registration form. "OK, here you go. I didn't designate a party yet. Hope that's alright. At least you found someone willing to listen."

"Uh, if you'd like to help, we could use another person on the quad for a Monday afternoon shift?"

"I'll think about it." I stood up, gathering my satchel.

"Well, maybe I can convert and *converse* with you over dinner sometime?" He remained seated, folding my registration form.

"My parents always said that you should never talk politics at the dinner table… But then again, a girl does have to eat." A grin immediately crossed my face. "My dorm address is on the form. Nice to meet you, Jacob."

CHAPTER 11
GO TIME!

JO-JO

I flew out of the Deli's doors carrying my handbag and two paper sacks of Danish. I glanced down at my highly unstylish, white lace-up, rubber-bottomed shoes; maybe good for running but not for making a good impression for my radio audience debut. Then again, my catsup-spotted white uniform and the paper cap bobby-pinned to my hair didn't help either.

There were several blocks between the deli and WOR on Broadway. I watched the minutes tick down while stopping at several busy crosswalks. I decided to ignore the caution lights and began dashing dangerously between cabs acting like an experienced New Yorker.

Reaching the station with minutes to spare, I banged on the back door. This time Sammy Shine opened with a smile. "It's the Stage Deli-Girl!"

"The name is Jo-Jo Anderson, Mr. Shine." I handed him one bag of pastries as I walked in trying to catch my breath. "Don't say... I never... gave you anything...Danny called... wanted me to get...here quick." I sat down for a second on a metal folding chair by the door.

"So, you're singing for us tonight?"

"I'm sure gonna try. Hey, is there a phone back here?"

"Yeah, near the janitor's closet, past the bathroom."

"Ok, wish me luck."

I turned and walked quickly toward the stage entrance as he called out, "Hey, Deli-Girl, you owe me a big kiss since you didn't bring my omelet."

I just shook my head. These guys! Everybody seemed to want something from me. But then again, maybe I wanted something too. I saw Danny standing in the wings off stage-left, holding a clipboard with a pencil behind his ear. Walking up behind him, I spoke softly, not wanting to interrupt the rehearsal in progress. "Hey there, I made it."

He turned and grinned as I held up his paper bag of Danish. "You guys are going to get so fat."

He pointed behind me. "There's two dressing rooms on this side. One for the women, one for the men. You can clean up and hang your coat in there. We'll need to run through your number a couple times soon and decide on some small talk to exchange with the host."

I held out the skirt of my stained uniform. "What can I change into? I can't wear this."

"Uh, rehearse in the uniform, keep the hat on, and I'll see what options we have."

"Really?" As I entered the dressing room, the tap-dancing twins greeted me. They were sitting there focused on stitching extra sequins on their short-skirted iridescent costumes. They had gorgeous costumes and all I had was a comb. Then I told myself, only seventy-five people would actually see me tonight, the rest of the nation would be listening in. My dress should be the least of my worries.

I pulled out a folded piece of paper which I'd tucked away in my wallet after rehearsing at the Ebb Tide. It had all the lyrics to Choo Choo Ch'boogie. Reviewing all thirty-six tongue-twisting lines, I tried to make sure I committed everything to memory, singing the number softly to myself in a corner of the dressing room. In the middle of my third rendition, Danny knocked on the door and yelled through the crack, "Deli-Girl, you're up."

Back on stage, I ran through my number twice, relieved the band director remembered the tempo I preferred. I thought the song was improving with each attempt. After the run through, Danny took notes from me on my background. These were topics Mr. King might ask me about on-air before my performance.

"Remember kid, the more memorable and engaging you are to the audience, the more chance of them voting for you. Gotta be honest, it's not all about who has the most talent. The act that wins is often the person who pulls the audience's heart strings, you know?" Danny chuckled and added. "Guess we're all a sappy bunch. By the way, I didn't have much luck finding any garments that suit you; but honestly, people might react better seeing you as the hard-working farm girl looking for her big break. I'd stick with the uniform. Makes you look relatable. There's some bleach in the janitor's closet to get the catsup out, and if you got the time, I'd hem the dress up shorter. Honestly, that dress you wore yesterday made you look a little old, maybe *too* successful. Get what I mean?"

I nodded. "I think so; hope you're right."

The stage director walked past us yelling for all the acts to get back to the stage area. Once we gathered around, he announced that everyone could take a one-hour break for dinner but had to return by six through the back door for a final run-through before the broadcast.

As the others left, I went to the pay phone and made a collect call to my parents. I recognized the voice of one of my old high school friends coming through the line at the Green Tree switch-board. "Anita, it's Jo Anderson! I need to make a collect call to my parents."

"Hi-de-ho, Jo-Jo! How's life in the big city? I'm so jealous!"

"Honestly, it's tough as nails. I'm just getting by, but tonight I caught a break. I'm scheduled to be on the Mutual Broadcasting show, Talent Jackpot."

"Jeepers! I'm definitely tuning in and telling all our old gang.

Knock 'em dead, Jo-Jo. Remember, you'll always be a big star here in Green Tree. I'm connecting you now."

She made me smile. I knew Anita would have half the town talking about tonight's show. I reached David at home, told him my news and asked him to tell Mom and call Sarah, so that she could also tune in. After saying my goodbyes, I darted into the bathroom and stripped down to my slip. I doused the catsup spots with bleach and water, and still feeling sweaty from my run from the deli, I gave myself a quick sponge bath with damp paper towels I'd taken from the janitor's closet. Luckily, I'd just thrown my uniform back on when someone knocked on the door. I unlocked it, staring at John King, who looked impressive in a perfectly cut, double-breasted, navy suit. He offered up a professional smile.

"Sorry, Mr. King, just cleaning up in here, I'll get out of your way."

"Thank you. So, Danny tells me you stepped in to replace the clogger?"

"Yes, I came straight from work."

Glancing at the uniform, he said, "I can see that. Excellent. Glad you could make it. I'm looking forward to hearing your song again. If you don't mind...Just a word of advice."

"Sure."

"Really try to milk that audience. Smile, wink, flirt with them and they're bound to fall in love with you."

"Appreciate the advice, sir. I'll do my best."

I raced down to the empty dressing room and saw the twins' sewing kit left open on the vanity. Based on Danny's recommendation, I took off my uniform again and began hemming up the skirt, using quick and messy long stitches my mother never would have approved of. I also noticed somebody had left a set of electric rollers next to the mirror and I was dying to try them, having only seen them in magazine ads. I plugged them in, finished my bad hemming job and hoped the owner of the curlers would stay away until the showtime lineup.

After rolling my hair, I noticed a burning smell and realized it was coming from me. Nothing smells worse than burned hair, except maybe cooked cauliflower. I was quickly taking them out when the door opened and the twins and a vocalist, who accompanied herself on piano, strolled in chattering.

The pianist immediately stopped their conversation in mid-sentence, asking, "Phew! What is that smell?" I was quiet, and began combing through my bouncing curls. "Wait a minute, blondie; did you just use my electric rollers? For all I know, I could get head lice from you!"

I couldn't lie. I turned around with an apologetic face. "Yes, I used them. So sorry. I just assumed the theater had them here for everyone's use before the show. But I can assure you, I do *not* have lice."

She brushed past me and picked them up. "Guess I'll have to wash each and every one of these when I get home. And what's with you anyway?"

"What's that supposed to mean?"

"I *mean...* you mysteriously showed up on stage for try-outs yesterday. I was the first to arrive--almost crack of dawn--and I never noticed you waiting in line like the rest of us. Then you show up today at the last minute, even though you didn't make it into the finals yesterday. Now you're hanging out in the dressing room all by yourself. I bet you got a lock with somebody on this show."

I shook my head and added a bold red lipstick to my mouth. "Look, I'm sorry about the curlers, but everything else you said is hogwash!" I bobby-pinned my paper waitress cap on at a jaunty angle, powdered my nose, turned toward the door, and said, "I wish you guys luck tonight. Break a leg."

One of the twins said, "That's really a terrible thing to say to a tap dancer."

As I closed the door, the pianist yelled behind me, "Something's fishy! Don't think I won't be looking into this."

After that little run-in, I walked off my stress taking long strides in the dark hallway behind the stage while thinking to myself, *great, now I have a target on my back. What was her name... Laverne? She's probably just jealous because she has a really terrible haircut. Like a frizzy bird's nest on top of her head. Maybe too many electric rollers? I'd be angry too.*

The stage director stopped me and asked, "Deli-Girl, mind gathering the other ladies. It's time for the final run through."

"Sure, and sir? The name's Jo-Jo Anderson."

"Hey kid, I got a lot of names to remember. For this week, you're Deli-Girl to me, and like I said, get the other dames out here."

We all assembled in a line behind the stage and the director shouted out commands like a drill sergeant. "First up, we got Billy-the-Wonderkid, singing *Oklahoma*." The other acts seemed to inwardly groan knowing he was maybe their stiffest competition. I noticed that his mother had added two side holsters and shiny, silver toy guns to his outfit. At least, I hoped they were toys. Because of his young age, his mother had been allowed to hover nearby backstage.

"Second, we have Roger and Donny. A second stool will be brought out for the dummy." After this comment, Donny swiveled his wooden head, blinked, and said in a comical voice, "Hey mister! Who you calling a dummy? And I'll take the best seat in the house please." I liked the ventriloquist; he and Donny were pretty funny.

The stage manager didn't crack a smile and kept right on with his proclamations. "Going third, we have the Terry Twins and their Tapping Toes." The twins were talented hoofers and very pretty brunettes, but tap dancing on the radio? Questionable.

"Next up, number four, we got soldier boy, Mickey O'Mally singing, *Danny Boy*." Mickey had a sweet face and voice. It didn't hurt that everyone still loved seeing a man in a military uniform.

"Fifth in the line up is Laverne Hall accompanying herself singing Bing Crosby's hit, *Sunday, Monday, and Always*. Laverne, we'll roll your piano out during a commercial break." Ugh, Laverne. She also better roll up her hair and get rid of that bird's nest.

"And to round out the night, we have The Deli-Girl, Jo-Jo Anderson, singing the *Ch'boogie* song." I was thrilled to be going last. I didn't know if they picked me to close the show because of my performance, or because they had already decided the order before the clogger twisted her ankle. No matter, but the pressure was on me to deliver a smashing closing number. The only downside was that I stood backstage next to nasty Laverne for most of the show.

The stage manager continued to address us. "Now, let me be clear. Everybody stays in order, in a line, stage left. You can watch *silently* from the wings, but you must stay in order, and absolutely no peeking out onto the stage. When you finish, go directly to the dressing rooms. No one is allowed into the audience after their performance. We got that straight?"

Everybody nodded and remained silent. Mr. Cheerios and two General Mill's jingle singers came backstage, shook each of our hands and wished us good luck. They were followed by Mr. King who walked past us, putting his script in order. From behind the stage, we could hear the audience being let into the studio, sounding excited as they found their seats. After a couple minutes, Mr. Cheerios walked on stage to applause. He talked about General Mills' sponsorship of the amazing show they were about to see and then introduced our host, John Reed King, to louder applause.

Before going on air, King explained to the audience that they had work to do. "Tonight, ladies and gentlemen, the fate of six talented new discoveries lies in your hands. Let me introduce you to Danny, our talent coordinator." Danny walked out pushing a machine on wheels called the applause-o-meter. It was attached to a long cord which was plugged in behind the back curtains. King asked the crowd to give Danny a round of applause. They all watched the meter's arrow move up to a midpoint as they clapped.

"So you see, we take your applause seriously, folks! If you really like an act, you have to show it with your hands, whistles, and cheers. Danny will record the height of the applause for each act. And for your information, this unique applause-o-meter has been approved and certified by the engineers at General Electric."

Then the stage director came out, shook Mr. King's hand, and tested all the microphones and announced, "OK, ladies and gentlemen, are we ready? We go live in ten seconds. So, let's start the show. Four, three, two, and one." Then he pointed to King, standing at a mic to his right, who began speaking in that magic voice of his. It was go time!

"A great big hello to all the families out there across the country tuning in tonight. As usual, the Talent Jackpot has six tremendous, talented contestants ready to strut their stuff, and a very excited audience who will be judging their performances. Remember, the winning act receives five-hundred-dollars and a week's engagement on a New York stage. Time's-a-wastin', so let's get started! First up, we've got a talented little cowpoke who's trying to lasso your heart and tie down your vote. He's singing a song about the heart of the U.S.A., *Oklahoma!*"

Billy the Wonderkid strutted up in his cowboy finery, offered up a few precocious responses to King's questions and then sang out high and clear to a very appreciative audience. At the song's end, the kid pulled out his cap guns and began popping them off as an additional finale. Danny had to eventually come on stage, take him by the hand, and lead him off stage so we could move on to the next act.

The ventriloquist, Roy and Donny, dressed in matching black suits, seemed to do quite well, and the tapping twins were good but their applause sounded fairly mild from backstage. As I had predicted, Mickey O'Malley, riled up the crowd, getting them on their feet with the tear he allowed to roll down his cheek at the climax of Danny Boy.

Laverne, still cautious of jumping head lice, was keeping her distance from me. But judging from the audience's luke-warm reaction to her piano and singing performance, it seemed that instead of singing Crosby's *Sunday, Monday, and Always*, Laverne would be singing the blues.

Now it was my turn. I was having my doubts, suddenly wishing I had my beautiful black dress on again. Why did I have to wear this awful uniform? I walked out on stage in a daze, but the polished Mr. King knocked me out of my reverie with his friendly questions. "So, Miss Jo-Jo Anderson, I heard you got plucked right out of work today to come and perform. Is that right?"

"Yes, Mr. King, I got the call and actually ran from the Stage Deli all the way to WOR."

"The Stage Deli? Near Carnegie Hall, correct?"

"That's right. I'd love to perform there myself someday. But right now I'm just serving up delicious sandwiches and pastries." *I was thinking, Max Asnas, that one's for you!*

"Well, tonight our lovely Deli-Girl is going to serve us up one of the hottest songs on the charts today. Here's Jo-Jo Anderson, who recently moved here from Green Tree, Iowa, singing Choo-Choo Ch'boogie."

My first stanza sounded a little wobbly. I was letting my nerves get to me again. Then I remembered Mr. King's words. I pulled the mic over, singing directly to the left side of the audience, offering up a flirty smile and then leaned over to the right side. I tried to relax and have fun, making train motions with my arms as they began clapping along to the song. It all was over so fast; I was ready to sing a second number. But the audience was up on their feet cheering for me. I might have won this thing!

I was immediately hustled off the stage, as Mr. Cheerios came back on and announced we'd have a short break from our sponsor. The Cheerios Kid, a cute little boy on the cereal box, was really voiced by a grown woman on the radio as she pretended to eat her bowl of wholesome goodness and protein, banging a spoon against a bowl, and asking, "Golly-willikers, Dad, can I have some more?" Then she and the man harmonized, singing the Cheerios jingle together.

While the commercial was going on, I headed backstage and noticed King, Mr. Cheerios, and Danny having a quick discussion about the applause-o-meter. I dragged my feet passing by, trying to eavesdrop, walking slowly back to the dressing room. After a minute, the stage director knocked, stuck his head in the dressing room, and told me to go over to the side stage again. Billy also joined me in the wings and while we waited, I noticed Billy, who was perhaps three-and-a-half feet tall, standing close to me and he appeared to be looking up my short dress. I inched away, frowning, as I looked down at him.

He responded abruptly saying, "What's buzzin' cousin?"

I questioned his uncharacteristic retort, but forgot about it when I heard King make his announcement. "Folks, looks like we have an unprecedented result this evening. We have two winning acts that registered the exact same applause ranking. Now, unfortunately, we can't have two winners, but I've checked with our sponsors and they've agreed to do a rematch next week, with these two performers doing three songs each, with the winner earning an unprecedented one-thousand-dollars! So let's give a big hand to tonight's two top tying performers, Billy the Wonderkid and The Deli-Girl, Jo-Jo Anderson!

CHAPTER 12
THE WONDER OF IT ALL
JO-JO

I was floating in a dazzling, glitter-filled dream. But no, here I was, standing in my serviceable white waitress shoes on the edge of the WOR stage, bowing slightly to loud applause, while smiling with absolute glee. After King's announcement, Talent Jackpot's gold and silver confetti rained down on us, and all I could think about was what a wild ride these last few days had been.

John King quickly moved center stage, between Billy and me, as the director motioned for him to quickly wrap. "So folks, we got ourselves a real barn burner next week! Tell your friends, tell all the family…tune in next week to watch these two massive talents going head to head." He saluted the audience and closed with, "This is John Reed King for Cheerios, signing off until next Thursday evening!"

Billy began shooting off his cap guns again, but his attractive mother hustled out on stage in a too-tight red dress, took his guns away, and then shook Mr. King's hand. King guided us all backstage where Danny filled us in on instructions for next week.

"Congratulations you two. Now, listen up. Here's what's been decided. Both of you will need to come up with three new numbers for next week. You'll have Tuesday and Wednesday mornings from nine until noon to rehearse with the band. Try to pick well-known tunes, maybe one ballad and two up-tempos." He looked at Billy's mother and asked, "Has Billy done any ballads before, Mrs. Kizinski?"

She nodded confidently. "No problem. My Billy can do it all. We'll pick some winners. Right baby?"

She pinched his round, rouged cheeks and he responded with, "Sure thing, Ma."

I bit my lip in concentration, immediately thinking of what songs I might choose.

Mr. Cheerios rushed backstage with a photographer in tow. "Alright Danny, we need to arrange some quick photos with our two winners. This show had an unprecedented response! Lots of people are calling into the WOR switchboard and the top guys at General Mills just rang me up. They want to promote the heck out of next week's show. Newspaper ads, taxi banners, radio promos, the works." Mr. Cheerios rubbed his hands together. "People just love a good competition! I'm thinking we'll promote it as The Blonde Beauty versus The Wonder Boy. What do you think, Danny?"

Mrs. Kizinski interrupted, shaking her head, and stated in a high squeaky voice, "No...No way. Billy's stage name is Billy the Wonderkid. *Not* the Wonder Boy."

Mr. Cheerios pushed us back on stage with the photographer, while explaining to her, "No worries, Mrs. K, it's all a work in progress. Hey, win or lose, it's free publicity, ma'am."

She looked me up and down, smirking. "Oh, you can bet my ass, we'll be winning. Billy's got the goods over The Deli-Girl any day of the week."

Cheerios then took her by the elbow. "Language, Mrs. K! There are children here." He guided Mrs. Kizinski and her bad attitude to the women's dressing room to wait, while the photographer began posing us in separate headshots and then together, smiling cheek to cheek, standing back to back, Billy taking aim at me with his guns, me leaning over him with my mic stand. After dozens of shots, I was ready to return to my room at The Dixie.

My adrenaline was running high, but I was tired from the emotional roller coaster of the long day. Then I remembered. I'd committed to meeting Damien at ten o'clock after *Annie Get Your Gun* let out.

After I visited the restroom, Sammy Shine opened the back door for me. "Hey, Deli-Girl, I heard you done real good today. Congrats!"

I gave him a peck on the cheek and said, "And thank you for everything." I stopped on the landing and watched Billy and his mom walking hand in hand down the alley. "Hey, Sammy, how old is Billy? He's so small, but obviously quite talented for his age."

"No idea, maybe four or five? But I know one thing; that mother of his…she's one hot tomato."

I shook my head and said, "Looks like she has her hands full with him. See 'ya Tuesday."

~

WHEN DAMIEN and I had made plans yesterday, he'd mentioned his parents would be in town briefly and wanted us to join them for a late dinner. Although exhausted, I went to The Dixie, changed into my new black dress, and met Damien at the backdoor of the Imperial Theater. When he saw me outside waiting, he grinned, grabbed me, and twirled me around. He was on such a high. His excitement was infectious and I immediately felt happy and proud of him in his temporary lead role in a top musical. As the cast all poured out, he introduced me to several of his fellow hoofers and I was in awe when I was suddenly shaking the hand of the show's star, the great Ethel Merman.

After breaking away from the other performers, Damien said wistfully, "Jo-Jo, wish you could have been there tonight. It was magical. I'll try to get some tickets for you before Ray Middleton comes back."

"I'd love that. Thanks."

We were walking briskly down the sidewalk when Damien said, "I've got a surprise for you. Tonight we're having drinks at the 21

Club. We're meeting my parents there. Afraid I can't afford their food, but drinks will be nice, right?"

"Absolutely." I was glad I'd worn the black dress. I'd heard 21 was the place to go in Midtown to check out celebrities.

"Yeah, Pops always wanted to go to 21 whenever we played in New York. I remember him saying so many times, "Next time kid, when we play the Palace, we'll celebrate at Club 21.""

As we waited at a crosswalk, I asked, "So did you?...Ever play the Palace?"

"Nah. Neither of those things ever happened. We were on the road a lot, but never got to play the top houses. About the time I turned twelve, vaudeville just started dying out. The better theaters put in sound systems and began showing movies. That's what most people want to watch now. There's still plenty of theaters that have stage shows before the films, but it's not the same. Right now my parents are featured performers on a river cruise boat. They're off two nights, before they head out again. But they love the life. That's all they really know."

"So you were part of their act?"

"Yes. Seems like from the time I could walk, I danced. They're a song and dance team and once I came along and picked up tap, the family act went by Jones and Company. I started performing at age four. They taught me everything I know."

"So you were a little wonderkid too! Oh, that reminds me. I have news... I got to perform on Talent Jackpot tonight!"

Damien stopped in his tracks. "What? What happened?"

"They called me a few hours before showtime today; another performer twisted her ankle."

"Bad for her, but fantastic for you!...So tell me about it."

"I tied for first! But instead of splitting the prize money, General Mills wants us to have a big rematch with lots of publicity."

Damien stopped walking and grabbed my arms. "Jo-Jo, this could really be a big thing for you! Two weeks in a row and *lots* of free exposure. Who are you performing against?"

I rolled my eyes, describing my competition. "Billy the Wonderkid, maybe five years old, but sings the heck out of songs, and he's so tiny. The audience loves him. But his mom…she's a real hustler, a typical stage mom."

"Well, kids are cute, but I'll bet you can out-sing him."

We made it into the bar at Club 21 where we found his parents drinking martinis. I shook hands with them both and got big bear hugs in return. They were an attractive, middle-aged couple, smiling, laughing, talking non-stop, who seemed capable of finding a stage wherever they went. They had already befriended people on either side of them, along with the bartender, and introduced us to their new-found friends.

The four of us broke away from the crowd at the bar and got a table close by. We decided to share a bottle of champagne to celebrate Damien's starring role. On our second glass and toast, Damien told his parents about me performing on Talent Jackpot with Billy the Wonderkid.

When Damien mentioned the name, his mom seemed intrigued and asked me, "So what does this Billy look like?"

"Honestly, the cutest little thing. Not much more than three feet tall. A blond kid, with a chili-bowl haircut with long bangs. Always has a miniature cowboy hat on. Kind of a little pixie face. But the kid can belt out a song! I have to say though, he and his mother seem pretty rough around the edges. Backstage tonight, I caught Billy looking up my dress."

Mrs. Jones nodded knowingly at her husband, "Ringing any bells for you, Gerald?"

"Sure does." Damien's dad leaned over and told me, "That little A-hole; pardon my French, Miss Jo. He stole a fifty-dollar-bill out of my trousers' pocket at a resort up in the Borscht Belt about six, seven years ago. Back then, I knew Billy stole it because he was the only other performer allowed in the men's dressing room, and I'd accidentally left my money when I changed into my costume." His father pointed towards me, "One other thing, Miss Jo. Billy the Wonderkid ain't no kid. He's one of those little people. By that I mean, he's a full-fledged adult, and that's no momma with him; she's his wife."

I was stunned, looking back between Mr. and Mrs. Jones trying to confirm this crazy story. "So, how do you know this?"

Damien's mother took over, explaining, "Darling, we've been around the block a few times. And the loss of fifty bucks is nothing to sneeze at, especially during those years. After the theft, Gerald and I went looking for the kid and found him in the back kitchen of the resort playing craps with the cooks. So, he's supposed to be five years old, yet he was swearing up a storm, smoking, and busy winning with our money."

Gerald jumped back in. "So I'm all hot and bothered, pick up Billy by the seat of his scrawny pants and shake him upside down, making stuff drop out of his pockets, yelling for him to give me back my money. Then, hearing the commotion, the mother dashes in, slaps me, grabs Billy and kisses him all over his face and then tells us, 'Billy may have a few vices, but he's no thief!' Then she scoops up all the money on the floor and walks away with Billy holding her hand."

Damien's mother took a sip of Champagne and chimed in, "Jo-Jo, we were dumbfounded. We thought we were dealing with a smart-aleck kid, but he was certainly not the five-year-old his supposed mother was claiming. So anyway, at our next gig in the Poconos, we opened for comic Jackie Mason, who's always doing shows up in that area. Apparently, Mason knew all about the kid."

Gerald took over with Mason's story. "Oh yeah, so he says Billy's parents did vaudeville all over the country as a clown act. They had this one skit that always killed. Billy's mom and dad would dress up as clown doctors, and their patient was a pregnant lady. So, she's on a rolling gurney going through labor and who should pop out under the sheet, but little baby Billy, in diapers, and he runs all over the stage out of the grasp of the two doctors and the mother who are all now chasing him. "Course at that time he probably was a kid, maybe did that from four to fourteen. Who knows?"

"My head is spinning. I had no idea."

Mrs. Jones added, "So, over the years, Billy and the girl playing the patient get a thing going. After they marry, she wants a more dignified act for Billy. They leave the clown family and vaudeville behind and have done pretty good for themselves out in the theaters with Billy as a singing act, but they always need to stay on the move so no one gets wise to Billy not getting any older."

Damien nodded. "You know, Jo-Jo, that's not really fair for you. A lot of people are voting for him because he's so poised and clever for his age, but if he's in his twenties, maybe he's not so spectacular."

I took another sip of bubbles, and nodded. "I agree. Look at Shirley Temple. People couldn't get enough of her back in the thirties. She was the number one film actress from 1935 to '38 and now she's box office poison. And she's only eighteen; still sings and dances, but people didn't want to see her grow up."

They all nodded, drank more Champagne and moved on, but I was in a dilemma. Thoughts immediately clouded my joyful mood. Should I let Billy rig the system and just hope I won the contest on talent alone, or should I report what I knew to Danny and maybe create a mess with the show? With my career and one-thousand-dollars on the line, I wasn't sure what to do.

CHAPTER 13
THE CHEERLEADER
SARAH

*A*fter receiving my stepfather's last minute call about Jo's performance on the radio, I ran down the hall to find Barbara in her friend's room. Once I told her about my twin sister being on Talent Jackpot's lineup, she quickly organized a listening party in our room with some of the girls from our hall and the eight of us crowded in, sitting on the beds, floor, and chairs.

After searching the dial, the static cleared, and we all stared excitedly at Barbara's radio, while listening to the deep voice of the show's host. As the show continued to go down the lineup, I was biting my nails hoping David had given me the right information about Jo being on the show. We listened through five different acts while the girls tried to envision what the performers all looked like.

Then King announced their final performer, Jo-Jo Anderson, while relief and then elation passed through me. This was really happening! My anticipation could hardly be contained as I passed around a photo of Jo and me taken at our high school graduation and the girls all agreed she was quite beautiful. Barbara shushed everyone, putting her finger to her lips. "Remember gals, we're here to listen to Jo-Jo sing. And it's the Ch'boogie song... I love that one!"

I wasn't sure which song that was. My study schedule rarely allowed me to spend time listening to the radio. I crossed my fingers for Jo, holding my breath, hoping she wouldn't flub a lyric, while all the other girls were snapping their fingers along to the beat, swaying back and forth. At the end, we all stood and cheered. The Deli-Girl was a big hit in room 221!

After a few minutes, they announced the surprising tie, and our room erupted again in massive applause. Girls from the other rooms stuck their heads inside to see what the commotion was about. All these girls were being so nice and supportive. Maybe I'd been too harsh in judging everyone earlier without really getting to know them.

The following afternoon, I had the urge to speak to Jo person-ally. Sometimes writing letters just wasn't good enough. Too much lag time. I really wanted to tell her how proud I was while listening to her on a nation-wide radio program. But, neither of us had phones and long distance calls were expensive.

Impulsively, I went down to use the phone near the reception desk in my dorm. I had to wait in line behind three girls while the phone was hijacked by a student having a big public argument with her mother. After ten minutes, I gave up and walked over to the library and used the payphone nearby. There was no wait and I asked the operator to connect me to The Dixie Hotel in Manhattan, which she kindly did after I dropped in four dimes. I hated spending the forty-cents, but having a real conversation with my sister was worth it.

"Dixie Hotel, how can I help you?"

"Hi there, my sister, Jo-Jo Anderson, lives in room 425. Is there any way I can leave her a message to call me back? Her room doesn't have a phone."

"You said Jo-Jo Anderson? Isn't that The Deli-Girl from Talent Jackpot?"

"Yes, that's her! "

"So, she lives here?" The operator asked excitedly. "I just saw her photo today on the subway and an ad in the paper. Isn't that a coinkydink!"

I had no idea what that was, but I said, "Yes, she's lived at The

Dixie for over six months now, but I really need to speak to her. This is her sister, Sarah."

"I could probably get a bellhop to go to her room and deliver a message but it might take a while. This is the time of day when all the guests are checking in. I'll tell you what, Sarah. I'll go pay her a visit myself. It's time for my break and I'd love to meet her in person. All of us operators are in the basement and we never see anything. Gee willikers! You think she'll give me an autograph?"

"I'm sure she'd be thrilled to."

"Give me your number and I'll have her call you back, and if she's not in, I'll let you know. By the way, I'm Willie, short for Wilhelmina. Let's say about fifteen minutes?"

"That's very kind of you."

"So Sarah, do you sing too?"

"No, I just study. Thank you Willie."

Now I had to pretend I was talking on the payphone for the next fifteen minutes, to avoid the phone being taken over by some other chatterbox. Maybe letter writing was easier after all.

Ten minutes later, the pay phone rang and I eagerly clicked on. "Jo-Jo, hi!"

"Sarah. It's Willie again. Just wanted to let you know that your sister's on her way down to use the pay phone in the mezzanine and, by the way, she's gorgeous! I'll be rooting for her Thursday and I'll tell all the other operators too."

I thanked her again, while thinking that poor Willie definitely needed to get out of the basement more. A few minutes later, Jo's call came through.

"My sister, the star! I'm so happy for you, Jo."

"Aw, thanks for tuning in. I'm glad you got the message from David. But one talent show certainly does not make me a star. Far from it. Now maybe if I win this thing Thursday, I'll get some mojo going. Part of the prize is getting a week's booking at a theater. Sarah, I'm really glad you called. I have a problem and could use your advice."

"I'm all ears, just like in the old days. You'd do all the talking and I'd just sit and listen."

"Sarah, even if you're quiet, you always give good advice." Jo-Jo went on to explain the dilemma about Billy the Wonderkid, his actual age, and whether she should tell the talent wrangler at WOR about it. "I'm just not sure if reporting it will only make things more complicated."

"I'm flabbergasted! What a flim-flam artist." I paused for a minute, thinking things through. "You know I don't mince words, Jo. I think you need to tell the talent guy right away. Then they'll decide what to do about it. And you'll need to go along with what they decide. I'm sure you'll still get to perform. And that's the most important thing, right?"

"That's true. I just don't want to come off as a sore loser...or create a commotion about the integrity of the show."

"As long as you're sure about the credibility of your story. You definitely don't want to spread false rumors."

"I'm pretty sure. Damien's parents seemed convinced. I'll try to verify a little more. So, enough about my problems. What's been going on with you? I'm so sorry about you and Tommy. I received your last letter and was shocked. How are you holding up?"

"I miss him... badly. Just knowing he's no longer going to be there when I come home for Thanksgiving or other holidays... It'll feel like there's a big hole in me. But Mom swears things will get better. She said it was time for me to let him go so he can start exploring a new life."

"She's right, as usual. If nothing else, I know the two of you will always end up as friends."

"I hope so. Oh, I do have other news, Jo. I have a dinner date this Friday!"

"You what? Sarah, you just said there's a big hole in your heart. I've never even seen you talk to another boy besides Tommy. Who with?"

"Jacob Riverstone. I joined a voters registration group and he's the president of the Young Republicans on campus."

"A Republican? That would be a first for our family."

"Slow down; we're just having dinner. Anyway, I'm sure there's plenty of good republicans out there. He seems quite smart."

"Sarah, if he's a nice guy, I want to hear all about it in your next letter. Hey, I hate to cut this short, but I have to go rehearse in a few minutes. The band at the Ebb Tide is willing to give me thirty or forty minutes of their time tonight."

"OK, big sister. Knock 'em dead. I'll be listening next week."

~

SATURDAY EVENING, I was sitting in a dark booth of the Hawkeye Hut with Jacob. While we were waiting for our order of burgers and beer, I noticed he was wearing a blue shirt with a small pin on his collar which confidently stated: **Dewey in '48!** I pointed to his pin and said, "You're a little ahead of the game, aren't you?"

"Not at all; it's less than two years before the next election. Dewey essentially hasn't stopped campaigning since he lost in '44. I predict he's going to have a big win. Mark my words, Sarah."

"Duly noted. If it's alright with you, I'd rather not talk much about politics and don't try so hard to pull me into your camp. I'll decide on my own."

He looked a little taken aback. "You're quite blunt."

I had to laugh at his comment. "Yes, I've been told. I believe in listening, considering, and then saying what I think. But, my abruptness does seem to ruffle a few feathers." Our beers arrived and I took a sip, "My twin sister says I need to learn the art of nuance and subtlety."

"So, you have a twin? There's two of you I have to convert?"

"Good luck with that. She lives in New York City."

"Interesting. Attending Brown or Columbia?"

Again, I laughed. "Actually, she barely got out of high school. No, she works at the Stage Deli in Manhattan and keeps trying to get into show business. She's also two inches taller than me, blond and blue eyed. So obviously, we're nothing alike, but we get along surprisingly well. As kids, Jo-Jo was always the leader and I was the follower, but in the last few years I'm learning to speak up more."

"That's what I like about you, Sarah. Well, that and your pretty brown eyes. So, about me... I already told you I was thinking about going into politics. I'll probably run for student body president this spring. My father is a judge in Des Moines and got me interested in politics early. Where do you see yourself once you graduate?"

"Somewhere in the education field. In administration eventually. I have a lot of ideas about teaching and curriculum. I'd like to make a difference."

"Interesting, in what way?"

At that point our burgers arrived and I focused on the food, but I was pleased with Jacob's questions. I couldn't recall anyone ever asking me what I wanted to do with my career. Most people didn't seem to take the teaching profession that seriously. It was as if it was something women did until they married and had children. I wanted to do more than that and improve things back in Green Tree.

Jacob took a big bite of burger and nodded. "We just had a new high school open in Des Moines. That makes three. I attended East High, but the city's really growing. Over one-hundred-and-fifty-thousand people now. I'm sure the district will be needing new teachers soon."

"It's funny, I've never even contemplated teaching any place other than Green Tree, but I suppose I should keep my options open."

"Absolutely, Sarah. There's a big world out there."

Later, Jacob and I strolled through downtown looking into shop windows and then crossed over to the campus. As we continued to walk, he slipped his arm around my waist, holding me close. Instead of me shying away, I found I rather liked it. The closeness, the sense of belonging. I felt a sudden stirring that was totally new. As we drew close to Currier Hall, I noticed the shadows of a few couples leaning against the trees, probably necking, before the girls had to go in before Saturday's eleven-o'clock curfew. I started feeling unsettled. Would Jacob expect me to do this too? Tommy and I had kissed, but never for a long period of time. I wasn't sure of his expectations.

Under the lights of the entrance, Jacob politely asked, "Would a good night kiss be possible, Sarah?"

I looked into his gray eyes and clear, pale face. "Sure." He took my chin and tilted my head up and gave me a brief peck on the lips. *Hmm, rather dry; certainly not titillating. What was I worried about?*

Then he pulled back and smiled. "Thanks, that'll do until next time. I'll leave you a message soon at the reception desk."

"Alright, good night, Jacob." I entered the dorm feeling rather disappointed. I'd thought there might be extensive lip locking, hugs, and perhaps warm whisperings in my ear. But no, just a simple little peck. I had better good-night kisses from my mother. This dating business was complicated. Maybe I should just stick to my studies.

CHAPTER 14
DECISION DILEMMAS
JO-JO

*T*he next day, as I arrived for the lunch rush, Mr. Asnas, Chuckles, the dishwasher, and the morning waitress, Myrna, all stopped working and applauded when I walked in. Asnas was apparently over the moon with the free lip service I gave the Stage Deli on national radio. As I tied on my apron, he announced, "So Jo-Jo, I was thinking. I'm going to put a big sign on the door: *The singing Deli-Girl works here. Tune in to Talent Jackpot next Thursday night!* What do you think of that?"

"Sure boss. Great idea. I appreciate your support." He continued following me while I punched the time clock. "Hey, my two coffee pals are here this morning sitting at the back table. Do your boss a favor; my friends would love to see you sing. They caught the show last night. Very impressed."

"Uh, sing right now? In the restaurant? Wouldn't that seem unprofessional?"

"Not at all. Go ahead, give 'em a thrill."

I felt like a wind-up toy he was wheeling out to amuse his friends. But I smiled, walking over to their table. I doubted there'd be an extra tip in it. The two men were a pair of frequent customers who often sat and argued with Mr. Asnas over everything from politics to how blue the sky was, usually nursing two cups of coffee over the course of a couple hours.

"Hi Gentlemen. Max said you might be interested in hearing me sing a song today."

One of the guys said, "Yes, we loved the train song. Do that one."

"Sure, but you have to help me sing the chorus." Soon, I had their table and customers at three more tables nearby, jumping on the Choo Choo Ch'boogie chorus. It was actually fun and everybody slipped change into my apron pocket as I passed. I suddenly had a deja vu moment of me and my childhood busking days in Hollywood, when I would tap dance for nickels and dimes in the foyer of theaters. I hadn't thought of that in years. Probably because it was during the time I lived with Nanette. I'd buried those memories pretty deep.

As I finished, Asnas noticed all his other employees leaning against the counter enjoying my little floor show. "All right... Enough fun and games. Everybody back to work."

By Saturday night, I was tuckered out. I flopped down in my bed, ready to rest my aching feet and listen uninterrupted to *Your Hit Parade* on my plastic Philco. Each week, the Lucky Strike orchestra and different guest singers performed the fifteen most popular songs in America, and the show always had a big build-up before announcing the number one song in the nation. I wrote down the titles of a few songs that tugged at my heartstrings, hoping to find three winners for my next Thursday performance.

This week, Frank Sinatra was the Hit Parade's guest singer. His voice was so smooth and dreamy. The last thing I remembered that night was Mr. Sinatra, casually holding a drink in his hand, walking into my room and sitting down at the foot of my bed, while he sang me to sleep crooning his top song, *Give Me Five Minutes More*. The next morning, I stretched, rubbing my eyes, hoping Mr. Blue Eyes was still around, but no. I added that song to my list, thinking, *Mr. Sinatra, you can have all the time you want.*

Somewhere between my dreams and reality, I'd decided that Sarah was right. I quit worrying about the pros and cons of alerting the station to the possibility of Billy's fraud and decided to take action. I called WOR Monday morning, and asked for Danny. I thought it best to speak to the talent wrangler, and leave it to him to take up the issue with station management.

"Danny Tucker here."

"Hello, it's Jo-Jo Anderson. Talent Jackpot?"

"Of course, my Deli-Girl! I keep seeing your and Billy's picture all over town. Lots of buzz going on with the show. Can't wait for rehearsals to start tomorrow."

"Yes, it's so exciting! First off, is this a good time for you? I don't want to interrupt your schedule."

"I have *Queen For a Day* auditions at two, but go ahead."

Listen Danny, I came across some information a few days back and was hesitant to come forward with it. Still, I think you should at least know about it and then have your bosses make their decision."

"This sounds ominous. What's the problem?"

I cleared my throat and steadied my voice. "Sir, I believe Billy the Wonderkid is not a kid at all. I'm not sure of his exact age, but he's probably in his twenties by now, and get this! Mrs. Kizinski is his wife, not his mother."

"What! Where did you get this? That's quite an accusation, Jo-Jo."

"I realize that. I've been thinking long and hard about it since I got wind of this…It comes from a reliable source."

"Ok, go on."

"My boyfriend's parents, Gerald and Wilma Jones, have been performing through the Borscht Belt as a dance duo for years and they told me they shared billing with Billy the Wonderkid quite a while back while at a resort in the Catskills. Even then, Billy was smoking, swearing, playing craps with the kitchen cooks. He's one of the little people--you know, miniature adults. But apparently, the act goes over better when the audience thinks he's just a young kid."

"You sure about all this?"

"Pretty sure. We all met for dinner last Thursday night and I described my competition, Billy, to them and they immediately knew who I was talking about. They even had it confirmed at another dinner theater with comedian Jackie Mason. He knew all about the kid and his wife's history. And I have to add, Billy said a few things around me that aren't typically child-like. Now, I know that's not proof, but I thought you should know. But I won't say anything about this to anyone else."

Christ-all-mighty, this could be disastrous. We have ads running all over the network and other big radio markets."

"I know. I just thought that if Mr. and Mrs. Jones knew about Billy, then probably a lot of other people in the business might also know. More people may talk, especially if he wins. But, whatever your bosses decide to do, I'm still on board with it."

"Jo-Jo, you were right to tell me. The problem is above my pay grade, but I'll speak with the guys upstairs. They may want to talk to you too, but in the meantime, rehearsals go as planned and just keep your mouth shut about it."

"Will do. Thanks for listening, Danny. See you tomorrow."

"See you Deli-Girl. Oh, plan on wearing the work uniform again for at least your first number. That idea really seemed to work."

"Will do, Mr. Tucker." Ugh! My smelly uniform, again?

Later, at work, Mr. Asnas arranged to let me off for rehearsals Tuesday, Wednesday, and the day of the show, as long as I tried to plug the Stage Deli another time on air. When I told him Danny wanted me to wear my uniform again, he got really excited, and called a pal of his in the garment business.

"Hey Milton, Asnas here at the deli. My friend...let's do a little bartering; Got a lovely girl working here who's on a big radio talent show this week. Yes...Yes, the very one! Anyway, the Deli-Girl needs a new waitress uniform ready by tomorrow. And I want the Stage Deli monogrammed in bright red across the top pocket, and on her hat. You do this for me, and you and your entire team get free bagels for the week. We got a deal? OK...make it bagels for two weeks. Perfect! You're a real mensch, Milton. Hang on, my girl's gonna give you her specifics."

Max handed me the phone and I gave Milton my size, measurements, height and asked that the skirt be hemmed above my knees.

Throughout the day, my regular customers were congratulating me, wishing me luck, and asking for songs at their tables. I picked up at least four extra bucks in tips while singing. Everything was going great until I got a call later from Danny, who told me the station manager and Mr. Cheerios wanted a meeting with me early tomorrow morning before rehearsals. The call made me unsettled, fearing I'd blown up our Thursday show by revealing Billy's secret.

CHAPTER 15
SWEATER WEATHER
SARAH

*J*acob was not the best kisser, and honestly seemed a bit timid in that regard, and yet he was so confident in other ways. But who was I to complain? My only extensive kissing experience had been with Tommy Martin. Maybe my smooch needed some work too? Either way, it was something that could be studied and improved upon. These were my primary thoughts as I headed over to the student union to meet Jacob for coffee on a cold, bright afternoon.

When I walked in, I took off my coat and tossed it over my arm. As I walked up, he smiled and said, "That must be your favorite sweater; you've worn that each time I've seen you."

My face felt frozen as I slowly responded. "Yeah… I like the color." How embarrassing. I felt like shrinking into the floor. I'd never thought twice about repeating an outfit. It was one of two sweaters I owned. They each coordinated with two wool skirts my grandmother made for me before I left for school. They weren't the most stylish, but seemed perfectly serviceable. Those items, along with a cotton print dress, dungarees, a few flannel shirts, and my church dress, were pretty much the extent of my wardrobe. I'd never given it much thought. Jacob would see them all quite soon if he stuck around long enough.

He'd already purchased my coffee as we sat, with a small table between us. Jacob sipped from his steaming cup and then asked, "Sarah, I was wondering if you'd like to help me man the registration table after your biology class tomorrow? For about two hours?"

I considered this for a few seconds. Wasn't I supposed to try to become a joiner, get involved? I was still a little hesitant. "Hmm, I guess."

"Honestly, It's a great way to meet other students and gives us a chance to talk to them about the upcoming election."

"As long as I don't have to promote any candidates, I'm willing to do that. Sure, sounds fun," I said with a forced smile.

"Great. We always wear some type of University shirt or sweater, just to show we're all part of the same group. Afterwards, if you have time, I'll introduce you to some of the other members. We usually meet for beers on Wednesday afternoons and discuss strategy. There's a couple of off-the-cobs in the group but most of the guys are good people."

"Off the cob? What's that?" I immediately thought he meant someone just off the farm? If so, that was definitely me.

"You know… someone who's a little crazy or silly. Certainly not you. You'll fit right in, Sarah. Don't worry."

Fit right in? Now, I *was* worried.

We talked about classes, irritating professors, and Jacob told me about the film, *It's a Wonderful Life,* which he'd seen a few weeks back. "You'll love it. If it's still showing, I'll take you next week."

Later, as I got up to leave, I said, "So, meet you in the quad tomorrow afternoon?"

"Yes, our shift starts at three."

"What if I don't have a university sweater for tomorrow? I've never thought of buying one." *Nor did I have the money to spend on one.*

"Don't worry. They sell them at the student union store. Probably only a couple bucks. See you tomorrow, Sarah."

I walked over to the little shop near the main entrance of the union and checked prices on their monogrammed sweaters. But I left without making a purchase. I didn't like them and was certainly not about to spend over three dollars on one. The Young

Republicans would have to take me as I was, with my old green sweater, or not at all.

The following day, I was in biology class. I'd attended two additional classes since my first run-in with Professor Carter. Although I detested his superior attitude, I continued to approve of his comfortable, confident lecturing style and his wide breadth of knowledge. He was not the doddering old Professor Jenkins he'd replaced. Jenkins was always losing his train of thought, meandering through musings that went beyond the need to know. Instead, Carter stuck to the material, often making biology the fascinating topic it should have been.

I was now a fan, despite his personal etiquette and attitude which definitely needed improvement. Before the end of class, Carter handed back quizzes taken during our previous class. I was pleased; I got everything correct including the bonus question. As he dropped the paper on my desk, he complimented me. "Good work, Anderson. I need to see you after class."

After the others left, I stood at his desk, waiting again for him to look up from the notes he was scribbling. I was supposed to be meeting Jacob and didn't want to keep him waiting. "Professor Carter, what is it that you wanted?"

He continued to keep his head down while writing. This man's manners were insufferable. He finally broke his train of thought, but continued writing with his eyes on the page. "What are your plans, Anderson? Your goals in life? Or are you still figuring all that out?"

"On the contrary. I know exactly what I want to do. I plan to get my degree in secondary education and then my masters in administration. I'd really like to change things regarding the curriculum of the schools in my hometown."

He finally looked up from his writing. "What a waste."

"I beg your pardon?" What an arrogant ass, to tell me my goals were meaningless. Now he was acting exactly as he had on the Greyhound bus. "Who are you to dismiss my goals? I think they have merit."

"You're thinking small, Anderson. Go bigger. You definitely

have the capacity." He pointed over to a chair behind me. "Pull up a chair and sit down, please."

I glanced at my watch and dragged a chair over.

"Your grade point average is ten percent higher than anyone else in this class. Both under ProfessorJenkins tutelage and mine. Have you taken a lot of biology before? You seem to grasp the concepts quite clearly."

I shook my head. "We were offered one basic course my sopho-more year in high school. But I generally do well in subjects I find compelling."

"Admirable. Let me get to it. I need a good lab assistant. Someone who is thorough, good with detail, and picks up the mate-rial quickly. You would help me set up the lab equipment and oversee other students' work, and of course, there would be a small university stipend involved. In addition, you get credit hours and it will benefit your resume."

I nodded, thinking it through. "That all sounds good. I was just thinking I could use some extra funds for incidentals. I'm on scholarship."

"I'm aware. I checked your records. In order to make your class schedule mesh with the lab schedule, I had to request different times for your English and history classes, but it shouldn't be a major obstacle.

"So you already switched my classes?" This was all moving along rather quickly.

He shrugged his shoulders. "It can be changed back. So you're in concurrence with these arrangements?"

"I...I guess so."

"Perfect." He handed me a printed form. "This would be a copy of your new class schedule. Just sign your approval here at the bottom. The classes are teaching the same curriculum as your previous ones so the transition should be smooth. But you will have to do some extra study on lab protocol. Are you certain you're inter-ested?" He took off his glasses and pinched the bridge of his straight thin nose, and looked over at me and attempted a hint of a smile.

I looked at the revised schedule and thought the paid position was worth the schedule changes. "Professor Carter, I'd be pleased to accept. Thank you." I extended my hand to shake on the arrangement, noticing his firm but warm handshake in return.

"Excellent. We'll talk soon then. How do I contact you?"

"I live at Currier Hall. You can always leave a message for me there." I stood up to go, taking my book bag from the floor. "I have to run. I'm supposed to be helping out at the voter registration table. I'm a little late."

"Yes. Thank you, Miss Anderson." He was already back to scribbling in his journal.

I left the building on a high note, almost catching myself skipping down the dark echoing hallway of the science building. A youngish, clever, albeit arrogant professor thought me to be mature and smart enough to assist in a biology lab. Maybe I *was* shooting too low for my capabilities? Why not go for a Ph.D, followed by the coveted Nobel Prize? Alright, don't be ridiculous. In reality, I'd been offered a small, part-time job to take care of stuff that stuffy Professor Carter didn't want to deal with. And I was fine with that. I wondered if there would be an official white lab coat involved? That might be nice.

I walked out to the quadrangle and looked for the table and gold sweaters of the Young Republicans. I spotted Jacob from the back; his short blondish hair gently blowing in the breeze, his back and shoulders solid and straight. I walked up in front of the table, still wearing my big, happy smile. "Hi there! Sarah Anderson reporting for duty."

"Sarah, you look happy today, but you forgot your team shirt."

"No, honestly, I didn't want to spend the money buying one, but the good news is my biology professor just offered me a part time job as his lab assistant."

" Are you sure you want to do that? Sounds like a lot of extra work. Hey, don't worry about the sweater, I've got an extra you can borrow."

Disappointed with his response, I said, "Thanks Jacob, but bright gold isn't really my color."

CHAPTER 16

THE BEAUTY VERSUS
THE BABY

JO-JO

*T*rying to think positively about the upcoming contest, I joined the band at the Ebb Tide again for practice. Dottie was now open to giving me tips on the best way to approach each song. She and the band helped me narrow down my list, choosing the three best numbers for my voice. We first decided on Glen Miller's, *In The Mood*, which was filled with fast-paced, challenging lyrics. After doing well with the *Ch'boogie* song, I chose another one in that vein, the Andrew Sisters' version of *Boogie Woogie Bugle Boy*. It was an older tune from '41, but always seemed to be a crowd pleaser. As my closer, the band leader, Slim, suggested the ballad, *Sentimental Journey*.

When we finished my practice session, Dottie came up and said, "Kid, don't let this go to your head, but your voice reminds me of Les Brown's singer, a little blonde songbird, Doris Day. She's gonna be one to watch for." Coming from Dottie, this was a huge compliment which had me smiling through bedtime.

I set my alarm extra early, knowing the following morning I needed to pick up the expected fresh Danish for Danny and Sammy Shine, and then race down multiple blocks to get to WOR for the managers' meeting before rehearsals.

I climbed into bed and dozed off and then saw myself walking out the back door of WOR and down the dark alley. Suddenly, a heavy wooden object struck my right ankle. The searing pain and shock knocked me onto my back. When I looked up, I was staring at tiny Billy holding a bat, with the fringe of his cowboy outfit blowing in the night breeze. Next to him was his mom/wife in her sexy red dress. They stood over me with gleeful smiles as Mrs. Kizinski pulled a black revolver out of her handbag, cocked it, and slowly pulled the trigger.

I woke with a muted scream and a blanket pulled over my face. My heart was still racing as I shook my head, telling myself it was only a ridiculous dream. It was three AM. I closed my eyes but didn't sleep a wink while I let the early morning hours tick away waiting for the morning alarm. As irritating as my wakefulness was, it was preferable to the nightmare of having my ankles whacked by Billy and shot in the face by Mrs. K.

Arriving at WOR, I felt guilty and anxious following Billy and Mrs. Kizinski up the stairs and into the studio offices. I had accused him of something pretty bad and I crossed my fingers that my information was correct. The three of us stared out uncomfortably at Mr. Cheerios, Danny Tucker, and the station manager, who were relishing the donuts and Danish I'd brought.

Danny opened the discussion with glazed sugar glistening on his chin. "Thanks for coming in early guys. We have a serious matter to discuss that involves everybody in this room."

Mr. Cheerios cleared his throat and continued. "We've had some recent phone calls with serious accusations that may bring the outcome of Thursday's show into question. And, I can assure you, General Mills will absolutely *not* be tainted with anything remotely scandalous."

I breathed in and out deeply, trying to calm myself. Thank God, he had not mentioned my name.

"Mrs. Kizinski, your son, Billy presents himself as a young child in his act. What exactly is his age?"

Not helping his case any, Billy, still wearing his cowboy hat, interrupted with a belligerent voice, "Who wants to know? Whatever they said, it's a bum rap."

Mr. Cheerios responded, "I'm not at liberty to say, but let me add, it's more than one person and we've done a little checking ourselves. Anyway, we've promoted this show as Billy the *Kid* versus The Deli-Girl. I just saw one tabloid doing a story with the headline: *The Beauty versus the Baby*. Now, we love the buzz, but everybody is assuming Billy is four or five years old, performing as some type of singing-child phenomenon. So, Mrs. Kizinski, what is Billy's actual age?"

Billy's mom wrung her hands nervously and said in a cloying tone, "Billy's just small for his age. He's almost seven now. We never claimed he was a certain age."

Mr. Cheerios shook his head. "If he's only seven, how can it be that he was performing this same act several years ago up in the Catskills. I have it on good authority that Billy is at least twenty by now."

She jumped up, grabbing her handbag. "That's preposterous! You're clearly mixing him up with his older brother, *Willy the Wonderful*. It happens from time to time. They look similar. Willy also used to perform, but he's retired now."

The station manager dropped his cigar in his danish and said, "Look, if you have another son that's in his twenties, you are looking amazingly young for your age, Mrs. Kizinski. We're gonna need to see some proof of Billy's age. You got a birth certificate?"

She sat back down looking indignant and responded. "Well, not *on* me. Does anybody in this room have one on them right now?" Everybody looked around with blank faces.

Mr. Cheerios slammed his hand on the desk he was sitting behind. "Enough of this ridiculous story of Willys and Billys. The integrity of this show is paramount. Mrs. Kizinski, you produce a valid birth certificate by tomorrow and we drop this discussion. If you can't, the show goes on as advertised, but under *no circumstances* does Billy win this thing. We'll pay you the five-hundred-dollars from last week's show, and then you're out of here with no discussion or complaints to any papers or radio programs. So, Mrs. Kizinski, will you be able to produce a birth certificate tomorrow?"

Mrs. Kizinski shook her head sadly. "No, it was lost when a

tornado hit and burned our house down. It'll be months before I can get a replacement certificate."

Billy chimed in. "This ain't fair. And what's this dame, The Deli-Girl, doing in here? I smell a low-down stinkin' rat."

Mr. Cheerios slapped his forehead in frustration. "Because she needs to know what's going on as well. If needed, the applause-o-meter will be adjusted this one and only time to reflect her winning and then Billy, you and your mother will be escorted to the bus station. And I would suggest, if you continue performing, that you do your act under another name. But if word of this ever gets out, you'll never work the Borscht Belt again. Also, the three of you need to sign an agreement to these terms."

Billy and his mother whispered to each other and his mother announced, "We'll just take our five-hundred clams and scram."

Mr. Cheerios became very firm. "No. The show has been advertised heavily nation-wide. Our General Mills brand is at stake. If you want the five hundred, you need to perform and then get out of town. Miss Anderson, are you going to be in compliance with these arrangements? You can't say a word to anybody about this."

"Yes sir. I understand"

Billy jumped up in anger. "Of course The Deli-Girl understands. Everything's going her way! This is highway robbery. It wouldn't surprise me if she was doing the horizontal tango with one of you guys."

I looked over at him defensively. "How dare you! At least I present myself as who I actually am."

Billy had now lost all pretense of coming off as a child. Throwing up his hands in anger, he explained, "Folks, folks. It's just entertainment, smoke and mirrors. Does a magician reveal his tricks? No, and we all know it's just a trick but we accept the illusion. That's all I'm doing. So, where's the harm?" Everyone continued to sit and stare at him, while his normally loud-mouthed mother remained meekly quiet. Then in frustration, Billy threw in the towel. "Oh hell…gimme the frigging papers to sign."

Danny stood, clapped his hands together and said. "Let's all calm down. Billy, if this wasn't a competition show, it might not be such a big problem, but on Talent Jackpot, people have to believe what they're seeing or hearing. And right now, we have a show to rehearse. The secretary outside has contracts for you three to sign. And then you need to follow me downstairs. The orchestra is ready to start rehearsing your song selections."

Following behind, I almost wished I'd said nothing. Now, I'd never know if I'd won this thing fair and square. Talent Jackpot would always feel tainted for me.

CHAPTER 17
SQUARE PEG-ROUND HOLE
SARAH

*A*fter working the voter registration table with Jacob, he suggested we join the Young Republicans' weekly planning and drinking session at Hesson's Tavern. As a hint of rebellion, I decided to postpone my evening with a biology textbook and be spontaneous. I laughed at myself while we walked, thinking that meeting a group of young republicans was hardly showing a madcap streak of independence, but maybe they'd surprise me.

The tavern was a small local pub which attempted to capture the spirit of old Germany with an elaborately carved wooden bar featuring a mirrored back. There were several small gnome figurines stuck in the corners, and rows of illustrated beer steins lining the dark walls. The bar was several blocks from campus and seemed to cater more to the townspeople rather than students. Jacob explained that their crew was allowed to monopolize a portion of the bar on Wednesdays as long as they kept buying drinks.

Once inside, he quickly introduced me to several men and a few women who were gathered around the back corner of the bar. As he waited for the busy barkeep, he said, "Sarah, why don't you find a place to sit while I order our beers."

I noticed two spare chairs at a crowded, large round table. I drew in a breath, offered up a pained smile, and sat down. I nodded at the other students who were in the middle of a robust discussion. I immediately felt like an interloper sitting in on their elite group.

One guy wearing a white shirt and wool blazer slammed his mug down on the wooden table, while looking around at his friends. "The League of Nations was a complete waste of time and resources. And what happened? It ended up going kaput. But now, what is our government doing? They're plowing all this money into the United Nations." He stopped and threw his hands up. "For what purpose? We need to stop sticking our noses into other county's problems." There seemed to be a light rumble of opposing comments when he noticed me trying to sink into my chair and be ignored. "Hey you, welcome to the weekly round table. What's your name?"

"Uh, I'm Sarah. Jacob asked me to join you guys today."

"So Sarah…let's get your perspective. What do you think of this ridiculous United Nations?"

"Well, honestly… I haven't read up on it much. But, after the last four years of international war, I'd say a body of nations wanting to maintain world peace isn't a terrible idea."

That did it. The table erupted into people talking over each other, pounding the table, with a few inflamed insults thrown about just as Jacob walked up with our two beers and scooted into the chair next to me. "Whoa guys, don't snap your caps. I leave Sarah for a few minutes and the table explodes into World War Three." He pointed to the loudmouth wearing the blazer and smiled. "Johnson must be grandstanding again."

The blazer guy pointed a finger at me. "It's just that your friend here doesn't know what the hell she's talking about."

Jacob came to my defense, putting his arm around me. "Stop picking on her, she's a novice. She'll come around, right Sarah?"

I gave this a few seconds thought and replied, "I'm not sure that I will. But I certainly think that the mention of world peace shouldn't result in condemnations and juvenile chest beating. I see nothing wrong with the premise."

Jacob offered a condescending smile. "That's the problem. It's merely a utopian dream--representatives of all nations coming together and holding hands in one building. Anyway, after creating the biggest bomb the world has ever seen, do any of you honestly think anyone will attempt to attack Uncle Sam again? I, for one, don't. Moving on... We need to talk about fundraising for the next election. Anybody have any fresh ideas?"

As they haggled and suggested, I finished my beer, visited the restroom and decided to leave. It seemed clear to me that I was not going to become a favorite among the young republicans. I'd tried being a joiner; attempted a little spontaneity, but I guess it simply wasn't in my nature. On my way out, I leaned over Jacob's shoulder and told him I had a quiz to study for and waved goodbye to the raucous round table.

~

I WAS LOOKING FORWARD to my first day as lab assistant to Dr. Carter. What a contrast! My sister might soon be rubbing shoulders with famous musicians on a New York stage, while I was looking forward to dissecting pig fetuses in a biology lab.

Growing up on the farm, it wasn't uncommon for a few small newborns to be crushed by a large sow right after birth, so I hoped I wouldn't feel too squeamish about the dissection. When you grow up around livestock, births and deaths are all part of the seasonal cycle. The professor had explained to me that the pig most anatomically resembled humans and that's why we used them for study of their internal organs and connective tissue.

For my training, Professor Carter was waiting in one of the smaller labs in the science building and looked up as I walked in. "Right on time, Anderson. I like that. Help yourself to one of the lab coats hanging by the door."

"I'm really looking forward to this," I said excitedly, selecting a white coat. I put it on and rolled up the sleeves. "I'm ready to get to work."

Carter was first showing me, one on one, so I could later help direct the lab students in proper dissection techniques. We stood next to each other at a lab table while he showed me the various dissection tools. He unwrapped two fetuses, stabilized them with twine, placed them face up over a lab tray, and began demonstrating the best cutting techniques, which I replicated. After cutting out the organ block, we were able to identify and examine the internal organs. I found the study fascinating and opened my notebook and began making a quick sketch, labeling all the parts.

As Professor Carter looked on, he said, "Anderson, surely you've noticed your text will have most of these labeled in a diagram."

"Yes, but illustrating and labeling everything myself helps cement the information more clearly in my brain. It's just the way I've always taught myself."

He nodded. "Impressive. Your attention to detail is quite good. All necessary techniques for a developing scientist."

I laughed a little. "Well, I'm no scientist, but I'm glad you appreciate the technique."

"But you could be, Sarah. If that was something you wanted to pursue. Don't sell yourself short. We could use more women in the sciences."

"Well, that's certainly true. I noticed almost all the faculty in the biology department are men."

He leaned over my shoulder, looking at my drawing more carefully. I couldn't help but inhale his heady scent, perhaps a mix of spicy aftershave, clean soap and...I took another sniff...Maybe Brylcreem? I looked up and noticed his short, sleek, perfect hair. Definitely Brylcreem. I smiled as I looked up into his eyes and he appeared to lock onto mine for a few fleeting seconds, and then Professor Carter backed away unsteadily, turned and immediately busied himself washing his hands.

"I, I think you've got this Anderson. Very good." He kept his flushed face and eyes downward while he started cleaning the tools and then quickly wrapped and rolled them in a dry cloth. "I look forward to your help with the students. You're free to go now."

"Oh, so soon? Alright. Thanks for your help, Professor." As I walked down the hall, I wondered...had I been studying biology or was that some instant chemistry bubbling up?

CHAPTER 18

BOOGIE WOOGIE BOONDOGGLE

JO-JO

*A*fter our morning meeting with the bigwigs, my rehearsal felt rough. I was feeling slightly off-kilter as Mrs. Kizinski sat in the front row staring daggers at me, while I tried to find the right pacing with the orchestra on my three new songs.

I stayed after and watched Billy's rehearsal, but the kid seemed unaffected by what had transpired upstairs. He belted out two more songs from the Oklahoma musical as if he was performing in front of a theater full of clapping admirers. Thinking it through, I realized he was a pro who'd sung on stages for years. This morning's incident was probably a minor blip in his checkered career. He and his wife had been duping audiences and theater managers for years and it wouldn't surprise me if they'd been caught at it more than a few times. But with the network expansion of national radio programs, continuing to keep their secret would certainly become more difficult.

By Wednesday's rehearsal, I'd concluded that the station's payout of five-hundred-dollars to Billy was far more than he would have earned in a month performing in the smaller venues. I shook off my guilt and fear about reporting him and, in return, I finally found my rhythm with the pit orchestra. I began relaxing my lyric pace and had fun performing with the musicians who showed amazing adaptability to different musical styles.

Before leaving, I visited the backstage restroom. As I came out, an older gentleman I'd noticed playing piano in the pit nodded and asked, "So, ready for your big day tomorrow?"

I smiled back. "Nervous and excited, but yes. I think I'm ready."

He shrugged the thin shoulders hiding inside the loose and faded black jacket of his suit. "Hey, nothing to be worried about. Heard a rumor; you got it in the bag, right?"

I looked back at him, my eyes popping in surprise. " News to me. Billy's a strong competitor."

He nodded, offered a dead-pan expression and said, "Yeah, sure, kid," as he shut the door on our conversation and the restroom.

That brief chat felt strange. Crap. Had somebody already spilled the beans? Hopefully, it was only band talk. Maybe the orchestra was impressed with today's rehearsal and presumed I'd win out over Billy.

After leaving WOR, I went to the army surplus store. I'd decided to create a costume for the *Boogie Woogie Bugle Boy* number that would give the song a military flare. There was a surplus warehouse on a backstreet off Times Square. Inside, the scent of the place was overpowering. Something like a mix of dusty canvas, mildewed woolens, and sadness. The store was bulging with used uniforms, boots, old medals, hats, helmets, tents, and equipment. It made me feel melancholy, looking around and thinking about so many returning soldiers selling off their uniform remnants for pennies on the dollar, probably to buy food or drink.

Most uniform items were for men, but I found a few pieces from a Women's Army Corp uniform. A fitted, olive-green wool skirt, a black belt, a khaki-color uniform shirt with epaulets, and a cute little field cap with a black bill. I could have bought several colorful bars and medals to adorn the shirt, but I thought that might be disrespectful to soldiers who served.

After buying my military duds, I dashed over to the deli and picked up my new uniform that Mr. Asnas had put a rush on. As I walked in, he waved at me and dropped the telephone receiver on the counter. He rushed to the back and came out with an ear-to-ear grin, so proud of his efforts. He carried my waitress uniform on a hanger covered in a long paper bag, and pulled the bag up, revealing it to me. "She's a beauty, Jo-Jo. Wear it proudly."

The white dress had a form-fitted bodice with a drawn in waist and had *Stage Deli* embroidered largely over the front left pocket in red and outlined in hot pink. "Wow, looks wonderful, Mr. Asnas. I can't wait to get it pressed and tried on. I have to run. Thanks for everything and wish me luck!"

So, I now had a costume change for each song. My deli uniform was for my opening piece, my black dress with the white collar and cuffs for my ballad, and the military uniform to close things out. This would all require some racing back and forth to the dressing room during the broadcast, but I wanted to look my best for each song and create a mood. I hoped that before or after the broadcast there might be photographers there taking snaps for the heavily publicized show. I welcomed the free publicity.

Dolly, a friend of mine, worked in The Dixie's laundry room. For months now, I'd paid her a buck a week, off the books, to wash and press my clothes. After retrieving my weekly load from my room, I caught up with her in the hotel basement and handed her my items, asking for a priority delivery for early tomorrow morning.

She smiled, accepting it eagerly. "Jo-Jo, my guy and I are tuning in tomorrow night. I'm so excited for you; and to think, you'll be wearing the clothes that I washed and ironed. I'll make sure they're perfect."

"Thanks, Dolly. I wish there was some way I could get tickets for you for the show, but they don't give us any extra. Guess they don't want us swaying the voting audience. But I appreciate your support."

"Sure thing; everything will be cleaned and delivered to your door by eight AM."

I had a restless night's sleep, but thankfully, no more recurring dreams with Billy's murdering mother. The following morning, I showered and wanted to try on the new Stage Deli uniform. When I opened the door there was no laundry hanging on the other side. Dolly had probably forgotten to have the bellhop deliver my clothes, or they were all running behind. In a hotel with over seven hundred rooms, the morning duties kept the crew of twenty-five bellhops racing.

I dialed and asked for the laundry room. After holding for a few minutes, Dolly came on.

"Morning, it's Jo-Jo. Just wanted to let you know my clothing isn't here yet. I'm happy to come down to get it if the bellhops are busy."

"That's odd. I actually stayed late last night and gave it to that cute new guy, Rudy, to take to your room."

"Oh gosh, please don't tell me it's missing! It's almost everything I own, plus what I was wearing for the show tonight."

"Don't worry. There's got to be some kind of mix-up. I'll try to get it sorted out real quick. I'm up to my eyeballs with sheets and towels right now. A big convention group is checking in."

"Sorry about that. Thanks Dolly."

I put on a floral print dress my granny made for me. The high, ruffled neckline made me look like I was singing in the Green Tree church choir. As I put on my makeup, my worry began to mount while I envisioned my performance without my costumes. In addition, Mr. Asnas would have a fit if the new uniform didn't get worn. I wanted to look professional-- not another hayseed fresh off the train.

A few minutes later, I got a call from Willie, the hotel operator who'd befriended me last week. "Good morning, Jo-Jo. Dolly-in-laundry filled me in on your missing clothes. Rudy, the bellhop, just clocked in and said he dropped them off last night before he left, but now he thinks he may have inverted the room numbers. It's looking like it got dropped off at room 524, rather than your room, 425. Rudy's checking now and should be back with your clothes in a jiffy."

"Bless you, Willie. Appreciate the update."

I unrolled my hair, brushed it out and continued waiting. I was so relieved when I heard a knock on my door. I opened it, staring at the handsome new bellhop with the worried face.

"I'm so sorry, Miss Anderson. I'm pretty sure I screwed the pooch last night and left your stuff at 524. Unfortunately, the clothes ain't hanging on the door any longer and nobody answered my knock. I even got a maid to check the room, but there was nothing hanging there wrapped in hotel laundry bags. I also checked with the front desk. Good news is that the guy in 524 hasn't checked out. I'll keep calling his room every so often. So sorry about all this."

The bellhop might have been handsome but he didn't seem too bright. I was really upset but tried to retain my composure. "It happens, but this sure was a lousy day for it to happen. I'm on Talent Jackpot tonight. The radio show? So, the clothes are quite important. I'm leaving soon for the studio, WOR. I'll write down their phone number. If you find my stuff, please call there, ask for Sammy Shine and he'll get word to me."

"Got it. I'll do what I can."

Wrapped in my overcoat, I walked briskly to the radio station. So much time and energy had been wrapped up in this show for the last few weeks. A thousand-dollars and a week's booking at a major theater was almost within my reach. I could almost taste it, but I prayed that taste wouldn't somehow go sour. At the back door, I told Sammy about possibly expecting a call from a guy who had my costumes, but I wasn't putting out much hope for them.

During dress rehearsal everything went smoothly and the Kinzinskis seemed resigned to the fact that they would get their pay-out and skedaddle. As the afternoon ticked away, I had to assume I'd be performing in my old church dress. While I was zipping it up the back, Danny knocked on the dressing room door.

"It's open."

"Hey there. Ready for a big performance tonight? Ratings expectations are over the moon!"

"Great, now I'm doubly nervous."

Danny laughed and leaned against the mirrored wall. "Don't be; your rehearsal was swell today. The sponsors seem pleased. Hey, this is strictly between you and me, but your week's booking might be at the *Copacabana*. Hard to top that, kid."

"You can't be serious!"

"Yeah, and they got a top flight band there, Shep Fields and his Rippling Rhythm Orchestra. This is all just a rumor, but I heard talk upstairs, so keep it to yourself."

"I won't tell a soul including myself. My hands are already shaking."

As Danny turned to leave, there was another knock. He opened the door and a handsome dark-haired man, wearing a Tuxedo, black overcoat and a hat was standing there holding a long bag. "Hello, anyone looking for these?"

I clapped my hands in excitement. "Yes! Thank goodness! I hope those are mine."

"Apparently they are. I grabbed the bag off my door this morning assuming it was my tuxedo. This afternoon, imagine my surprise at work, changing into my tux and instead, finding these lovely frocks."

I rushed over and took the bag, checking the contents. "Yes! Everything's here. Thank you so much." I reached out to shake his hand. "I'm Jo-Jo Anderson. It's so thoughtful of you to bring them here."

"James Appleton, happy to oblige." He took his hat off, while introducing himself. "You have a heap of people looking out for you at The Dixie. Five associates working there swarmed me at the desk when I brought this bag in and asked about my missing tuxedo. When they told me you were performing on Jackpot tonight, I quickly changed and jumped in a cab to bring everything over."

"You're too kind."

"It's no bother. It was on my way."

This pleasant man had gone to a lot of trouble and I wanted to show my appreciation. "Mr. Appleton, would you have any interest in watching the show from the wings tonight?" I glanced over at Danny still standing by the door. "Danny, would that be possible?"

Danny looked the guy over. "Fine with me. But you'll need to stay out of sight and keep quiet. I'm meeting with the stage director now. I'll tell him. Have a great show, Deli-Girl. We go live in ten."

Mr. Appleton returned his hat to his head and looked at his watch. "Hmm, sounds fun. So the broadcast starts soon?"

"Yes, ten minutes."

"Miss Anderson, I'd love to accept your invitation... on one condition."

"Sure, what is it?"

"Come with me to a party afterwards. It's a company thing. We'll only be a little late arriving."

"After the week I've had, I could use a party. I'd love to. Thanks!"

"Fantastic. I'll let you finish getting ready and go find my spot."

After Mr. Appleton left, I jumped into my new deli uniform and struggled to zip it up from the back. This new one fit much snugger than my standard one-size-fits-most that I was used to wearing. But after looking at myself in the mirror, I loved the more flattering cut. I hung my other two outfits on a rolling rack and unbuttoned things for quick access during my costume changes. I pulled out a dozen black-n-whites and some oatmeal and raisin cookies from a sack that Mr. Asnas sent over, and arranged them on a platter. I planned on carrying them out to Mr. King when he introduced me tonight. While I rechecked my makeup and hair in the mirror, the stage manager knocked on my door.

"Deli-Girl, quick, stage left."

I took a deep breath, exhaled and deftly balanced my platter of cookies on my right palm, plastered a big grin across my face, and walked out standing silently next to Mr. Appleton and Billy the Wonderkid. An overhead light was shining down on us and I suddenly noticed a slight five o'clock shadow under Billy's makeup and rouge. Guess the kid was getting careless about his farewell performance.

I turned my attention to John King, who was on stage, and listened to his smooth, velvety voice. "Tonight's show is the most highly anticipated contest that we've ever presented on Talent Jackpot and we have two extremely talented singers who'll be duking it out while showcasing their vocal chops for you, so let's get to it! First up--she's a beautiful blonde from Green Tree, Iowa. But you know her as our favorite Deli-Girl, Miss Jo-Jo Anderson. Let's welcome her with a big round of applause!"

I walked out swaying my hips just enough, holding my platter and waving to the audience with my other hand. King looked at my plate of cookies and took the lead.

"Well Jo-Jo, looks like you came well prepared tonight. What did you bring us?"

"Just a few of my favorite cookies from the Stage Deli."

"Thank you! I happen to have a sweet tooth myself, but I'm sure the crew will make these disappear quickly. They look great! So, what do you have planned for us tonight?"

"Three numbers, Mr. King. I'm so excited. I picked two swing tunes and one new ballad."

"All right. I'm going to munch down on some delicious cookies while you lucky people in the audience will be treated to a Glen Miller favorite, *In the Mood*, sung by Deli-Girl, Jo-Jo Anderson. Take it away boys."

I was now on the stage alone, listening for the familiar opening notes from the trumpet, then the trombones came alive, sliding in, and I was off and running, singing a crowd favorite.

The show could not have gone better. Both Billy and I performed well, but I really began to make the audience jump out of their seats on my final number when the band started up the popular Boogie Woogie Bugle Boy. I sprung into the song with exuberance and chomped at the five stanzas of lyrics, not missing a word.

In my heart, I felt I'd won the show fair and square, whether the applause-o-meter was properly working or not. Billy and his moth-er/wife stood looking on from the wings as I walked off the stage. Mrs. Kizinksi sighed deeply, took Billy's hand and said, "OK love, I got the five hundred. Let's grab your stuff and get the hell out of this joint." Then she looked over at me. "You surprised me, Deli-Girl. You did OK out there."

Seconds later, I found myself standing between John King and

Mr. Cheerios after they announced my name. I was shaking their hands, surrounded again by falling silver and gold confetti, accepting their accolades and the audiences' applause. When I heard Cheerios announce that I would soon be singing for a week at the Copacabana, I couldn't believe all this was real. My dreams were actually coming true.

As the studio audience began to filter out, several photographers rushed to the edge of the stage, snapping my photo while I stood next to King. Flash bulbs were blinding my eyes, while the accompanying reporters shouted out questions directed at me.

"Deli-Girl, is it true you're having an affair with someone connected with Talent Jackpot?"

"Miss Anderson, we've had credible sources say the results of Talent Jackpot may be rigged. What's your response?"

"Deli-Girl, how is it you got on this show without going through try-outs?"

"Hey, where's the Wonder-Kid? We need a quick interview with the kid."

Even with Mr. King's protective arm wrapped around my shoulder, I began panicking. I'd just experienced one of the happiest moments in my life, but now I felt like a pack of dogs had raced in and were circling me and I didn't know what to say. As questions continued to be hurled, I looked up across the pack of snarling reporters, my face frozen, staring into the beady eyes of former disgruntled contestant, Laverne, the pianist with the bird's nest hairdo. She stood behind the gaggle of reporters with a malicious grin across her face.

CHAPTER 19
ABSENTLY MINDING THE PROFESSOR

SARAH

*T*hursday, I'd carved out time from my study schedule to tune into Jo's final competition on Jackpot. My roommate, Barbara, was beside herself about listening to the show again and was terribly proud and excited to tell everyone at Currier Hall that her roommate, Sarah, was the twin sister of The Deli-Girl from the radio show. Unbeknownst to me, she had organized a lobby listening party downstairs. She had cajoled the house mother of Currier Hall to plug in multiple radios throughout the lobby so everyone could cheer on my sister in her competition.

I was overwhelmed with the celebrity status Jo-Jo seemed to have taken on. At breakfast, Thursday morning, everyone in the dorm seemed to be talking about it and asking me questions about Jo-Jo. This Talent Jackpot show appeared to be a very big deal. I had a few photos of Jo in my scrapbook from plays she'd starred in while in high school. Barbara insisted I bring those to the lobby and pass them around so that everyone could see what my sister looked like while we listened to her perform.

Before the show started, a quarter of the dorm residents had crowded into the large formal lobby, which was furnished with heavy draperies, a piano, and numerous groupings of couches and wing chairs. All these girls had come in ready to cheer on Jo-Jo

Anderson. I wished I'd owned a camera to take a photo of this moment so I could show my twin what a fan base she now had at my school. Barbara had reserved us the best seats, sitting next to a large wooden RCA radio with excellent speakers. All the room chatter miraculously quieted down as soon as the host with the golden voice started the show.

Jo's first number, *In the Mood*, wowed the room. This was one of band leader Glen Miller's most popular tunes. Even I knew this one. Jo was singing with such enthusiasm and the lyrics were surprisingly complex and fast. I had no idea how she managed to memorize them all. It was followed by Billy the Wonderkid's rendition of *Surrey with the Fringe on Top*. Songs from the musical, *Oklahoma*, seemed to be his specialty. I had to admit, he was good. Although Jo had told me his real age, I didn't share that piece of news with the Currier Hall girls. On his final song, *Oh What a Beautiful Morning*, his voice broke a few times. It was probably a poor choice for his range. But when Jo-Jo came out for her finale, she riled up the studio audience with Boogie Woogie Bugle Boy. Everybody at Currier Hall was clapping, swaying, and singing along.

Then the room got quiet again during the commercial break while we listened to the Cheerios Kid talking up the deliciousness of his regular morning cereal. We were all anxiously waiting for the applause-o-meter outcome. When John King revealed the winner, everyone jumped up and applauded, then patted me on the back, congratulating me, as if I had won the darn show. I was so proud of my sister and decided to write her a congratulatory letter tonight that would go out first thing tomorrow. But as everybody wandered back to their rooms, my elation for Jo was followed by an uncomfortable feeling. I knew at that moment something may have changed the relationship between Jo and me .

If she became successful and well known, would fans turn her head? Would Jo ignore our family? Would she hate coming home to Green Tree after living the highlife in New York City? And where did I fit into this picture? Debating political issues certainly was not my forte' and this whole entertainment world seemed so strange, yet it utterly fascinated most people. I was the simple country mouse who had an eerie feeling about the whole thing.

While dressing the next morning for class, I felt a sense of urgency. I couldn't wait to get to the lab. As prickly as he was, Professor Carter also intrigued me. Hard to imagine that someone I had disliked so much on our first meeting could now possibly be an infatuation. Or was my infatuation caused purely by his reaction and attraction to me? I definitely noticed him checking himself the other afternoon, suddenly shutting down our work before allowing himself to get too close to me. That power of attraction felt intoxicating and I liked it. Odd, that an older man, an intelligent professor, might possibly be interested in me.

I looked at my watch and quickly brushed through my long hair, plaiting it into one thick dark braid. I glanced into the mirror on my way out. Perhaps I should cut my hair? Nobody was wearing it like this anymore. Instead, I opted for a touch of lipstick. Walking down the dorm stairs to the lobby, I considered the variables of Dr. Carter. Not unattractive, nice hazel eyes, thin severe face, a good head of hair, definitely intelligent but with a superior attitude, well spoken, easy to anger, and mature. I liked that part; a fully baked man that had studied all manner of things and seemed worldly. Whether I agreed with him or not, I liked that he was sure of himself.

But perhaps I would walk in today and see that all my morning musings amounted to a hill of beans and were simply my vivid and busy imagination. Perhaps instead, Professor Carter had only felt an odd reaction to the pickled formaldehyde the pig fetuses were emitting? Either way, it was something to ponder and I looked forward to assisting him at our first student lab class.

Walking out of Currier Hall, I noticed Jacob leaning against a tree by the entrance. I assumed he was waiting for me. "Hi there, Jacob. What brings you here?"

"I figured you were heading to the science building about now. It's on my way."

I looked surprised. "How do you possibly know my schedule?"

"I'm just observant in that way. So, I take it you didn't care much for the Young Republicans meeting the other afternoon? You left so early."

I settled my book satchel on my shoulder as we began walking. "I'm sure many of the members are quite admirable and interesting people. It's wonderful that they're so committed. But I felt uncomfortable because I'm just not knowledgeable in politics. I haven't taken the time to create informed opinions. I don't want to just parrot my parents' conversations or, for that matter, somebody else's ideas. Right now, I just can't put the time into doing that. I hope you understand."

"I guess I get it. But it's just so important to stay involved. For our country's sake."

I shook my head and explained, "Jacob, maybe we're just not a good match. Our interests don't seem to be meshing."

"Well, I'm disappointed to hear that. I think you're great and was looking for more. Perhaps even as a partner interested in helping me expand my political pursuits. It's something we could work on together."

"Yeah, I guess that's not me. I will be voting though and you've certainly made me more aware in that regard. I'm also going to take the time to read the editorials in the paper more often. But I can see that I'm just not the right girl for you."

He stopped walking and looked at me, pondering my statement. "Sarah, I hate hearing that."

He leaned over and gave me a peck on the cheek. *No... still nothing, no chemistry whatsoever.* It had run its limited course. Now I'd have to explain to Mother that my first foray into joining a club and dating had ended abruptly. I'd have to seek out other diversions.

As Jacob took a different fork in the sidewalk through campus, I knew it wouldn't be long before he'd find the perfect running mate; whether it be in his love life or his first political campaign. Jacob would be just fine. I tried to fight off the urge to smile, but a grin popped out anyway.

I entered the science building, followed by a tall, young man behind me on crutches. I held the door for him, while he hopped in. He had his right trouser leg cut short and sewn up to where a knee should have been. I had to wonder if the leg amputation was caused by a war wound or disease. He looked so young, with ruddy cheeks, bright eyes, and longish fly-away hair that reminded me of yellow straw.

"Thanks for getting the door, miss. Don't suppose you know how far lab 1-D is?"

"Sure do. I'm headed there. Just four doors down."

"Good." He pointed to his wooden crutches. "These are new. The padding is lousy and this campus is darn big."

"I can help you with your book bag. It looks heavy."

"Thanks. I'm fine. I first had to go to the registrar's office and get a schedule change. They originally stuck me in a lab on the third floor." He shook his head and said, " Ever tried three flights on these sticks? It's no picnic."

"I'm sure you're right. So, you're in Professor Carter's lab?"

He stopped in the hall and took out a piece of paper from his shirt pocket.

"Uh, yes ma'am. Dr. Carter."

"I'm Sarah Anderson. Dr. Carter's lab assistant. I can help you get set up."

"You?" He looked down at me and seemed surprised. "I'm Lester Adams. Pleased to meet you." As we walked into the room, I directed him to a tall lab table that he would share with another student.

"So, we do the lab work while standing?" He looked puzzled.

"Yes, most of the time. Will that be a problem?"

"Kind of; if I use my crutches for balance, my arms and hands don't work so well. Maybe I'll get the hang of it in a while." He cursed softly to himself as his face turned red. "I'll be getting my wheels soon, but when I sit, the table's gonna be too high."

I nodded, looking around. "I never considered that. Let me see what I can do. Just sit at the professor's desk for a minute. I'll be back."

I went further down the hall and glanced into an empty class-room. It was filled with four rows of ten wooden desks and chairs. Surely they could do without one set. I took the chair from a back row and carried it down the hall into the lab, and then returned for the desk. By now, other students were starting to file into the lab as I pushed the desk down the hall.

Then I heard, "Anderson, what are you doing?"

I turned around and smiled, but it appeared Professor Arrogant had taken over the body of Dr. Carter again. "You have no authority to remove supplies or desks from one class to another. They're set up according to need."

"Well, that's perfect then because we are in *need* of a desk and chair in the lab. Dr. Carter, we have a student named Lester with an amputated leg who is unable to stand through the lab work. I was attempting to correct the problem."

"Let me look into this. You get everyone into a lab coat and there's a new box of gloves in the cabinet. Issue one pair to each student."

I nodded and added, "I had another thought regarding Lester. Once he gets his wheelchair, we could have a low ramp and plat-form built so he could work alongside other students. Make might him feel more included."

He dismissed the idea immediately. "Sarah, I can't rebuild the lab room for a single student."

I went back in and asked everyone to select a lab coat and then dropped two pairs of gloves at each workstation. While I was doing this, I saw Professor Carter speaking to Lester and then saw the boy painfully attempt to stand up, grip his crutches, and move to the desk and chair I brought into the room.

"Anderson, you can partner with Mr. Adams when you're not busy helping others."

The rest of the lab went well, with Professor Carter giving instructions and pointing out organ features from a large anatomical drawing he pulled down from a scroll mounted over the blackboard. I started working with Lester and he seemed to be comfortable with the first instructions, so I quietly moved around the room, stopping at each station, and offered advice if someone looked lost or had trouble making the correct cuts. Some people were squeamish, but it was nothing more than I anticipated. I really enjoyed the work but my mind kept returning to Lester and his disability. I knew he felt singled out, working alone while he really only wanted to blend in.

After two hours, everyone cleared their spaces and left. I was looking forward to a one-on-one discussion with Carter; perhaps he would even invite me for coffee?

"Anderson, well done today. Thank you for your assistance."

I removed my lab coat and hung it up. "Happy to be doing this, Dr. Carter. I'm really enjoying the work. More than I thought I would. I just wanted to ask about…"

"As long as we're working together, out of class, you may call me Beckham. No need for formalities."

"And Sarah is my *preferred* name. So, what kind of name is Beckham? I guess calling you Becky is out of the question."

"My parents didn't believe in pet names. Beckham is fine."

"I wanted to discuss something with you. Any interest in going for coffee or tea, Professor?" I couldn't believe I'd just asked him that. My boldness was growing by leaps and bounds.

He pulled out his old fashioned pocket watch. "I have fifty-two minutes to spare. And there's a teapot and hot plate in my office. Shall we go there?"

We climbed to the third level of the building which was a hodge-podge of offices and lab space. He directed me down a hallway across from a restroom. "Here we go, my own little cubby hole. It was the only space they could offer me, being a mid-semester replacement."

There was a desk, two chairs, a sad looking potted plant, and books and files scattered in haphazard piles. I laughed and said, "Someone needs to do some tidying up."

Beckham walked in ahead of me, stepping between the piles of textbooks and plugged in his hotplate sitting on top of a file cabinet. "Actually Sarah, I was thinking you might be able to help me with that. The tidying up bit. I remember on the bus you told me you were good at organizing."

"Yes, I remember that, and recall that you sniggered smugly and immediately turned down my offer to help."

"Hmm, I didn't know I was capable of sniggering, but I think we've moved past all that now. By the way, during that bus trip, I was stressed at being called down to the university at the last minute and had a thousand things on my mind."

"I understand. I'll go ahead and take that delayed apology now." I sat grinning at him, while he fussed with tea bags.

He sighed deeply, taking two mugs off the cabinet. "I think these cups need rinsing out. I'll make a quick trip to the restroom with these, and Sarah…I am sorry for dismissing your offer so quickly."

He closed the door and I thought that was probably the only apology I was going to get from Professor Arrogant. After he returned, while we were sipping steaming cups of black unsweetened tea, he asked, "So what did you want to ask me about?"

"So, I was thinking about today… with Lester, the amputee. Thanks for letting him use the desk, but I think the school needs to do more. He's bound to be feeling isolated, separated from other students."

"What am I supposed to do, Sarah? We can't bend to every person's whims and needs. There's standards we adhere to. For now, we are accommodating him."

"It seems like a new injury, since he's waiting on a wheelchair. I'm not sure if Lester was injured in the war but there's bound to be a slew of men with different debilitating injuries that have started attending the university and many more to enroll soon. These questions have to be addressed. Think about it. President Roosevelt ran the whole country from a wheelchair! Certainly we can figure out a way to accommodate some students in a simple lab setting."

"All right. Calm down, Sarah. I said I would look into it. Maybe we can figure something out. Please drink your tea, and let's change the subject."

"Good. I'm pleased. And I'll think about doing something for them on my own end too."

He shook his head and added, "I said *maybe,* but I have no doubt you'll find a way to disrupt things. Then he stood up with the tea kettle and asked, "More tea for my stubborn, hard-headed assistant?" Finally, a slight smile emerged from one side of his mouth. "Even with your obstinate streak, I quite enjoy working with you, Sarah."

CHAPTER 20
RESCUE ATTEMPTS
JO-JO

*M*r. King placed both his hands, palms up, in front of himself to quiet the reporters. Thankfully, he had a loud and commanding voice when he needed it.

"That's enough! Let's all calm down. Hey, look fellas, I have *no* idea where you're getting this cockamamie story, but I can assure you that Miss Anderson has won this competition fairly and I *don't* doubt that the millions of listeners tonight feel the same way. It's true, Miss Anderson didn't make the first cut for last week's show, but she was called back at the last minute when a dancing clogger twisted an ankle. And regarding the Wonderkid, he had another out-of-town engagement that he and his mother were traveling to tonight. They've already left the building."

A gangly looking reporter with an enlarged Adam's apple jumped in as Mr. King and I turned to leave the stage. "Johnnie Simms, New York Post. What about all the rumors of Jo-Jo's affair with some top guy at the station. Deli-Girl, any response?"

Now I was angry. I stopped in my tracks, turning toward him. "There is no rumor, Mr. Simms, unless you start a false one. The idea is preposterous and was probably started by a disgruntled former contestant." While saying this, I looked again at Miss Bird Nest and didn't flinch.

King tugged on my elbow and announced, "There is no story here. That will be all the questions we have time for, boys. Let's clear the studio or security will throw you out." Mr. King and I walked backstage but I could tell he was clearly ruffled. He looked around for Danny and yelled at him. "Where in the hell did all that come from? Find the source and kill it." Danny and I stood quietly next to him, as he questioned us. "Either of you two have anything to add to this?"

He stared at both of us while I watched Mr. Appleton slip quietly away down the hall. I decided to speak up. "Mr. King, at the original tryouts, I was suffering from a nervous stomach and had to use the backstage restroom. I began practicing my song there because I liked the tile acoustics. Danny was walking by, heard me singing, liked my style and asked me to join the other people on stage for try-outs. So, in that regard, my audition was unusual." My story was about seventy percent true and would keep both Sammy and Danny from getting into hot water.

King responded, "All right. We can live with that. Danny, anything you care to add?"

"No. Everything else was pretty normal. This nonsense probably comes from Billy shooting his mouth off at some bar. He's trouble with a capital T. It's my fault that I wasn't able to spot him as an adult at the initial auditions. Maybe we should check everyone's ID going forward."

Cheerios walked up from the side curtain and said, "Agreed! Miss Anderson, we'll be calling you soon with details regarding the show at the Copa. We need to let all this bru-ha-ha die down first. On the bright side, I have your check." He handed it to me with a little bow. "Congratulations to you, missy. You put on a great show."

I held the check gently and gazed at it. "This is wonderful, thank you for everything." I was upset by the reporters' questions which spoiled an almost perfect evening, but at least I now had more money than I'd ever seen in my life. I glanced around for Mr. Appleton, thinking I should change into my black dress for his party. But during all the shouting, he seemed to have disappeared. I didn't blame him. I gathered my things from the dressing room, still wearing my military uniform, put on my coat and headed to the backdoor. Walking down the darkened hallway, I saw a tall, familiar woman leaning against the wall smoking a cigarette.

She blew a smoke ring toward me. "Finally…Didn't think you were ever leaving. Well Jo-Jo, you've got yourself in a little pickle, don't you? Seems like you're in need of a good agent."

I waved at the smoke and walked past her and stopped. "I have no need of your services and I know who you really are, *Nanette Jorgenson*. I rarely forget a face, even though you're starting to look old." I knew that comment would stab her to the quick.

She laughed while stepping on her cigarette butt dramatically. "You were always a stubborn little brat. But your voice has developed, I'll give you that. Jo dear, you have no idea what kind of hornet's nest is out there waiting for you. Trust me, you're going to need some help and guidance."

"Maybe I do, but not from the likes of you. If for no other reason than my own mother would probably disown me if I took you on as my agent. After all those years, you are still her least favorite person."

Nanette looked up and then shook her head. "Dear simple Mariah…she never had a clue about your talents. If we hadn't had the FBI on our backs, I'm certain you would have become a major child star. But instead, you ended up just like I thought you would, on a farm in the middle of nowhere."

"Yeah, and I turned into a normal, healthy kid with two loving parents."

Her tone softened for a few seconds. "Jo-Jo, I always loved you. I just wanted more for you. Mariah could never see your potential."

"Whatever makes you sleep better, Nanette, Nan, or Fran… whatever you're calling yourself now. By the way, how did you get back here?"

"Sammy Shine. He's a regular on my payroll. I've slipped a lot of clients onto this show. But honestly, you were impressive out there tonight. Here, take my card. You're going to need it. I have a car waiting at the backdoor. And if I know the press, they're right behind that door waiting for you."

I threw the card in my bag. "I'll take my chances and walk."

"Have it your way." Nanette pulled a white fox stole over the shoulders of her black suit, and nodded to Sammy as he opened the door to both of us.

"Good night, ladies."

The second I stepped onto the cold, wet steps outside, I knew Nanette was right. She broke through the group of reporters, parting them like the Red Sea and climbed into a waiting black car, while I was left engulfed in a nest of gossip mongers with cameras. I tried pushing through them, keeping up a smile, saying, "I have no idea what all these questions are about."

Within a few seconds, I felt a tug on my arm and a strong grip pulling my hand. I looked down the stairs and saw Mr. Appleton. With his clasped hand, he led me through the throng, and put me quickly inside a waiting taxi. He jumped inside the other door and told the driver, "Club 21 please. We're in a hurry."

CHAPTER 21

HEROES AND HEART THROBS

SARAH

a few days after my encounter with Lester Adams, an idea bloomed. I scheduled a meeting with the Director of University Student Services, Mrs. Hortence Miller. She was dressed in a severe brown suit, with her hair pulled back into a tight bun, and after motioning me into her office, Mrs. Miller scrutinized me thoroughly. I sat across from her desk and began by discussing Lester's difficulties working with the tall lab tables while balancing on crutches. As I paused for a breath, she continued to look at me with a confused expression.

"So, as lab assistant to Dr. Carter, I was wondering what you would suggest the university could do to accommodate Lester's needs. He has one amputated leg and he simply can't stand at the assigned lab tables to do the required work. I'm assuming he's a recent war veteran."

"Hmm, so Miss Anderson, you're saying he is unable to do the lab work standing at a table?"

Hadn't I just said that? Perhaps she was deaf. I slowed my speech and increased the volume. "Yes, that and the fact that students work together as lab partners, so he's also missing that collaborative learning experience. Oh, and obviously, numerous stairs are an issue too."

"Well what in the Sam Hill am I supposed to do about stairs?"

"I guess we first have to acknowledge the potential problems and then consider that Lester will be one of *many* disabled students who have come home from the war and will be taking advantage of the GI Bill's coverage of college tuition. Some of the issues should be easily addressed and some will take more time. But in the meantime, I had a thought."

She was now resting her cheek against the palm of her hand, frowning at me and looking as if I had thrown a big monkey wrench into her day. "By all means, share your thoughts, Miss Anderson."

I took another deep breath, exhaled, and continued. "Well, I've never organized a group before and need your help. I was thinking the school should organize a club of volunteer students interested in assisting the university's disabled student vets. They would match up student volunteers with these student vets who might need help having wheelchairs pushed, or books carried, perhaps offering help with tutoring, touring the campus, and offering simple camaraderie. I suggest we call the group, Help for Heroes, unless you have a better suggestion?"

She remained silent and I continued. "We could promote the program in the dorms and the school paper. I'm certain a lot of students would like to do their part in helping. What do you think, Mrs. Miller?"

She was nodding and the glazed look had disappeared. "Yes, I can see that would be helpful. The idea has merit, but *you, Miss Anderson*, as head of this organization, would need to match up the volunteers with the disabled and handle scheduling. It could be a massive task. I simply wouldn't have time for that. There's a form here you need to file if you want to start an officially sanctioned campus group, so just fill that out, get a minimum of ten students on board, and I'll try to get it approved for you."

"Oh, I didn't plan on doing all the coordinating. I have studies and homework to take care of."

"As we all do, Miss Anderson. But it's your idea. *You* need to get it up and running and jump through all the necessary hoops."

Hoops? The idea seemed solid but I certainly wasn't hoop

jumping material. It would involve a lot of people to talk to, class schedules to coordinate, time commitments. "But you're the student services director?"

Hortence forced a smile and said, "The key word in that title is *student.*"

"And what about the need for a bio lab bench for students that are unable to stand?" Every lab should have at least one or two. Then there's all the stairs."

Now Miller had gone from nodding to shaking her head. "That sounds more complicated and expensive. You do your part on organizing the volunteers and then, later, I'll put the lab table suggestion on an agenda to discuss with the dean, but I wouldn't get your hopes up. So, does that about cover it?"

I suddenly felt overwhelmed and disappointed with her response. Maybe this wasn't a good idea. "I guess. I'll get the form back to you when I can."

As I stood, she said, "Don't be discouraged. As I said, the idea does have merit, Miss Anderson. See what you can do with it."

I left the office unsatisfied. I wanted to present a brilliant idea and let Hortense take it from there. But apparently if it was my idea--it would be my responsibility. By filling out the form and finding ten members, I would at least have an official sanctioning of the university.

Then I had another thought. I honestly knew very few people on campus, but the two people I did know fairly well were my roommate, Barbara, and Jacob of the Young Republicans. And both of them seemed to know a lot of people and were definitely effective at getting others to do their bidding. If I could get those two on board, I could probably get the group organized. But I'd have to be persuasive.

In the afternoon, I went to the biology lab early to set up equipment. Dr. Carter was already there, scribbling notes. I couldn't help but notice the afternoon sunlight coming through the window highlighting his auburn hair as he bent over. He did have a nice head of hair. "Hello Professor, how are you doing?"

"Good." He actually looked up and smiled. It was a full toothed smile rather than his regular disappointed half-smirk. "You look nice today."

"Thank you?" It was a highly uncharacteristic compliment as I looked down at my tired, plaid skirt and green sweater which I'd worn numerous times. I reached for a white lab coat and covered my old clothing.

He said, "It's your hair. It's different, correct?" My hand went to touch it and I remembered that I'd been in a hurry and worn it long and loose. "You should wear it like that more often."

This was quite different. What happened to my curmudgeonly professor? "Uh...just so you know, I met with the Director of Student Services today to discuss ideas I had regarding Lester Adams and other possible disabled students."

A touch of exasperation crossed his smile. "So, you're still trying to solve that problem? I appreciate your determination. I just hope it doesn't interfere with your lab assistant duties."

"I hope not. I'm considering starting a group of volunteers to assist vets on campus."

"You are relentless."

"Any news regarding the lab table for Lester?"

Professor Carter suddenly looked quite pleased with himself. "Well, believe it or not, at your urging, I spoke with the building maintenance supervisor and he located an old stool from the basement. It just needed some minor repairs." He pointed to the new addition. "I placed it right there, next to your table. Hopefully, that will solve Lester's problems and you can stop harassing me about it."

I walked over, sat on it, and was pleased. It even swiveled up and down a few inches. "This should be perfect, providing he can pull himself up a bit. Thanks for arranging this, Beckham."

He glanced at his pocket watch, got up, and closed the door. "Sarah, I hope this doesn't sound too out-of-the-blue, but I would like to invite you to dinner this evening. I'm not really sure of the protocol or rules regarding students and teachers, but I'd like to see you outside of the classroom."

I paused, giving it a few seconds thought. "Uh, dinner? I suppose. Why not? We're both adults, correct?"

He raised his eyebrows. "Well, one of us is more adult than the other."

"Beckham, how old are you?"

"Thirty-two."

I nodded, thinking it through. Thirty-two sounded really old, but he didn't look too ancient. In fact, today, he actually looked quite handsome. The occasional smile did wonders for one's appearance. I should try it more often myself. "I'll be twenty in two months. I guess that's an acceptable difference."

"Well, good. How's seven?" He scribbled something down in his journal and tore it off. "Here's my address, and a little map. It's an upstairs apartment, not far from campus." As he handed it to me, his hand brushed over mine and we touched a tad too long. He nervously coughed and turned away to reopen the door. "So, let's get those frog cadavers out of their packaging then."

A few minutes later, Lester hopped in on his crutches and looked around. "Hi Sarah. Looks like they moved that desk that I used before."

"Yes, but you have something better! Actually, Dr. Carter had a maintenance worker locate this stool for you." I patted the back of it and turned the handle underneath the seat. "Look, it swivels to a lower position to sit down. This way you can work here with a lab partner."

Lester came over, leaned his crutches against the table, swung his good leg over the seat of the stool, and then pulled the rest of his body over. I turned the seat around a few times, raising the height of the stool for him.

"Jeepers, it's perfect." He looked over at Dr. Carter sitting at his desk and called out. "Dr. Carter. Appreciate your help."

Carter nodded back. "Glad that worked out."

I brought our dissection tools over and asked Lester quietly. "Do you mind if I ask? Did your leg injury occur during the war?"

He looked down as he softly spoke. "Battle of the Bulge. But you know…I always felt kind of lucky about it. I came out alive. Most of my unit didn't, but I don't like to talk much about it." His eyes looked back up at me. "So anyway, what are we gonna do with these frogs?"

～

LATER THAT EVENING, I was anxious about seeing the professor. This was new territory for me. Sure, I'd been in Tommy's room several times, but I'd grown up with him, almost like a brother. This was something entirely different. It was a man's apartment, a thirty-two-year-old college professor's apartment.

It was actually rather exciting. I purposely tied a ribbon around my head and left my hair down long and wavy because he mentioned he liked it. The temperature had really dropped and I decided to wear trousers and a pullover sweater under my coat.

Barbara noticed me putting on lipstick and immediately became suspicious. "I thought you broke it off with Jacob, although I don't understand why. He's so cute."

"I did. I'm not seeing Jacob. I'm going to study biology."

"Sarah Anderson, I've seen you put on lipstick once since we've lived together and you're putting it on to study at the library?"

"Yes. But maybe there's a handsome new librarian working there. If you ever studied, you might find out." I laughed and waved goodbye to my nosey roommate.

Following Beckham's directions, I easily found the apartment a few blocks off the main street from campus. It was a white, two-story clapboard home with an outside stairway on the side that led to Beckham's place above. I knocked softly and he immediately answered.

He was wearing the same well-worn blue cotton shirt and pleated black trousers he'd had on at school, but he'd removed his necktie which made his face look more relaxed. "I love that you're so prompt, Sarah."

"Family trait I guess. My parents seem to think promptness is next to Godliness. And besides, I do recall your scathing lecture when I showed up late for your first class. You were so insufferable."

"Well, you haven't been late since. Guess it worked. Come in." He opened the door wider, while I walked in tentatively. "I haven't done much with the place. It came furnished as is. The couple downstairs rent it out exclusively to university associates, but not students. They prefer it quiet."

I nodded and whispered, "I'll try to refrain from breaking into song." It looked to be a simple three-room place with a front sitting room, a small kitchen off to the side, and a bedroom at the back, which I assumed had a bathroom. I sniffed, noticing there was a smokey, burned smell permeating the small place.

"Nice. Are you looking for a house? Something larger?"

"Not now. Perhaps in the future. I'll have to see if they renew my position after this semester. Please, have a seat. Are you hungry?" Beckham seemed nervous, possibly more than me. "Do you drink wine, Sarah?"

"I've only had it a few times. I'll try a glass."

There was a small square table in the kitchen area set for two. He opened the bottle of wine and poured me a glass. "It's a Riesling. This one's pretty sweet, but I thought you might like it with your dinner. I've prepared chicken and rice."

"Thanks." I took a sip and sat down. "Yes, nice." I didn't know a Riesling from a bottle of moonshine, but was trying my darndest to seem sophisticated. "So, do you cook much?"

"Honestly, no. I've eaten every meal out since arriving here except breakfast. I can make eggs, bacon, and oatmeal."

He pulled the chicken out of the oven and cut slices from the breast. The skin appeared pretty dark, possibly burnt, but when he cut into the meat, it looked quite pink. In my experience, chicken was not to be served almost raw. The white rice was dry but edible. I pushed the food around on my plate and focused on the wine.

Beckham took a bite, noticed my still full plate and said, "Sorry. This is bad; isn't it? I did try. There's a small container of ice cream in the fridge. Maybe we should just try dessert and move on to the couch."

"I do love ice cream." I glanced over to a nubby two-seater sofa with a coffee table placed in front and thought, dessert already? This date was moving forward quickly.

Beckham fiddled with bowls and ice cream in the kitchen, while I brought our glasses and the wine bottle over to the sofa. I took a few more sips of wine, anticipating an expected kiss. How would it go? Surely, considering his age, Carter had much more experience in this department than Jacob had.

I watched as he approached holding the bowls. "Here you go. It's simple vanilla but it's good."

"Better than the chicken?" I asked, smiling as I took it.

"Much better, I promise."

We each dug into the soft ice cream. I held it in my mouth, savoring the sweetness and creamy texture. "Oh, so good! Guess I'm really hungry."

"Yes. me too." Then he set his bowl down on the small table in front of us. He put his hand gently on my face, tracing the side of my cheekbone while sending chills down my spine.

I looked up into his face and placed a hand on his shoulder as he bent over and placed his lips on mine. He whispered, "I've been wanting to do that ever since you stayed after class and told me how much you were fascinated by cell division."

I had to laugh, interrupting his soft, lovely kiss which I quickly reciprocated. This second one seemed to last for several glorious minutes. As our hands and mouths began to explore, Beckham pulled away, taking off his glasses. "Sorry, these are useless. They're all fogged up now."

"Good, I always thought you had nice eyes. Now I can see them better."

He looked surprised. "Seriously? I never thought you ever really looked at me--in that way, I mean. You're always so engaged in the lecture material."

I nodded. "I've been known to do two things at once." Then I took the initiative and began kissing him, more forcefully. Some deep desire had kicked in and it was overruling any of the inhibitions I had while coming here. Maybe it was the wine, but the kisses felt and tasted delicious.

His fingers began running through my hair, while I arched my back as he placed several burning kisses down my neck. Was it possible to overheat and combust? As we groped and explored I felt myself exploding into tiny pieces and floating across the room above me. I'd never experienced feelings like this before. Tommy and I must have been doing things all wrong.

Suddenly Beckham pulled up a bit and created a slight separation. "Your lips, like a ripe delicious strawberry. It's hard to stop. I'm sorry, Sarah. I don't want to take liberties with you. This is going too far, too fast. You intrigue me, but I had no idea I'd get so carried away. Maybe it's best if we just finish our wine and I'll walk you home."

I was dying to continue, but he was probably right. I certainly wasn't ready to go all the way. And if I did, it would require some further study on my part. I looked at him with a pout, shrugged my shoulders, kissed him again and pulled away. "Maybe you're right, Professor. A walk home would be nice though."

CHAPTER 22
THE INNER CIRCLE
JO-JO

I sunk into the warmth of the taxi's back seat, pulling my coat close, digging my hands deep into my pockets. I looked over at this handsome stranger. "Thanks for the rescue, Mr. Appleton. That was overwhelming. The closest I've come to a crowd like that is when my customers are clamoring for coffee warm-ups."

He laughed. "It's not often I get to rescue damsels in distress."

"When John King started yelling backstage, I noticed you leaving and didn't blame you for aborting the evening."

"Thought it might be a good idea to have a cab waiting. So, have you been to 21 before?"

"Just once, recently. But I can't go in there wearing this? It's a WAC military uniform. When I was there before, some women were wearing evening gowns. I'll look ridiculous."

"Hey, you're The Deli-Girl, a celebrity. Tonight you can wear whatever you want. Just wear it with attitude. And keep the military hat on. It looks cute."

I suddenly felt exhaustion creep in from a mix of tension and hunger. I shrugged and sighed. "Whatever you say, Mr. Appleton."

"Call me James, please."

"Alright then, and if you don't mind, no more Deli-Girl. Jo-Jo

Anderson is fine. By the way, what type of party are we going to? Personal or business?"

"A little of both. I'm a producer of sorts. Currently working on a project for MGM. Pulling together the financing."

My mouth dropped. "So, you're in the movie business? MGM… as in Metro Goldwyn Mayer, the one with the lion?"

James laughed a little. "Honestly, right now I'm more of the money guy. Trying to talk a few connected people into putting their money into a big new musical the studio is wanting to produce. On my end, it's not very glamorous. Some of those investors will be here tonight."

"Ah-ha, so more like a business meeting with a party atmosphere."

"You're catching on quick."

Then the cabbie turned around and said, "21 West 52nd Street, sir." James took my hand as we slid over the backseat to his door which was curbside. "And here we are, Miss Anderson."

He paid the driver and we both looked up at the well-lit building featuring numerous colorful statues of lawn jockeys lining the steps. "So James, what's the story behind all the jockeys?"

"Last I heard, one of the restaurant's early patrons was an avid fan of horse racing and gave the club owners one as a gift. Eventually, all the elite stables from the area began donating them, as a way to promote their colors."

"Hmm, there must be a lot of gamblers eating here."

"You're definitely right about that. Seems like everything is a big gamble in the Big Apple. It's freezing out here. Let's go in."

As we walked into the lobby, James took my coat and bag of clothing to the coat check. I was glad I wasn't walking into the dining room wearing my old overcoat. It had been perfectly acceptable our junior year of high school when Mother ordered it from the Sears and Roebuck catalog, but now, in New York, it looked old fashioned and a bit threadbare.

After checking his own hat and coat, we walked over to the maitre'd and James explained that we were late arriving, but were joining a table for ten under the name of LB Mayer.

"Right this way sir. Follow me."

When I was at 21 with Damien, we'd only had drinks near the bar. Now, as we were led through the dining room to the table, I was overwhelmed with the flying toys and memorabilia hanging from the ceiling overhead. From airplanes, blimps, autos, to racing horses, it was a child-like feast for the eyes, strung up across the room from every angle. We were directed to a long table in a more secluded corner alcove.

As we approached, I saw numerous men and a few women seated, dressed to the nines, sharing animated conversations. James spoke up loudly over the din from the table, while tapping the side of a crystal water glass with his spoon. "Friends, welcome! I believe I've previously met almost everyone here. I trust the waiter has been generous with appetizers and delicious cocktails from the bar?"

Again, there was chatter and nods, with one man clamoring, "Still waiting on that lobster dinner you promised, Appleton."

"On the way soon, and the best you'll ever have. I'm sorry Mr. Mayer couldn't be here himself tonight, but I'm James Appleton, sent by LB to treat you to an amazing dinner."

One of the older gentlemen interrupted with a chuckle. "OK James, if I know LB, he's looking for money. Somewhere down the line this dinner's going to end up costing me something." Everybody seemed to laugh in unison.

James quickly replied with a smile. "Well, Mr. Rockefeller, looks like you're on to me. Honestly, LB and I are both excited to offer this elite group a whiff at a fantastic investment opportunity that we believe you clever people will be interested in. Before I begin formal introductions all around, let me introduce another new friend. Don't let the WAC uniform fool you, folks. This was one of her costumes while singing Boogie Woogie Bugle Boy tonight on WOR's Talent Jackpot. This is Jo-Jo Anderson, a very talented vocalist."

After his announcement, most of these people looked a little confused, offering up mild applause. This was definitely not a Talent Jackpot kind of crowd.

The table seemed to be a collection of older men, a few accompanied by their bejeweled wives. James made all the introductions.

These were men who represented large banks, Wall Street investment companies, an owner of an independent theater chain, a former ambassador, a current senator, and a producer from the National Broadcast Company. If they didn't know each other before, their moneyed background seemed to immediately admit them to the club, as everyone began exchanging financial and political gossip, of which I knew very little about.

Bandied around the table, I heard talk of new home construction on the rise as a result of all the soldiers coming home. The Wall Street guy was talking up a firm called Levitt and Sons. "Honest to God, they're building almost thirty homes a day, creating swaths of brand new communities. Following in old Ford's footsteps; they've created a damn assembly line house-factory. Now, that's a company to keep your eye on."

A banker added, "And automobile sales are headed sky-high. Mark my words. The savings rate in this country is at an all time high--twenty-one percent of income. And believe me; people are ready to spend on the big stuff."

The senator sitting across from me mentioned, "You're right. In Michigan, they're already retooling the factories. I never imagined how quickly we'd be able to transform back to peacetime products." He rubbed his hands together. "I definitely feel a big bull market coming on."

I was quickly feeling like a fish out of water, having little to add to the conversation. The last thing I needed was for someone at this table to ask me if I was The Deli-Girl. I wasn't even a high-class waitress. I pushed bagels and pastrami sandwiches and was thankful for my pile of nickels and dimes at the end of each day.

Martinis were brought for James and me and food was ordered for all as I busied myself laughing occasionally at an off-color joke, smiling, sipping, and eating. James, who was seated next to me, leaned close to my ear and asked, "So, what do you think?"

I whispered back, "Honestly, it's like getting to walk into Saks Fifth Avenue knowing I could never buy anything. I feel like I have nothing to add to the conversation."

He patted my hand and looked at me sympathetically. "That's

OK. You're young. Take advantage of the situation. Just listen and learn. There's a boatload of knowledge at this table, and a lot of malarkey too. You're doing just fine."

"You sure about that?"

"Absolutely."

As the meal wound down, James drew in everyone's attention again and explained that MGM had plans for a major new musical that was highly anticipated as a follow-up picture for actress Judy Garland, after the great success of *Meet Me in Saint Louis*. This film would have the best team of composers, a top-name director, and the most popular co-stars from the MGM stable of actors.

One lady, dripping in diamonds, interrupted and asked, "Why the hell did LB get rid of all his top stars at MGM? Garbo, Crawford, Loy, Shearer? All those beautiful women. Didn't make sense to me."

James replied, "Well, I agree, all talented women, but LB's always focused on the future. Who and what will be popular and profitable next month, next year, and for the years beyond. Audiences are hungry for new and they are loving big, splashy, colorful musicals, with talented actors and dancers. Today, Americans want to be immersed in the fantasy and carried away from their everyday lives."

I noticed everyone had put their forks down and all eyes were on him. He was working his magic, drawing everyone in for a piece of the action.

"This new film will be all about that. People close to the project are already talking Oscar-worthy. Now, don't make your decision tonight. I'll connect with you individually and offer up more details. Tonight is just about celebrating this opportunity." Then he held up his freshly filled glass, clinked my glass and led everyone in a resounding toast. "To grabbing the brass ring."

My steak was probably the best piece of meat I'd ever eaten and the liquor seemed top notch, but I was still a fairly inexperienced nineteen-year-old and I felt like I'd been faking it all night. After the dinner finally broke up, we were standing curbside while James attempted to hail a cab. He asked me if I'd consider going dancing, but I was exhausted.

"Hopefully, some other time, James. This has been an illuminating night, but I think it's time I get to bed. I actually have to work at the Stage Deli tomorrow. It's back to reality, I'm afraid."

"I'm sure it was a long day for you. Maybe just a nightcap in my suite at The Dixie? You're only a quick elevator ride away."

"Sorry, not tonight, but thank you for a really delicious dinner."

As we pulled up to the hotel, he took my hand and walked me into the elevator. "So, maybe I'll call you tomorrow. I'm in town for a few more days. I'm sure I might be able to offer some career tips and advice if you're interested."

I told the elevator operator, "Fourth floor please," and told James, "I'd really appreciate that. Just leave a message with the desk. My room doesn't have a phone. Thanks again for everything. Goodnight James."

The next morning, around ten, I was leaving for work. As I crossed the lobby, Rudy, the bellboy who had, in his words, 'screwed the pooch' on my laundry delivery, stopped me. "Miss Anderson. Holy smokes! Congratulations on your big win. I take it that the man in the tuxedo got your costumes back to you in time?"

"Yes, Rudy, *just* in time. Thanks so much for staying on top of things. That meant alot to me. By the way, the gentleman, Mr. Appleton, where did he find his tuxedo? Who did that get delivered to?"

Rudy took on an odd expression and hurriedly answered. " Uh, a lost tuxedo? News to me. That man came into the hotel with your clothes in a bag wearing his tuxedo, a fancy overcoat, and hat. A swell looking guy."

"Ok, that's odd. Thought it had been lost. Thanks Rudy."

CHAPTER 23

ATTRACTIONS AND DISTRACTIONS

SARAH

*O*ver the weekend, I was floating in a glorious two-day bubble, thinking about Beckham Carter. I'd never been this distracted. While reading The Odyssey, Beckham's green eyes continued to pop up, interrupting Odysseus' attempts to return home. Trying to pivot to trig, his voice kept interrupting my concentration, telling me how long he'd been waiting to kiss me. In my favorite library study carrel, I gently touched my cheek the way Beckham had, and could feel my temperature rise and my neck get hot. This was getting out of hand. I needed to refocus on my studies and do something about the Help for Heroes group. So far, it was a group of one.

Sunday evening, during meatloaf night at Currior Hall, I attempted to enlarge the group. I sat down next to Barbara and several of her devotees. I wasn't sure how to broach the subject of the volunteer group but I offered a wave and took a bite of the ketchup covered meatloaf. I rarely joined my roommate and her crew, usually preferring to eat by myself while reading at a table in the back. The girls were in the middle of an animated discussion about a recent movie they'd all seen.

I jumped in the middle of their conversation, opening with, "So, am I wrong, or is tonight's meatloaf especially delicious?"

The seven of them stopped talking, looked at me with either confusion or indifference, and then continued their conversation. Barbara said, "I know what you mean, Deborah. When that young sailor returned home with hooks instead of hands and then tried to light those soldiers' cigarettes... I just wanted to cry. He was trying so hard to be accepted."

Deborah nodded and said, "I know, and then that officer with the family... his kids were so happy to have him home and he just couldn't adjust to anything from his old life."

Wait a second--were they talking about a movie about wounded veterans? This might play right into my hand. I interrupted again. "So, what's this movie you're talking about?"

Deborah explained with a huff. *"Best Years of our Lives.* Gosh Sarah, seems like everybody's seen it by now." The girls all nodded and murmured in unison. I was out of the loop as usual. But honestly, who had time to go to the movies?

Barbara quickly explained, "It's about three soldiers coming back from the war and having a hard time trying to fit back into their civilian lives. It really makes you think."

I had my perfect opening. "OK, this is going to sound strange, but I am starting a group to help returning injured student vets on campus. I can't believe you guys are talking about this movie! There's a student in my bio lab who has an amputated leg. He's on crutches and really struggles with the stairs." I looked at the girls and pointed to them. "You ladies know a lot of the gals on campus. Do you think there'd be much interest in a group helping out students with disabilities like that?"

Barbara looked at the others. "I don't know? My plate's pretty full with the sorority's big fundraiser."

I had to turn this around. Barbara could sway the whole table for or against this. "Barb, I don't know much about your sorority, but isn't it supposed to be about community service? What could be more important than helping fellow students that fought for our country and got maimed in the process?"

Deborah, put down her fork and was quiet for a moment. "My

cousin came back partially blinded by a landmine. I could probably squeeze out a little time each week, Sarah."

Yea! I had one person, a group of two.

Barbara then chimed in. Maybe we could rack up some volunteer points for our sorority, right ladies? And all for a good cause."

"Yes!" I said. "You know, a lot of these returning vets will need help having wheelchairs pushed to classes, or finding their way around campus. Maybe helping carry books, or offering simple friendship. Who knows what all they would need?"

Deborah nodded. "I can see how that would be helpful."

I continued. "And, Barbara, the group would need a volunteer coordinator. Someone who can match volunteers with vets in need. You'd be *so good* at handling that."

"You think so? I guess that is my strong suit. So, who else is involved?"

I was thinking--*just us*--but I said, "Well, they haven't fully committed yet, but Jacob Riverstone and several of the Young Republicans seem interested. And I could probably handle publicity."

Barbara said, "No offense, Sarah, but Abigail is excellent at garnering publicity." She nodded to the girl at the end of the table. "It's Abbie's thing and her major is with the advertising and communications department. I'd highly recommend her."

"Sure. Abigail, you sound perfect. So, I'll check with those guys in the Young Republicans and get a list of disabled vets from the administration office to see who's in need of volunteer assistance, and then Barbara, you could get people signed up for shifts."

Barbara nodded enthusiastically. "Let's go ahead and start a list of volunteers. Who at this table is interested?" Deborah and Abbie's hands shot up. "Come on ladies. I know each of you have one or two afternoons off each week. Surely you can give up a little time." The four remaining women sheepishly raised their hands, as Barbara wrote all our names on her list.

I was excited, slapping my hand down on the table. "This is great. That makes eight. We only need two more students to start an officially sanctioned student activity group. We're on our way, girls."

Barbara quickly looked around the dining room and spotted a few girls from our wing. "There's Emily and Franny sitting with a couple others. I'll go talk to them."

I was amazed by her bulldozing confidence. Five minutes later she put the sheet down in front of me. "I got three to join, that's eleven, Sarah. We're official. I'm glad to hear Jacob Riverstone is interested. Find out how many of the Young Republicans are joining us and then we're up and running."

I think Barbara was more interested in rubbing shoulders with Jacob than the disabled vets, but I needed her power of persuasion. The following day, I looked down the quadrangle hoping to see Jacob working the voter registration table, but the weather was so cold there were no tables out. I couldn't remember which dorm he was in, but I checked the directory at the student union, found his address, and walked over. I asked for him at the desk and they sent a runner upstairs. A few minutes later, Jacob came down the staircase looking like he'd just woken up, with messed hair, rubbing his eyes, uncharacteristically disheveled. When he saw me, he didn't smile.

"What are you doing here?"

"Uh, just wanted to talk to you for a minute. Can we sit down in the lounge?" He walked ahead of me, not saying anything, and sat down in an armchair. I took the one across from him.

He looked down at his watch. "I've got stuff to do; what do you want, Sarah?"

This was going to be harder than I thought. Why did I tell Barbara that Jacob was interested in joining? It seemed that he now detested me. "Well, I can see I hurt your feelings last week. I'm really sorry. I guess I just didn't want to waste your time. I think you're a great guy, but we're just from two different worlds."

"All right. Is that about it?" He stood up to go.

"Wait, hold on. My roommate, Barbara and I are starting a volunteer group to help disabled veterans returning to school. I was curious if your crew of Young Republicans might allow Barbara and I to attend your next meeting to speak about their needs and see if your members would be interested in joining us. So far, we have eleven girls committed to volunteering, but we'll need some men too. And you never know, I'll bet a lot of vets have a vested interest in politics after returning from the war. Might be a new area of recruitment for you. By the way, my roommate thinks you're really cute and wants to meet you."

He nodded, but offered no eye contact. "Honestly…it's not a terrible idea. So, this Barbara… she thought I was handsome?"

"Very. You two should meet. Shall I tell her to come to Hesson's Tavern this Wednesday? I'll be there too."

Jacob sighed and looked at the floor for a few seconds. "Alright. Bring her along. We'll listen to your ideas and decide. But no promises. See you then, Sarah."

Well, that wasn't a ringing endorsement, but it wasn't a no.

IT WAS FINALLY Tuesday--four days and five nights since I'd been with Beckham, but who was counting? I was walking down the hall for my afternoon biology class, and as I walked into the room, I couldn't help but blush a little. Could everyone else see it? Surely something looked different about me. Would Beckham still be interested or had I acted too aggressively and scared him away?

Throughout the lecture, there were no furtive looks directed my way by the professor, no glancing over to my desk with that hint of a smile. It was straight lecture, the occasional question, a few chalk board terms written for emphasis. Nothing that indicated, *yes, I've been thinking about you. Yes, so glad to see you. Yes, you look especially desirable today.*

I could hardly keep my mind on his lecture. I was watching Beckham's mouth move, noticing how he tilted his head, how his trousers hung a little too loose on him, and his necktie was somewhat crooked. But I took no notice of what he was saying. I looked down at my notepad and saw I'd written down two sentences. Is this what happens when people feel they're in love, or in lust, or whatever this was? It was impossible to concentrate on anything. This was terrible.

After class, I hung back, slow to gather my stuff together. As the students filed out, I slowly walked to the front as he watched me approach his desk.

"I got nothing from your lecture today. I'm going to have to glean everything from the text and reread that chapter. Did you steal my brain the other night, Professor?"

"Hmm. Maybe you left it in my office. Want to join me there for coffee?"

"Only if you actually have coffee."

He stood up, turning to go. "Yes, I do and I bought you your own mug."

That was it. I was his.

Upstairs, in his still-cluttered office we attempted to rehash his latest lecture while sipping from our cups of instant Nescafe. "Beckham, these files all over the floor are driving me crazy. You really lack organization skills."

He shrugged and laughed. "It's all your fault. Each time I come up here I'm too distracted thinking about you." He got up and locked his door. "Hope that's OK, I just don't need any students interrupting us right now." He took my hand and pulled me up from the chair and leaned against the wall, holding me close. I looked up and we kissed again. It was long, lingering, and passionate, like a delicious coffee-flavored confection. "Your eyes, Sarah, they're mesmerizing."

I was so happy. He *was* still interested in me. Last Friday night had not been a one-time aberration. This was happening. Hands were touching, moving from face to shoulders to breasts. I was hot everywhere, about to explode again. My hands went inside his shirt. I felt his hands pushing up my sweater, rubbing my breasts. After several minutes I pulled away. I didn't want to, but felt I had to. "Sorry Beckham, that's as far as I'm prepared to go, especially in this office."

Nervously looking about for something to do, I turned and started picking up piles of file folders off the crowded floor. "So...do all these need to go in that metal cabinet?"

He was still catching his breath, trying to tuck his shirt back in. "Meet me at my apartment again. Please. This Wednesday night?"

"So I file these?" I was still holding the manilla folders. "
Alphabetical, by date, or subject?"

He looked distracted. "Christ, I don't know. Alphabetical?"

"Yes, that's probably the best approach. But, to answer your
question…Yes. I'd love to come over again, provided you get a new
chicken recipe, but Wednesday's not good. I have to meet with the
Young Republicans to try to get them on board with my Help for
Heroes group."

He looked at me slightly upset. "Christ, that again? Well, come
after and why are you letting that take up your time?"

"Because it's important to me and my roommate, Barbara, is
coming with me. She'll think it's odd I'm going somewhere else
afterwards. Thursday's good for me though. Or Friday?"

He nodded and slightly smiled. "Thursday then. Friday afternoon I have to go to Minneapolis for a few days."

I pulled out the file drawer and then laughed. "Hope we don't
combust before then. So, alphabetical? Looks like I'll have to make
some letter tabs first. For someone who is so articulate and methodi-
cal, your filing system is terrible." Glancing at my watch, I said, "I'll
get this all sorted for you. You better hurry along. Your next class
starts in four minutes."

"Already?" He hurriedly returned to his desk and gathered his
notes. "How do you even know these things? You see, Sarah. I need
you in my life." He grabbed his briefcase and left, while his parting
words were like a perfect song which played over and over in my
head through the remainder of the day.

CHAPTER 24

MAMMA MIA!

JO-JO

*P*ulling my hat down and keeping my coat close, I walked against the bone-chilling wind, while my mind rehashed the conversation I'd just had with Rudy, the bellhop. There was probably a simple explanation, but James Appleton clearly told me his tuxedo was misplaced and he had received my clothes in error. But Rudy told me that James walked into the hotel wearing his tux, hat and coat. If he already had the tux cleaned and delivered earlier, why would he have taken the bag of clothes hung on his door to work? None of this made sense, but I was sure it could be cleared up in a New York minute once I spoke to James again. I hoped I'd see him later tonight, before he left town. It was exciting to chat with someone who seemed to know most everyone in the business. Especially someone who was on a first name basis with LB Mayer.

As I turned the corner approaching the Stage Deli, I saw several men hanging around outside. They were all smoking, leaning against the walls, casually chatting. Then I noticed a few were carrying large cameras. It was the reporters again, still attempting to create their fabricated gossip-mongering story. Publicity was good, but not this kind. I decided to cross the block early and enter through the deli's back door from the alley. It was usually left unlocked for smoking employees to use during their breaks.

Once inside, I saw Benny, the dishwasher. He had his back to me as he rinsed and stacked plates for washing. I walked over to the rack in the corner and hung my hat and coat. Underneath, I'd worn my new uniform, wanting to show it off to Mr. Asnas.

"Hi-de-ho, Benny. How's your day going?"

The stooped, older man with grizzled gray hair turned around surprised, his bright brown eyes smiling. "Well, hello Miss Deli-Girl. You was really cookin' with gas last night. We was all listening at my place. You done good, girl!"

"Thanks Benny. So nice of you to tune in. It was exciting! Hey, do you know anything about those men hanging around outside? That's why I came through the back."

He shrugged. "Not really sure, Miss Jo. Mr. Max say they's asking for you. Probably wants to congratulate you, I think."

"OK, thanks. I better clock in." I entered the dining room from the back and found the owner shaking hands with a few customers he knew. I walked over, struck a pose and tapped him on the back shoulder. "What do you think of the uniform, Mr. Asnas?"

He turned around surprised, grinned and then pushed me to the back room. "Hey Jo-Jo, love the uniform and the good words you spread about the deli last night, but you got big problems outside. Since I unlocked the damn door this morning, it's been reporter after nosy reporter slinking in asking me questions about you. Asking what did I know about some romance going on with you and some guy at WOR. I started making them all stay outside, but they don't seem to be leaving. This looks bad; bad for you and my business."

I stomped my foot in anger. "The whole story is ridiculous, Mr. Asnas. I've done nothing wrong and certainly have not had any relations with men at that studio. How would I even have time for that?"

Asnas nodded and said, "I'm glad to hear this. Can't have these ugly rumors circulating around here. For now, I think it's best if you take the rest of the week off. Myrna wants more hours anyway." He made a shooing motion with his hands. "Go now. Go enjoy your big win. Probably all the reporters will get bored and just go away."

"You think? But, Max, I still need this job. Just because I won that show doesn't mean I don't have to work. But maybe this would be a good time for me to start those dance lessons."

"Yes…good time for that. You just won some very big money… go enjoy it. I'll tell the reporters that you're taking some time off."

I sighed deeply, hating to go out in the cold again and wouldn't have minded eating my free sandwich. "OK, I'll leave out the back first and please don't tell any of them where I'm staying."

He patted my back and said, "Of course not. Good luck Jo-Jo. Take care of yourself."

I looked at him with a puzzled face. "I *will* be back, Max. It's just for the week. I need this job."

He nodded. "You know, over the years I seen so many waitresses come and go, many of them dreaming to be on a real stage. For some reason, I don't think you'll be back." Then he made his shooing motion again. "Enjoy that money. Come back and see us when you're a big star."

I laughed while closing the back door and said, "Sure thing. I'll see you next week."

I walked back towards The Dixie and looked at my watch. It was still early enough in the day to check out possible dance studios. I wondered if Damien had any recommendations. He'd learned from the best in the business--his parents. Come to think of it, it had been over a week since we'd seen each other or spoken on the phone. He was probably busy with his show. I returned to The Dixie and stopped at the row of phone booths near the lobby and tried to call Damien, but nobody picked up.

As I passed the registration desk, Leonard, one of the guys who worked the desk, called out to me. "Miss Anderson, you have a few messages." I walked over and waited as he checked an older couple out. Leonard was young, with round, wireframe glasses, and always looked so professional in his starched white shirt, checked tie, and gray Dixie Hotel blazer. As I stepped up, he said, "Hey, Jo-Jo, congrats on your big win. One of the bellhops told me about it. Let me grab your messages." He turned to the huge board of key boxes pigeonholed right behind him, one for each room, and handed me my memos. "Oh wait, something else just arrived for you. I'll be right back."

I leafed through my messages and saw that Mother had called and asked me to call her collect. There were also a few requests from reporters wanting me to give them interviews regarding my win. One was from that pushy Post reporter from last night. How did he know I lived here? I wondered if granting interviews would be a better way to get publicity and get rid of these negative rumors. But I had no idea on who to trust; it seemed most of these guys were just looking for dirt.

"These recently arrived." I turned around and Leonard placed a large vase of tall, bright, exotic flowers on the wooden counter.

"Oh, they're lovely! Thanks Lenny." I'd never been given flowers, with the exception of a small rose corsage at a school dance. Back in Green Tree, flowers like these were reserved for funerals or weddings, and never looked this nice. I carried the large vase over to the elevator and peeked in the bouquet for a card and pulled it out.

Thanks for being my perfect guest last night. I'm busy with work today, but would love to take you out for dinner tonight. How about the Copa at eight? Your friend, James Appleton.

My heart soared at his generosity and of course I was impressed with the extravagant flowers. It would be thrilling to have dinner there and get an early view of the Copacabana as a guest, especially if I was performing there later. I placed the large bouquet on my small nightstand, then sat down and gazed at it for a few minutes. I wiggled out of my deli uniform and changed into black trousers and a black turtleneck sweater. Remembering my Jackpot check, I took it out of my pocketbook and stared at it, wishing I could frame it. I'd learned many things during my upbringing. This prize money was not to be squandered. I had to make every penny count. I wished my mother was here for her advice. I really missed her at these times and was eager to make that collect call.

Going through my purse, I also noticed Nanette's gold edged business card, printed with a delicate black script which read: *Fran Jordan-Talent Agent to the Stars*, with her phone number and business address listed below. I was certain she could offer strategic tips on handling interviews and would be happy to tell me the best place for dance lessons at a good price. Even though I was feeling a little overwhelmed, I refused the idea of asking for Nanette's help, and dropped the card back to the bottom of my purse. Perhaps James might be a good resource. I would find out tonight.

First on my agenda was making the call to Mom. I went back downstairs.

"Green Tree switchboard, how can I help you?"

Once again, I recognized the voice of my high school pal, Anita. "Anita, it's Jo-Jo. How's it going? I need to make a collect call to my mother."

"Absolutely, but first let me tell you something. I told everyone about that Jackpot show and got the whole town tuning in. And guess what? Mr. Odenmeyer from the Coffee Cup is naming a sandwich after you! *The Jo-Jo Rye*. It's cheddar and roast beef on rye. What do you think of that?"

"Fantastic. Tell him the next time I'm in town, I'll come in and order one and I'll let my parents know too."

"Well, I'm just jumping for joy about all this and we're so proud of you, Jo-Jo. OK, I'm connecting you now."

I smiled listening to Anita and Mom chattering back and forth before Mother talked to me. When Anita finally clicked off, Mom said, "Jo, we were so proud of you last night! Your Dad and I just wanted to let you know that. David's going to be so upset that he missed your call."

"Thanks so much, Mom. I was thinking of you yesterday before I went on. About your confidence and always pushing yourself forward on your own. Even though you didn't know it, my memories of you helped me through that program last night."

"Aw, thanks, Jo. You're making me cry. Sorry. Hold on"…I heard her sniffle a few times…"All right, I'm back now."

"Mom, I did want to ask; what do you suggest I do with my winnings? I've never had enough money for my own bank account before."

"Get one open right away, Jo. Living in a hotel, keeping a lot of cash around cannot be safe. I suggest you open a checking and a savings account. Banks are much better now. I'm sure you don't remember, but back in '33, the Bank of Green Tree closed without warning. In fact, it happened all over the country.

"Well, that certainly doesn't sound safe."

"But things have changed so much. Now the government guarantees your money up to five-thousand-dollars. I'd put a couple hundred in a checking account and the rest in savings. Let your money earn a little interest."

"All right. I'll try to do that today. Mom, I know these calls are adding up so fill me in on everybody really quick before we have to hang up."

She caught me up on Green Tree gossip in record time. Brother Sammy had gotten into a few fights at school, but nothing too serious. David had decided to grow alfalfa on his newest acreage this spring. And all three of Mom's boarding houses were fully rented. Life sounded pretty darn good, except for the poor boys my brother punched in the nose. I hung up smiling, thrilled to have a conversation from home. It was just the ticket for fighting off homesickness and so much better than just a letter.

Back at the desk, I left a note in James' box, letting him know I'd be happy to meet him for dinner at eight, then I asked Lenny what bank The Dixie used for their deposits. He told me the name and location of the bank which was not too far from Times Square. I figured if it was good enough for the hotel, it was good enough for me. On the way over to open an account, I considered buying a new dress for tonight, but decided I shouldn't splurge again after buying my black dress only two weeks ago. That dress would have to make do for the Copa.

I did allow myself some pampering though. I passed a swanky salon, took a deep breath and went in. I got a bold red manicure and had my hair washed, trimmed, and curled for tonight. I asked for something sophisticated and the stylist parted my hair in the middle, created two large rolls on each side at the crown and twisted the back into a classic chignon. It was the first time I'd ever had my hair professionally cut and styled and I left feeling movie-star glamorous. After leaving the salon, I noticed it was past three, and unfortunately, the bank had just closed. Opening my own accounts would have to wait until Monday.

Promptly at eight, James knocked at my door, just as I decided to cut a red rose from his bouquet and pin it on my white satin lapel. Opening the door, I was taken aback at this handsome man. James was looking sharp in a dark navy suit, his brown hair slicked back. He looked at me dressed and ready to go. "Love a girl who's ready to roll on time. Impressive!" He gave me his arm and asked, "Shall we?"

Coming off the elevator, I felt like I was on the arm of a prince as I swished across the tiled lobby floor while imagining I was wearing a French designer gown. Although, a large wall mirror opposite the elevator reminded me that I was still in my bargain-rack dress from Macy's. But James had reminded me last night--it was all about attitude. If you believe something fiercely, others will believe it too.

Once we slid into a cab, James looked at me and took my gloved hand. "So glad you decided to join me. You're going to love the Copa. It's going to blow your socks off."

"Gosh, I hope not. I just put on my one and only pair of silk stockings."

He laughed and kissed the top of my hand. "I wouldn't worry about that, Jo-Jo. I have a feeling you're going to have all the silk stockings you need."

CHAPTER 25

COMMITMENT

SARAH

Dearest Jo,

I have to admit this to someone. I'm about to burst. Jo, you're the closest friend I'll ever have. I am unabashedly head-over-heels in love. How can this be happening? Wasn't it a mere six weeks ago that I was crying my eyes out over losing Tommy Martin to the navy and another girl? Isn't this too fast, could my feelings possibly be real? You're the only person I trust to discuss this with. The man I'm mooning over is a biology professor, thirty-two years old, somewhat handsome, intelligent, stubborn, rude, but someone who seems to admire me and my mind, and he happens to have the most amazing kisses! I honestly tingle to my core when I think about him. It's really quite extraordinary.

This is all new for me, Jo. I know he is probably too old, and if the university knew of the relationship they would certainly frown on it because I am both his student and his lab employee. But I absolutely must be with him again. At this point, we have not consummated the relationship sexually, but I don't know how much longer either of us can hold out. The bond is so thrilling that it has distracted me from much of my studies and has me even thinking of a career in biology rather than education. I seek your immediate advice! You've always been more worldly than me in affairs of the heart.

Write or call soon. I hope all is well in Manhattan and that you'll be

singing soon at the Copacabana. All the dorm girls admire you so much!
You must write to me and describe the place in great detail. Who knows if
I'll ever get there myself.

 Your loving sister always,
 Sarah

J had to tell someone how I was feeling. Jo had always been my confidant, although in the past I'd had little to confide about. Growing up together, Jo-Jo was always the one asking me to keep her secrets. Nothing too terrible, but I recalled her occasional sneak-outs to meet a boy from the next town, skipping school on a few crucial test days, playing sick instead of going to church. I generally went along and backed up her stories, but I truly doubted Mom and Dad were not wise to her tricks and just put up with her.

Before I tore my gushing letter to shreds, I quickly folded it and popped it in an envelope. President Truman's face seemed to be looking at me with disapproval as I licked the back of his three-cent stamp, placing it with guilt onto the envelope. Then I ran downstairs and dropped it in the mail slot. There! It was done and my secret was out, at least to one person who lived far from the university.

I took a deep breath and took my time releasing it. "So Sarah, what are you up to?" I jumped, turning around to see my roommate, Barbara, walking past the reception desk. With her gossip-prone tendencies, I considered what a field day she would have knowing the contents of the letter I'd just mailed.

"Hey there, Barb, just dropping a letter to Jo." We turned toward the stairs as I said, "Oh, don't forget. We have our meeting at five with the Young Republicans. I told Jacob I was bringing my very attractive roommate."

Her face quickly blushed, although it might have been from the flight of stairs. "Sarah, you little minx. I hope you didn't say that. I wouldn't want to disappoint him. But I didn't forget. I came home to freshen up."

Back in our room, I unbraided my hair and brushed through the waves. I put on my light rose-colored lipstick again. I justified the use of cosmetics knowing I would be speaking in front of a group of people and should look my best.

Barbara and I were sharing the small mirror on our door, as she touched up her lashes with mascara. "Sarah, please don't take this the wrong way, but if you'd like to, you can borrow a sweater my mother recently sent me. The deep-red color would look great on you, and honestly, it's a little too tight for me across the chest."

"Sure. I know I rarely show interest in clothes, but I'm starting to see their occasional importance. Thank you." She also lent me a matching red ribbon to tie back my hair. I felt almost stylish.

An hour later we were standing amongst a crowd at the bar in Hesson's Tavern, sipping from beer steins, and introducing ourselves to the predominantly male members of the Young Republicans around us. I quickly realized I never could have done this without Barbara at my side. She was shaking hands left and right, gathering names, and spreading the word about our fledgling group, Help for Heroes.

I saw Jacob walk in and waved him over. "Jacob, this is my roommate, Barbara. We're so excited to speak to your members today." He was back to looking neat and tidy, wearing his gold Hawkeye sweater and black blazer.

Barbara took over from there, shaking his hand and moving in. "Jacob, so good to meet you. I've seen you around campus and heard great things about you from Sarah. I'll let you grab a beer and then would you mind if I bend your ear for just a moment about our project? You'd be the perfect person to join us." He smiled, nodded, flagged down the bartender, and then their heads were bent together discussing strategies, politics, or perhaps the size of Barbara's breasts? I was happy. They seemed meant for each other.

Turning around to grab a bar stool, I noticed Lester, attempting to navigate his crutches through the heavy double doors of the bar. Earlier, I'd mentioned the meeting to him and my idea about the volunteer group we were organizing, but I was surprised he'd actually shown up. I quickly walked over, opened one of the doors, and greeted him. "Lester, so glad you could make it. Hope it wasn't too far for you."

He glanced around, seeming a little intimidated by the crowd. "Actually, my cousin dropped me off. Good news though. I just heard, I'm getting a wheelchair next week and maybe in a year or two, a prosthetic leg. I've been on a waiting list with the VA for a while."

"That's wonderful! You'll be zipping around campus in no time. Hey, beers are half-price now if you'd like a drink."

He offered up the first genuine smile I'd ever noticed from him. "I'm never one to turn down a cheap beer. Lead the way."

We wedged into a space at the bar waiting to place our order, while I spoke loudly over the din of student voices. "Once every-body settles in, my roommate and I are going to speak briefly about Help for Heroes. Lester, honestly, you were my inspiration for the idea. Do you think you'd like to speak, for just a few minutes? Tell people what you think about the idea, or some of the issues that you deal with daily."

He looked down at the scratched surface of the bar. "I'll think about it. Haven't done much public speaking."

I shrugged and said, "Me neither. Guess there's a first time for everything. I think your story would certainly have an impact."

"I'll let you know how I feel after a drink or two."

Eventually, people settled down into chairs at several round tables. I quickly counted the group. There appeared to be about thirty-five members present. Jacob kicked things off.

He clanged a spoon against his glass mug a few times and brought the rowdy group to attention. "We have a couple guest speakers here tonight who are creating a new volunteer organization on campus, and now that I've thought and heard a little more about it, I think the idea is something members here should really consider joining. Some of you may recall meeting my friend, Sarah Anderson, a couple weeks ago. And we'll also hear from her roommate, Barbara Thompson. So, if you can keep it down for a bit and give these girls a listen, I'd appreciate it."

There was a little grumbling and a smattering of applause as I took Jacob's spot, nervous as hell. I coughed a few times, tugged on my sweater, and plowed forward, trying to make my voice more forceful above the conversation.

"OK folks, listen up and imagine this. You fought hard for your country during the war, possibly lost a limb, an arm, or more in battle and was sent home. Eventually… you find out that vets are being given a wonderful opportunity to attend college through the new GI bill. Doors are now open to you, you're excited to learn, you start dreaming about a new career… but, once you're on campus you find you can't even get up the stairs to attend your first class."

I looked around. Eyes were now on me. Some appeared interested, others had their arms crossed and looked unmoved. "It's difficult to even manage the simplest act of opening the front door of a classroom while in a wheelchair. Maybe you can't reach the book you need on a library shelf and have to find help. Perhaps you feel isolated because your injury makes you look different from the other students, or you're a few years older and feel out of place. Honestly, for an injured vet returning to school, the list could feel endless. Barbara and I have formed Help for Heroes, and we need more students who will volunteer an hour or two a week to help turn things around. Disabled vets don't want special treatment. They just want access to the simplest things that able-bodied students take for granted. They only want to be put on a level playing field. Barbara will talk to you more about the nuts and bolts of coordinating student volunteers with our disabled students. We need to make this idea a reality."

Before Barbara could take over, one guy stood up from a table, leaning over, and said, "My older brother lost his hand on a ship out in the Pacific. He's back at the farm, doing just fine. Nobody's helping him."

Another guy at the bar chimed in. "Not so sure about all of this. Maybe these guys don't want help. Probably don't need any extra attention."

I took back the floor before everyone started piling on. "Thanks for your comments. I've been doing a little research. Actually, back after the great war in 1919, a college right here in Iowa started a program for disabled vets, retraining them in several areas of farming: orchard grafting, bee keeping, farm machinery repair, dairy production. It was quite successful and ended up training over 2,000 vets for agricultural positions. Unfortunately, after 1925, the program was dismantled. From what I read, those men had great appreciation for the skills they learned. And if you'd like to hear directly from someone with a debilitating injury, I'd like you to meet a friend of mine." I looked over at the bar and saw Lester staring at me with fear in his eyes. "Lester Adams, would you like to step up and say a few words?" I was hoping he'd decided to speak. *Please come up Lester…don't leave me hanging.*

He drained the remains of a beer down his throat, grabbed his crutches and hopped over to where I stood. His light hair shone brightly under the overhead lights as he began speaking with a slight uncomfortable stutter.

"Guess I'll say my piece. I'm not m-much for talking to groups, but I came here to-today because Miss Sarah asked me to. Lost this leg here when I was hit in France. It was m-mangled by a landmine. But anyway, everything Sarah said is correct. There's so many things that ch-challenge us disabled folk that most others take for complete granted. There's a lot of us that could use just a little help here and there. In my case--help with stairs, maybe creating some kind of plywood ramps. So, please consider her request. This could be a groundbreaking effort allowing a large community of people to come out from the shadows. Appreciate you letting me speak."

I was so proud of him that I began clapping loudly and a few others followed suit. Then it was Barbara's turn. She was immediately in her element, already relaxed and taking charge, telling students what might be required of them, that it was their duty and now time to do their part after others had already given so much. She was loud, friendly, and cajoling. I hoped Jacob noticed that she was the true politician here.

Barbara and I passed out sign-up sheets. Several were not interested but we convinced about half the people to commit. That would now bring our group up to twenty-eight. Barb and I thought it was a good start. Later, as we gathered our coats to go, Jacob came by and invited us to join a few others to go for burgers. I declined the offer, saying I had a test to study for, but Barbara accepted.

Walking home, I couldn't stop smiling to myself. The whole evening had taken me totally by surprise, making me feel good about myself and our commitment. Who knew that Sarah Anderson, the slightly obsessive, nose-to-the-grindstone scholarship student could be a group leader, a hoop jumper, and possibly successful matchmaker? Well played, Sarah!

CHAPTER 26
THE CLUB OF DREAMS
JO-JO

*T*he cab driver slowed the car and turned his head toward us. "Sir, 10 East 60th Street, the Copa."

I stared out the window, looking up the stairs of a five-story brownstone. I'd seen ads and news stories about the Copa; the place was legendary. "That was quick. Alright James, I'm ready to be impressed."

The cab pulled up close to a well lit canopy where a uniformed doorman, wearing a long navy coat with gold buttons and epaulets, opened our door. He greeted us in a deep New York accent. "Evening, folks. Welcome to the Copacabana." He offered his gloved hand while I stepped out of the cab. So far, as promised, I was impressed. There was a long line of people waiting to get in, but we walked directly to the door opened by a second doorman. On the first level, we checked our coats, then a host wearing a dark suit greeted us and James said, "Appleton, reservations for two,"

"Right this way, Mr. Appleton." We walked downstairs into the main dining room next to the stage. The maitre d' turned and said, "Right next to the dance floor, as requested. First show is just about to start." The host pulled out my chair as I sat and gazed about. "Enjoy your evening."

Our waiter quickly approached with menus and asked about

drinks. James looked at me and said, "I think a bottle of Champagne is called for. Whaddaya say, Jo-Jo?"

"I agree!" I took in the room, as we waited. We were seated inches from the dance floor which also seemed to be the stage for the performers. Behind the dance floor was a tiered band stand which was curtained on each side with clusters of shiny palm trees encased in fabric and backed by a beautiful painted mural of a tropical scene. Within minutes of our cork being popped, the members of the Copa's orchestra began to file in, take their places, and began tuning up. By the time we'd toasted and swallowed our first glasses of Champagne, the dance floor was filled with eight Copa girls. They were costumed in bright ruffled sleeves with shirts tied above their midriffs and short lime-green sarong skirts split up the front exposing the dancers' long, shapely legs. The dancing was fun, the ladies were beautiful, but the most impressive part of their act was their ability to balance wide flower-filled hats on their heads while attempting high kicks.

The band was playing a Latin samba-inspired beat that sounded all new to me, but I loved it. The featured brass section of the band jumped up and moved in rhythm together, blowing out the sensual tunes for the gyrating dancers. As James poured our second glass, his eyes never wavered from the stage. "So what do you think?"

"Love it! So colorful."

"After the dancers, there's usually a comic and then a headline singer. I think Frankie is singing tonight."

"Frankie?"

"Yeah, Frank Sinatra. Standing a few feet away from us. Not bad, right?" He laughed as if it happened to him every day.

It had only been a couple weeks ago that I'd dreamt Frank Sinatra was at the foot of my bed crooning me to sleep and now he'd actually be standing near us. I had to shake myself to make sure I wasn't dreaming again. After the dancers did a few numbers, they left the stage and the band leader brought down the music temperature, having the band play a few low-key tunes so that waiters could scramble around to take dinner orders. The menu offered only Chinese food. I chose egg rolls and sweet and sour pork. James went with dumplings and a hot soup.

"Just so you know, the food here is decent but not great. Most people come for the show, ambiance, and ridiculously priced drinks." He brought his voice lower and moved his chair a little closer. "Also, the place is definitely mob controlled. You don't want to get in too tight with the owners or sooner or later they own you. You know what I mean?"

I looked at him with a blank stare. "Actually, I don't."

"Jo-Jo, really?"

"Don't forget. I'm from Green Tree, Iowa. Not a lot of mobsters mixing it up with the Norwegian farmers there."

"True. OK, the mafia--usually big connected Italian families, often out of Sicily and some Eastern European Jews too. Most started with bootlegging, running speakeasies, and number games. But since prohibition ended, they've moved into all kinds of enterprises: facets of entertainment, betting, prostitution, drugs. And they control most of Vegas. But if you don't get too close, they're OK people."

"Really? I find all that hard to square. Sort of like, admire and dance on the rug, just don't look underneath it?"

He nodded. "Yes, kind of like that."

I had to absorb that for a minute. "So we have a Brazilian inspired nightclub, run by Italiens and Jews, serving Chinese food, and we're drinking French Champagne."

He laughed again, "Yeah, welcome to New York City, Deli Girl."

"James, I did have a question for you." I inched my chair closer so we could talk over the raucous crowd. "Yesterday, when you brought my clothes to me at the radio station, you mentioned they were mixed up with your tuxedo which hadn't arrived back from the cleaners."

A cloud passed over his face. "Yes, something like that."

"Well, this morning, walking through the lobby, I ran into Rudy, the bellhop. I asked him about your tux and he told me you had it on when you came back to the hotel with my clothes. So what's the *real* story?"

A look of embarrassment came to his face. "I should come clean with you. I promise. It's nothing sinister."

"Good, I'm ready to hear it."

"As you know already, I work for Mr. Mayor and MGM. I'm kind of his fixer. I started off purely as a finance man, but now everytime he has a problem or an itch that needs scratching, he calls me. So, a few weeks ago, on his bidding, I lined up all those potential investors for a dinner here in Manhattan, the dinner you attended last night. Anyway, lately LB has been relentless about signing up new talent. Especially young female talent. A lot of the fillies in the stable are aging out--his words, not mine."

"That does sound pretty awful."

"True, but it's a fickle business. You can be the hottest thing in the country and suddenly you do one off-color thing or get a few years older and nobody wants to see you again. Anyway, there are a few new young talents now on Broadway he'd heard about, and you. He'd seen a poster for the Talent Jackpot contest with your face on it in LA and called me when I got here and wanted me to check you and these other ladies out while I was here for the meeting at Club 21. My job was to find out if these young ladies are the real deal...The age they say they are, see if they're able to carry on conversations in front of intelligent people, whether they have drinking or drug problems, boyfriend issues. And most importantly...do they have that special spark, that magic quality the camera can capture."

At this point, the waiter brought our plates of steaming food, but my attention was all on James and I was getting impatient for a real answer. "And?"

"Maybe that sounds easy, but as soon as I tell actors that Mr. Mayer might be interested in them, they change. They try to be someone they aren't. Granted, I was a little deceitful with you. But I thought an easy way to get to know you was to come to your rescue with the clothing. Be your knight in shining armor, so to speak. It was nothing really thought out. It just sort of happened. I'd called

WOR and found out you stayed at The Dixie, and approached a bellhop when I checked in. I guess he was this *Rudy* character you mentioned. Anyway, I asked if he happened to know if the Deli-Girl was here today. He said he'd seen you come though the entrance earlier in the afternoon. Then he mentioned that he was coincidentally on the way to deliver your clothes to you for tomorrow's performance. I offered him a twenty, told him I was an old friend of yours and would be pleased to deliver them myself to you by tomorrow afternoon. On Rudy's behalf, it was a pretty large tip to ignore and he didn't feel any harm would really be done."

I rolled my eyes. "Except the anguish of waiting for them. But, I guess your ploy worked. I was overwhelmed with gratitude when you showed up holding that bag. And then when you dragged me away from the tangle of reporters at the back door, that was the cherry on the top. But now, I have to say, a lot of shine has dropped off the knight's armor."

"Well, that's the way it goes. Maybe I should have just brought them to you straight away, but I wouldn't have gotten to see you perform from the wings, or see how you reacted with all those big-wigs last night. I feel like I'm seeing the real you. A nice, beautiful girl from a little town who's holding her own, trying to make it in a tough business. I admire you and hope you will forgive my little charade. I don't get caught at it often, and I'm a little embarrassed."

"Don't get caught often? Do you make it a habit to lie?"

He shrugged. "My job is to keep LB happy. If the job requires that little white lies pop up occasionally, so be it. I'm not proud of it but it's a necessary evil in my business."

I shook my head, disappointed with James' response. "Maybe I'm just too innocent. But I wonder if people could just be honest with each other."

He nodded back. "I agree. I'd like to try." He forked into his soft, fat dumpling, took a bite and said, "Jo-Jo, please, your food is getting cold. It seems to taste especially good tonight, after all that truth telling."

I had to laugh and forgive him a bit, but a different side of James Appleton had emerged and I wouldn't forget it.

"While I'm disclosing, let's start with a clean slate. He raised his glass in a toast. As I clinked against his crystal glass, he said, "By the way, would it make you happy to sing a duet with Frank Sinatra tonight?"

"What?" I almost dropped my glass as my hand began to shake.

"Don't be totally surprised if he walks over and asks you to join him on stage for a few moments."

I could only look at James with sheer terror mixed with a tinge of delight while thinking, oh my God, the dream had become a reality and I was scared to death.

We finished dinner, dessert, and drained our bottle of Champagne, while listening to more Latin infused numbers from the orchestra. Comedian Buddy Hackett came on with some funny stories and bad language that would have had my parents yanking me out of there. Mr. Sinatra did eventually appear on the band stand to massive applause. The noisy revelers around us all quieted down as the orchestra's piano player started a brief intro and was then joined by the rest of the band, followed with the horn section taking the lead. Sinatra calmly stepped off the band stand and centered himself in the middle of the stage caressing a mic stand and jumped into his latest hit, *Five Minutes More.*

I'd been hearing it on the radio, but having Sinatra sing that song in person was so much more thrilling. From my ring side seat, I paid attention to his style, the way he held his microphone, how he used his singing voice in an almost conversational tone, and watched how he engaged with the audience. This man was a master and I was ready to absorb all the nuances of his performance.

About six songs in, he stopped the orchestra with his hand to keep them from starting the next number. "Ladies and gentlemen, I know you're getting tired of staring at my skinny mug. Well, I have a treat for you tonight. There's a young lady out here on the front row, pretty as a picture, and sings like a song-bird. You might have heard of her recently as The Deli-Girl on Talent Jackpot, but tonight let me present to you, in person, the lovely Jo-Jo Anderson."

As he began my introduction, the nerves had kicked in and taken hold of my body. This was really happening. My mouth refused to form a smile, as he casually walked over, reached out to take my hand, and gently pulled me up from my chair. James warned me this might happen; in fact, I was pretty sure he had paid a few key people off to make sure this would happen, but I still couldn't believe it. I was performing a musical number with Frank Sinatra right now!

As we turned, walking back to the center of the stage, the singer draped a comforting arm around my shoulder, and whispered in my ear, "Relax doll. We're gonna do this together. You sing *Sentimental Journey*, right? We'll go back and forth on the verses. I'll lead, you join me. Watch for cues."

I nodded, hoping my face would drop the mask of terror. Just a few minutes ago I was feeling loose and free from the Champagne. Now I couldn't recall a single lyric from the song except the opening line. Maybe I could hum along melodically?

He put his arm around my waist, probably hoping to keep me upright. "Alright folks, tonight the Deli-Girl and I are gonna take a little trip together, a nice, soft cruise." He turned to the orchestra and said, "Boys, how about a little Sentimental Journey." As the band began the breezy, melodic song, he whispered to me with a smile, "Don't worry Jo-Jo, it'll all come back to you."

Frank Sinatra was holding the mic stand, staring at me with his deep blue eyes, singing the opening line: "Gonna take a sentimental journey"...I was entranced. He sang the words so smoothly, like golden honey. Then I recalled Dottie from the Ebb Tide band telling me I'd reminded her of Doris Day. I had to do Miss Day proud. Sentimental Journey was her top hit. I couldn't screw this up. *Think...what's the first line of the second verse!* Nothing. Nothing was coming to me. Frank finished his first verse. I still had a blank stare on my face and he graciously covered for me, gliding into the second verse as I stupidly hummed along.

Then suddenly the bridge of the song burst through my frozen brain. As he finished the second verse, I took the mic and sang out *"Seven, that's the time we leave, seven,"* and I kept going through the bridge and continued with the third verse. To wrap up, our heads bent close together, we shared the mic repeating the first verse together. God, I hoped he wasn't inhaling my garlic infused Chinese-food breath.

The performance was not polished nor memorable. I had stumbled with one of the nation's most famous singers, but I finished and was still standing to whistles and applause. I quickly apologized to him while the audience was clapping. "So sorry I froze. My mind went blank. Thanks so much."

He shrugged. "Hey, it happens." Then he looked out at the audience and said, "Miss Jo-Jo Anderson, everybody. Give her a hand!" Several flash bulbs popped while we stood together for a few more seconds holding hands. As he walked me back to my table, he whispered, "Lucky for you that blondes aren't my thing right now. Thanks doll." He kissed my hand, gave a slight bow and continued on with his show. I was in a total daze, and didn't really come down to earth for several minutes.

I tugged on James' sleeve as he stared out at six of the Copa girls dancing around Frank to another hit song. "James, where do you think those photographers were from?"

"Uh, pretty sure it was The Post, Times, and the Journal. Those were the three papers I called anyway. Wait until Frank's finished and we'll talk about it."

He sang a few more numbers and ended the floor show, which apparently started up again at ten, midnight, and then again at two AM. These performers did not have it easy. In between shows, couples began dancing to the band.

James turned his attention back to me. "So, once I got word that Frank would agree to ask you to join him in a song, I called the three biggest papers in town. We need to get people talking about something other than that bullshit story printed in The Post today."

"What story? I haven't had a minute to pick up a paper."

His eyes opened wide in surprise. "Oh sorry, just assumed you saw it. There's a big picture of you and that talent show host, John King, with his arm wrapped around you and you looking up adoringly at him. I saw it happen; you were scared of all the reporters' questions at the end of the radio show. Nothing more. Once again, the story is all hearsay and false rumors contending that there's some impropriety going on at Jackpot, and then of course they wait until the end of the story to quote you and King denying everything.

"Oh my gosh! I think I'd rather not see it."

"So my thinking was, we show everybody a great photo of you performing with Frank. Shows the readers that you're moving on to bigger and better things and let's hope everybody forgets about that stupid radio show."

"Wow, I'm really green to this stuff. Thanks so much. But, I have to ask...Why are you so concerned about me? This all seems really above and beyond."

"Jo-Jo, I'm a businessman and good at my job. Mayer might be interested in you signing with the studio. Of course, you'd need to do a screen test and interview first, but he doesn't want damaged goods. When it comes to his actors, he hates bad press and scandal. He's the king of producing wholesome, lavish musicals. I'm just cleaning up a little mess and enjoying myself in the process."

"After hearing all the details, it makes sense and I appreciate you." I patted his hand and he stiffened a little.

"By the way, just so you know, I'm a committed married guy with a beautiful wife and a young son. I'm just here to help you, Jo-Jo, if you want to come along for the ride."

I leaned back in surprise. "Sure, sure. I am a little confused though...why did you ask me to your room for a drink last night?"

He raised his eyebrows and shrugged. "Just a little test. You passed."

CHAPTER 27
I'LL TAKE MINE SCRAMBLED
SARAH

*T*hat evening I walked in the direction of Currier Hall, but as I crossed Clinton Street, I thought of Beckham and felt drawn like a magnet to his apartment. I wondered what he would have thought of tonight's meeting. He'd probably disapprove of me taking time away from my studies. But I was on a high from our talk to the group and wanted to share that with somebody. Within a few minutes, I was heading up his stairs.

I checked my watch, it was only seven-thirty. Each time I stepped on one of the creaking wooden stairs, I was afraid the older couple downstairs would pop out of their door and interrogate me. I knocked twice and was almost relieved when he didn't answer. He was probably out having dinner.

Why was I rushing this? He told me to come Thursday, only one day from now. Surely my sex-addled brain could wait another twenty-four hours. Besides, didn't I have more important things to do than kissing my biology professor? Hmm, debatable. I continued walking down the dark sidewalk back to my dorm, forcing myself to forget the warm embraces, roaming hands, and delicious mouth.

I forced my thoughts back to the meeting. The Young Republicans hadn't given us overwhelming support, but we'd signed up enough new members to give Help for Heroes more clout. I thought it was important that we had both a male and female representation. I didn't want people thinking we were a bunch of women offering pats on the back and handing out milk and cookies. I wanted this group to make a difference and hoped, when our numbers were stronger, we could push for more substantial changes, but in the meantime, being a friend and a helping hand would be a good, positive thing.

As I crossed Clinton street, I noticed the headlights of a truck slow down next to me. I turned and saw Lester rolling down his window. "Hey, that you Sarah?"

"Hi there! I just made a wrong turn. I'm heading back to my dorm."

"My cousin and I are going back to the house and cooking up a mess of eggs and bacon. Wanna join us?"

I gave it two seconds' thought and my stomach guided the decision. "Sure, scrambled or sunny-side up?"

He smiled and said, "Whatever way you want 'em. Hop up." Lester opened the door and slid over to the middle of the truck's bench seat.

I stepped up on the running board and got in. Leaning across Lester, I offered my hand to his cousin. "Sarah Anderson. Thanks for the invitation."

"Conrad Adams. Appreciate the volunteers you're trying to pull together. Lester told me all about it. Quite admirable, Miss Anderson."

"Thanks, but Lester's the admirable one. He spoke so eloquently tonight. Sorry I put you on the spot, Lester, but you really came through. So, you both live close by?"

"Yeah, we're just a mile south."

Lester explained, "Conrad keeps all the boilers running on campus. He's a building maintenance supervisor and the reason I'm here. Offered to house and feed me while I went to school."

"That's wonderful. You know, I didn't realize how hungry I was until you said bacon and eggs. Barb and I left for the meeting before the dining hall served dinner." We quickly pulled up to a simple one-level home with a small front porch. "I'm happy to help. I used to scrambled a lot of eggs back home, especially when my mother was working."

Conrad pulled Lester's crutches out of the bed of the truck. I slid out and Lester followed behind me. We entered through a side door into a small kitchen, with room for a refrigerator, sink, a short counter, and a stove. There was a square table pushed against the wall, covered with a faded floral print cloth, and two miss-matched chairs pulled up on either side.

Conrad appeared to be a bachelor, sharing his home with his cousin. He didn't seem too talkative and looked maybe five years older than Lester. He headed into another room while Lester turned on the radio, which blared out some swing dance tunes, and we got to cracking eggs, frying bacon, and toasting bread in the oven. Conrad returned with another chair from the parlor, sat down and smoked a pipe while we cooked. Soon the place was filled with the comforting smoky aroma of hearty breakfast food.

As we all sat down, I said, "Gosh I miss this. Cooking a big breakfast of good food. We always had at least a farm hand or two pulled up to the table most mornings."

Lester cocked his ear to the radio and said, "Hey, there's a tune I haven't heard in a while. *Pennsylvania 6-5000.* You know, it's kind of funny. I actually learned to swing dance to this song at the USO. A year later, my dancing days were over. Sorry, don't mean to sound bitter."

"Don't you dare apologize. But you never know Lester; maybe those new legs they're coming out with later might have you dancing yet."

We moved on to other topics of our future hopes and dreams. He was seriously thinking of doing research in a lab setting, while I mentioned I'd probably become a teacher. We talked about different books we'd read recently and our home towns. The time passed quickly when I suddenly realized I'd be late for curfew if I didn't leave immediately.

Lester asked his cousin, "Conrad, you mind running Sarah back to Currier Hall? It's getting late."

"Sure thing. I gotta check on a problem in the admin building basement anyway."

Lester said his goodbyes outside and Conrad drove me back to my dorm. When I opened the truck door to leave, he said, "Miss Sarah, thanks for being a friend to Lester. He needs a few right now. This coming here for school…it was a big step for him. He had a lot of doubts about it. Still does, actually."

"I can only imagine. Appreciate your hospitality, Conrad. Hope to see you around campus."

When I got to the room, Barbara was already in her nightgown reading in bed. "So where did you slip off to? You're so mysterious lately."

"Nothing mysterious about eggs and bacon. On my way home, Lester Adams and his cousin invited me to join them for a late breakfast. I guess I was hungrier than I thought. We really had a great meal and a good time getting to know each other. How were burgers with Jacob?"

"Dreamy. Did you know his father is a big judge in Des Moines?"

"Yes, he mentioned that. Must be a favorite subject of conversation on his first dates."

"Well, he wasn't bragging about it; it just happened to come up. And did you know he's planning on running for student president this spring and possibly run for state office later, after law school?"

"Yes."

"I know I'm really jumping the gun here, but just imagine, Sarah, being the wife of a state senator or representative. That *has* to be exciting."

I shrugged, while undressing. "Maybe. Might be more exciting if *you* were the state senator, Barb. I watched you tonight. You should think about going into politics. You really have all the skills." I put on my robe and grabbed my toiletry bag.

"Don't be ridiculous, Sarah. How could I do that with a family of kids to raise? You know that's what I'm planning on. Trust me. That will be work enough."

"Don't sell yourself short. You could handle it, Barbara. I'm serious."

She laughed while closing her book. "You're funny. Thanks for tonight, Sarah. I know you made all that happen. With Jacob, I mean. Oh, one other thing. Watch yourself with Lester. I know, he's a nice guy, but you don't want to end up supporting a cripple."

I shook my head and closed the door, heading to the showers. I had no words.

CHAPTER 28
EMPTY POCKETS
JO-JO

*M*idnight was approaching. Before James and I left the Copa, I met one more important person as we were stepping away from our table.

"Leaving so soon Miss Anderson?"

I turned and stared into the face of a smallish older man with glasses, wearing a tuxedo. "Sorry, we didn't get a chance to chat. I'm Monte Proser. Thanks for coming in. Really enjoyed your number with Frankie. By the way, I own the joint."

I reached over and shook his extended hand. "Thank you for giving me the opportunity! I was obviously overwhelmed, but it was such an honor to sing with Mr. Sinatra."

"No, kid. You did OK, really." Then he looked over at James, squinted his eyes, and reached for his hand. "So, you're Mayer's guy... Appleton, right? Monte Proser. Good to meet you." As they shook hands, I noticed some cash changing hands from James to Proser. I was honestly not surprised; there was no other way I'd be on Sinatra's radar. "Sorry you two gotta rush out, but I guess you heard, Jo-Jo, you're doing two weeks at the Copa soon, right?"

"Two weeks? Fantastic! Really looking forward to that but I hope I'll be able to rehearse with the band first."

"Sure, kid. The band always rehearses with the singer. I'll be in touch."

"Terrific. I stay at The Dixie Hotel. Just have someone leave a message with the desk."

"Yeah, The Dixie. I think I knew that already. Got a nephew that works there. Enjoy your evening." Then he was off, walking toward another person, giving them a bear hug and pat on the back.

James took my arm and held it close as we walked to the coat check, saying under his breath, "Good, now you're on his radar. Monte Proser, he's a real mover and shaker around the area. This will be a good first step for you."

Back at The Dixie, James walked me to my door. "I'm headed out early in the morning, back to LA, but Jo-Jo, it's been a pleasure. If you can get through your two weeks at the Copa with no issues and some good reviews, we may be in touch. Just keep your nose clean."

"Don't worry. I plan on it."

James gave me a peck on the cheek, turned and then called out, "Oh yeah, happy Thanksgiving."

"Thanksgiving? I'd entirely forgotten. When is it?"

"Uh, a week or so. Best of luck to you."

As he walked back to the elevator, I called out, "Wait, James--do you have a card?"

He looked at me and nodded. "We'll be in touch."

I WOKE up the next morning feeling refreshed and somewhat settled. After all the excitement from the past few weeks, it was a good feeling. I had a full free day ahead of me. No job, no dates, no obligations. I decided to enjoy it while I could, hoping to get confirmation on the Copa performances soon. I'd slept in until ten and decided to treat myself to a breakfast at the Stage Deli as a customer. I especially wanted to speak to Chuckles and give him a twenty for turning me onto the Talent Jackpot show in the first place. But perhaps I should try to contact Damien again. We hadn't seen each other in a while and so much had happened.

I took a quick bath, pulled on my sailor dungarees and striped top, and went to my sock drawer to get some cash that I'd saved for this week's rent and food. I reached back into the corner and pulled out a flimsy striped sock, getting a panicky feeling. There was always a round soft roll of cash pushed into the toe. My heart jumped as I stuffed my hand inside knowing immediately it was empty. Perhaps I'd rolled the money but forgot to put it in the sock? Could fifty-two dollars be gone? I quickly ruffled through my undergarments, throwing everything out on the bed. Shit! Not only was my cash gone but my one-thousand-dollar prize check was missing too. I could hardly breathe.

How could I be so stupid! On our phone call yesterday, hadn't Mom told me to get an account opened right away? Instead of putting my check in a safe place, I'd opted for a new hairstyle at a salon. So ridiculous!

I felt violated and so vulnerable. I'd lived in this little room for months now and never had a problem. I'd befriended all the people in housekeeping, most of the bellhops and desk guys. Who would steal my money? Then I shook my head, thinking, wake up Jo-Jo. Everybody knows you just won a thousand dollars and you're too damn trusting. What was the best action to take? The police? The hotel manager?

I decided to go downstairs to lodge a complaint with the manager. As I walked the hallway to the elevator, it occurred to me that the thief might possibly be Rudy. He'd taken a twenty dollar bribe and gave my clothes to a total stranger, and from what he had told James, he seemed to be aware of my comings and goings. If he was brazen enough to do that, maybe he was comfortable stealing. I decided to speak to him first, threaten to go to the manager and check his reaction.

Walking through the tiled floor of the lobby, I noticed Ted, the bell captain standing at the podium by the doors. He scheduled all the bellboys. I approached with a smile that I didn't feel. "Hi Ted. Just curious, was Rudy working last night?"

"Hi Miss Jo. Uh, let me think…yeah, he did. He was working the door when I left."

"And what about today? Is he here yet?"

Ted glanced at his watch and said. "Yeah, you can probably catch him downstairs in the break room, should be getting ready to come on shift. Anything I can help you with?"

"Not at the moment. Thanks."

Below the first floor, along with the large laundry room, there were separate locker rooms for the female and male employees to change into their uniforms, hang their coats and hats, and store personal items. Below this level, there was a large city bus terminal, so many hotel associates had the advantage of taking the bus and being delivered straight to their place of work. I asked one of the men entering the locker room if he could see if Rudy was inside. A few minutes later Rudy came out, combing his thick, dark hair before putting his uniform cap on.

He looked over at me and said, "Hey, what brings you down here with the poor folks, Miss Jo-Jo?"

I plucked up my nerve and said, "I have a few questions for you. Is there somewhere we can talk for a minute?"

"Sure, let's go into the stairwell. It's my favorite smoking spot."

I followed him through a utility door into an echoey landing on the back stairs and leaned against the railing. "Look Rudy, I know for a fact that you accepted a twenty dollar bribe and gave my clothes to a man you didn't even know and then lied to me about it. I also know you worked the late shift last night while I was out, and this morning I came up missing a roll of cash *and* my check from Talent Jackpot. I know you guys have an in with some of the maids with pass keys. If you hand over my money and check now, I won't report what I know about you to the manager."

Suddenly, he went from cute, innocent bellboy to thug. He immediately pushed me into a corner of the landing, held a hand across my throat and whispered in a menacing voice, "If you even think about telling the manager or Ted about those missing clothes, you'll be sorry. And you got no proof I took that check or the money. I got family connections that you don't even want to think about. So suck it up, little Miss Deli-Girl."

He began pressing harder on my throat, cutting off my breathing. "You need to be careful and don't say a word to nobody." Then I heard voices echoing downstairs as some people were coming up. He lifted his heavy hand off my windpipe, while I took in a deep wheezing breath and pushed him out of my way.

I walked to the door quickly, not saying anything and then couldn't help myself and turned back. "I should have known something was up the first time I heard your weasley voice and stupid, ridiculous excuses. You should be ashamed of yourself."

I ran quickly to an open elevator and shut the door. Should I heed his warning or tell somebody? I was conflicted. Could it be that he was the nephew who the Copa owner mentioned? That fifty dollars was needed to pay my weekly bill at The Dixie which was due today, and also cover all my expenses for the coming week. Since Mr. Asnas didn't want me working right now, I had no income coming in. Then I thought about changing hotels. The Dixie had come to feel like home; the price was right, the location was great...but the bellhops? Dangerous.

I was on edge, frightened, hungry, and couldn't think straight. I checked my wallet in my purse. I had one dollar and a few coins. Why hadn't I deposited that damn check or at least kept it in my purse! I felt so stupid and careless. I went to the phones and tried calling the talent wrangler at WOR to ask if he could cancel the stolen check and issue me a new one. My heart was pounding as a station receptionist answered the phone.

"Hello, is Danny Tucker or the station manager in?"

"No, not on weekends. They're usually here by nine on Mondays."

"Uh, What about the guy from General Mills?"

"No, sorry he's generally here Tuesday through Thursday."

"Thanks for your help." Hanging up in frustration, I couldn't think who to call. Maybe Damien might have some advice? I hated calling with a problem. Seemed like I always needed something from him. I tried calling anyway, but once again, nobody answered the hall phone.

Food! Food and coffee would help me think. But now I was too embarrassed to go to the Stage Deli. I couldn't even afford a sandwich and a drink, much less give a decent tip. And I'd be way too embarrassed to ask anybody there for a loan. I walked into a drug store with a lunch counter and ordered the special advertised in their window: two scrambled eggs, bacon, and coffee for fifty cents.

The breakfast filled my stomach but was not great--too much grease on the eggs and bacon, giving me a queasy feeling. I was close to Penn Station and decided to check out the newsstand in front, wondering if last night's Copa photos had made the papers. Once there, I recalled the guy working there. He was the first person I spoke to after I'd arrived in New York.

I picked up The Post and flipped to page six. There it was, above the fold, a five by seven photo of Frank Sinatra and me, with the headline reading: ***New Paramour? The Deli-Girl and Frank Sinatra Get Sentimental***

I quickly scanned the article below which was just a brief mention of Sinatra's Copa show and me being called up to join him for a cozy song and hug. It also mentioned we harmonized well on the closing verse of Sentimental Journey. Not bad at all. The only thing that was slightly titillating was the headline, but that always seemed to be the case with these types of newspapers. And I actually looked decent in the photo, with a broad toothy grin, smiling confidently. Glancing at a few other gossip sheets, I saw there were no other mentions of the John King--Deli Girl scandal. The *nothing-there* story had simply evaporated for now. James Appleton definitely seemed to know his business.

"Hey blondie, you actually going to buy something? This ain't no library."

"Yeah, I'll take The Post. In fact, I'll take two." I handed him his dime and said, "You know, I met you the first day I arrived here from Iowa, about eight months ago. Ring a bell?"

"Blondie, I'm in front of Penn Station. Do you know how many new kids and tourists buzz by here every day?"

"I guess that's a no. Anyway, you told me to go back home to Iowa before the city broke my heart. And honestly, today, something happened that made me feel like doing just that, but you know what?"

He stood there looking bored with his arms crossed against his chest. "Tell me before I die of curiosity."

I opened the paper to page six again, pointing to the photograph. "Look, that's me singing at the Copa, arm and arm with Frank Sinatra. Ha! How do you like those apples?"

He leaned over, squinted at the picture, looked at me, nodded and shrugged. "Hey, once in a blue moon, I get it wrong. Congrats, kid. Although… you kinda look better in the picture." Then he moved on to the other end of the stall to sell some postcards.

I stood on the corner hugging my newspapers, waiting for the walk signal, while deciding what to do next. I had fifty-five cents to my name. My hotel bill was twenty-four-dollars with tax, but I had no cash to pay it. I really wanted to move out of The Dixie, still feeling the threat of Rudy's heavy hand on my throat, and I suddenly had the strong urge to go home to Green Tree for a week of refuge, but I couldn't leave until I knew my performance dates at the Copa. Having a weak moment, I thought to call James Appleton and ask for a quick loan, but he'd left this morning. I felt stuck standing on that cold corner.

Then the white pedestrian light flashed on and off as a mass of people moved me forward. I suddenly knew what I needed to do.

CHAPTER 29

INTOXICATION

SARAH

*T*he other bio lab students were slow to leave while I wiped down all the tables and put away equipment. I was dragging out my work, waiting for confirmation from Beckham that we were still meeting tonight at his place. Finally, the last student left. Beckham continued to look down, writing notes in his infernal notebook. I would love to have a look at whatever he was writing. Perhaps it was all gibberish and he did it just to prolong my agony.

I hung up my lab coat, gathered my books, coughed lightly, and said, "Guess I'm done here. Anything else you need from me?"

He glanced up, appeared distracted and looked around. "No. Everything looks good. Thank you, Sarah."

That was it? No invitation for coffee upstairs? No mention of tonight? My heart chilled. I was so confused by today's lack of attention. I picked up my satchel and headed to the door. As I pulled the knob, I turned back, swallowing my disappointment. "Alright then. Have a good evening."

He was back to looking down, writing in his book. "Yes. You too."

I was devastated and confused. I had walked around all day bubbling with excitement and anticipation about tonight's invitation, but now all that was dashed. Maybe I should blame my mom. She was the one who had encouraged me to meet new people and go out on dates, making the most of my university surroundings. So, I'd fallen for someone and now I was wasting hours thinking about him. Although… I guess Mother hadn't mentioned the need to fall for one of my professors.

As I walked briskly toward the library, I shook my head in anger. Where was the old Sarah? The focused, organized Sarah who knew the right thing to do. Where had she gone?

That evening, after dinner, I pulled out my history book. We were now whizzing along to year 455 as the Germanic Vandal tribes invaded Rome. Barbara was out for a sorority meeting, so it was a good, quiet time to review for an upcoming quiz. I had to force myself to concentrate on the words I read and made notes so that my mind wouldn't wander. A knock on the door interrupted my studies. I got up, opened the door and recognized one of the girls working at the front desk.

"Sarah, there's a gentleman downstairs asking for you."

This never happened. Surely it wasn't Beckham. He wouldn't reveal himself like that at the dorm. "Alright, thanks. I'll be right down."

I quickly brushed through my hair, pinched my cheeks, and headed downstairs. There, standing at the bottom of the stairs was Professor Carter. He was leaning against the desk, holding a file, within earshot of the two women behind the desk. Yes! He'd come for me. I was thrilled.

"Professor, what are you doing here?"

He handed me the file folder. "Sarah, was it you that left this in class? I thought you might need it. It was on my way."

The folder wasn't mine but I played along. "Oh, thanks. I'm so relieved. Thought I'd lost it."

He smiled slightly. "Alright, see you in class."

I turned and went upstairs, eager to open the contents. Inside was a note, written in his almost unreadable scrawl.

Dearest Sarah,

I convinced myself this morning that our infatuation needed to end. It's not good for my career and probably a distraction for you from your studies. But honestly, tonight, I find I can't do that. I'm thinking about you constantly. Your hair, your soft touch, your lips. I apologize for brushing you off earlier. If you still can, please come to my apartment tonight, but only if you feel the same way. Sometimes it's hard to overrule our common sense when our bodies and brains are telling us otherwise.

Yours,

Beckham

My hands shook as I read the note. This was confirmation of everything I wanted to hear. He still wanted me. I had to go. It was a little past seven and the week-night curfew was ten. I waited fifteen minutes and then briskly walked to his apartment. As soon as I came to his door, he pulled me in and embraced me, kissing me almost immediately.

He whispered in my ear. "Forgive me for being so conflicted. I'm grateful you came."

I nodded in agreement. "I was so happy to see you at the dorm."

We touched and then kissed again, our bodies pressing hard together while leaning into the wall by the door. It felt as though we couldn't get enough of each other; as if we were trying to drink each other up. Then he took my hand and led me into his bedroom.

It was a simple room, with one exposed ceiling light bulb, furnished with a chair, dresser drawers, and a double bed. Our breathing slowed as he stepped back and gently took my coat off. He softly said, "You're so beautiful. A simple, natural beauty." He smiled slightly and asked, "May I?" I nodded as he helped me pull my sweater over my head and then unhooked my bra, dropping both on his bed.

Beckham looked down at me in admiration and kissed each breast. "We can't rush this, Sarah." I nodded and clumsily began unbuttoning his shirt. Was this the way it was done? He undressed me, so now I undress him? My fingers fumbled on his buttons.

Beckham quickly yanked the shirttails out of his trousers, pulled the shirt over his head, and took care of his own belt and trousers.

He said we shouldn't rush, but I was quickly out of clothing. I removed my panties with shaking hands, embarrassed to be standing naked in front of him. Pulling the quilt and sheet down on his bed, I quickly scooted underneath, feeling the chill of cold sheets against my skin.

I tried to keep the tremor from my voice, not wanting to reveal my nerves. "I appreciate you not wanting to rush, but I do need to be back at my dorm by ten." Why did I say that? I'd immediately taken all the excitement out of the room.

He didn't respond, but instead turned off the overhead light. And just as quickly as I admonished myself, I forgot curfews, Germanic Vandals, and the old couple living below. This was about right now. This moment. Nothing else mattered. I felt a sensual touch I'd never experienced before. From head to toe, Beckham's fingers and tongue were softly probing, exploring, taking me to new heights I'd never come close to experiencing.

Guiding my hand toward his firm penis, he showed me how he enjoyed it being rubbed. Eventually, he entered me. It was painful at first but followed by a thrill I never expected. A warm flush invaded my brain. No one had told me how wonderful this would feel. I never wanted to leave this warm bed. It was intoxicating!

Later, my head fit perfectly in the space between his shoulder and chin, as I softly touched the light hair on his chest. He turned and glanced at a small clock on his dresser. "Sorry Sarah, it's close to ten."

I checked my watch and jumped out of bed. "Oh my goodness! I hate to leave but I'll be sprinting all the way to make it back in time." I threw my clothes on, while Beckham did the same.

"I'm not much of a runner, but I'm happy to join you."

"Honestly, I'm fine getting back by myself. Thanks, but I have to go." We kissed quickly and I was out the door. I dashed back to Currier Hall in the dark, running over uneven sidewalks, and catching my loose flying hair on low hanging branches. I approached my dorm as the house mother closed the latch on the double doors. From inside, she shook her head at me and reluctantly unlocked the door again.

"Sarah Anderson, it's not like you to be so late. And you look like you just fell out of bed. Tidiness is a virtue. Remember that, Miss."

"Sorry Mrs. Henderson. I was studying late, the sacking of Rome. Fascinating stuff. It won't happen again."

Catching my breath, I took my time climbing the stairs. A few girls were still in the lounge, while upstairs, others were heading to the showers wearing their robes and caps. I opened my door to darkness and tiptoed in not wanting to wake Barbara. While hanging my coat, she switched on her desk lamp with a yawn. Her hair was clipped up in her nightly pin curls and tied with a scarf.

"Late again, Sarah? What was the little scholar up to tonight?" She sat up in bed and stared at me expectantly, probably probing for a minor scandal to share with our cell block.

"Just studying. I have a history quiz tomorrow."

Barb looked down her nose at me, examining me like one of our frogs in the lab. "I don't know...sure you were studying? Something's different about you."

I gathered my toiletry bag and turned toward her. "I lost track of time and had to run home from the library."

"OK... but then why is your sweater on inside out? Sarah, have you been a naughty girl?"

I grabbed my nightgown and robe and slammed the door behind me and stood in the hallway for a few moments, calming down, trying to collect my thoughts. Then I reentered the room and switched her light back on. Barb sat back up and said, "What is it now?"

I attempted to keep my voice steady and strong. "Barbara, there's a couple of things I need to get off my chest. One, if we are going to remain friends and roommates, I don't need you questioning my every move, or discussing my whereabouts with others. Two, if you truly want to be a part of Help for Heroes, you can't say the things you said the other night, like suggesting I don't want to end up supporting a cripple. If you don't understand why, there's no point in you helping lead our group."

Barbara looked shocked that I'd had the gumption to speak to her so frankly. She flicked off her light, turned in her bed and covered her head with the covers. Before leaving again, I added with a softer voice, "Barb, I want to continue to be friends, but keep in mind... words have consequences."

CHAPTER 30

WHO DO YOU TRUST?

JO-JO

*A*s I neared Central Park, I turned west on 59th. Waiting at the crosswalk, I was surprised and happy to see Damien on the opposite side. I waved and dashed across right before a cab honked madly and almost mowed me down. Safely on the sidewalk, he twirled me around and we exchanged a light kiss. "Damien, I can't believe I'm running into you! I just tried to call a few hours back. How are you?"

"Living life, but busy!" Groups of pedestrians flowed around us and Damien gently tugged me away from the curb and held me close while we stood next to the wall of an apartment building. "Yeah, sorry we haven't been able to connect. By the way… congratulations on your big win. I read about it in the papers."

"Thanks, and I hope you ignored those stupid stories about some made-up romance between me and John King. Totally ridiculous! But tell me about you…How's the show going?"

Damien pushed his gloved hands in his coat pockets as the wind picked up. "Apparently ticket sales are going through the roof and the producers seemed pleased with my stand-in as Frank Butler. The best news is, they just offered me the lead role when the show goes on tour."

"My goodness... that's fantastic!" We both beamed at each other.

"Yeah, Fran thinks it's a great career move and, of course, the salary increase will be nice. Rehearsals with the touring cast are scheduled to begin in January and they just signed Mary Martin for Merman's part. There's twenty cities booked so far."

"Wow, you're rubbing shoulders with some great leading ladies. First, Merman and now Martin!" I looked down and took a deep breath. "Well, I'll certainly miss you, but I'm really happy for you, Damien."

We both stood closer as the biting wind continued. "So, Jo-Jo, what brings you over to 59th? Not working today?"

"Yeah, taking a break from the Stage Deli, but I was hoping to drop in on Fran to see about a little loan. Someone stole some money from my room and I thought she might be willing to help me out. Guess I think she still owes me something from years ago."

He took out his wallet and pulled out a bill. " I got a spare ten-spot if that helps."

"Aw, thanks, but keep your money."

."That's funny though, you going to Fran's. I *just* left her apartment. She negotiated a great contract for me for the touring show. I literally signed the papers ten minutes ago. She'll probably help you out. Yeah, go talk to her, but watch out on those interest rates of hers."

"I've been reluctant to get tangled up with Fran, but I'm feeling a little desperate today."

"Hey, Jo-Jo, I hate to run but I need to get to the theater. I'm really late. Got a two o'clock matinee. Good luck with everything; I'm rooting for you."

"You too! Take care." My heart was beating fast. I wished we'd had more time to talk. Damien...such a great guy, but something felt different. It was as though our lives were passing each other by. We kept missing any real connection. And both of us were simply too busy to get off the train.

I kept walking and soon recognized the awning and doorman.

He admitted me and I asked a second man sitting at a desk, "Uh… Fran Jordan, is she in?"

He looked me over, apparently deemed me acceptable, asked my name and made the call. "Miss Jordan, there's a Miss Jo-Jo Anderson here to see you in the lobby. Yes, ma'am. Will do."

He nodded at me and said, "You can go up. Fourth floor, 4C."

I was disappointed at myself for how quickly I'd caved. It was only two nights ago that I'd told Fran that I absolutely had no need of her services and now here I was, knocking on her door. Was this my only possible solution? Damien seemed to think it was a good idea. I knew I needed help and guidance in this business and felt so vulnerable right now. I knocked on 4C with trepidation.

She opened the door wearing a long black silk robe with her auburn hair in curlers. I couldn't help but notice the few strands of gray popping out along her hairline, but even with the hair up, she was still a beauty. She looked at me without a smile, while holding the door slightly open. "I knew you'd show up sooner or later. What's the problem?"

"Sorry to bother you, Nanette, but I may need your help temporarily."

She shrugged, left the door ajar, turned and walked down her hallway, calling after me, "Might as well come in. Close the door behind you." A typical Nanette move; she already had me following along behind doing her bidding.

I couldn't help but notice, her apartment was darn ritzy. The entryway floor was a checkerboard of marble squares in deep green and ivory. This led into a plush paisley-patterned carpet in a spacious living room, with a picture window overlooking the park. I walked over to the window. "Wow! Fabulous view, Nanette. You're doing well."

She sat down on a chaise lounge and lit a cigarette, blowing out smoke and waving it in my direction. "Please Jillian, if I'm going to help you, you have to call me Fran or Miss Jordan. I haven't gone by Nanette in years."

I turned and sat down across from her in a comfy, hunter green armchair with fringe trim. "Yes, that's right. Didn't you change the name to Fran when the FBI started looking for you? And, by the way, you were the last person to call me Jillian--and that was thirteen years ago--so it's back to Jo-Jo, please." I let out a deep breath and thought, *Good come-back!*

"Sorry, yes, slip of the tongue." She looked across at me and stared intently. "So, almost thirteen years. Not so long ago, but *so* much water under that bridge. You've gone from a very young child to an almost-adult. Just look at you…Stunning, really." She blew out another plume of smoke.

"And you went from photographer's assistant to agent to the stars."

She ignored my comment, looking at her nails. "So, back to the present. Miss Jo-Jo, why do I have the pleasure of your company?"

"Well, first and foremost, I need a fifty-dollar loan to pay my hotel bill and to cover food expenses. I only need it until I get my bank issue settled."

"Good God, you just won a thousand-dollars. I hope you didn't get involved in some high stakes poker game and lose it all."

I waved my hands in front of me. "No! Nothing like that. I was planning on opening a bank account this coming Monday, but someone broke into my room last night and stole my spare cash and my Talent Jackpot check. That cash was all the money I had until I could deposit my winnings and now I don't even have that."

"Jesus, Jo, live and learn! You should have gone first thing and deposited that check."

Hearing those words reminded me of my mother. Shaking my head in frustration, I said, "I realize that now, but in the meantime, what can I do? I have nowhere to turn. I tried calling WOR this morning, but none of the guys in charge will be back until Monday morning. On top of that, I questioned a new bellhop at The Dixie who seemed suspicious, and he immediately threatened me, putting a fist to my throat. If he's innocent, the violence seems way out of proportion."

She stared at me shaking her head. "Rough morning. OK, let's break this down. It shouldn't be an insurmountable problem. I'll loan you the fifty and we'll go together to WOR first thing Monday morning and ask the ad sponsor to cancel the check and reissue another one. I'm hoping you weren't foolish enough to endorse it, right?"

I looked at her quizzically. "Endorse?"

"Signed the back of the check? My God, Jo-Jo, you're as green as those corn fields you came from. Tell me you didn't do that."

"No. No, I left it blank."

"Let's see…If the check was stolen Friday night, and all banks are closed today, there's no way the check was cashed yet. So, we're safe there. You *must* be more careful. Are you still working at the deli?"

"No, that's my other problem. The owner let me go because the reporters were causing too much of a commotion around the place. I could probably talk him into rehiring me, but I'm supposed to begin a two-week stint singing at the Copa soon, so with rehearsals and all, there's really no point in going back right away." I looked around, sniffing the aromatic scent of coffee and noticed a cup next to her chaise. "Hate to ask, Nanette…I mean Fran, but any chance I could have a spare cup of coffee? I could really use a hot cup right now."

"Certainly." She pointed in the direction of the kitchen. "Help yourself. There's a percolator on the counter and cups and saucers in the cabinet overhead." She lifted up her empty cup. "Jo, dear. I'll take a refill too."

She never stopped. Always trying to get the upper hand. But that's OK. I'd play her game until I got my money. "Sure, Fran. Cream or sugar?"

"Both please, there's a tray next to the pot, just bring everything over."

I passed a beautiful ebony wood dining table at the end of the room and went through a swinging door into a bright, airy kitchen. I took down a cup and saucer, poured coffee into both cups, and put the sugar bowl and a small carton of half and half onto the tray. I walked back in saying, "Service with a smile, ma'am."

"Perfect." I watched her drop in three sugar cubes and a generous portion of cream, and I sat back down. She patted her rollers. "Sorry I look so undone. I didn't have any place I needed to be today until later. But it's not like you've never seen me in rollers before," she chuckled. "Remember, every night, when I used to tie your hair up in rags and make those cute pipe curls? You were adorable." She stopped to sip her coffee. "You were just like a little doll back then, tap dancing on those sidewalks. By the way, I caught your song with Sinatra last night. I was sitting at the Copa bar. I could tell you fluffed the second verse, but you landed on your feet. I was proud of you. Can't be easy singing next to a big star."

I was surprised. "I can't believe you happened to be there! And you're exactly right. My brain and memory froze but everything eventually defrosted as the bridge finally came to me, thank goodness."

She put out the remains of her cigarette. "Jo-Jo, I didn't just *happen* to be at the Copa last night. Like I said before, I *know* people. I'm friends with one of the cooks, and more importantly, the Copa band leader. I called him in the afternoon and asked him if you'd been scheduled to perform yet. He hadn't heard anything but told me Frankie was going to bring you up for a song or two. That was probably your audition last night. They'll get you on board soon. But watch out. The place is crawling with the mob. The club owner, Monte Proser...He's a bit of a drunk, but really knows talent. He manages all the entertainment. But there's another guy, Jules Podel, that runs the kitchen and bar. A total asshole. Stay away from him."

"Yes, that's what James Appleton told me. Said the place was connected."

"Yeah, word on the street is that mobster Frank Costello seems to run things behind the scenes. That's certainly not unusual around here. Anyway, as long as you pull in fresh customers, Monte will be happy. But you don't want to stay on too long there or the club thinks they own you. You know what I mean?"

"I guess I'm beginning to."

"That's why you need an agent. A good one. I say you do two weeks at the Copa and then we move you on to something else."

"Yes. James said if I get good reviews and keep my nose clean, he'll bring me out for a screen test at MGM."

"What? Are you serious? So, who's this James guy? I've never heard of him."

I noticed her eyes light up like a slot machine when I mentioned MGM might be interested. Were those dollar signs spinning through those green eyes of hers? "James Appleton. He works for Mr. Mayer at MGM. Told me he was his fixer, whatever that means. He said Mayer was interested in bringing some new, young talent into the tent. That might be me, Fran. Imagine that! He's also the one who paid the Copa owner to have Sinatra bring me up to sing."

She nodded her head. "Impressive move. A few years back, Jo, did you ever see that Walt Disney movie, Bambi?"

I stood up to get a coffee refill. "No. Believe it or not, there's still no movie theater in Green Tree. But I've heard of it."

"Well kid, you're like Bambi. You're a wide-eyed baby deer lost in the woods and there are some people in this business that are gonna eat you for breakfast if you don't have someone looking out for you. Nobody will help you like me. I promise you that."

"I'm not sure I need all that, Fran."

"Look, I promise you, you're not gonna make it on your own. I know all the backstage people in town and a lot of the casting directors. Sign with me today. I make ten percent off any jobs I have a hand in getting you. I will always try to get you top dollar and get you signed up on the best projects possible. You're new, fresh goods. We have to handle your career carefully. Jo-Jo, let me be a part of that."

Still standing, holding my empty cup, I hesitated to answer and just stared out the window, gazing at the canopy of empty tree branches in Central Park. I was on the fence about any long term relationship with Nanette. I wanted the fifty-dollar loan and her help getting me another check issued, but I wasn't sure if I wanted her as my agent. Knowing our history together, I just didn't trust her. Not to mention how my mother would feel if she knew. Her hate ran deep.

"Jo-Jo, I can have all your earnings and payments go directly through my management accounts. You don't have to worry about financial entanglements. You'll have enough on your plate. You just do your thing on stage, screen, or radio and I'll do the rest."

"Hmm… I admit, I could use your help, Fran. Especially in negotiating contracts. But I would want my own bank account and I'd be in control of my earnings and then pay you through them. As an agent, you would work for me, correct?"

"Honestly, I see it as a partnership. One hand helps the other and vice-a-versa. Let me be your partner, Jo-Jo."

I nodded, thinking it through and sighed. "Deal. But I handle my own money."

She raised her eyebrows and laughed. "It's your problem then. We already know how well you did with your first big paycheck."

"Fran, I'll learn from my mistakes. But I really appreciate you helping me with the check thing at WOR Monday morning."

Fran stood up facing me, shaking her head. "Jo-Jo, you just told me you didn't need my help with any money matters and now you expect me to go down to WOR and beg them to issue you a new check? So, what's it gonna be? Are you all in or not? Trust me, I only have your best interests at heart."

Damn, she was good. I supposed I could always renegotiate our contract later. I hesitated, wondering what Sarah would think of all this. She was way too smart to fall for all of Fran's claims. But then again, I did have the Copa contract coming up and Damien said Fran was shrewd when it came to negotiating. At that moment, I felt I had no choice. "Alright. I'm in."

"Good. Time for me to get dressed. The two of us are going over to pay Monte Proser a visit right now. Knowing you're a newcomer, he's going to try to lowball your weekly rate at the Copa. But I'm not about to let that happen. Trust me, you're going to be glad we're back in each other's lives."

"Wait…what do you think about going to the police about my missing check? Do you think I should report it?"

She stopped before going to her bedroom. "The police? I'd say no. After talking with Proser, we'll have a little chat with your hotel manager or that bellhop you mentioned. I might be able to squeeze him a bit. We'll see."

I turned and walked to the kitchen for that second cup of coffee. I placed my head down on the counter, dizzy and still reeling from what I'd just agreed to.

CHAPTER 31
PAY DIRT
JO-JO

I sat in her living room waiting, and in a matter of minutes Fran quickly went from a floozy, flaunting her flimsy black robe, to a confident business woman, wearing a black skirted suit, cream silk blouse, and a multi-strand string of pearls. After leaving the apartment, her doorman hailed us a cab that took us quickly over to the Copa. When we neared the club, I asked, "Fran, it's kind of early. Should we have made an appointment? Mr. Proser may not be in."

"He'll be there. From what I hear, Proser spends his afternoons drinking Dewars while scheduling and auditioning talent at the Copa. Hopefully, he'll talk to us. I like to catch people off guard before they've contemplated an agenda."

"All right, you're the agent."

Fran ignored the front entrance. I followed behind as Fran went directly to a back door she seemed familiar with. A few Asian kitchen workers, dressed in white uniforms, were sitting around a table eating. Fran waved to one of them. "Hi there, Jon-Jon, boss in yet?"

In mid-bite, he turned his head and said, "Podel not here yet. Proser over by stage now. You want eggroll, Fran?"

"Maybe later. Thank you."

We went down a long hallway passing a few dressing rooms and a closed office door. We continued and came through a side entrance to the stage. Fran stopped and whispered to me, "Remember, let me lead. Only respond if he speaks directly to you. Usually, the talent's never at these negotiations." I followed her, walking down the terraced rows of tables and chairs to the edge of the stage. A string of eight Copa girls seemed to be working on new dance steps, while Proser sat at a table wearing a white shirt and dark suit, drinking from a glass and smoking a cigar, with paperwork scattered in front of him.

Stopping about four feet from his table, Fran said. "Monte Proser, hard at work, I see. No wonder you're the most successful club owner in town!"

He looked up, squinted and put his glasses on. "Hey...we've met before, right?"

"That's right, Fran Jordan. I've represented a couple comics you booked. Anyway, Mr. Proser, I know you're a busy guy. Won't take much of your time. I was thrilled to hear you're hiring my client, Jo-Jo, for a couple weeks' stint. We needed to knock out some dates for her schedule. Big things are coming her way fast."

He looked over at me while puffing out a smoke ring. "You didn't waste any time hooking an agent, did you? Yeah, I get it. Saw her with Mayer's guy last night." He nodded to the chairs around him. "Take a load off."

We pulled out the chairs and sat down. He grabbed a notebook and leafed through several pages. "Ok, I'm light on vocalists the second and third week of December. Had a canary back out on me. By the way, how's your dancing?" While asking the question, he looked at me.

"Honestly, I'm a little rusty..."

Fran immediately interrupted. "She's being modest, Monte. She's been a tapper for years and catches on like a pro. After a few rehearsals, she'll be tap dancing her way into your heart."

After that exaggeration, I was praying Proser wouldn't ask me to jump up and dance with the girls on stage.

"OK... if you say so. No bullshit, Jordan?"

"Absolutely not. And I had a few ideas for her act. Here's what I was thinking....a medley of all the current big hits on Broadway. A few costume changes, and we should incorporate the dancers into some of the songs. A real crowd pleaser. You'll have customers lined around the block."

He looked straight ahead, staring at his dancers and then shouted loudly, "Jeanne, get those kicks higher. You're top girl in the lineup. Remember, anybody can be replaced." Then he looked back at Fran. "Yeah, I like it. Broadway medley--sounds nice. All right. Two weeks, four shows a night, five days a week. I'll pay her fifty dollars a week. Goes to seventy-five for the second week *if* we see a twenty percent increase in traffic. With an option for two more weeks if I like the response."

Fran laughed. "I hope you're joking. Even with days off, that amounts to less than three-dollars a show. Ridiculous!"

Podell took a sip from his cup. "You're pretty quick on the math, Jordan. But she's a nobody, an unknown entity. I'm taking a big risk here."

"Not true. You're getting a triple threat, Jules. Beautiful, fresh goods. Just off a national radio show that featured a lot of publicity, especially in New York. And I saw The Post today; a big photo of Jo-Jo and Sinatra. Page six, no less."

He looked back and shook his head. "You're trying to rob me, Jordan. Take the offer or walk. I've got agents lined up waiting to get their talent in here."

I suddenly panicked. Wait a minute. I wanted this gig really bad. "Uh, Fran, maybe..."

Fran interrupted me. "Let's go, Jo. He's low-balling you. You deserve to start at a hundred a week. We have two other clubs we can go to."

As we headed up the stairs, we heard. "Shit. Ok...Ok. Get back here." We promptly turned around and listened. "We'll start at seventy-five a week and go up an extra twenty-five if the door's up the following week, but I'm not paying for any of her costumes or extra backdrops. That's on you guys."

Fran had walked back to the table with me standing behind her.

"We'll agree to eighty-five for the first week, and then an extra twenty-five. When should I come round and sign contracts?"

He threw a pencil across the room. "Fuckin' agents. OK. Eighty-five a week. Come by in a couple days. Tuesday around four? Oh, and sex her up a bit. She's too damn wholesome."

Fran nodded and added, "I suggest you invest in taxi signs for the booking, something like-- *Deli Girl Does Broadway. Exclusive at the Copa.* Tourists will eat that up!"

He shrugged, "Sounds expensive, but not a bad idea." Then he looked up and stared at me. "Don't disappoint me little girl. I'm expecting big things."

I gulped, smiled, and nodded. Fran turned to leave again when I had a thought. "Mr. Proser, last night you mentioned you had a nephew working at The Dixie Hotel. I've lived there for a while. Maybe I've met him. Lots of great people working there."

He puffed on his cigar. "Yeah, good looking kid, young, nephew on my wife's side. Name is Rudy. Rudy Canotelli. The kid wanted to work here, but I figured, at his age, he'd spend all his time ogling the dancers, so I lined him up with a friend at The Dixie."

I gave him a friendly nod. "Rudy…thanks. I'll introduce myself if I get a chance. Looking forward to working for you, sir."

Fran didn't say anything until we entered the kitchen. The crew was now up at their stations, chopping and peeling. "Jon-Jon, I'll take four of your hottest egg rolls." She handed him a buck and he put four hot and greasy ones in a bag for us with some napkins. "You're the best, Jon. See you next Tuesday."

Again, Fran was quiet while we waited for a cab on the street. She waved one down and slid across the back seat, saying, "Dixie Hotel." Then she turned to me, handed me an eggroll wrapped in a napkin and said, "Don't you *ever* say you can't do something when a club owner, director, casting agent, or producer asks you a question. The answer is always *yes*. You say yes, you book the job, and then after…you start learning how to do it. Got it? Besides, you were always a great dancer."

I was taken aback by the ferocity of her tone and softly muttered, "Yeah, when I was five."

Tearing into a crunchy eggroll, Fran ignored my comment and said with equal venom, "Now, we're going to find that fucking little Rudy and set him straight. By the way, good job finding out the goods on him with Proser. Smart thinking."

I felt like I'd just been slapped and kissed in the past ten seconds. *The Whiplash Witch*. I smiled thinking about my new nickname for Fran.

She asked the cabby to pull up half a block from the main entrance of The Dixie and told me to walk into the lobby, sit down and wait. She waited a few minutes, then walked up and spoke to the doorman who used the phone at the podium. Soon, Rudy showed up all smiles. He followed Fran into the lobby, with the two of them standing near me and Fran asked, "Hi Rudy, just saw your Uncle Monte. He had a message for you. Is there somewhere we can talk?"

"Sure thing. How's my uncle doing?"

"Oh, working hard, as usual." Fran nodded for me to follow, while he led us down to the same landing where he had threatened me earlier today. When he noticed me following, he started looking jumpy.

Rudy glanced around at the empty, echoing space, "This spot is good. What's the problem?"

I stood back as Fran took over. "There will be no problem, you little shit." Then she shocked the hell out of me and Rudy when she abruptly slapped his face sideways. "I know for a fact that you, and probably some hotel maid you screwed, stole this young lady's check, and since it's Saturday, there's no way you could have cashed it yet. I'll give you exactly five minutes to produce that check or I'm going to the hotel manager, the police, *and your uncle.* Jo just signed a contract to perform at the Copa and I'm sure Monte Proser would be upset if his new star performer got roughed up. And if you *ever threaten* to harm a hair on Jo-Jo Anderson's head, you'll find yourself at the bottom of the Hudson. Is that understood?"

Rudy nodded, while rubbing his slapped face, then he became defensive and asked, "So, what makes you think I got that check?"

"Because, you idiot, first of all you're an admitted liar. Second, if you hadn't stolen it, why would you threaten Jo-Jo? Don't screw with me, you brat. You're now down to four minutes and thirty seconds. We'll wait here."

Rudy dashed down the hall as Fran leaned against the railing and lit a cigarette taken from a gold case in her purse. Then she looked at me and said, "Don't ever start smoking; it's not good for your voice."

Within two minutes, Rudy walked briskly back from the employee locker room, carrying a lunch bag. A bright red mark still glowed across his cheek. He pulled out a folded piece of paper. Fran took it, opened it, held it to the light, checked the back, and then said, "Don't forget, you little piss-ant. I'm watching you."

We took the elevator to my room, and once inside, I sat on the bed in a slump, exhausted from the tension of watching Rudy fall apart. I said, "I can't thank you enough, Fran. You've been an immense help. A few hours ago, I couldn't think straight; I was so upset."

She opened her purse and pulled out a fifty-dollar bill. "Here, use this to pay your hotel bill and get some dinner. Also, here's a card for a seamstress. She's in Chinatown. She's cheap, good, and fast. Get her to sew you up a few evening gowns, something simple, elegant, with shimmer. I'm hanging onto the check. I'll pick you up Monday morning to go to the bank. We'll get an account opened."

"That sounds wonderful."

"Just so we're clear, ten percent comes off the top of this check for me, and of course, ten percent off your earnings at the Copa."

"But Fran, I won that check and got the Copa booking before you were even my agent. That's not really fair, is it?"

She glanced at her watch, "According to my calculations, I've been working for you for the past four hours and you're already over twelve-hundred-dollars ahead from what you would have had earlier today. I think I've earned my keep. I'll see you at eight-thirty Monday morning. Be waiting outside."

I sighed, sat down on my bed, drained from the hours spent with Whiplash. "I'll be ready."

She headed to the door and then turned. "By the way, if I were you, I wouldn't bother pursuing your little boyfriend, Damien Jones. He's busy rehearsing for the touring show and I have it on good authority that he swings for both teams...if you follow my drift." And with that, she slammed the door.

I sat in a daze, staring at the blank wall. On the one hand I was exhilarated for prospects to come, but on the other, I was worried about the sticky, dark web of a world I'd just stepped into. Much needed--a sudsy bath and a trip home to Green Tree to cleanse myself.

CHAPTER 32
TIES THAT BIND
SARAH

*T*he Thanksgiving break was fast approaching. For the upcoming holiday, school would be closed Wednesday through Sunday. After my Thursday night introduction to sex, my libido was seriously entertaining the idea of five full days spent in Beckham's apartment, with endless hours of making love without fear of curfews and class assignments. I envisioned days of really getting to know each other, sharing jokes, favorite novels, reading in bed with heads and hands touching. The idea sounded absolutely wonderful. Of course, my parents would be mad if I didn't come home, but I could come up with some sort of excuse. Barb seemed to know I was up to something, but she still had no clue I was seeing Beckham. I assumed she thought Lester and I might be heating things up, but I remained totally mum on the subject of my evening absences.

On other matters, my roommate and I seemed to have managed a truce from the other night. The next morning, she was up, got dressed, and never said a word about my comments. Yes, she continued to be outgoing, bossy, and in the know on everyone's business, but that's who she was.

Barb suggested we should go together to meet with the Director of Student Services and relay our news. We were excited to tell Hortence Miller about our new twenty-eight members. For her part, Mrs. Miller had a list of a few dozen names of students who had indicated on their school applications that they were part of the GI scholarship program and in some way disabled. Because our organization's goal was to aid these students, she agreed to give us a small budget for postage and flyers to inform students about the program. But that was all the university was willing to offer. Now that we had some volunteers, the key was getting disabled students interested in signing up and open to discussing their needs.

Barb and I divided the work load and decided to send out letters to our new members and disabled vets after Thanksgiving. All the dorms were shut down during official holiday breaks and Barbara was planning to return home to Des Moines. She was conveniently catching a ride in Jacob's car. He seemed to be one of the rare but lucky students on campus with their own vehicle.

I was curious what Beckham would think of my idea about remaining together in Iowa City. On Monday afternoon, while we were sharing coffee in his office, he asked, "Which bus are you catching on Wednesday for Green Tree; the seven AM or the noon?"

Leaning against his desk, I stared into my coffee cup. Should I go for it? Was I being too bold? What would Jo-Jo do?

"Well, honestly, I was considering spending time with you, Beckham. Dreaming about five full days without a curfew, staying in your cozy apartment. What do you think?"

He coughed a bit in surprise. "Sounds lovely, Sarah, but I've got family obligations up in Minneapolis. My parents are expecting me."

How stupid of me. The thought never occurred to me. He had family too. "Oh… I see. You never speak of them, so I didn't realize. I suppose it's just as well. I'm sure my parents expect to see me too. But it seems like such a perfect time for us to be together. Guess I'll take the seven AM bus Wednesday."

"Good. Family time is important. Well, you should be off. I need to prepare final exams for December."

I was a little startled at his abruptness. "Will I see you before we leave? Sometime Tuesday?"

"Doubtful. I bought a noon bus ticket for Tuesday, since I'll be done with my classes. So, I guess this will be it for a little while."

"Really?"

"Sarah, it's only a week. Go home and enjoy yourself."

I put my cup down on his desk and acted as if it was nothing. "Not to worry. I will. Goodbye."

"Sarah… turn around please." He stood up and put his arms around me and offered a brisk kiss on the cheek. "I will miss you tremendously. Think how excited we'll be to see each other again."

I looked up, my eyes starting to tear up a bit. "You're right. I'm being a baby about all this. See you next week."

Coming into the dorm later that day, I checked my mailbox and was excited to receive a postcard from Jo. It was a colorful one, featuring a photo of the Copa girls dancing in short, bright yellow, ruffled skirts. I ran upstairs to read it in private.

Dear Sarah,

Here you go, as requested, a fun look at the Copacabana, my future stage for two weeks. I begin my dates there in early December. So, I'll be home for Thanksgiving at least through Sunday. I'm looking forward to having our secret chats about this interesting older man in your life. I want all the details when I get there and I'll fill you in on my life. One word of caution…go slow with this guy. Lots of love! Jo-Jo.

Well, it was too late for the go-slow warning, but I was thrilled Jo and I would see each other soon. It was almost as good as spending time alone with Beckham. As much as I wanted to show off the Copa postcard to Barb and the other girls on our wing, I didn't dare risk some Nosey Nancy reading Jo's message on the back. I quickly tucked it in my underwear drawer before curious eyes grabbed and read it.

I headed downstairs to book a bus ticket and give my parents a call to relay my travel plans. When I called the station, both of the Wednesday buses passing through Green Tree were totally booked. I should have known better than to wait so long. My only options were to catch the Tuesday noon bus, the same one Beckham was taking, and miss two of my afternoon classes, or book the noon Thursday bus and be late for Thanksgiving dinner. I opted to miss classes with the added bonus of spending five more hours with Beckham. Mother was thrilled with the news that she'd have both her girls home for several days.

Tuesday, I finished my morning classes, picked up my suitcase at the dorm, and dashed to the station, making it just minutes before my bus pulled out. I climbed up and searched for Beckham and a vacant seat on the crowded bus. I didn't see him or an empty seat.

With the bus engine rumbling and ready to go, I turned back to the driver. "Excuse me, sir. I don't see any seats available, but I *have* to make this trip."

He grumbled about women always running late, got up, and announced in a booming voice, "Listen up. Any of you got an empty seat next to you, raise your hand."

Across the back of the bus, there was a long bench seat. These seats were the stiff and uncomfortable ones that didn't lean back. Everyone on the back row shuffled over and created one extra space and then a young man slowly raised his hand. The driver turned to me and said, "There you go, middle back row, but it looks like all the overhead space is taken. You gotta hold your luggage for now. I got no time to store it in the cargo space." He glanced down at his watch and climbed behind the wheel. "I should have left two minutes ago."

I lurched down the aisle as the driver pulled out and turned onto the street. I was not happy. Five hours crammed like a sardine in a long tin can, holding my suitcase, without even a window to look through. And where was Beckham? I had wanted to surprise him. Maybe he had missed the bus? He was a little absent minded. I pulled Wuthering Heights out of my satchel and prepared for a long, bumpy ride.

~

WHEN THE BUS finally pulled up to Gottlieb's gas station in Green Tree, I was thrilled to get off. It felt so good to be home again and see Mother waiting for me. She was patiently leaning against the gas pump with her arms crossed, as the bus rolled to a stop. When I walked down the stairs I heard, "There's my girl! Sammy, Sarah's here." She hugged me tight, patting my back. "I'm so glad you came. I've missed you so much and I can use your cooking skills. We have two pies to bake today and so many other things to do. Jo's train doesn't get here until tomorrow at two."

I laughed and said, "That's fine. She's useless in the kitchen anyway."

Sammy came out holding a large Tootsie Roll. "Sarah!" He ran toward me and gave me a big hug around the waist. "Buy me this candy, pleeease?"

Well, hidey-ho to you too, Sammy." I reached in my purse and gave him five cents and watched him run back into the store to pay.

I put my bag in Mom's trunk and sat in the front, as Sammy raced back out with his unwrapped Tootsie Roll, joining us in the backseat. Mom pulled out and said, "We're going to need to stop at Whitmiller's for supplies." We headed a few blocks down Main Street and pulled up to the only grocery store in town. I loved stepping inside, hearing the bell tinkle as we walked in, and the slamming of the familiar screen door behind me. Sounds and smells of the familiar felt so comforting--the creak of scuffed floorboards and the scent of fresh baked bread placed near the register.

Mother efficiently directed the shopping expedition, "Sarah, grab a five-pound bag of flour, a bag of sugar, a can of Crisco, and another of pumpkin filling. I'll get the rest of my list. Sammy, you can pick out *one* box of cereal. Only one!"

He went down his favorite section, yelling, "Rice Krispies!"

"Mom, does he ever slow down? Gee willikers! Were we like that?"

Mom picked up a basket and began gathering some canned goods from a shelf. "He's all boy, that's for sure, but David seems to have him under control. And no, you two were not like Sammy. Sarah, you were often so quiet, but also stubborn, with a bit of a temper. Then there was Jo, always on the go and a big talker. You two were so different."

I nodded and laughed. "Yes, I remember. I've heard it a million times. Jo was the leader, I was the follower and she got most of the attention. Occasionally, I resented it back then, but that's all water under the bridge now." I turned and went down another aisle, saying, "I'll go find my part of the list."

Once we had over a dozen items up on the counter, Miss Whitmiller, an old school friend of Mom's, rang up each item on her massive cash register. "That's $4.25, Mariah."

"My goodness, prices are up, aren't they?"

She nodded back with a sigh. "I know. Ever since the government controls ended in June, prices keep climbing. Trust me, I hear it from every customer, every day." She whispered to us and looked back to the stockroom, "That's why my mom doesn't want to run the counter any more. Too many complaining customers. But some of it's caused by all the food we're sending to Europe right now. The higher the demand, the higher the prices."

Mom nodded, loading items in her carry bags. "I know, Milly, I'm not blaming you. I'm just glad we live on a farm and still raise half of what we eat."

As we were leaving, another friend of Mom's came in. Sheila Elkins--her parents owned the local paper, the Sentinel. "Mariah and Sarah! Look at you, Sarah! So grown up. Let's see...you're at the University of Iowa now, correct?"

I nodded as Sammy wrestled between us to go out skipping on the sidewalk. Mom jumped in saying, "Yes, Sarah's doing great, wants to get her Masters in Education. Oh Sarah, tell Sheila about the club you recently started at school. It's a wonderful idea."

I looked over at my doting mom and said, "We're just getting started but it's called Help for Heroes. We're organizing a group of students to help all the recent disabled vets that are attending the university. I have thirty volunteers so far."

"That's so interesting. Sarah, I'd love to do a little piece on that for the Sentinel. We're always trying to gather fresh news with a local angle. It's hard to come by some weeks. How about, I stop by on Friday, maybe around noon? It won't take long."

I looked over at Mom, who nodded. "Fine with me. We'd love to have you join us for lunch too. Noon it is. Great to see you, Sheila, and be sure to tell your folks happy Thanksgiving."

The next morning, Mom and I were up with the chickens, rolling out pie crusts, peeling potatoes, and cutting up old bread and celery for stuffing. We had to put Thanksgiving prep on hold to make a big breakfast of eggs, sausage and oatmeal for Dad, Sammy, two hired hands, and Uncle Billy. My Uncle was called Billy-Boy by almost everyone else and was Mom's business partner, her sister's husband, and David's best friend. I had numerous uncles around Green Tree, but Uncle Billy was always my favorite.

He was enjoying the last of his sausage links as he asked me, "So Sarah, you still bossing around all those professors on campus, telling them what's what?"

My memory flashed on Beckham's face in bed last Thursday night, and I blushed. "No, Uncle Billy. I usually let the professors take the lead. But my grades are going well."

"Great. We need you back in town and get you teaching these kids here something useful. So, when you coming back for good?"

"If I do summer classes, I could wrap up my teacher's certificate by the end of next summer, but I may continue with my masters. We'll see."

"I surely admire your focus, Sarah."

That afternoon, while Mom was resting her feet and taking a quick nap in a living room armchair, I took the car into town to pick up Jo at the train station. We hadn't seen each other in nine months. Happily, her train from Chicago arrived on time. I stood on the depot platform waiting for her to climb down the stairs. I waited as two men and a well dressed lady got off, continuing to keep my eyes peeled on the train's stairs.

When no one else got off, I became worried. Surely, Jo hadn't missed her Chicago connection?

CHAPTER 33
SISTER SECRETS
JO-JO

J stepped off the train feeling rather silly in my travel ensemble. The blustery wind had me grabbing the wide brim of my peaked hat with one hand, while my other hand kept the long navy, double-breasted coat from blowing me backwards. Not an easy feat in three-inch matching pumps. This outfit felt perfectly stylish for the train stations in New York and Chicago, but definitely a little over the top for Green Tree.

Two men walked in front of me, one of whom had offered to carry my heavy suitcase. Seeing Sarah, I thanked the man, lugged it a few steps on my own towards her and wondered why she was just standing there staring forward like a statue. "Good God, Sarah! No hugs for your sister?"

She jerked her head back in surprise and reached out her hand, flipping up the brim of my hat. "Holy smokes. I can't believe I didn't recognize you. I swear, I'd have bet you were Ginger Rogers if you'd come dancing down those stairs."

I held out my arms, saying, "Oh, shut up and give me a hug."

After our big embrace, Sarah pushed back and looked at me again, while shaking her head. I can't believe I didn't recognize my own twin! Where did you get these clothes? They look like they cost a fortune."

"They probably did. Don't worry, I borrowed them from a friend. She wanted me to look my best and give the hometown something to talk about."

"Oh, trust me. You'll turn a few heads." We began walking to the car, both of us helping carry my suitcase.

Climbing inside Mom's car, I asked, "So, where should we go?"

Sarah looked at me with a shrug. "It's either the Coffee Cup or the pool hall."

"So many choices," I laughed. "Hey, remember Anita from our class? She's one of the Green Tree operators now. Anyway, she told me Mr. Odenmeyer at the Coffee Cup named a sandwich for me after winning Jackpot. I promised her I'd go in and order one."

Sarah checked her watch, attempting to keep us on a schedule. "OK, we have a little time. Fine with me, as long as you're paying. Let's go try the Jo-Jo Anderson special."

We drove past the courthouse and parked a few spaces down from the cafe. The Coffee Cup was a Green Tree institution. While I was with Nanette last week, even she had reminisced about meeting with highschool girlfriends at the Coffee Cup for cherry sodas and weekly gab sessions.

Getting out of the car, Sarah said, "Remember, after school? This was our regular hangout. I studied here most afternoons."

"Yeah, you studied books and I studied the boys. But we always had to fight over table space with the retired farmers, usually sipping their tenth cup of coffee."

Sarah opened the door and I went in, walking up to the glass counter to salivate over the baked goods. I hadn't eaten since Chicago and was hungry. Mrs. Odenmeyer was behind the counter. "Hello, Mrs. O. It's Jo-Jo and Sarah... Mariah's daughters."

"Well, I'll be! It sure is. And you're even more of a beauty than you were in high school, Josephine. Hold on a second." She walked into the stockroom calling for her husband. They both came out with big smiles on their faces.

"Jo Anderson, as I live and breathe, look at you!" Mr. O. exclaimed. "You put our little town on the map, Missy. Don't know if you heard, but I named a sandwich for you after you won that big show."

"Aw, thanks. That's why we came in. Sarah and I are gonna split one please, and two Coca Colas."

"All right then, one Jo-Jo Deli-Girl on rye and two Cokes."

Sarah came up and reminded me, "Don't tell Mom. She'll be mad knowing we're eating so close to dinner."

I nodded and turned, looking at the few tables that had customers, but didn't recognize anybody. I did notice, though, that they all had stopped eating to stare at us. Anything new or different in town was always a novelty and subject to extended conversation.

We sat at a table closest to the back of the cafe. I lowered my voice and said, "So Sarah, tell me about this professor. I want all the details."

She took a deep breath and brought her voice down to a whisper. "Gosh where to start? It was the day after Tommy Martin broke my heart." Looking up wistfully, she added, "That seems so long ago now. Anyway, I'm on the crowded Greyhound heading back to Iowa City and this fussy man in glasses, wearing tweed, doesn't let me take the seat next to him. He was too busy sorting his papers, so I picked them up and they fell to the floor. As I sat down, he was so hostile, he wouldn't talk to me the rest of the trip, even after I apologized."

"Not a very auspicious beginning Sarah. He sounds terrible."

"Oh, it only got worse. After I arrived on campus, I went to the dorm, changed clothes and showed up late to my biology class, and of course, who was lecturing as I walked in? The same mean man from the bus! My old professor had been called away abruptly and his replacement, Professor Beckham Carter, was angry at me, again, for disrupting class."

Just then, Mrs. Odenmyer walked up with our sandwich and drinks. "On the house, girls. Enjoy."

We both thanked her and Sarah leaned over and said, "Well, aren't you special. She's never given me anything free in nineteen years."

We both had a good laugh and began eating. "Sarah, you need

to hurry your story along to the point when you two stopped hating each other, or you'll have to catch me up once we get home."

Sarah looked around for eavesdroppers and then continued. "Well, let's say it was a good thing that I'm fascinated with biology. He was impressed with my grade point average and my passion about meiosis cell division."

"Only you, Sarah, could attract a man with a love of cell division."

"That's true. So, within a couple weeks, he asked me to be his lab assistant--a paid position." She leaned in close and said, "But things started heating up after that." She raised her eyebrows and added, "Details to be continued later tonight."

"Aren't you the mysterious one, Sarah." We took a few bites of our sandwich halves and I said, "I have news too." From my purse, I pulled out my clipping of The Post's story and photo of me singing with Sinatra. "Take a look at this. Last week, I unexpectedly had a chance to sing with *the* Frank Sinatra. I still have to pinch myself when I see this photo. I really can't believe it happened."

Sarah grabbed the news article and slapped her hand on the table. "My sister is singing with one of the biggest crooners in the country. Jo, I knew in my heart you'd make it big. It was just nine months ago when I made my prediction at the train depot." She read the brief article and shook her head. "Golly! This is unbelievable."

I folded the clipping, returning it to my purse. "It was pretty incredible, but keep in mind, singing one song with Sinatra at the Copa does not mean I'm close to making it big. In fact, I was so nervous when he invited me up on the stage for the duet, that I forgot the first verse. It was so embarrassing."

"Oh my! What did you do?"

"Hummed along like an idiot, and thanked the Lord that the second verse and chorus came back to me. That's show business, Sarah. The craziest stuff happens. But thinking back on it, it was pretty magical."

"I bet. My roommate, Barb, will go crazy when she hears that story. Now for myself, I'm more of a Bing Crosby fan. I don't really understand the appeal of Sinatra. Sure, his voice is good…but he's so skinny, isn't he?"

"Well, thin or not, he's got dreamy blue eyes and such personal style on the microphone."

We sucked down the last of our Cokes. "We'd better get going before Mother sends David out searching for us," Sarah announced.

I pulled out a buck and left it on the table and we thanked the Odenmeyers again. Sarah laughed as we walked down the side-walk. "Now that you're a celebrity, guess you have to tip like one. The Odenmeyers probably haven't seen a dollar tip since they opened."

"Well, tips are easier to give when the food is free."

Everything was ready and waiting when we walked into the house. Mom had finished making a huge pot of chicken and dumplings, steamed green beans, and fresh buttered yeast rolls. Along with the family, Uncle Billy and his wife, Aunt Arlene, were there. Hugs were shared and Mom ushered us into the dining room. The best damask tablecloth and matching napkins were in use and places were set using David's late parents' good china.

Once seated, the conversation quickly turned to questions about my life in Manhattan. All manner of queries bubbled up. Uncle Billy was first. "So, I gotta know, Jo, what's it like living in a dang hotel for months on end."

"Well, Uncle Billy, if you like someone cleaning your room and making your bed everyday, it's pretty sweet. Besides, instead of having friends all over town, most of mine work at the hotel. So, it's almost like living in a small town. There's two bars, three restau-rants, 700 rooms, and even a bus station in the basement."

"That's pretty amazing, but I bet they don't have a farm and implement store. Uh, pass those dumplings please."

Between bites, Aunt Arlene asked, "I just have to know, Jo. Is John King as handsome as his voice makes him sound on the radio?"

"Simple answer, Auntie, yes! Tall, dark, and handsome with the most perfectly cut suits. And he smells good too. He must use some amazing after-shave."

Arlene and Mom nodded knowingly. "I knew it! That's exactly how I imagined him."

As I managed to squeeze in bites of food, the questions continued. The family wanted to know how I managed to memorize all the words to my songs? How did I do my laundry? Was the Talent Jackpot show rigged? What was it really like at the Copacabana? Had I met many stars working at the Deli?

When I started repeating my Frank Sinatra story, everybody laughed, shaking their heads, assuming I was pulling their leg. At this point, I noticed Sarah was silent and then began frowning, while clearing everyone's dinner plates. But the rest of the family wouldn't believe I sang with Sinatra until I showed them my clipping. Hell, I wouldn't have believed me either.

After dinner, I presented my family with the gift of a Monopoly game. We'd all certainly heard about the board game before, but our parents had never bought one, thinking it a frivolous expense. After dinner, instead of gathering around the radio, listening to Mom's favorite, The Ford Dinah Shore Show, we all played the game instead. Sarah volunteered to be the banker and keeper of the peace. Mom quickly became fascinated with it, buying up choice properties with relish, while Sammy cried every time he had to give up some of his colorful money. I went bankrupt quickly, Billy would only buy the cheap properties, and Aunt Arlene kept getting sent to jail, but David and Mom duked it out to the end. Mom made a gamble on several expensive hotels and David finally claimed victory with his wise, prudent investments.

Sarah laughed as she divided up all the money and organized it back into its box. "Well, that's pretty telling. Mom, you better slow down on converting those old houses into apartments."

Billy nodded, standing up and stretching. "Yeah, Monopoly or the real world, the inexpensive single housing unit is the wave of the future. So many couples are getting hitched right now and wanting their own place. Small, simple houses--that's where we need to put our money, Mariah."

"Agreed," Mom answered.

Mother's sister, Arlene, stood up, picking up her purse and said,

"All I learned from that game is that I don't enjoy being put in jail, especially every time I get a paycheck. Time to go, Billy-Boy. I'll be helping Mom and Dad with Thanksgiving dinner all day tomorrow. Will we see you folks there later?"

Mom answered, "Probably so."

After Sarah and I washed and dried dishes, we headed upstairs. I'd had twenty- five hours of travel and was exhausted. Later, lying in our childhood beds in the dark, Sarah continued her story from the restaurant.

"So Jo, in your postcard you warned me to go slow with the Professor. You're the only person I've told and I'm a little ashamed to admit this, but... we did the deed just the other night. It was so thrilling. I was in utter heaven."

"Goodness! So, tell me about the utter heaven part."

"It's too embarrassing to go into detail. All I'll say was that it seemed to involve a lot of tongue."

"Wow! Was not expecting that. I'm really happy that it all went well for you, but just be careful, Sarah. Remember Kenny Miles... when he and I disappeared after the senior picnic?"

"Of course. Most of the girls in town still have a crush on him."

"Well, all I can say about that was that I was *underwhelmed.*"

"So you and Kenny did it?" Sarah said in a disappointed tone. "And here I thought, at long last, I'd been the first."

"But it sounds like you and Beckham had a much better time. And you two seem to have more in common. I'm really happy you've found somebody, Sarah."

"Thanks, I just wish we didn't have to meet secretly. Hopefully that will all change this spring. He won't be my teacher then."

"Yeah, that would be difficult. Skulking around, hiding from the world. Listen, I also have a secret. Promise me, you won't breathe a word of this to Mom and Dad."

Sarah turned on the light and looked at me with concern. "What is it?"

"Remember the name, *Nanette Jorgenson,* the lady I stayed with when Mom had to work at the Martin farm after Dad died?"

Sarah nodded. "Of course, although, to this day Mom refuses to say her name. I do recall how upset she was when the two of you went missing. We were barely five, but I remember Mother being in agony."

"I know. It was terrible that Nanette didn't tell Mom when she dragged me to Hollywood. But anyway, the strangest thing happened. Believe it or not, I ran into her in Manhattan through Damien, that guy I was dating. She's his agent, although she goes by Fran Jordan now. At first I wanted nothing to do with her, but recently, she's been helping me out."

Sarah looked at me with surprise. "Jo! What do you mean by helping you out?"

I whispered back, "Lower your voice. Fran negotiated a good contract for me with the Copa, and she's lent me some money... only until I get my funds from the bank. She even let me borrow the clothes I wore today. I really believe I need her help right now. She knows so many people in the business and she's tough as nails. I'll learn a lot from her."

Sarah did not look happy about my admission. "Jesus, Jo. And I thought I was living dangerously. It sounds kind of like you signed a deal with the devil."

I looked at her, not expecting such a negative response and replied in kind. "Well, you might be doing the same thing with the professor," I hissed back.

Right then, Mom popped her head in. "So, everybody's already in bed?"

"Yeah Mom, it's been a long day of travel. I'm bushed. Thanks for the great dinner."

"Always a pleasure. I'm so proud of you both." She leaned down and kissed us each on the cheek, and turned off the light. "My amazing pair of ones. Goodnight girls. Sleep well."

THANKSGIVING DAY I gobbled up all the family favorites, turkey with stuffing, mashed potatoes and thick brown gravy made from turkey giblets, canned carrots and peas from Mother's summer garden, along with my favorite, Norwegian lefse rolled up with butter and brown sugar. I continued to eat with abandon, knowing my weight had gone way down since arriving in New York.

After our mid-day meal, we joined most of my mother's family at my grandparent's farm. It was great seeing everyone inside one very crowded house. I counted thirty-four of us at one point, but conversations spilled out from the living room onto the front and back porches, over the sink and kitchen table, and into the back yard where many of the men were smoking.

Passing by one group of men, I heard them speaking of the young vets who'd recently returned to Green Tree from the war, the climbing price of milk, and upcoming elections. In the kitchen, the women were gossiping about neighbors who were newly pregnant, a possible movie theater opening downtown, an increase in school taxes, and the latest styles selling at Magees. Out front, a cluster of my cousins were having a discussion about duck hunting, and a truck and auto dealership opening between Green Tree and Blue Earth.

My head was spinning while I walked from one conversation to another, trying to jump in, but realizing I was totally out of the loop. I felt like I'd been living on a different planet for the past nine months.

On Friday, Sarah and Mom prepared a nice, small lunch for her friend, Shiela, from the Sentinel. After the meal she was going to interview Sarah about her school volunteer group. Before Sheila arrived, I went upstairs to rest. I was no longer used to the five AM wake-up time that our household always operated on. Just as I was dozing off, Mother knocked on the bedroom door.

"Jo-Jo, Sheila heard you were in town and wants to know all about the Talent Jackpot show and the upcoming Copacabana appearances. She brought a photographer with her too. Hurry down, dear."

I rubbed the sleep out of my eyes and dabbed on a little rouge and lipstick. When I came downstairs, Sarah was washing up the lunch dishes, while I sat down across from Sheila. I answered much the same questions that I had my first night here and then gave, yet, another rendition of the Frank Sinatra story. Pictures were taken and then the reporter announced she needed to leave soon and had better get some information about Sarah's club. We all looked around and noticed Sarah had quietly left the kitchen. Mom went to look for her in the living room, while I checked upstairs. She was nowhere to be found in the house, so Sheila left.

Later in the day, Sarah returned and went upstairs to read. I followed behind her asking, "What happened to you? Sheila was all ready to ask questions about Help for Heroes, and we couldn't find you."

She pulled a textbook from her satchel, keeping her eyes down. "I think she got what she wanted. To talk to you… take pictures of you… ooh and aah over you. It's tiresome, Jo. It's always about you. You sang a song on the radio, while I'm trying to do something meaningful that could help injured people. Does anybody really care? No. All anybody wants to hear about is Jo-Jo the Deli Girl."

"But Sarah, that's not my fault…"

"I need to study. Please…either take a nap or go downstairs."

CHAPTER 34

THE LITTLE GREEN MONSTER

SARAH

*S*unday after church, Mother drove Jo and I back into town. The mood between the two of us remained frosty, and I knew it was primarily of my making. I was leaving on the noon bus heading to Iowa City and Jo was catching a one o'clock train to Chicago. Mother filled the void of conversation between us with small talk about the mayor's wife singing off-key in the church choir. "Well of course, it could hardly be helped, with the organ being so out of tune." Suddenly, she paused for a second and said, "I don't know what's been going on between the two of you since Friday, but I can tell when something's wrong. So, out with it and make amends. Trust me, you don't want to leave each other with some silly argument hanging between you two."

Sitting in the front seat, I huffed, crossing my arms against my chest. I turned around to look at Jo. She was staring out the window and calmly stated, "Sarah's just jealous because Sheila from the Sentinel wanted to talk to me *and* her. As I told you before, Sarah, she was only trying to get two stories instead of one. I bet our visits home will probably be front page news."

Mother laughed and said, "Don't think so highly of yourself, Jo. There's a new hybrid corn seed that will surely take precedence over the two of you. But to my point, is that true, Sarah? Are you angry at your sister because Sheila asked her questions about the Copacabana for a story?"

I continued looking straight ahead. "Guess I'm just irritable. It's been a tiring weekend. But I really don't understand why everyone is so fascinated because someone sings a song on the radio? Even all the girls at my dorm seem to know more about *Jo-Jo the Deli Girl* than they know about me. It's annoying."

Jo leaned forward talking to the back of my head. "But, Sarah, why is that my fault? Everybody's obsessed with the movies and entertainers. It's been like that for years. Think about it this way. Good old Harry Truman is doing lots of important stuff in the White House right now. Signing bills left and right. Some people may talk about it, but most of us would rather read about the new record Doris Day just put out, or the latest movie Ingrid Bergman or Cary Grant is in. It's just a way to escape from the serious day-to-day stuff."

I turned again and spat out, "So I get compared to Harry Truman and you get to be Doris Day? That's typical. It just all seems so trivial."

I stared out the window again while Jo whined behind me. "Well, it's not always easy being compared to the smart one either. Yes, I sing and dance, but I could never get through the courses you're taking now. I know what teachers at Green Tree used to say behind my back. 'If she could only be more like Sarah.' I almost laughed as Jo mimicked the voice of our old principal perfectly.

But, instead of laughing, I twisted my head around and said, "Well, you could have tried studying a little harder."

"And you could stop being such a baby about all…"

Mother then pulled the car over and broke hard. "That's enough! You both have your strengths and weaknesses. And despite your differences, you've always gotten along."

We both got very quiet as Mother started the car again and eventually pulled up to the bus stop. "Sarah, if you honestly feel your club at school has merit and is doing something important, then you need to tell Sheila about it. It was rude of you to leave when you did. I want you to write her a nice letter of apology about skipping out before she had a chance to speak with you and then go on to explain all the details of Help for Heroes. Will you do that for me?"

I wasn't thrilled about doing it, but growled out a "Yes." As much as I hated being told I was in the wrong, I knew Mother was right.

I got out of the car and went to the back to pull out my suitcase. Mother also got out and followed me to the back of the Ford. "Will you please give your sister and best friend a hug. If you don't, you'll be kicking yourself five minutes out of the station."

I looked down, embarrassed I was acting so immature. I opened Jo's door and said without inflection, "Mom says we have to hug and apologize. Do you forgive me?"

Jo gently pushed me back and stood up. "Of course, you big baby. You're forgiven. Now give me a real hug." We stood and held tight to each other for a full minute as tears came to our eyes. After separating, Jo said, "And Sarah, I honestly should have asked Sheila to include us together in a picture when the photographer came in. That was my mistake, I'm sorry. Come to think of it, how did Sheila even know I was in town?"

Mom came between us. "Well, if the two of you hadn't gone to the Coffee Cup and snuck in a Jo-Jo sandwich before dinner last Wednesday, she probably would never have known. Don't think I didn't hear about it either. People talk around here; especially Mrs. Odenmier. And never forget, girls, your sister will be the best friend you'll ever have. Don't burn that bridge."

As the bus pulled in, I thought about my actions and words. If I was honest with myself, I knew I still felt the same way about the situation. I was tired of Jo always getting the glory, and yes, I was jealous. That little green monster had definitely climbed up on my shoulder and was busy whispering in my ear. My apology was a hollow one.

Looking for a seat on the bus, I'd hoped to find Beckham on board. He wasn't. Again. I assumed he must have taken the really early morning bus from Minneapolis instead. I spent the first hour of the bus ride concentrating on making notes about the letter Mom asked me to send to Sheila. I would explain that Help for Heroes was now a group of thirty-one committed students trying to make the university experience more welcoming for disabled vets. No. That sounded very blah. I began thinking of the benefits a news story like this might offer. I considered donations and realized I should boldly ask for the need of money to fund the building of ramps on campus, student backpacks, and other simple solutions for barriers facing the disabled. I would also explain that the university currently had no budget for this. In conclusion, I would add that if anyone wanted to mail a check to help our cause, we would send them updates and photos of our progress.

Why hadn't I thought of asking for donations before? Although most students had minimal funds, people at home, especially those who had lost loved ones, might certainly want to contribute as a way of paying back those who had survived the war. I was now very much hoping that Sheila at the Sentinel would agree to print the story for their next edition.

I was getting excited thinking about the story's possible ramifications. I needed to contact our publicity director, Abigail. I decided to give her an outline of this letter, ask her to rewrite it with more pizazz, and then send it out as a press release to all the newspapers in Iowa. And why not also send it out to all the VFW organizations in the state? As a group, we needed to think bigger. My ideas kept snowballing as the bus rolled along.

By the time I returned to campus, I'd written up a lengthy list of people to contact and things to do regarding Help for Heroes. I had become re-energized and put the row I'd had with Jo on the backburner.

That evening, the dorm cafeteria was serving a light dinner of turkey sandwiches and lime fruit Jello. Barb and many of the girls on our floor had yet to return. I stopped and checked my mail slot and was surprised to find a note from Beckham. I immediately opened it and read it on the way to the dining room.

Dearest Sarah,
Hope your Thanksgiving weekend was enjoyable. I missed you and look

forward to being with you soon. If you'd like to come by Monday evening
around seven, it would make me quite happy.
    Beckham

Rather dry and antiseptic, but the note made me glow inside anyway. As I sat down to eat by myself, I realized that for the first time in weeks, my head had *not* been focused on Beckham and that was refreshing. With the professor in my life, I was always swinging between exaltation or disappointment, often coupled with a fear of something I was doing wrong.

I slipped some cubes of Jello down my throat, while rereading Beckham's short note. Exaltation or disappointment be damned, I felt sure that by Monday evening I'd be skipping joyously to his apartment at seven.

SETTLING BACK in after the Thanksgiving break, I had contacted Lester and asked him to take on the position of Treasurer for Help for Heroes. I wanted someone other than me to handle the funds if we started receiving donations and Lester seemed pleased with the responsibility. Abbie was also eager to dive into her position as publicity director and got busy sending out press releases and dona tion requests.

After that first week back, the winter doldrums settled in around campus, but I remained upbeat. I tapped on my window, opening it just a crack to put out dried bread crumbs for a few hungry sparrows flitting across nearby tree branches. Snow covered the ground across the campus in deep white drifts, muffling the sounds of student life. The freezing temperature and gale-like winds kept most of us indoors at Currier Hall except for attendance at our mandatory classes. Finals were coming, which always seemed to put a look of desperation into the eyes of procrastinating students, as they frantically sought out the notes of others who'd not been cutting classes.

Although I was still far from popular, my reputation as a top student started to garner me attention with several of the dorm girls who requested tutoring sessions and exam reviews. I accepted the challenge and began charging twenty-five cents an hour for services. It didn't sound like much but it was starting to add up, especially when I tutored two to three students at a time taking the same class.

I found most every minute of my waking day filled with tasks: attending classes, biology lab responsibilities, tutoring sessions, and holding meetings with the officers of the Help for Heroes team, which included Barb, Jacob, Abigail, and Lester. The club had become a driving force for me and I was thrilled to see things coming together.

My nights were also busy, primarily with Beckham. We were now up to three nights a week, still meeting secretly at his apartment. Sometimes we shared meals together, often we read together, cuddled up under bed covers, but most certainly, we shared sex. I felt the bond building between us getting stronger with each meeting. And the love-making continued to improve as I became more comfortable and knowledgeable about what we both enjoyed.

I couldn't believe my life. For the first time in my recollection, I felt so complete, so driven, and successful in my pursuits. I was a lucky girl. I had to wonder, how was Jo doing? But I didn't bother to call or write to her, or mention Jo's Copa engagement to the girls at the dorm. I felt sure her name would be up in lights soon enough.

After Abbie's first round of press releases went out, Lester came into the lab, wearing a big smile under his wool cap and ear flaps. He now easily pulled up on his raised stool and spun around to face me.

"Lester, what has you grinning like the Cheshire cat?"

"Got good news for us, Sarah. Right as I left for class, I checked the mailbox and found three checks that came in for Help for Heroes. One, for ten dollars from the Green Tree Business Association, twenty-five from a Des Moines VFW hall, and another twenty from the Iowa City Chamber of Commerce."

I was so pleased I gave Lester a quick unexpected hug and clapped my hands together in excitement. "Do you think it's enough to build our first stair ramp?"

Lester's cheeks were flashing red. I didn't know if it was the cold weather or my enthusiastic hug. "I doubt it, but maybe. I'll have to check with my cousin about all that, and of course the building superintendent will have to approve everything."

"This is great news. Looks like we're ready to open a bank account and make a fifty-dollar deposit. It's important that everything is documented, Lester, and please give Abbie a call and ask her to send out thank you notices."

"No problem. Hey Sarah, after the lab we should go celebrate. Conrad could drop us at the Hawkeye Hut. Maybe we could study over a beer or two."

A few other students had started meandering in, but I knew Beckham, sitting at his desk, could have easily overheard our conversation. Would he care about that? It wasn't a date, just a simple study session. I shrugged and nodded. "Sure, why not. We deserve a celebration."

After lab, I told Lester he'd need to wait about ten minutes while I stored the equipment properly. Then Beckham walked over and asked Lester if he could have a few minutes alone with me to talk about lab exams. Lester nodded. "Sarah, I'll be waiting in the hall."

Immediately after the door was closed, Beckham waved his hand in front of me, asking, "So, what's this all about? Sarah, it looks like you're putting way too much thought and time into this group of yours. I knew that was bound to happen."

"Lester and I are studying together and celebrating our first donations. That's all. The amount may be enough to have our first ramp built."

Beckham frowned and crossed his arms. "Don't forget your priorities. Your studies and our time together. We both need that right now, don't you agree?"

I looked at him thoughtfully and suddenly became irritated. "I'm very concerned with my priorities and my 4.0 grade point average should reflect that. As far as time with you goes, I'd say I've been quite generous. I do enjoy our time together; quite a lot, actually. But I can certainly make my own decisions on who to study with and talk to. Now, was there something you wanted to discuss regarding the lab exam?"

"No. You're free to leave."

Without saying another word, I turned and continued wiping down the desks and microscopes, and stacking the culture plates. On completion, I put on my hat and coat, grabbed my satchel and walked to the door. As I turned the knob to go, he said, "I hope you'll find the time to come to my place Friday evening." I glanced behind me. He was sitting at his desk, looking down, scribbling away in his damn journal.

"Sure. Goodbye, Beckham."

While leaving, I wondered if I would be jealous if Beckham showed interest in another female student needing his help. Would I be angry and demand he give me more attention? Probably not... Well, maybe? And what was he writing about in that journal? Probably cursing me and my lack of focus.

I saw Lester leaning against the wall on a crutch and watched his smile widen as I walked his way. I did know one thing. I didn't like fretting about what Beckham was thinking. Life was too short.

CHAPTER 35

DOGS, DRESSES, AND DITTIES

JO-JO

From Green Tree to Chicago, I dozed, waking up in fits and starts while stopping at endless small towns along the train route. I thought about Mom's final words to Sarah and me and felt bad to see Sarah still pouting as she climbed onto her bus. I felt sure she'd forgive me as time passed. But was anything really my fault? Could I help it if the people of Green Tree wanted to hear about me performing in Manhattan versus her life as a top student in Iowa? Really, Sarah?

Once I arrived in Chicago, I had a layover and extra time to grab a late dinner between trains. Walking through the impressive Grand Central Station, I decided to try the famous Chicago Dog I'd heard so much about. My heels clicked down the shiny marble floors, passing massive fluted Corinthian columns and wide arched windows. I followed signs to a restaurant located in the station, with a casual lunch counter built along the side. I stepped up to one of the round swivel stools and was quickly greeted by a man in a white shirt, white pants, and a paper cap. I immediately felt an alliance with his uniform.

"Hey pretty lady, whatcha need?"

"People keep telling me about the Chicago Dog. Thought I'd order one if it doesn't take long to make."

"As long as you got three minutes, you made a good choice. How's about a beer to wash it down."

I shrugged, knowing I still had another eighteen hours of travel before I reached Manhattan. "Why not? A cold beer or two and a dog."

As promised, within a few minutes, he brought me a large beef sausage wrapped in a long poppy seed bun, topped with yellow mustard, pickle relish, chopped onion, sliced tomatoes, Italian peppers, and a dill pickle spear. It was so large and messy, I didn't know where to start, so I drank the beer and contemplated the dog. I noticed it was missing one thing and asked the man sitting to my right to pass the ketchup.

He started to pass the red bottle over my way, looked at the dog, and then pulled back. "Can't do that, miss. You might get arrested."

"What are you talking about? I always put ketchup on my hotdogs."

He shook his head and laughed. "Not here you don't. Against the law in Chicago."

I took the bottle from him. "I'll take my chances. I'm feeling lucky today."

He pulled several paper napkins from the dispenser in front of him and said, "Better keep these handy. That blue coat is too pretty for mustard stains."

"Thanks. You must be from here, right?"

"Born and bred. He reached out his hand before I made a mess of mine. "Justin Winkleberg, attorney at law."

"Hello, Mr. Winkleberg. Do you always state your profession as part of your name?"

"I believe in cutting to the chase. I figured we'd probably get to discussing it sometime during the course of that dog. And you are?"

Holding up the hot dog, I replied, "I'm starving. But I'll get back to you with a name and my aspiring occupation after a few bites."

He looked at his watch and lit a cigarette. "I can wait. My train to New York doesn't leave for another fifty minutes."

I chewed for a full minute, enjoying the mix of spicy condiments with the meat and bun. Then dabbed my mouth and chin, looked at my watch and said, "Me too. We're probably on the same train. By the way, it's Jo-Jo Anderson, triple threat, or so says my talent agent."

"I enjoy watching you eat. With so much gusto!" He offered me a cigarette, which I declined. "So, you must be an entertainer then. In a Broadway show I might have heard of?"

"Unfortunately, no. I'm just getting started. But I will be singing a medley of Broadway hits soon. Just signed to do a two-week run at the Copa. That's why I need to get back to Manhattan. I have rehearsals."

He nodded, sipped the foam off a new beer and said, "Fascinating. I do love a good Broadway tune. Maybe I'll drop in and see the show. The Copacabanna is a hoppin' club." Then he quickly downed his beer, finished his cigarette, and handed me his card. "Miss Anderson, good luck with the rest of the dog and your Copa run. It was a pleasure meeting you."

"And you as well, Mr. Winkleman. Enjoy your trip."

On the train to New York, I gazed out at beautiful snowy vistas of forest, lakes, and farmland. After a brief nap, I began to focus on work.

Before leaving Manhattan, I'd discovered a wonderful music store selling all kinds of instruments and sheet music. I asked the salesman for his recommendation of the twenty most popular Broadway tunes and bought the music for all of them, knowing I'd need to narrow it down to probably seven or eight songs for a set. I thought I'd be able to study the music while in Green Tree, but I never found the time and didn't dare run them by Sarah after she turned so sullen towards me.

I went through the twenty songs, humming away to myself, and then selected a mix of ballads and up-tempo hits that would work best with my range. I was anxious to test them out in pre-rehearsal with a band. I didn't want to go into the Copa rehearsals cold, without a clue. After returning, I planned to ask Slim at the Ebb-Tide to practice with me, but this time I'd pay the band.

Between money for rehearsal musicians, new gowns, a decent pair of evening shoes, and sheet music, I was anxious to actually start earning a paycheck from the Copa. I was grateful that Nanette had helped me recover my thousand-dollar check, less her one-hundred dollar cut, but those funds would quickly disappear with all the expenses I would be incurring.

My hope was to keep a cash reserve of five-hundred-dollars that would cover costs getting me to Hollywood and into the MGM studios, *if* James Appleton liked my Copa reviews.

My train pulled into Penn Station early the next morning. I grabbed some breakfast at the station, dropped my bag at The Dixie, and walked to my bank to take out more cash; another hundred dollars. This withdrawal brought my balance down to just above seven-hundred and I had a two-week wait before my first Copa check.

I then ventured into Chinatown via the subway. I got off at Mott Street and began searching for Nanette's recommended gown designer, Angie Chin. I had her address on a business card but all signage on the storefronts and offices used Chinese symbols which were useless to me. I stopped three different people for directions which led me down several narrow, winding streets. I eventually located the address and climbed four flights of stairs passing the open doors of gambling rooms, a few already crowded with tables full of people playing cards and mahjong at ten AM.

Breathing heavily, I arrived at a crowded studio space filled with hundreds of tall rolls of shiny satin, silk, and brocade fabric. I saw no organization of color, style, or fabric type and couldn't imagine how anyone could keep track of what was in stock. As I wandered through the towering bolts, the narrow trail on the scuffed linoleum floor led me to four women sitting in a row, busy at work behind sewing machines. None of the four ever bothered to look up. Over the whir of their machines, I called out. "Hello. Good morning? Hi-de-ho!" Still no response.

I continued walking forward through the narrow space. Reaching the end, I stood next to a closed door with lots of yelling going on behind it in a language I assumed was Chinese. I waited a few minutes, but the yelling continued. Then I knocked, opened the door, and poked my head through. A middle-aged woman of Asian descent, wearing a slightly askew curly blond wig, was speaking loudly into a large desk phone and stopped mid-sentence, eying me suspiciously.

"Hi there. I'm looking for Angie Chin? Fran Jordan sent me."

Without comment to the person on the receiving end, she hung up the phone with a loud clunk and stood up. "Ah yes, Fran. Very good customer, very beautiful, like you. What you want? You want gown? Nightclub sexy? Many styles to choose. Come. Sit. Sit." She patted a chair next to her desk. I nodded in agreement, and she began showing me countless pages of illustrated pattern choices.

For my Copa debut, I had visualized opening my act wearing a strapless, knee-length, cocktail dress, then perhaps changing into elegant palazzo pants and a midriff blouse, and finishing with a long one-shoulder sheath gown. I pointed at a few pattern pictures that came close to my vision and Angie said, "Yes, yes. Best choice. Come. You follow."

As we reentered the fabric forest, she asked, "What color you like? You like blue? Blue very good for you." She grabbed a roll of sky-blue satin and another of icy pale blue. "And looking good in gold, I think. Very sparkling, very rich." She dug into a shelf heaped with bolts of material and pulled out two shades of metallic fabric. "Maybe pink? Sweet, young. I think very nice for you." While holding all six heavy bolts, Angie opened a closet with her other arm and shoved me inside. "Underwear only. You change now."

I was in a tailspin following this small but commanding woman around her crowded studio. I undressed, hoping I'd worn decent undergarments and stuck my head out waiting for further instructions.

She motioned me to step out. "Come, come. Lilly measure you." She yelled loudly and a tiny, older woman hobbled over from some hidden cubby-hole carrying a foot stool and measuring tape. She began pulling the tape taute against every angle and limb of my body and jotting numbers down on a scrap of paper. After measurements were taken, Angie held the chosen bolts of fabric up next to me, clicking her tongue, squinting her eyes, mumbling yes and no, then dashed off for second choices and seemed happier with new selections. She busily wrote figures down on the back of a postcard, clicking her tongue again like an internal adding machine and announced, "You pay seventy-five-dollar. Ready in two days."

Even with Angie doing a rushed two-day job, the price seemed quite high. I recalled feeling guilty buying my five-dollar dress at Macy's basement. In comparison, this seemed exorbitant. I tried to hide my shock at Angie's asking price and then imagined what Fran Jordan, Agent to the Stars, would say. How would she counter the price?

"No, sorry Angie. What if you take three days to sew them and I'll pay thirty dollars total?" Ten dollars per outfit sounded reasonable to me.

She started laughing, as she walked over to the four women behind the whirring machines, and began speaking loudly to them. In unison, the four stopped sewing, looked over at me, and laughed hysterically for about thirty seconds, and then went back to their work. Obviously, my haggling skills needed work.

"Miss Jo-Jo. Angie Chin is top designer. Fashion artist. Use best fabric. Make perfect for you. Because friend of Miss Jordan, you pay *sixty dollars*."

I knew I had the one-hundred dollar bill burning a hole in my wallet, but I had budgeted that hundred to last me until my first Copa check. Between a near starvation diet and the money needed to pay the Ebb Tide rehearsal band, I quickly calculated the very highest I could pay Angie was forty-five dollars.

"I'm sorry Angie. I'm sure they'll be beautiful, but it's just too expensive." I shook my head, walking toward the door, crossing my fingers.

As I touched the door knob, I heard, "You pay fifty-dollar cash, no check."

I turned and smiled. "Forty-seven dollars, final offer." I whipped the hundred dollar bill from my wallet and waved it.

Angie shook her blond wig vigorously but agreed. "Quick. Follow me. I give change."

∾

LATER THAT DAY, as I crossed through the lobby of The Dixie, I warily glanced around, watching for Rudy the Punk, but once I was safely in the elevator, I decided that his threat was minimal. I was tired of being afraid of other people. I needed to get tougher and wise up if I was going to survive this crazy business. I unlocked my door and bounced down on my springy bed, closing my eyes with an exhausted sigh. I took a needed restful nap and felt at peace. As I had explained to Uncle Billy, after nine months, The Dixie felt like home.

The band at the Ebb Tide kept a loose schedule. They generally started playing around seven. Or at least the band members began to shuffle in around that time. That evening at 6:30, I meandered downstairs and noticed the combo's leader, Slim Wallace, sitting at the bar downing a bourbon and Coke. I took the empty stool next to him and told the bartender, "Water with lemon, Jerry. So, Slim, how's it going?"

Slim was an excellent piano man but also loved bourbon as much as the piano. He mumbled as I moved in closer. "Oh, more of the same and none of the new. How's about you, Jo-Jo?"

"I actually have big news. Got a two-week engagement at the Copa."

He jerked his head up and his bloodshot eyes stared back at me. "Whoa! How you manage that? That's top of the top, kid. Can't do no better than that in this town."

"Thank you! I have a proposition for you and your band if you have a minute."

He shrugged and sucked a sip of bourbon through his teeth. "Let's hear it."

"Your guys and Dottie were such a big help preparing me for Talent Jackpot. I just can't go into the Copa rehearsals cold having never sung my song selections without a band. If you guys have a little extra time this week, I'd love to pay you an extra twenty-five to rehearse with me for an hour or two."

He folded his hands on the bar and looked down, shaking his head. "Little girl, you're heading into the big leagues now. You're going need a heck of a lot more than your good looks and an hour or two. Let's plan on three sessions this week, starting around five o'clock for seventy-five bucks total, and then we'll bring you up on stage in front of our little audience for a while each of those nights. You'll need at least that much time to truly prepare."

I winced at the price tag but knew Slim was right. I did need the extra practice, and performing in front of the audience at the Ebb Tide would be invaluable. If I came into the Copa stiff and scared, I could easily see Monte Proser canceling my contract if he thought I wasn't ready. I could tell when he hired me, he thought I was a little too hayseed for the Copa. In my head, I subtracted another chunk from my bank balance, nodded at Slim and said, "You got a deal. When can we start?"

Money and time spent with the Ebb Tide combo proved to be a wise investment. The next afternoon, I showed Slim and Dottie the music for the eight songs I'd selected. After glancing through them and taking a look at the lyrics, the veteran jazz singer, Dottie, gave me a good piece of advice. "Sweet cheeks, these lyrics just aren't gonna cut it in a sophisticated nightclub. There's nothing wrong with the cornball songs if you know the story that goes along with 'em, but singing them outside of the story is gonna be tough."

I nodded and chewed a nail while giving this new problem some thought.

Slim piled on, laughing at the lyrics to a song from the musical, Oklahoma. "Dottie's right, listen to this line from I Cain't Say No--- *I hate to disserpoint a beau, when he is payin' a call.* I've heard this number before. Might as well be a barnyard hootenanny."

"Yeah, I see what you mean. I just thought the lyrics were cute and funny. What if we slow it down and I try to sing it more sultry and sexy. I could take out the hick accents in the lyrics. It might give it a whole different feel."

With a cigarette dangling from the side of his mouth, he said. "Let's try it. Your funeral, Jo-Jo."

I crossed through the lyrics, correcting the words written to suggest a rural accent and made them sound more cosmopolitan. Instead of singing, I almost spoke the song's lyrics in my lowest register, while Slim and the band slowed the tempo. It completely changed the feel of the song and we all began to really like it. I quickly decided I'd use it to open my act.

I envisioned my first headline: *Jo-Jo Anderson--The Girl Who Can't Say No.* I'd show Monte Proser that I wasn't the simple, wholesome Deli-Girl he thought I was.

CHAPTER 36

UNEXPECTED BUMP IN THE ROAD

SARAH

*B*eckham and I never discussed our little argument from earlier in the week. I wasn't ready to risk my new friendships because of one jealous man, but I was glad I didn't have to. When we met on Friday evening, perhaps as an unspoken apology, he made another attempt at preparing a good dinner. I walked into his small apartment and was enveloped in the scent of baked ham dotted with pineapple and side dishes of corn and salad. Beckham was still wearing a long apron over his shirt and trousers when I arrived and I couldn't help but picture him sweating over every meticulous detail. This time, he'd purchased a meat thermometer and actually followed a recipe. I was touched seeing an open copy of *Aunt Sammy's Revised Recipes Cookbook* on his kitchen counter. My mother had used the same one for years.

"Beckham, I'm surprised. This looks delicious!"

He smiled, looked down and kissed me. "Well, you've been very patient with me. I haven't treated you to a well-cooked meal yet. We can't count my first attempt."

"You're right. We absolutely can't count that." We both laughed as the tension broke between us, helping us get past our earlier quarrel. Our dinner conversation turned into a biology lab discussion and then I questioned him about his Christmas break plans.

"Let's see, two weeks from now? Guess I'll be doing more of the same-- up in Minneapolis with my family."

I was disappointed at Thanksgiving when he hadn't been on the bus, but I had never questioned him about it. I didn't want to sound like an anxious, prying girlfriend. But my curiosity got the best of me. "So last time, for Thanksgiving. No Greyhound bus?"

"Yeah, I actually ended up getting a ride with another prof from the history department. She has a car and we split the gas and drive time. Worked out pretty good. I'll probably try to hitch a ride with her again."

"I see. Uh, not sure how my mother would feel about it, but I could probably join you in Minneapolis for a few days if you like. I'd love to meet your parents."

His face froze momentarily as he tried to hide his discomfort. "Tempting, but best not to push it. I don't think my mother would like the idea of one of my students showing up at her door. Might be awkward. Give it time, Sarah."

I kept eating my dinner and didn't respond.

As the days slipped by, we continued to keep up our student-professor facade in the classroom and lab, but then released all our pent up sexual tension with each meeting at his apartment. Unfortunately, our time together always felt so rushed because of my dorm curfews. But hopefully, once I was no longer his student and lab assistant, it wouldn't have to be that way.

Things weren't perfect. I knew he was controlling. He'd exhibited that tendency on the first day we'd met on the bus. But I was stubborn and tried to hold my own with him most of the time. On the following Friday night, we were each tearing off our clothes, when he complained to me, "Why haven't I seen you since Monday? This is really becoming unacceptable."

"Beckham, I told you after class Tuesday, I scheduled tutoring sessions every night this week. It's the last week before finals. Everyone is cramming and needing help, and I have my own exams to study for."

"Then why are you taking on all these extra tutoring sessions?"

"Because, I'm trying to save money. You know the lab job doesn't pay much. A couple bucks a week."

He cupped my breast and reached down and kissed it, asking in a whisper, "And what are you saving for?"

"Life." Then I took his hand and pulled him over to the bed and continued explaining, "There's so many things that I go without. And I hate asking my parents for anything. I know they'd help me if I really needed it, but by a certain age, I like feeling more independent."

"I do like that about you. It's admirable, especially for a woman."

I looked at him with a squint and said, "That's a rather backhanded compliment." I pulled his arm out across the bed and climbed on top of his hips. "I'll show you who's boss now, Professor."

DONATIONS CONTINUED TO TRICKLE IN, with Lester giving me weekly updates. The balance brightened for our account when Abigail, our publicity director, had a big interview with the university newspaper. The story was featured on the front page and then got picked up by other school papers and the Associated Press in Iowa. The story gave us a windfall of donations from civic groups across the state. A week after, Lester dropped by my dorm with exciting news.

We sat down in the lobby, but Lester was practically jumping out of his chair. "Sarah, you'll never guess what our bank total has climbed to."

"Uh, let's see. Have we hit a total of five-hundred-dollars yet?"

His smiling face was suddenly crestfallen. "How did you know that?"

I leaned toward him in my chair. "Because, Lester, last week you said we had two-hundred-and-fifty and I knew Abigail's story was drawing a lot of attention. So I took a wild guess. And I think that's wonderful!"

His giant smile returned. "Well Conrad thinks that might be enough to build two ramps, depending on where the school wants to put them. So it's time for you and Barb to go talk to the people that make decisions."

"Excellent. Why don't you join us Lester. You're a big part of our group."

"Really?"

"Absolutely."

Following up on our amazing news, Barb and I scheduled a meeting with the student coordinator to announce our good news. A few days later, in her office, Hortense Miller stared across at the three of us in a confused daze. "You've done what? What are we talking about?"

For someone whose sole job was coordinating with students, Mrs. Miller always struck me as someone who was ill at ease with anything having to do with students. I explained at a slower pace. "A ramp...something that can be placed near or over a section of stairs so that wheelchairs and crutches can operate more smoothly."

She leaned over, attempting to understand each detail. "I see. Well that has to be discussed. We can't have these ramps just put up willy-nilly."

Barb, who always knew the better way to turn a phrase, said, "Yes, of course, Mrs. Miller. That's why we're meeting with you first. We'd like you to tell the administration that we can pay for supplies and the maintenance crew's time if they can build the ramp, and then of course, the administration should decide which building would benefit the most with our first ramp."

"Your first ramp? So there will be more?"

I couldn't help myself and jumped in. "Well one ramp is certainly only the beginning. Eventually, every building on this campus should have one. Don't you agree?"

"Well, I don't know. It might look unsightly. Why the need for so many? I'll have to take this up with those people above my pay grade, won't I?"

"Apparently so." I huffed impatiently, a bad habit I was trying to break. "Mrs. Miller, we understand that these decisions have to go through channels. We just wanted you to know the funds are ready and Help for Heroes is merely waiting for a selection of high priority spots where the administration wants the ramps placed."

Barbara added, "Also, we'd love a good photo to send to the press once the ramp is put in place. One featuring our treasurer here, Lester Adams, a disabled vet, wheeling up the ramp. And perhaps you, Mrs. Miller, cheering him on."

Lester looked at us confused with this information. "As the group's treasurer, I don't know if I should also be your gimp pin-up boy. But, to be honest, I wouldn't mind showing off my new wheels on a good ramp."

Poor Hortense shook her head and pointed to Lester. "I have no idea what this young man just said."

I explained, "I think he is looking forward to being in a newspaper photo with you, Mrs. Miller, demonstrating the proper use of a ramp."

"Well, why didn't he say that?"

Barbara concluded the meeting for us. "Mrs. Miller, please remember to remind the dean that this could be a wonderful publicity opportunity for the school. I'm certain there are hundreds of prospective disabled students who would feel more welcome attending a university with such a progressive campus project. Wouldn't you agree?"

She looked across at us and nodded slowly as she digested each morsel of information. "Well I suppose it might. I'll bring this information up with the dean at our next meeting."

My goodness, Barbara was good. Such technique! I needed to work on my skills of persuasion.

IT WAS one day before I was to go home for Christmas break. I had my last final coming up, and felt exhausted. With great effort, I pulled on my clothes and made it to the dining hall for breakfast before the final serving. I had my usual morning scrambled eggs, a piece of fruit, a slice of toast and jam, and coffee. I sipped the coffee and an incredibly bitter taste slid across my tongue. I took a bite of almost-cold eggs to mask the taste of the bad coffee, and I suddenly couldn't hold anything down. A huge rush of heat spread across my forehead and I could feel the little that was in my stomach was about to come up. I raced to the bathroom in the downstairs lounge and made it into a stall just as an acidic yellow liquid, along with a bit of egg, shot up from my stomach.

Just my luck. A touch of the flu was hitting me right as I needed to complete my final exam and then make the uncomfortable trip home on the bumpy bus. The flu wasn't uncommon this time of year on campus, probably a combination of the cold weather keeping everybody indoors, students wearing themselves out studying, and eating poorly. But it was uncommon for me.

My health had always been strong and I attributed it to a good diet, a strong gene pool, and pure tenacity. But it felt like those three things were failing me at the moment. I still had over two hours before the exam. I went back to my room to lie down.

I set my alarm for an hour later and dropped into an exhausted sleep. When I woke up, I felt stronger and made it through the exam. By four in the afternoon, the same symptoms came back. Later, as Barb came into our room, I explained that she might want to bunk with another friend tonight, so she didn't catch what I had.

"Good idea, Sarah. I'd hate to ride home with Jacob and get him sick too. So when did you start feeling bad?"

I described this morning's symptoms and then explained that another bout of nausea had just come up unexpectedly.

She looked at me earnestly and said, "If I didn't know you better, I would say it sounds like morning sickness. But I guess that's not possible, right?"

I looked at her in shock. The pregnancy idea had never occurred to me, plus Beckham had used condoms often during my most fertile times. We'd been fairly careful. He complained about using them and their cost, but felt it was important to be cautious.

I shook my head and told Barb, "No. Absolutely not possible. Hopefully, it's just a passing virus. I bet I'll be down for the day and will pop back to normal tomorrow."

"Well, if it's all the same to you, I'll bunk with Susie down the hall. Her roomy left for home last night. Jacob and I are heading out in the morning after his last final. I'll check in with you later. Get some rest." She grabbed her packed suitcase and toiletries and went down the hall.

I was taking the seven AM bus in the morning. I hoped I'd be up and feeling better for the long ride tomorrow. When I woke, my stomach felt stable and I was relieved. As a precaution, I put four handkerchiefs in my satchel. The dining hall wasn't open when I left, but I bought some crackers and juice at the station. I ate just a bit, hoping to keep my nausea at bay. As the bus pulled out onto the street, my stomach lurched and I yanked out a kerchief and held it to my mouth. I could tell, this was going to be a rough trip.

My mind went immediately to Barbara's comments. Could I be pregnant? Had I been too careless? Hopefully, this was only a touch of the flu, but what did I think about the idea of having a child? I honestly wasn't opposed to having children but I saw absolutely no upside at this stage in my life. It would compromise all of my plans. It would delay or possibly derail school for the time being. There were no pregnant women on campus, at least none that I was aware of. There must have been many from time to time, but they seemed to conveniently disappear. I'd never thought much about that before. What would Beckham think? Would he be happy? Was he ready for a family? And what would my parents think? Sensible, stable, clever Sarah, now possibly pregnant? Not a smart move.

The questions were exhausting. I placed my hot forehead against the cold and damp windowpane of the bus and closed my eyes to the passing empty fields. It was probably only the flu.

CHAPTER 37

THE GIRL THAT CAIN'T SAY NO

JO-JO

*F*ran Jordan sent a bellhop up to my room with a message asking to meet her downstairs for coffee. It was Saturday morning. I'd just finished three nights working with Slim and the Ebb Tide band and was eager to tell her how it went. She was waiting in The Dixie's Rise and Shine Cafe. I never ate there because it was twice as expensive as other breakfast joints down the block, but I was happy to join Fran there as long as she picked up the check.

Once again, she was perfectly outfitted in a navy belted suit and peaked hat with a cute little feather. I wondered if I would ever be able to afford clothing like that. In contrast, I looked like I'd been dressed from the church donation box. I was wearing a bulky hand-knit pullover and plaid pleated skirt, another leftover from my high school wardrobe.

I walked up to her table. "Morning Fran. You look great."

She looked me up and down with her cold, appraising eyes. "Wish I could say the same for you." Fran appeared to be intermittently sipping orange juice and inhaling a menthol cigarette. "Have a seat. There's a lot on my plate today. Just wanted to check in and see if you're ready for Copa rehearsals. I got a call from Monte's stage director, Lou. He wants you there Tuesday at two PM."

245

"I think I'm ready. My set list is complete and I jotted down a copy for you. I was curious about your take on it." I pulled a sheet from my bag and slid it across the table. "I practiced these with the band here at The Dixie. They offered good advice and let me sing all the numbers in front of their early crowds. It really helped my confidence."

Fran pulled up my list and looked it over. "Good idea using the band. Now let's check these song choices. *I Cain't Say No*--Hmmm, maybe? *Oh What a Beautiful Morning*--Really sappy. *Got the Sun in the Morning and the Moon at Night*--Not bad, upbeat tempo. *There's No Business Like Show Business*--Good closer. *Chattanooga Choo-Choo*-- Crowds still love that one. *The Trolley Song*--Yeah, good. *The Boy Next Door*--Slow and cloyingly annoying."

She nodded and folded the sheet to keep, "Alright. Not bad. These last two, they're not from Broadway shows though, are they?"

"No, but they're from the musical, Meet Me In Saint Louis. It's one of my favorite movies. Actually got to see that in Clear Lake a few years back. James Appleton mentioned that Mayer, at MGM, was looking to make another big musical, so I thought it might be a good idea to put those two in my show. Doubt if Mayer will ever hear about it, but you never know."

Fran looked at me and said knowingly. "I'll try to make sure he does. Clever idea. Ready for a cup of mud?"

"If you're buying, yes, and some pastry please. I'm starving."

Within minutes, I was forking into a Danish that, in my opinion, wasn't near as good as the ones from the Stage Deli, but it didn't keep me from eating every crumb while we talked. "So, I'll be picking up my dresses later today from Angie Chin. I'm excited to see how they fit."

Fran was now scanning ads in the entertainment section of the paper while listening to me. "They're good seamstresses. Should be perfect."

"Hope so. They ended up costing me forty-seven dollars."

That caught her attention as she looked up. "For three? That's actually fantastic. I've never gotten her to go that low. I'm impressed."

I smiled. Any time Fran mentioned she was pleased or impressed, it was a huge compliment. "I just asked myself, what would Fran do? I got Angie down from her original quote of seventy-five."

She laughed and touched my hand on the table. "My God. You're just a younger version of me."

My eyes opened wide as I pulled my hand back and took a big slurp of hot coffee. *The Whiplash Witch? I certainly hoped not.*

～

TUESDAY, my music file was in my bag, I'd picked up my dresses from Angie Chin, and bought a pair of gold heels and a simple day-dress from Macy's to wear for rehearsals. I had even prayed this morning for a good rehearsal, but that didn't help calm my fears.

Fran picked me up in a cab and, as moral support, agreed to attend my first Copa rehearsal. She wanted to introduce me to Shep Fields, the Copa band leader. According to Fran, Fields and his Rippling Rhythm Orchestra did not suffer fools or novices. He'd been leading different orchestras for the last twenty years and had made numerous recordings. I needed to at least act like I knew what I was doing.

Once again, we entered the Copa together through the back door and walked down to the stage where the musicians were settling in and warming up. Fran waved to Shep. He was sitting on a chair, nursing a drink in front of the band stand. He had a thick dark mustache and wore black frame glasses, looking quite professorial.

Fran reached over for a hand shake. "Shep, Fran Jordan. Great to see you again. Let me introduce you to my client, Jo-Jo Anderson. Got the voice and face of an angel and she's a ducky shincracker too."

Shep shook his head and laughed. "You agents...you never stop selling. Anyways, guess we'll find out real soon." He turned to me and said, "Yeah, I remember you from a few weeks ago. You sang with Frankie right?"

"That's right. Mr. Sinatra was kind enough to bring me on stage for a little duet. Hope I won't be as nervous this time."

"Nothing to it. Just like singing in the shower."

Fran asked, "Will Monte be in this afternoon? I wanted to get his take on the set."

Shep looked around. "Probably. He usually plays the ponies, shows around three, and then heads to the office for a nap around five." He laughed again and shrugged. "Not a bad life, huh?"

I handed Mr. Fields my music selections and while he leafed through them we heard a big commotion upstairs. It began with what sounded like pots and pans banging together, followed by intense yelling, climaxing with a kitchen worker suddenly thrown through the side stage entrance and knocking over a table and a few chairs on his way down. I immediately ran up the stairs to help him, while everyone else just stared at the loud intrusion.

" My goodness. Are you alright?" The young man had a big red mark on his face where it looked like he'd been punched but he seemed able to stand as I gave him my hand.

He nodded, rubbed the back of his head, and spoke in a thick Italian accent. "I'm OK. No worry. Grazie, grazie. I go now."

"But, what happened?"

He raised his hands in front of his face, speaking softly.. "I make a little mistake. I go now."

The door swung open wide behind us, and a menacing looking pitbull of a man in a dark suit and a chrome-dome looked down at us. "You still here? I told you to get the hell out! Now."

The poor guy was shaking in fear as he limped behind the man and scurried away.

Then the tough guy looked at me, made a difficult attempt at a smile on his red, beefy face and came toward me. "Hey, you're The Deli Girl, right? Welcome to the Copa, Miss Anderson. Jules Podell, manager." He reached out his hand and I reluctantly reached forward and shook his. "Sorry for that little dust-up. Can't take any more thieving assholes. I look forward to hearing your set."

"Uh, thank you? I thought Monte Proser ran the Copa."

"Yeah, kind of a team effort. He does entertainment. I run all the receipts for the kitchen and bar. Hey, have a good rehearsal, Miss Anderson."

As soon as he left, I heard murmurings among the band members. I walked over to Shep and asked, "Does that happen often?"

The band leader looked a little shaken. He cleared his throat and said, "Uh, the guy keeps a tight ship. Let's just say Podell runs a little hot and we'll leave it at that." Then he turned his attention to the band. "OK boys, let's get started. Miss Jo-Jo Anderson has some Broadway melodies for us this afternoon. We'll do a run through and then get the dancers out here around three-thirty or four."

Dancers? I'd forgotten all about doing some dance steps. Wasn't sure if my mouth and feet still worked together at the same time. After the first hour of rehearsal, it was clear that Shep and the Rippling Rhythms were total pros. I'd offer a slight suggestion of how I wanted a certain song to go and within a few minutes the band would work it out, follow Shep's lead, and have it down perfectly.

Eventually, the band took a smoke break and eight Copa girls wandered out in rehearsal shorts and fitted cropped sweaters. One of the lead dancers, Jeanne, was also their choreographer. She explained to me that most of the girls could also do a little background singing if I needed that. I gave her a list of my tunes and she and I decided which ones might work best with some dance and singing accompaniment.

Jeanne quickly came up with some great ideas to incorporate with *The Trolley Song* and also for the *Sun in the Morning and Moon at Night*. She improvised some simple steps, with the lineup of dancers in a row behind me bobbing up and down as if on a street car. I loved the idea and so did Fran.

Then Monte Proser walked in. I couldn't help but notice him in his dapper duds. Although a small, older man, he had a noticeable presence. Carrying a drink from the bar, he was wearing a beautiful checked sports jacket, a red pocket square, black trousers, and black and white wingtips.

"So, Fran, how's our Deli Girl doing so far?"

Fran looked up from her table. "Terrific. She came up with a nice song selection and Shep's been doing a good job keeping her sound unique with his arrangements."

Monte continued to stand near the edge of the stage. He was slurring slightly. Could it be that Mr. Proser was drunk at three in the afternoon?

"Terrific, let's get a run through. Where's the damn orchestra?"

Jeanne looked up and said, "They'll be back in ten. We're still working on dance steps."

Monte pointed at me. "So I hear Jo's a good tap dancer. Jeanne, help her pick a song to tap to."

Fran called out, "I don't know if Jo-Jo's worked out any steps yet. But by tomorrow she'll have something."

Poser grabbed the chair next to Fran. "No. You told me before. She's a great tapper and I want to see her sing and tap." He called out to me, "Jo-Jo, you bring your tap shoes?"

"No sir. Not today. I'll bring them tomorrow."

"Yeah, you do that. Get yourself a drink and get ready to sing. I gotta see what I'm paying for. I'm running ads on this thing next week and I expect you to deliver."

"Absolutely, Mr. Proser."

Fran stood up from the table. "I'll get drinks, Jo. What do you want?"

"Just water with lemon please. Thanks."

Proser then handed Fran a ten-spot. "Come on, get yourself a real drink on me. It's almost four o'clock, you're allowed. Sit down and drink with me."

I walked over, smiled, and sat down, feeling like I was walking on cracking ice and about to fall through. "OK Fran, I'll take a glass of red wine, but with water on the side, please."

The Copa girls ignored Monte and kept practicing Jeanne's dance steps.

"So Jo-Jo, let's see your line up." I handed him the list and he glanced at it, nodded and said, "Yeah, good. Big hits. I like that. The crowd here always loves hearing the familiar tunes. Stuff they can relate to, you know?"

"Yes. That's what I was hoping for. I'm really excited about this opportunity, Mr. Proser."

"Yeah, you should be. Every singer and comic in the country wants a crack at the Copa. And here you are…just a kid. You got chutzpah, Deli-Girl. Oh yeah, that reminds me. I want you to open wearing that Stage Deli uniform, the hat, the tray, everything. It's cute; it's your shtick."

"Yeah…But I don't work there anymore."

"Don't worry. I know your old boss, Max Asnas. A real cheap-skate. He'll love the free publicity."

"But I just bought a really gorgeous cocktail dress. Remember, you told me not to look so wholesome."

"You're right. I did say that. Hmm." He looked up at the ceiling for about thirty seconds and then snapped his fingers. "I got it. I see it all very clearly." He yelled out to the dancers on the stage. "Hey, girls. We still got that folding screen somewhere in the back?"

Jeanne responded, "Yeah, it's in our dressing room. With all you guys tramping through there, it's the only way we can change sometimes."

"Good. Have one of the kitchen guys bring it to the stage now." Then he turned back to me. "OK, so here's my idea, Jo-Jo." He was pointing to locations on the stage, as if he was already seeing me there. "You're gonna tap dance out on stage in your uniform with a platter full of bagels. Maybe we have the Copa girls follow along behind you, tapping away. Then, you wander through the front tables, asking men in the audience who wants some hot, soft buns. You'll toss them all out to people, while flirting with the men, then you go back to center stage and talk about how you're from No-where Iowa, having a tough time making your way in Manhattan."

"Well, you're right about that, Mr. Proser."

"Yeah, but then you tell the audience your deli days are over and it's time for a change. So, you step behind the screen, and the Copa girls will help cover up your backside, as you quickly change and step back out in the sexy cocktail dress."

"Interesting?" I said with some hesitancy.

"Then, you're gonna go up to the mic on the edge of the stage and sing that first song, *I Cain't Say No*. The audience will go wild. I guarantee it."

I wasn't quite sure how to respond. I nodded with a frozen smile. "Well, that's different. You think it's a good idea Mr. Proser?"

"Hell yes, it's a *great* idea! That's why I do this for a living. I've been creating and promoting acts since way before you were born." The band members started filing in from break, and Monte yelled out, "Shep, get the band in their seats quick. I need to hear The Deli-Girl sing all her numbers. Come on, time's money, Shep."

I stood up from the table as Fran came downstairs from the lounge with my wine. I took a few sips as the band quickly filed in. It was now my time to shine, but I was suddenly feeling hot and flushed. Here I was, wanting to impress the man who'd seen and heard everybody who's anybody in the business. Who was I kidding? Why did I think I could do this?

I took several more sips. The wine began to calm my anxiety, but Shep had to start my first song three times before my vocals melded into the melody smoothly. By the end of the song list, some-how, I was able to sell Monte on the act. His tone turned a touch more sympathetic. Hopefully, he was starting to see more promise. Monte suggested I rehearse at least three more times with the band before my opening gig. I think he sensed I had a bad case of self doubt. If he was willing to give me extra days of rehearsal time, I was certainly going to take it.

After meeting the menacing Jules Podel who managed the back-end of the Copa, I felt slightly more at ease with the boozy but professional Monte Proser running the front end. After my final run-through on Thursday, Monte called me over to his table, put his arm around me and said, "Kid, you're gonna knock 'em dead tomorrow night. The lights will be on you. Don't worry about all the big shots that might be out in the audience. They're coming to drink, eat, dance, and impress somebody they brought with 'em. You're just icing on the cake."

"Got it, Mr. Proser. Like singing in the shower, right? That's what Shep told me."

"Sure. Except keep your clothes on and bring the energy.

Remember, the more people talk about the show, the more others will come. The bigger the crowd, the more I pay you next week. Got it?"

"Absolutely."

He took another gulp of his Scotch and motioned upstairs, to the bartender, for another. "Did I ever tell you, years ago I managed Texas Guinan, Queen of the Speakeasies."

"No sir, sorry I'm not familiar with the name."

He appeared lost in his memories. "Another time, another era. Anyways, she wasn't the prettiest, or the best dancer, not even the best singer. But she had charisma, you know? A big, ballsy blonde. The bar crowd always came to every club she opened, just waiting to see what crazy shit she'd do next. Her opening line each night was, "Hello suckers!"

I laughed. "Not really my style, but I understand what you're saying. I need to find something unique about me and work it. Something special."

"Exactly. Go home now. Rest up. You gotta show up tomorrow by seven. First show's at eight. You'll come on after the comic and dancers. Keep the spark and enthusiasm up. You got four shows to do each night. It's the major leagues now."

CHAPTER 38
IT'S SHOWTIME, FOLKS!
JO-JO

I didn't sleep a wink Thursday night. My brain continued to go through every lyric, each dance step, even the rehearsed winks and nods. But I woke up with energy, fueled by fear and adrenaline. I went to the Stage Deli Friday morning to eat a good breakfast and say hi to the gang. I was also supposed to pick up extra paper hats and aprons for the Copa dancers for a little number we'd worked out for the opening.

Walking in, Max Asnas immediately dropped his phone and greeted me, "Hey Jo-Jo, appreciate the free buzz! We're sending the bagels and Danish over daily around four. And kid, whatever you want on the menu today, it's on the house."

"Thank's Max. Appreciate that." I smiled at his generosity and stepped into the back and greeted the dishwasher and baker. At the grill, while giving Chuckles a hug, I whispered, "I'll put your name on the list for tonight's eight o'clock show if you can make it."

He looked up from his sizzling liver and onions and thought about it. "Guess I'd have to wear a suit, huh?"

"Yeah, probably so."

"For you, I'll pull mine out of mothballs and try to show up. Last time I had it on was for a funeral. Uh, can I bring a lady friend?"

"Of course. Who's the lucky girl?"

"Marina, from the corner market. I buy a paper from her every morning. Now I got an excuse to ask her out."

"Glad I could help. Oh, by the way, Chuckles, I'd let that suit air out for several hours if you want Marina sitting anywhere near you."

"Smart, thanks Jo-Jo."

I stuffed myself with bacon, eggs, fruit, and pancakes, knowing this would probably be my only meal, unless I could scrounge a few egg rolls from the kitchen.

I took my time bathing, got my hair and nails done, went over my sheet music and lyrics a hundred more times, put my garments in a carry bag and took a cab to the club. I hated spending money on that, but I thought it might look cheap if the Copacabana headliner was riding the subway to her gig.

I walked in through the back and hung my clothing and makeup bag in the dancers' dressing room. Headliners had their own dressing room but Joe E. Lewis, a well known comic, was already set up there. I felt more comfortable with the Copa Girls anyway. I walked into their noisy mayhem, stepping over street clothes and coats dropped on the floor, and passed by three rolling racks of costumes. There was makeup and hair rollers strewn on top of the vanities with mirrors, and three of the girls had received large vases of flower arrangements from admirers.

The conversation seemed to bounce around the topic of men: current boyfriends, guys from the audience who'd sent flowers, a big spender who Jeanne hoped was taking her out for a decent meal, and talk of a potential Hollywood producer who was scouting the Copa Girls. Amongst the squeal of conversation, I heard someone call out my name.

One of the security guys was at the door, eager to ogle the dancers in mid-dress, although they seemed oblivious to his stares. "Jo-Jo Anderson! These just came for you. Appears you got a fan already." He was holding an arrangement of tall red roses.

I was surprised that anybody would send me flowers. Maybe my parents or Chuckles? But no…neither would ever spring for that kind of expense. I took the vase, curious to read the card.

I'm coming to the ten o'clock show. After your performance, I'd love to take you to dinner and watch you eat.

Your Chicago Dog advisor

Justin Winkleman, Attorney at Law.

The card made me laugh, remembering the outspoken man from the Chicago train station. I thought to myself, why not? He might be interesting.

Today, I'd bought my first set of false eyelashes from the drug store and asked Hester, one of the dancers, to put them on me. She was the one who suggested I try them. As Hester leaned over me with glue and tweezers, she said, "Jo-Jo, you're going to flip when you see how great you look in these. By the way, us dancers always treat the new kids to our favorite drink, Vin Mariani. You gotta try it. Most nights workin', the seven of us go through at least three or four bottles of the stuff. You'll love it."

She poured me a tall stemmed glass of the deep red liquid and the other girls crowded around, with their glasses held high. In unison, with big smiles, my new girlfriends clinked glasses together and shouted, "To Jo-Jo!"

I took a sip, licked my lips, and stared into the mirror at the pale face with thick black lashes, rosy cheeks, and bright red lips looking back. "Hester, I love the lashes and this wine. Thank you! But doesn't drinking red wine all night make you groggy and clumsy?"

"Usually, but not this stuff. It's from Paris, France! Podell gets it in for us under the table. Apparently, it's illegal in the States, but It's good red wine with cocaine added to the blend. That's what makes you feel real zippy. Amazing stuff."

"Hmm, I have no idea what that is, but I like the idea. Wine for my nerves and cocaine for my energy. Sounds like a winning combination!"

"I guarantee you'll love it."

I changed into my deli uniform and Jeanne generously offered me the use of her heated rollers while I touched up my hair. I added the paper hat for the finishing touch, then I leaned back, tried to relax, and sip my drink. Soon the stage director, referred to as Lookie Lou by the dancers, stuck his head in the door and yelled, "Copa Girls, all asses on stage immediately."

Over the clamor, Jeanne yelled back, "Lou, a little respect, please!"

"Hey, I respect you just fine. I respect those long legs of yours, I respect those short skirts you wear…"

Jeanne interrupted his irritating banter, "Yeah, yeah, Lou. Girls, hustle up. On stage now!"

In the quiet of the empty dressing room, I suddenly realized I was calm but excited in a good way. I'd worked extremely hard for this night and I wanted it to be perfect. I turned the radio on and restudied the lyrics of the little song I'd come up with to sing while I passed out the pastries. I placed all the baked goods sent by the Stage Deli onto my platter. I closed my eyes and took deep calming breaths. Finally, Lookie Lou knocked and asked, "Jo-Jo, you're up. You ready?"

"Absolutely!"

"Great, that's what I want to hear. OK, we've got the aprons and hats for the dancers, I need your dress and heels for the change-out. Let's go."

I followed him down the back hallway, inhaling the strong scent of chop suey and garlic. The dancers had just come off the stage and were taking off their ruffled skirts, and tying the short deli aprons around their black leotards.

I waved while passing the line of Copa Girls, keeping my ear to the orchestra leader as he announced, "Ladies and gentleman! A special treat for you tonight. You know her, you love her. It's Manhattan's own special Deli-Girl, Miss Jo-Jo Anderson!"

To my great relief, I heard loud applause and whistles. I was on cloud nine. Wearing my black shiny tap shoes, I shuffled, balled, and heeled myself out to center stage with a full platter in one hand, my other hand on my hip, and a giant smile across my face. At the mic stand, I sang to the beat of a snare drum:

It's your favorite Deli-Girl with treats for you.
Do you want something sweet? Sure you do.

I have bagels, Danish, got some hot buns too.

Just wave and wink when you see me coming through.

As I wrapped up the ditty, the Copa girls tapped on stage behind me and kept chanting the line: *"She's got bagels, Danish, and hot buns too! She's got bagels, Danish, and hot buns too!"* while I was weaving through the audience, handing out baked goods. People called out as I smiled and waved. I didn't know if it was me, the free food, or the dancers, but the audience seemed happy.

My platter quickly emptied and I came back and sat on the edge of a stool placed on stage in front of the mic, just as Monte had envisioned it the other day.

"Not sure if many of you know my story, but I'm a farm girl, grew up in the small town of Green Tree, Iowa. It's quite a lovely little village, but I always had the urge to be in show business. Somehow, I knew one day I'd make my way to the Big Apple. I gotta tell you folks, it's been pretty tough. I've worked for months now at the wonderful Stage Deli over by Carnegie Hall. But I finally got a big break and now I'm performing at the Copacabana. Can you believe it! So here I am and I've decided tonight, maybe it's time I change my image."

I stood up and walked over to the side of the changing screen. "What do you guys think? Why don't I change into something more...I don't know...something more New York?" At that second, the drum and horn section began playing a vaudeville style strip-tease beat while I went behind the screen. With the dancers' help, I quickly stepped out of my deli dress and tap shoes and into my gold heels and the bright-blue strapless, cocktail dress with matching elbow-length gloves, courtesy of Angie Chen.

I stepped out from the screen, raised my arms and asked, "So, what do you think?" Loud whistles and applause followed as I walked back to the mic and did my own special rendition of *I Cain't Say No.*

It worked! Monte Proser, sober or drunk, knew what the hell he was talking about. With the excellent help of a fabulous band and the gorgeous Copa Girls, I sailed through my next six songs and had so much fun doing it that I hated to stop. But then I reminded myself, I had to repeat the show three more times tonight. No need for an encore now.

The crowd really seemed to love *The Trolley Song* and of course, the show stopper, *Chattanooga Choo-Choo*, although reception to *The Boy Next Door* seemed tepid. Fran had been right about that, dammit. At one point while on stage, I'd noticed Chuckles sitting at a small table with his gal, Marina. After the final applause, I came back down the stairs and surprised him with a greeting. "Chuckles, so glad you made it." I couldn't help but notice the whiff of mothballs permeating my hug. "Thanks for coming and for everything else you did for me." He introduced me to his date who seemed sweet. "So, what did you two think of the show?"

Chuckles grabbed my hand and said, "Best night of my life. Can't believe I'm here. To think, Joe E Lewis was right there in front of me. And wow, those beautiful Copa Girls, and then *you*, Jo-Jo, topping off the night. Doll, I got no words on how good you were. I'll have to tell Max all about it. He'll be thrilled."

It was great seeing him so happy, but I was ready to get back to the dressing room, cool down a little, and have another glass of Vin Mariani. The band was on a break and the waiters were busy taking orders while I headed to the employees' bathrooms down the hall from the kitchen. I knocked before entering and I heard a female voice call out, "Hold your horses, why don't you?"

As I stood waiting, I couldn't help but overhear a shouting match coming from the kitchen area. I wandered over a little closer to catch the excitement. It was Podell again, yelling at a bartender I recognized.

"And if I ever catch you giving away long pours or comping customers at the bar, I'll throw you outta here on your head and it won't be pretty."

The older bartender spoke up. "Jules, I been here since the place opened and Monte wants certain people comped. He demands it."

"Yeah, well Monte ain't running the bar. I do. And if he wants to hear from Frank Costello about this, then so be it. But you do what I say, or you're out!"

I sighed and shook my head. Just more problems between the

two bosses, making it tough on everyone. After another minute, the bathroom door opened and a shapely cigarette girl and the band's sax player came out together, brushing white chalky smudges off their noses. The sax player looked over and said, "All yours, Deli-Girl."

After the ten o'clock show, I spotted attorney Justin Winkleman, who stood up and waved as I was taking my final bow. After I left the stage, I came back down and greeted him. "Mr. Winkleman, your roses were gorgeous. Thank you! So, were you still interested in watching me eat?"

He nodded, saying, "I might even join you. I've heard the Scotch and water diet is unsustainable. What are you in the mood for?"

"Anything but egg rolls. We can go elsewhere but I'll need to be back a little past midnight."

He stood up and put on his suit jacket. "I noticed a bar and bistro a few blocks down. Why don't you grab your coat and we'll tap dance over."

"So, you're a dancing lawyer? Didn't take you for a hoofer."

"I do have a few moves, but unfortunately tapping isn't one of them."

"And here I thought I'd found the perfect partner. How about I meet you by the front door in five?"

I still had my one and only wool coat and knew it would look hideous over my satin cocktail dress. Going into the dressing room, I noticed several fur stoles on the costume rack. Most of the girls were out on the floor drinking with patrons, but Jeanne was still there touching up her makeup.

"Hey, Jeanne, I've got a date for dinner. Any chance I can wear one of these stoles over my dress for about an hour?"

Holding a hand over her eyes, she laughed. "I never saw anything. Just don't let anybody else notice. Monte insisted on buying real mink and *nobody* is allowed to take home the costumes."

"Got it. I'll carry it under my arm until I get out."

Walking up to the front door, I now felt like a thief and hoped the door man would take no notice of the fur. Justin was waiting by the entrance. The door man opened the heavy double doors, while I offered a big smile and winked. "See you back in an hour or so, Dutch."

"Sure. See ya' Deli-Girl."

The bistro was the perfect place. Dark and quiet, with each table lit by a candle in a reflecting glass holder. The menu offered simple sandwiches and drinks. I ordered a roast beef on rye and a glass of water, while Winkleman ordered soup and another Scotch.

"I'd join you for a drink but I've been tossing back Vin Mariani since seven o'clock and I need to clear my head for the midnight show."

"Ahh, that explains your energy. I gotta say, you were high octane on stage tonight. Very impressive for your first official gig. But watch it on the Mariani. You know that stuff has been banned for a while now?"

"One of the dancers mentioned that but she claims it's harmless. Keeps everybody's energy up. Apparently the guy running the bar gets it in for the band and entertainment."

"Yeah, I'd be careful with that."

We clinked glasses and Winkleman said, "To your success. I'm happy for you."

"Thanks; I appreciate you coming to the show. So, when do you head back?"

"Oh, I live here. I grew up in Chicago but went to law school here. Been in Manhattan for about eight years now."

"Fantastic. Well to new friends then. Cheers!"

An hour later, Justin and I said our goodbyes outside the Copa, and forgetting Jeanne's warning, I waltzed through the doors hugging the mink across my shoulders. It felt so luxurious. As I passed down the employee's hallway, Lookie Lou, gave me a second look and then stopped.

"Hey, isn't that one of the Copa-Girls' stoles? Did you leave the club with that on?"

"I'm certainly not stealing it, if that's what you're asking. I had to step out and clear my head for a bit. It's cold outside. Sorry, guess I should have asked."

"Yeah, you should have and the answer would have been no. Absolutely, no costumes leave the premises. Now I gotta report this to Mr. Proser."

"Why? I'm putting it up right now."

"Rules is rules." Then he leaned toward me and lowered his voice. "Unless, you wanna do me a special favor later. If you do, the mention of this theft will be sealed in the vault."

I was confused and then my eyes opened wide at his lizard-like face. "Are you saying what I think you're saying?"

The creep nodded, "I think you're catching my drift." He pointed behind him. "This bathroom…after the final show."

I refused to answer and continued to push past him to the dressing room. "I have a show to do." I slammed the door in his face. My heart was beating so fast I couldn't think. The dressing room was full again and the cacophony of womens' voices seemed even louder. I quickly hung the mink stole back with the others. Staring at my hot and angry face in the mirror, I thought about my career ending before it really began. There was no way I was having sex with Lookie Lou. I replaced my red lipstick, powdered my face, and made a quick decision.

The midnight show would start in ten minutes. I walked down the hallway and peeked out, looking up to the lounge, searching for Monte. He was there clapping some guy on the back, in the midst of a lively conversation.

I waited a minute and then approached him, waiting for a lull in their discussion. "Mr. Proser…so sorry to interrupt, but may I have a quick word with you?"

"Sure kid. Gentlemen, this is my new little discovery, Jo-Jo Anderson. Isn't she cute?" I shook hands with a small circle of men and then the two of us stepped away from the group.

"I apologize for coming to you with this, but I wanted to tell you something stupid I did earlier. A friend of mine invited me for dinner after my ten o'clock show. It was so cold outside, so I borrowed one of the fur stoles on the costume rack. I had no idea it was real, but anyway, when I returned, I found out no one is allowed to remove costumes from the premises. I only borrowed it for forty minutes or so but I wanted you to know. I promise I'll never touch anything again."

"Hey, I appreciate the honesty. You're right. Those stoles are the real deal. Monte Proser doesn't skimp on the cheap stuff. I guess you can understand why I can't have anyone even borrowing the costumes. Right?"

"Yes sir. I'm very sorry."

Monte looked to be considering my admission of guilt and didn't seem all that upset about it. "Alright. I trust you. Besides, Dutch, the doorman, already told me about it when you walked back in." Then he laughed. "Stick with me kid, and you might end up owning a mink of your own some day."

CHAPTER THIRTY NINE
Holiday Surprises
Sarah

As THE BUS RIDE PROGRESSED, my nausea eventually subsided and I convinced myself it was only a passing virus. Nothing to be concerned with. The Greyhound finally pulled into Gottlieb's station and I saw my stepdad, David, waiting to pick me up.

He gave me a warm hug, put my case in the back of his truck and wished me a Merry Christmas. "Glad to have you back, Sarah." Once we were rolling down Main Street he said, "Your mom has a little surprise waiting when you get home, but I'll let her tell you all about it."

"That sounds mysterious. Let me guess…The Luthern church finally bought a new nativity set."

"Not even close."

"Uh, the VFW hall just put in a jukebox."

David looked at me with mild exasperation. "Just be patient, Sarah."

"That reminds me. I have a little money to spend on Christmas gifts. Any suggestions for Mom and Sammy?"

"Hmm, Mariah's slippers are looking pretty shabby but she won't give them up, calls them her *old friends*. As far as Sammy goes, he's already getting a new bicycle and a few other things. Keep your money. I know you've been working hard for it."

"I like the slipper idea. Thanks"

When we walked in, Mom was in the middle of making dinner. She turned and held one arm out to me while holding her mixing spoon in the air. "Hooray, the bus must have been right on time." She hugged me tight and then released me with a kiss. It felt so comforting to be home. "David, take Sarah's case upstairs please." Then she turned to me and asked, "Just wash up and help me set the table. We're having one of your favorites, pork chops."

There were two farm hands I knew well, who joined us for dinner. As the six of us said grace and passed around the platters of chops, potatoes, and vegetables, I asked, "So Mom, David says you have a surprise to tell me."

Mom looked at David and shook her head, laughing. "For someone who's a man of few words, you let that slip out pretty quickly. Well, I have *two* surprises, one of which I'll share with you later. But the big one is that I decided you and I are going to Manhattan to see Jo-Jo! She can't come home because of the Copa engagement. So...I decided that the two of us should go and have a high time in the Big Apple."

I gave a little whoop of excitement. "I certainly wasn't expecting that. That's exciting!"

"We're getting a room at Jo-Jo's hotel. The city should be fun this time of year. Imagine the wonderful decorations in all those big stores. And, of course, we'll go see the show at the Copa. For once in my life I'm going to splurge."

Jo-Jo and I hadn't talked or written since our Thanksgiving dust-up, but hopefully, all would be forgiven when the two of us arrived. Our family had planned to go a few months after Jo first left for New York, but we could never align our schedules. This news was all incredibly surprising.

"That sounds wonderful. But what about David and Sammy?"

David shook his head, saying, "Can't think of anything I'd

rather *not* do. Fight Christmas crowds and dress up for some fancy-shmancy night club." The two field hands grunted in agreement and continued eating. "You girls go. Sammy and I will hold down the fort." David put his arm around Mom's shoulder and gave her a squeeze. "You deserve it, Mariah. You've been wanting to go to Manhattan for years now, way before Jo-Jo ever went. Business has been good. It's your time. Go have fun."

Then Sammy yelled out. "No fair! I want to have fun too."

David looked at Sammy and said, "Guess I'll have to find another little boy to drive my tractor down the drive."

"No! That's my job, Dad."

"Then you better stick around here, son."

I watched my mom and stepdad look lovingly towards each other and felt so lucky to have them as parents. "So, when do we go?"

Mom passed the dinner rolls, with their crusty tops shining with golden butter. "I got a hold of Jo-Jo yesterday and she reserved us a room for four days, starting the day after Christmas. So, we'll leave Christmas day. David picked up our train tickets this afternoon."

"Wow, what a wonderful gift! Thanks so much."

Later that night, once I was in bed, Mom came in with her other news. My light was still on as I tried to get ahead on next semester's required reading for English lit.

"Still awake and reading a textbook, no less. Sarah, this is your break time."

"I know…but between tutoring, lab work, the volunteer group, and other stuff, it seems like I never have enough time." I closed my book and looked up expectantly. "So, what's the other news? You sold another house?"

Mother sat down at my bedside and took a deep breath. "No, I can't believe I'm saying this but…David and I just found out that I am three months pregnant."

"What!"

"I know, I'm not as energetic as I was at eighteen, but I'm still healthy and strong, and, honestly, we're so much better prepared now. And come to think of it, your grandmother had Arlene at thirty-nine and everything turned out fine."

"My goodness! I'm so happy for you both." I reached over and hugged her as I fought back a few tears. I wasn't sure what to think. I suddenly felt incredibly emotional. Once again the dynamics of our family would change.

Mother looked relieved telling me her news. "Thanks, I'm just grasping the idea myself. Can't believe it's happening, and for now, we're only telling family, so keep it to yourself. But I have to say, David seems really excited. He's hoping for another boy, so Sammy will have a playmate and someone he can boss around."

I laughed, wiping away my tears. "Sammy already bosses everyone around and has David wrapped around his little finger."

"You're right about that. Well, that's all the surprises I have for you today. I'm so glad you're home, darling. I'll say good night now. You know how early the mornings come around here."

"Yes, no need to remind me. Love you, Mom, and congratulations. Really, it's totally unexpected, but wonderful news."

I turned off my light with thoughts about the unique and strange possibility of mother and me being pregnant at the same time. What a contrast we were. She was overjoyed, but the mere possibility of a pregnancy filled me with dread. Worries and doubts continued to swirl through my head until I finally fell into a twisted sleep.

A FEW DAYS later we were on the train to New York enjoying ourselves. Mom and I played endless games of gin rummy and when we tired of that she napped and I stared out at the passing bleak but beautiful rural scenes. We both enjoyed pleasant meals in the formal dining car and felt rather posh sitting at the white linen-covered tables complete with small vases of flowers. But that night, my sleep was restless in our reclining chairs. The following morning I felt motion sickness as I stood up and stretched, but seemed to feel better after I forced myself to throw up in the restroom.

We eventually pulled into Penn Station, the most enormous train station I could imagine. After numerous stairs and tunnels, twists and turns, following signs and exit arrows, we spotted Jo-Jo leaning against the wall near the main exit, looking disheveled, chewing her nails. Her blonde hair was rolled up in twin large coils on the top of her head and the back was twisted and pinned up.

She ran up to us with hugs, kissing Mom first. "I can't believe you both have come. This is so wonderful!" Then she looked at me, keeping her distance. "So, have you forgiven me, Sarah? For hogging the limelight? You know darn well, I just can't help myself."

I gave a sheepish grin. "Yeah, I was being silly. I've known for years you're a glutton for attention. Why else would you be wearing two sausage rolls on the top of your head?"

"Jo-Jo laughed and did a quick modeling pose. "Ladies, I promise you, this is the latest style. I can't wait to take you both to a nice salon. We're going to get the works: hair, makeup, nails. You'll love it!"

I backed off with a nervous giggle. "No one's cutting my hair. I know someone who appreciates it long and wavy."

Mom added, "I'm not saying absolutely no, but I've had the same hairstyle for the last twenty years and I think it has served me well."

"That's the point, Mom. Change is good. I thought we could enjoy a little champagne brunch to kick the day off. What do you say?"

Mother looked at her watch. "Drinking champagne at ten-thirty in the morning? Is that what New Yorkers do?"

"On their day off, after working twenty shows, five days straight...yes! That's what we do. Now come on, girls. We're on holiday!"

Mother looked at Jo-Jo warily and said, "Well, you're in charge, dear. We'll follow your lead."

Jo picked up Mom's suitcase and turned to leave the station. "By the way, I have good news. Monte, the club owner, just gave me a raise, so I decided that we're going to the swankiest place in town, The Plaza Hotel. I've heard so many customers mention it. But first, let's drop the bags and I'll let you two freshen up. Can you both handle a half-mile walk?"

Mom snorted. "Jo, you know I do that every single day just going to the mailbox. I'm not ready for the rocker yet."

We meandered through the heavy pedestrian traffic on the broad sidewalks and then dashed between the non-stop yellow cabs in the crosswalks. Of course, I'd looked at numerous photos of Manhattan, but seeing it in full color, with all the sounds and smells, surrounded by the three dimensional height and architectural grandeur…well, let's just say it was overwhelming.

The Dixie was impressive too. I was surprised at how large it was and Jo appeared to know everybody that worked there. She briefly stopped to chat and introduced us to her hotel friends as we made our way across the lobby to the elevator. Our room was fairly basic, but we did have our own tub, telephone, and radio. As Mom quickly bathed, Jo and I returned to the lobby and caught up, sitting comfortably on upholstered, floral-print armchairs. As we chatted, a nice looking young desk clerk wearing glasses caught my eye as he leaned over and greeted Jo.

"Leonard, let me introduce you to my twin sister. She and my Mom have finally come to visit. This is Sarah."

"Miss Sarah, I have to say you look nothing like your twin, but yet you're still as beautiful. Enjoy your stay."

"Thanks Leonard." I was really beginning to like this town. "So Jo, tell me about your raise. What changed at the Copa?"

"Well, like I said, the gig was originally just for two weeks. But according to Fran, Monte has been pleased with the crowd I've been bringing in as the headliner, so now he wants me to hang around longer as the primary singer with the Copa orchestra. Says I'm bringing in a new, younger audience."

"That's impressive. But what about that guy from MGM? Seems like you were pretty interested in doing a screen test for them."

She leaned over and spoke more softly. "Yeah, Appleton hasn't contacted me yet. But Fran negotiated with Monte and he boosted me to a hundred-and-fifty a week if I stayed for a while."

I opened my mouth in surprise. That was a lot of money for a young woman. "My goodness! So how do you feel about it?"

"Fran thinks it's a good idea to stay. Says I'll be getting excellent exposure at the Copa. Although, I gotta say, these afternoon rehearsals, coupled with four performances each night, make any kind of normal life incredibly tough. I feel like there's no time for anything else. I'm either working or sleeping. These last few weeks I've felt so tired."

"I believe it. I noticed you looked a bit down at the train station. I've never seen you with dark circles around your eyes before."

"What? What are you talking about?" She pulled out a small hand mirror from her handbag and gave herself a close look. "Jeepers creepers! You're right. I look like someone in one of those horror movies. I really need to get better sleep, and just yesterday I took an energy shot."

I raised my eyebrows. "And what is an energy shot?"

"Don't look so worried. Several people at the club get them once or twice a week. They're administered by a doctor who Monte recommended. Apparently, they're loaded with all kinds of vitamins. Especially vitamin B, I think. They really seem to help. Yesterday I was feeling so up and energetic, although for some reason, not as good today. I think I'll get another one when Dr. Max comes by later this week."

I was concerned. "Jo, be careful. I've never heard of anything like that. You need to ask exactly what's in the shot and let me know. I can look up stuff like that at school if you like."

Jo waved away my alarm. "You're always such a worrier. Even Monte's wife takes the shots, along with some of the dancers and band members. They just help us make it through the late night shows. The doctor himself said he saw them give amazing benefits to soldiers during the war. That's when he first began administering them. Trust me, I'm more than fine." Then she looked at her face again in her mirror and started powdering around her eyes. "Oh, Sarah, remember....don't bring up anything about Fran when Mom is around."

Seconds later, Mother tapped me on the shoulder. "Your turn

Sarah. The bath did wonders for me. So, what are you two whispering about?"

I turned to look up at her, feeling guilty about keeping secrets. "Oh just night club gossip. Jo will catch you up. I'll be quick." I stood up to go to the room and said, "Oh, by the way, Mom has some big news to share with you, Jo."

Within the hour, the three of us were walking into the lobby of The Plaza, heading to the Oak Room for Champagne brunch. I was trying not to gawk and let my jaw drop as we walked through the opulent hotel oozing with elegant chandeliers, richly carved dark wood paneling, intriguing old paintings in heavy gold frames, and beautiful groupings of furniture in textured art deco designs. Mother seemed to be playing everything down, but I'm sure she was dying to point out details of every decorative furnishing we passed. We walked up to a massive door, manned by a maitre'd.

"Yes, ladies. How may I help you?"

Jo-Jo took a deep breath, probably pushing away her fear of feeling out of her depth, and said, "Yes, three for brunch please. The Champagne brunch."

A flicker of a smile approached his lips. "As much as we would love to serve you three ladies, I regret to say that the Oak Room is for business *men* only. I would be happy to welcome you back this summer. We have recently allowed women to drink and dine at the Oak Room during the summer months, so please join us then."

We were all rather stunned at this. Mother stepped forward and stated with indignation, "Young man, we are on the cusp of 1947. For God sakes…that is the most archaic policy I've heard in quite a while. You can be assured that we will *not* be coming back to spend our money during any season, much less the summer, when your bosses see fit to seat and serve us. Please inform your managers that this policy is an outrage to all business *women* everywhere."

We quickly walked out, hurrying to release our righteous indignation outside The Plaza. We crossed over to Central Park and began laughing hysterically and patting our glorious mother on the back for her outspoken ways.

Jo said, "You sure told him, Mom! But I'm still in the mood for a cocktail. How about we try Tavern on the Green. It's dreamy at night with all the lights and trees, but it should be fine for brunch. It's in the park; not too far from here."

We sat inside the busy restaurant and enjoyed a delicious lunch and drank orange juice mixed with Champagne. Jo-Jo appeared to be in good spirits leading the toasts, but I could tell something was off. I knew my sister as well as I knew myself. Even with the bubbling Champagne flowing, life was not perfect in her sparkling world.

CHAPTER 39

WISHING ON A STAR

JO-JO

*E*ach week blended into the next. I was surprised on my day off when I walked out of The Dixie around noon and noticed I no longer needed my heavy coat. It was late March, the sun was out, the sky was blue, and the wind was low. I couldn't believe I'd been at the Copa for almost four months. When did the winter disappear?

On reflection, I knew at least where the time had gone. I was sleeping past noon each day, rehearsing duets with new headliners, learning another new song with the orchestra, performing four shows a night, and going for breakfast until four AM with a crowd of Copa Girls and band members. Throughout all that time, I was drinking Vin Mariani and taking energy shots. Wash, rinse, repeat.

I was grateful for the opportunity and the money, but I wasn't sure I could keep up the pace. The shots helped at first, but by early March I was feeling anxious and on edge within about eight hours until I got the next one. And a lot of club employees seemed to be lining up out the backdoor when Doctor Max was administering his medicine. On the days he didn't show, a lot of us were snapping at each other and easily irritated. I loved the euphoria after the shot, that feeling of being sharp and at the top of my game during the shows, but that reaction never lasted long enough anymore.

Maybe it was time to stop. Not everyone took the shots. Perhaps the side effects were becoming worse than the cure. I should follow Sarah's advice and find out what was in the vitamin cocktail. What I probably needed was more sunlight and fresh air. Instead, I was surrounded by cigarette smoke and low lighting each afternoon and all night. And once I finally returned to my room, it was hard to sleep after the adrenalin rush of the shows, which made it even more difficult to drag myself out of bed after I finally went to sleep.

Anyway, today would be different. I was going to embrace the day, ignore my cravings, and eat a healthy meal. I was walking to the Stage Deli when I was distracted by a Loews Theater marquee showing *Life With Father*. I'd heard several of the girls mention this movie and a feature was just about to start. I hadn't been to the movies in months. I decided I'd eat popcorn instead of my favorite deli sandwich.

I plunked down two quarters and bought a ticket. Inside, the theater was huge, seating well over two thousand, but today there were perhaps only a few hundred in attendance. Above the floor seating, were two balconies and beautiful swagged curtains on the stage that pulled back as the movie began.

Walking out later, I felt entranced by the film. It was a comedy about a well-to-do family of red-headed boys, a controlling father, and a lighthearted but conniving mother. In addition, my eyes were glued to the screen whenever a young beauty named Elizabeth Taylor was in a scene. She appeared to be a teenager and I immediately longed for her job.

This movie was the type of family centered films James Appleton had explained to me that MGM was striving to produce. That's probably why their studio was considered the gold standard in Hollywood. Maybe MGM was where I should be? Not hanging out in some dark, smokey bar singing to inebriated diners. I knew the Copa was an amazing place to grow as an entertainer, but I felt I wanted to do so much more.

Maybe it was time I talked to Fran again about this.

I stopped at a drug store and called her apartment, catching her at home. "Fran, it's Jo-Jo. Just wondered if you had time to meet for coffee. Need to talk to you today if possible."

"What's so urgent?"

"Just wanted to discuss some issues."

"How about we meet at that coffee shop at The Dixie, The Rise and Shine? I've got a half hour gap in my schedule at four."

I returned to my hotel and got there early and ordered a bowl of canned fruit cocktail and a Coke. After the long movie, I needed something to perk me up.

Fran eventually sauntered in and looked down at what I was eating and just shook her head with disgust, while taking off her calf-skin gloves. "What's so damn important?"

"I was curious if you ever sent my latest Copa reviews to Mr. Appleton and let him know I was still interested in doing a screen test?"

"Sorry, I did, but got no response. There's no rush. You're doing great at the Copa. Some singers wait their entire careers to get the spot you're in now. And the money's decent too."

"Honestly, I have as much interest in acting as I do in singing and dancing. Remember, you called me a triple threat. I guess my third talent is just itching to come out."

"Jo-Jo, you still have almost three months on a six month contract and I'm pretty sure Monte will want to keep you on after that. I can probably negotiate even more money at that point."

"Six months? You never told me about a six month contract! I never agreed to that. You only told me Monte wanted me to sing with the orchestra for a little longer. The money is nice, but I'm ready for something different."

"No, I'm sure I told you. You were excited about your raise and probably weren't listening to the other details. I never brought a contract for you to sign because it was a verbal agreement worked out on a cocktail napkin. You know how Monte is."

"I'm certain I would have remembered six months."

"Besides, Jo-Jo, you're at the top club in the country. You're getting great exposure there."

"I was hoping you could get me scheduled for a screen test. I could take a week off and maybe visit the MGM studios."

Fran looked up at the ceiling, sighing deeply, "There's no point until you complete your contract. What's the rush?"

"Remember the day we were talking about working at the Copa, before we went in to talk to Monte the first time?"

"Jo-Jo, I have numerous clients. I can't remember everything I say."

I took a big sip of Coke and looked up at her. "You specifically said the Copa was run by the mob and I shouldn't stick around too long or they think they own you. I don't want to be owned by anybody, especially the mob. There's a lot of shady people coming in and out of there. In fact, that comedian, Joe E Lewis? He told me he can't sing any more because some mobster in Chicago cut his tongue and face up and he was so badly beaten he was hospitalized for months. And all he wanted to do was leave a mafia controlled club to perform at another place in Chicago. I don't want to end up like that."

"Jo-Jo, you can't believe half of what some of these comedians say. They're always exaggerating. Just think of singing at the Copa is like being at the Harvard of nightclubs and you're earning a Master's in entertainment."

I was getting frustrated at her refusal to even consider contacting MGM again. "But it seems like all the best young stars are under contract with MGM. I'd like to be a part of that world."

"Yeah, you and every other starry-eyed girl in America." Fran stood up and slid her handbag under her arm. "Look, I gotta run, but trust me when I say the movie business isn't all sunshine and rainbows, Jo. There are producers promising the world to get young starlets on their casting couches. Then there's the temperamental directors who are a pain in the ass. And don't get me started on all the jealousy between actors. The old ones hate the young ones and everybody's gunning for someone who might take their part. Not to mention, the whole damn town of Hollywood is a hotbed of sex, drugs, and communists."

"Well, Mr. Appleton seemed quite polite and he told me Mr.

Mayer took care of his actors as if they were his own family. Some of them even call him Papa."

"Ha! And some of them call him the Devil. Jo-Jo, you're my top girl. Keep doing all the great stuff you're doing and I'll look into the Hollywood angle in a while. We'll talk soon. OK?"

I nodded and watched her walk away. I felt despondent, although I should have felt on top of the world. Maybe ordering a new outfit would make me feel better. I left and spent the remainder of the day at Angie Chin's studio.

CHAPTER 40
THE TALK
SARAH

.

I was no longer taking Beckham's biology class for the spring semester, although I did continue to work as his lab assistant. I initially asked him if we might now go out together in public since I was no longer his student, but he felt it was still too early for him to be seen dating a student, and perhaps it would be best to wait until summer.

My bouts of nausea had been sporadic but not daily, and I had spotted in early February so I thought I might be in the clear on the pregnancy scare. But then came March. I waited anxiously each day but I had no menstruation whatsoever. After my nightly shower, it was late and I was alone. I examined myself quickly in the full length mirror. There it was, clear as day. My body had changed slightly. My breasts appeared a little larger and there was a perceptible roundness to my belly which was normally quite flat.

I'd been in denial. I was now sure I was pregnant. How could I have been so blind. And how would Beckham feel about father-hood? Hopefully, he'd be excited and we could marry during the summer. We had so much in common and sharing the love of a child would strengthen that bond, wouldn't it? If we married, we wouldn't have to hide our relationship. I could continue classes at school and hire a few students for babysitting. The timing wasn't the best, but nothing was impossible. My own mother had twins at my age and then four years later had to raise us on her own when my father died. I needed to talk to Beckham.

We'd been meeting quite regularly, especially on Fridays. After Thursday's lab, I asked if we were still on for Friday night. He looked up from his office desk. "Sure, see you at six. There's something important I'd like to talk to you about. I'll make spaghetti and buy a nice bottle of wine; how does that sound?"

"Great. Uh, I have some news too, but let's talk tomorrow."

Friday afternoon--I put more effort into my appearance, washing and rolling my hair. As a finishing touch, I added a bit of rouge and lipstick. I wore the new dress Mom bought me during our visit to New York. I loved it back in December when Jo had picked it out for me. It had a cinched waistline and was cut slim through the hips. Hopefully, my stomach wasn't too noticeable, but the dress already felt tight on my waist. I'd often heard the saying that women had a lovely glow when they were pregnant. Unfortunately, my glow was all cosmetic and underneath was a nervous pallor of white fear.

Friday evening, Beckham opened the door to his apartment and gave me a long hug. "You really look beautiful tonight. I'm glad you're here. Want a glass of wine before we eat?"

I suddenly wondered if wine might affect a baby. Maybe at this point it didn't matter too much, but why risk it? "Actually, I'm kind of trying not to drink. Starting to gain too much weight."

"Well, I'll pour you a very small glass then. Have a seat." I sat down on his small couch and Beckham brought over the wine glasses and took my hand in his very gently, sitting next to me. "Like I said yesterday, I had something important that I wanted to discuss with you. Sarah, I'm nervous, so please forgive me. This relationship has been wonderful. But I think it's time we change things up."

Oh my goodness. I suddenly realized he might be proposing. This was terribly exciting. I'd never gotten a sense of that from Beckham before.

He looked me directly in the eye, our faces only inches apart, while I smiled in expectation. He coughed, took a sip of wine, and said, "I really don't know how to say this, so…I'll just spit it out. Uh, Sarah, I'm getting married this summer at the end of July. We just made it official."

"Wait…what? You and me? Beckham, yes! That would make me very happy."

He shook his head and closed his eyes for a second. "No. I'm sorry. That came out wrong. It's not you. It's someone else. But I promise that we were broken up when I first met you. I guess things kind of changed over the Christmas holidays. You understand how these long-distance relationships go."

My heart stopped for a few seconds. What was I listening to? Then as the full realization of what he was saying came together, I wanted to scream and scratch his eyes out. He looked so calm while I was dying inside. Who was this *we*? It didn't matter. I now hated Beckham's smug, arrogant face. He was talking, explaining, making weak excuses, but I only heard an indistinct buzz. Nothing he said mattered anymore. How could I have thought I loved this person? Had I been so blinded by the sex and his words of affection?

"And all that is supposed to make me feel better?" I shook my head in anger, unable to comprehend his duplicity. "Let me just clarify…things *changed* over the Christmas holidays but you continued making love to me for over three months and never said a word about it?"

I stood up in anger and tossed the wine from my glass in his face. I only wished I'd asked for a fuller glass. He sat there looking up at me from the couch with a stunned expression as red drips ran down his face onto his white shirt.

"Sarah, I expected a little more maturity from you."

"How *dare* you act so sanctimonious." I picked up the dinner napkins he'd brought over with the drinks, wadded them up and threw those at him also. I raised my voice suddenly, no longer caring about the elderly neighbors below. "I'm not *only* hurt, confused, and angry, I'm *pregnant*, you idiot. Pregnant with your child. How could you even *think* of continuing to have sex with me while you were getting back together with someone else. What were you doing? Just hedging your bets, in case things didn't go well back home? Keeping your little student fling burning bright until you had to finally cut me off?"

He was now looking down, wiping the wine off his glasses with the crumpled napkin. I should have thrown the actual glass at him, not the napkins. I would have loved to see it shatter on his thick skull.

"Sarah, I find it hard to believe you're pregnant. I've been pretty cautious."

"I guess *pretty* cautious isn't quite cautious enough…and you're supposed to be the ace biologist! I trusted you. Guess you'll need to reread that procreation chapter a little more carefully. And while you're doing that, you can find a new lab assistant. I can't work for you or even *look* at you one more second. You disgust me!"

I guess my pregnancy admission was beginning to sink into his brain. "Are you certain about these accusations? And what exactly are your plans? Are you keeping the baby?"

"It's not an accusation; it's an announcement. And you just lost your right to any further consideration regarding me or my body." I grabbed my purse, slamming his door, as anger turned to tears which were pouring from my eyes. Plans? My plans were now unplanned. What should I do? Go back to denial? I suddenly felt sick as I climbed down the outside stairs of his apartment and retched violently on his neighbors' bushes in front of their living room window, as they looked on in surprise while listening to their radio program.

Who to talk to, what to do…what were my next steps? Perhaps first, an absolute physical confirmation from a doctor. Someone that had no connection to the school or my hometown. Barb and Lester had become some of my closest friends but I definitely didn't feel like confiding with either of them. Mom? God, no. She would be so angry with me and already had her own pregnancy to deal with. Just the disappointed look in her eyes would send me running out of Green Tree. Jo-Jo? No, she was too busy and seemed exhausted with her own issues. She didn't need to be plagued with my problems. Besides, I could already hear her voice saying, 'And all this time, I thought you were the *smart* one.'

Then I considered school. Would my scholarship be dropped? Possibly. Probably. They didn't like giving out university money to girls with loose morals, or at least those who got caught.

I started backtracking. My first bouts of nausea occurred right before Christmas. It was now mid-March. That would put me at possibly three to four months pregnant, with a due date sometime in August? If I was showing slightly now, what would I look like at the end of semester in late May? Hopefully, I could make it through the end of term without anybody of importance noticing. If not, my scholarship might be in jeopardy. That could not happen. My degree was too important to me. And all that work I had already done this semester... school had been my focus for so long. I couldn't stop now.

I stomped down Beckhams's street and reached campus but continued to walk the sidewalks around the university buildings, oblivious of where I was going. I bounced so many ideas around that my head hurt, trying to balance Beckham's horrible deception against my future at the University. My hatred for Bekham's lies would continue to seethe for a long time, but right now I needed to make decisions which included the best means for me and this new life within me to succeed.

CHAPTER 41
FRIEND AND FOE
JO-JO

*J*eanne Templeton had become a close friend. She had just turned twenty-six and was considered the elder statesman of the Copa Girls. She and I often chatted during our early morning breakfasts together before heading home to our beds. Monte trusted her guidance with the girls and rewarded her well for her stability, skills on stage, and management of the dance team. She'd been dancing at the Copa for three years after doing a grueling two-year high-kick stint at a Las Vegas casino. When arriving in Manhattan, Jeanne's big dream had been to make the chorus lines of some Broadway musicals but she ended up staying at the Copa for the security and favorable appreciation of the club owner.

From the stories Jeanne told me, most of the girls on the team arrived with dreams of stardom and eventually seemed to settle for a middle-class tourist businessman who took them home to places like Topeka and Peoria.

We were lingering over our second cup of decaf in a twenty-four hour cafe, packed with formica coated tables, lit by stark fluorescent bulbs. I was dumping a second packet of sugar into my cup as the rest of the girls and guys from the club headed out. Jeanne was yawning, holding her pretty head up with her hand. "So, Jo-Jo, you're still living at The Dixie, right?"

"Yes. It'll be a year at the end of this month. In some ways, time has flown by so fast."

"You know, with the money you're making now, you could probably get a decent apartment."

"Maybe, but I've been considering moving to a suite at The Dixie. Those rooms come with more space, a little seating area, and a phone. Honestly, I like it there. So convenient, and a lot of the people working at the hotel have become close friends. We kind of take care of each other, like a big family."

"That's nice, sweetie. I just thought with your big raise you could do better. Two-fifty a week for a baby like you is nothing to sneeze at."

"Where did you get the idea that I'm getting two-fifty a week? It's one-fifty. I'm grateful for it but you know how quickly money spends around here. Especially paying for all those vitamin shots."

Jeanne looked confused. "I could swear back in late December, your agent and Monte were sitting where he always does, near the stage. During a break in rehearsal I overheard their conversation. Monte told her he'd pay you two-fifty a week if you stayed on. She kept mentioning you wanted to go to auditions in Hollywood for MGM. Please don't think I'm a big eavesdropper, but Monte really doesn't hide much from me anyway. He knows I'll keep things to myself."

"Are you sure that's what you heard? Fran told me my raise was for one-fifty and she hadn't heard anything from the people at MGM. "

Jeanne shrugged. "Sorry kid, but I'm pretty sure about what I heard. I remember because I was really happy for you with the raise he offered. I wanted you to stick around. But hey, don't get me involved. You'd better check things out with your agent. Maybe there's some shenanigans going on. You been with her long?"

I closed my eyes and sighed with exhaustion. "In a way. But that's another long story."

"I'd start asking some questions. There's some unscrupulous

agents out there. I mean, your agent looks legitimate, but you never know."

"Yeah, thanks. I should do that." I was stunned. I knew Fran was tough and selfish but was she an outright thief?

Jeanne inhaled the last of her cigarette and stubbed it out. "Kid, I could tell that afternoon that Monte really wanted you to stay at the club. He likes you; it's nothing sexual, as far as I know…but he sees you as an asset. You're a great little songbird, a hard worker, and easy on the eyes. He appreciates that and generally rewards loyalty. That's why I'm still there."

"Thanks for the info. And Jeanne, please keep all this to yourself." I looked down at my watch, groaning at the late hour. "Hey, want to split a cab? It's already four."

Jeanne pulled up from the table. "Sure, and by the way, all that Vin Mariani? I'm asking Podell to stop carrying that stuff."

"Why?"

"At first I liked it, but I swear it's too addictive. It's definitely bad news for the dance troupe. It's the Cocaine mix--it's dangerous. I've been looking into it. I don't know if you've noticed, but I've been weaning myself off of it. Hardly touch it now. But Hester and a few others are a total mess. She keeps a bottle going all the time. I'm going to have to let her go if she doesn't straighten out."

"Thanks for the tip. I'm in pretty deep too. Was it hard to stop?"

"Yeah, real hard." We both left some coins for a tip and headed out.

The following day, Jeanne's comments about Fran were fresh on my mind. I decided the best approach to find out my real weekly salary was to ask Monte about my latest contract and bypass speaking to Fran for now.

Proser had a new male singer he wanted me to rehearse a duet with and asked me to come in early. I walked into the club and saw Monte at his table, sipping his Scotch, talking to a young, good looking guy.

"Ah, here comes my little yellow canary. Jo-Jo, come meet Eddie Fisher. His agent is one of my best friends and he swears by this guy.

Apparently, Eddie stole the show last summer at Grossinger's Hotel."

Eddie stood up and shook my hand. "Monte's been telling me great things about you, Jo-Jo. I look forward to working with you this week."

"Yeah, me too. Any suggestions, Monte?"

The boss stood up from the table and said, "I'll let you two work it out. I need to take care of some business. Pick something the crowd will be familiar with that works well for both of your voices. You know the drill, Jo-Jo. You two should be terrific on stage together. Eddie's just a kid too. Barely nineteen, right Eddie?"

"That's right Mr. Proser. Thanks for this opportunity."

Monte nodded and started to walk away. I was still standing and said, "Uh Monte, before you leave, may I have a quick word with you in private. It won't take long."

"Sure, walk with me. I gotta go down the street and put some money on a sure thing. Eddie, she'll be back in a minute."

Monte and I stepped onto the busy sidewalk as he lit a cigar. "So, how can I help you?"

"I just needed confirmation, Mr. Proser. I never got a chance to see the new contract Fran Jordan worked out with you late last December. I needed to clarify that. What was the length of my engagement and my weekly rate? Fran mentioned six months. Was that correct?"

"Yeah, as long as we're happy with the performances, we wanted to keep you on for the next six months at, let's see, I think I told her two-hundred a week?"

"I see. Not two-fifty? I thought it was two-fifty but I wanted to be sure. Fran handles my money."

I'd have to check my books. I got a ton of employees, kid. But I think we agreed on two a week. So, whaddaya think of Eddie? Cute kid, right? But I hear he's a little weasel. Watch out for him. Anyways, I think the crowd will love you two together. I'll bet the farm on that one."

"Sure. It'll be fun performing with someone close to my age."

Monte stopped walking and turned towards me. "So, Jo-Jo, let me ask. Are you happy at the Copa? You gonna stick around for a while?"

"Yes, I'm happy, but I have to admit, the schedule is pretty daunting."

"Yeah, I've always been in the club business so the night owl hours are normal for me, but it's not for everyone. Now that you mention it, you're looking kind of tired and really thin. Have you tried any of those vitamin shots from Doctor Max? They really do the trick for me."

"Yeah, not sure if those are working out so great for me. What's in those shots, anyway?"

"Who the hell knows. The doctor, hopefully, right?" He laughed after saying that, as if it was a big joke. "I just know they rev me up." Monte continued to chuckle as I began to shudder. What had I gotten myself into?

"Anyway, Monte, that was all I needed. Thanks for your time. I'll get back to the club and work out something with Eddie. See you later tonight."

"Anytime, sweetie."

So, was I supposed to be getting two hundred or two-fifty? Either way, it wasn't one-fifty and someone was stealing from me and I had to assume it was Fran. I'd have to deal with her later. For now, I had to try to sing a duet with cute Eddie Fisher and try to cut back on Vin Mariani. Maybe one glass though... Only to help me get through a rehearsal with the weasel.

CHAPTER 42
THE BIG REVEAL
SARAH

*I*t was a beautiful, chilly day in April and I was standing next to Lester, Barbara, and Jacob as the Governor of Iowa's wife and Hortence Miller stood on either side of us for a few newspaper photographers. Our first major ramps were recently installed at the back of the administration building and Mrs Miller was hoping to garner more publicity for the university and our Help For Heroes group. She was friends and former classmates with Governor Blue's wife and thought her presence at the ramp's christening might give our project more clout.

The ramp was built in a zig-zag design to make the steep angle easier for wheelchair use. Before the group arrived, Lester and I gave it a test drive as I easily pushed him in his new wheelchair up the ramp.

He was positively gleeful. "We damn well did it, Sarah! I can't believe it." After the push upwards, he glided down the ramp with ease under his own power.

Later, in front of the press, Mrs. Blue said some kind words about our efforts and hoped that our work at the university could continue with additional donations given by the generous citizens of Iowa. When I'd been told the governor's wife was coming, I had hoped she'd announce we were getting state funds to assist our mission, but no such luck. Although having Mrs. Blue promoting our work was certainly a plus and guaranteed our group some extra press. The First Lady gave a short speech, and then she pushed Lester in his wheelchair up the first leg of the ramp, as they both waved and smiled to the cameras.

After a few questions from reporters, Mrs. Blue took my elbow and walked with me down the sidewalk. "It's Sarah Anderson, isn't it?"

"Yes, ma'am. That's right."

" I understand from Mrs Miller that you are the organizer of this admirable group,
young lady."

"Yes, that's correct. But I've certainly had help from our avid volunteers."

"Well, I'm impressed. So, you're a mother, a top student, and a charity organizer. I don't know how you manage to find the time. I have two teenagers and barely have time for anything else. Will this be your first, or do you have other kids?"

I immediately felt the color drain from my face as I tried to find the words to respond. Nobody before had ever mentioned they thought I was pregnant. Was it really that noticeable?

I tried to respond nonchalantly. "You're very kind with your compliments, but I must tell you I *am* a busy student and tutor, but certainly not a mother. Maybe someday, but I have my hands full right now with my studies. I hope you and Mrs. Miller have a lovely lunch." I wanted to leave quickly before she elaborated or felt compelled to apologize.

"Well, I insist you should join us for lunch, Sarah. Hortense and I always go to a quaint little tea room downtown."

All I wanted to do was scurry away and hide in my room. I came up with an excuse immediately. "That's such a generous offer, but unfortunately, I'm meeting a student for tutoring at noon. I'm certain though that my roommate, Barbara, would be thrilled to join you. She's our group's coordinator and is a big fan of both you and the Governor. In fact, she and her boyfriend, Jacob, are part of the Young Republicans on campus."

"All right then. I suppose I should speak to them as well. You take care."

I quickly waved goodbye to the rest of the group. I had hoped I could make it until the end of the semester without drawing attention to my pregnancy, but if a total stranger noticed it within minutes, what were other people thinking?

As I passed the reception desk at Currier Hall, one of the girls called out to me. "Sarah, phone message for you. Your sister called."

I took a look at the message. Jo wanted me to call her back soon. Apparently, she now had a phone. We had not talked since our December visit and, come to think of it, our letter writing had come to a halt these last few months. This might be an important call. I decided to walk to the phone booth outside the library.

After reaching The Dixie Hotel operator, I asked her to reverse charges and connect me to Jo-Jo Anderson's room. "Sarah?" I barely recognized Jo's voice on the line. It was raspy and slow.

"Jo, what's wrong? You sound terrible."

"I feel terrible. Aching all over… fever and shakes. Haven't slept in days. I'm miserable, Sarah. I didn't know who to call." At that point, Jo began crying in sharp jagged howls, sounds I'd never heard from my sister before.

"My God, Jo, what can I do to help? Is it the flu? Should I call a doctor for you?"

"No. I think…it's those damn…shots. I tried to quit taking them…Now I'm seeing things, hearing voices. Sarah, I think I might be going crazy. Had to call in sick. I hate to ask, but can you come? I need you so badly."

Without hesitation, I said, "Yes. Just hang in there for one more day. I'll come, Jo. Keep a cool, wet towel over your forehead. Take some aspirin for the muscle aches. Drink plenty of water, and no matter how bad you crave those shots, stay away from them . Do you hear me, Jo?"

"Yes."

"Jo, you're the strongest girl I know. You can do this. You'll probably feel miserable all night long but only talk to people you trust and do not let that doctor from the Copa come by. I'm sure he'd love to pay you a house call. First, I need to arrange some time off from school and then I'll take the train to Manhattan."

"I'll wait, Sarah. Just ask the desk. I'm in a new room."

I then went directly to the administration building to speak with the Dean of Education. The timing was not great. Semester finals were only a month away. "Dean Campbell, my sister is on her own in New York and is quite ill. I need to take an extended leave of absence to help her, but I desperately want to keep my scholarship."

The dean opened up a manilla folder and was scanning my files. "Sarah, you've been an admirable student. I can see by your grades that you're an excellent reflection on this school." He looked up and clasped his hands on the desk. "This is what I'm allowed to offer for a medical leave of absence. You'll be given incompletes in all your courses for the spring semester and then have ten weeks to finish any remaining course work or final exams for this semester. We'll send a memo out to all your instructors." He looked down at my file again. "Uh, I see here that you also work as a lab assistant for Professor Carter. Should I contact him as well?"

"No, not necessary. I had to quit that job. I had too many students to tutor and Dr. Carter seemed to think I could be easily replaced." Had I said that with a little too much vehemence? A simple 'no' would have sufficed.

The dean looked up again. "Very well, I'll take Carter off the list."

"Yes, let's do that." I thanked him profusely and told him I looked forward to coming back as soon as possible and left Jo's address at The Dixie for any follow up communication. I went back quickly to my dorm and explained to the Currier Hall director of my dilemma and asked to use the phone to check on train times. There was a final train to Chicago at six. After packing my small suitcase, I took my meager roll of cash from the sock drawer and realized that I didn't have enough for a train ticket. I was at least twenty-five or thirty dollars short. Now I was stuck.

I thought of Lester and all the money which was recently donated to our Help For Heroes fund. Maybe as treasurer, he'd allow me to borrow fifty dollars, which I'd pay back after getting it from Jo. I went downstairs again and made the call, hoping he was home.

Thankfully, he answered. "Lester, so glad you're there."

"Sarah, you missed a good lunch. Well, honestly the sandwiches were way too tiny but it isn't every day you get to rub elbows with the Governor's wife. Jacob, Barb and I all got invited. Sorry you had a dang tutoring session."

"Yes, that was too bad. Lester, I have a big favor to ask, but tell me if it's against the rules."

"Shoot, what's the problem?"

"I need to borrow fifty dollars from our Help For Heroes fund. My sister is really ill and I need to take a leave of absence from school to be with her in New York. I'm trying to catch a six PM train tonight."

"But what are we going to do without you? You're the center of our group. Sarah, it all comes down from you."

"You guys will be fine. Between you, Barb, Abbie and Jacob, Help For Heroes is in great hands. But the money I need for--"

"I got money, Sarah. You're welcome to it. My VA check came in a week ago. I'll borrow my cousin's truck and come take you to the station."

"Oh, bless you, Lester. You're a God-send!"

"Not a God-send. Just a good friend. I'll be there within an hour with the money."

At five o'clock, Barbara had still not returned, so I dashed off a quick note telling her of Jo-Jo's alarming illness and a phone number where I could be reached by tomorrow night. I let her know I might not be able to return before the semester's end and thanked her for keeping up the spirit of our group.

My closing thoughts to her were: *Most of all, Barb, I thank you for our developing friendship and your indomitable spirit. You never fail to amaze me. Your roomie, Sarah*

It was hard to think back on how much I had disliked her several months ago, but now I valued her as a close friend.

I hurried downstairs and found Lester parked near the curb. I put my case in the back and got into the front seat. "I had no idea you could drive. When did that happen?"

"I've been driving since I was sixteen, but my cousin just had to rig this up with a handbrake and gear shift."

"Fantastic, he's pretty wonderful."

"Yup. The brother I never had."

It didn't take long to get to the train depot, but I still needed to purchase my tickets. "Lester, I can't thank you enough. I promise I'll send the fifty dollars soon."

"No need. I owe you way more than that. Sarah, I knew nobody on this campus before we met. You befriended me and made me a part of something special. You're really remarkable. I hope you know that. Whatever problems you have ahead of you, count me in and I'll be there."

I needed hearing that from somebody so badly, but hadn't realized it until Lester said the words. I leaned over quickly and kissed his scruffy cheek and turned quickly before he could see me wiping my eyes. I pulled my case from the back and called out, "You are amazing. Goodbye, Lester."

CHAPTER 43

THE GOOD DOCTOR

SARAH

*A*rriving in New York City was so much more daunting without Mom and my sister. It was beginning to get dark and the men leaning against the walls of Penn Station looked menacing. The air felt sootier, making it hard to breathe and the traffic never stopped. Everything felt faster, including the people talking on the streets. I knew The Dixie wasn't too far, but coming out of the station, I was turned around. I thought I'd recall everything clearly, but today it was a tangle of numbered street corners.

I stopped at a newsstand outside the station to ask for directions. "Excuse me, sir. Can you tell me which way I might find The Dixie Hotel in Times Square?"

He leaned back and crossed his arms, glancing at my suitcase. "You're either from Northern Iowa or Southern Minnesota. Which is it?"

I was amazed. "How did you know that? It's Iowa."

He shrugged. "I got an ear. Hear at least a hundred different accents every day." He turned and took a nickel for a newspaper from another customer and then returned to me. "Now, I could give you directions to The Dixie but I'm a busy guy with a business to run. On the other hand, you buy one of these color-coded

Manhattan maps and you can find everything without bothering me any more."

I pulled one out of the holder and started to open it up. He grabbed it back and said, "Nothin' doing. That's fifty cents, lady."

I was exasperated. Why couldn't he just simply point me in the right direction. "A half buck for this little thing? That's ridiculous." I took out my wallet, and grudgingly put two quarters on the scuffed counter.

"Well worth it, Iowa. It's got the answers to all your prayers. Go see the sights and then go back home. I can tell, it ain't gonna work out for you here."

"Well, I'm in agreement with you there. See you on my way out of town."

I looked up at the corner street signs. I was at the intersection of 34th Street and Seventh Avenue. I found it on the map and simply walked up eight blocks on Seventh to 42nd Street where Times Square was colored in red. Easy breezy. Look at me--I'm a Manhattanite! Once I reached the area, I turned in all directions hoping to recognize the top of the large hotel. There it was... on the west side of 43rd.

As I walked in, the lobby was buzzing with guests and employees. I waited in line at the desk to ask for Jo's room number. I recognized the handsome desk clerk with glasses from my December visit. "Hi, I'm here to visit Jo-Jo Anderson. She told me she has a new room number. Apparently, she's moved."

"Yes, ma'am, the Deli Girl moved on up to the suite life. Guess she's doing pretty well at the Copa. Hey, I remember you, the twin sister, right?"

"Yes. Good memory. I'm Sarah Anderson."

"Alright, if she's expecting you, you can go on up. Room 512." He pointed to the elevators.

Up on the fifth floor, I knocked a few times at her door--no answer. Hopefully, she was only sleeping soundly. I tried again with no response. I went back to the lobby and used the house phone to call her room. Again, no answer. Now I was beginning to panic. I went back to the desk and waited for the same clerk. I checked his name badge, and lowered my voice. "Leonard, so sorry to bother you again, but I came to stay with Jo because she called telling me she was quite ill. She's not answering her door, so I was hoping someone could let me in. She's either sleeping very deeply or too sick to get to the door."

"Hmm, I'm really not supposed to do that, but now that you mention it, I haven't seen her in the lobby for a couple days. She's usually so friendly to everyone. Tell you what, I've got a break in ten minutes. I'll take you up there myself."

I waited in the lobby getting more anxious by the minute. How was I supposed to treat an addiction to a vitamin shot? I didn't even know what it was. What could I really do for her?

"Let's go up." I was startled, lost in my thoughts when I heard Leonard's voice next to me. Back on the fifth floor, he knocked loudly with no response. Then he unlocked the door. There was a small seating area in the suite and a door left open to her bedroom. I ran in and saw the tangled sheets of her bed, but no Jo-Jo. The bathroom was also empty.

"Leonard, I'm sorry to have bothered you, but it appears she went out. Maybe she's feeling better? I'm really confused. Any chance I can get a spare key in case I need to leave?"

He looked reluctant, but said, "I suppose… Hang onto this one, but don't tell anybody you got it from me."

It was already past seven in the evening. I noticed she had a sheet of phone numbers next to her phone, which included the club's number. I called the Copa. It was answered by a man of few words with a deep resonating voice. "Reservations."

"Sorry to bother you, sir, but would you possibly know if Jo-Jo Anderson is working tonight?"

"Hold on." I waited less than a minute before he came back on. "Yeah, just saw her on stage with the band. They're warming up for the eight o'clock show."

"Thank you. Is there any chance I can leave her a message? I just arrived from Iowa to visit her."

He sighed and asked, "Name and number?"

"Just tell her Sarah has arrived and she should call me at her place as soon as she can."

"Call Sarah at Jo-Jo's place. Got it."

"You're so helpful. Thank you sir." This was followed by a quick click on the other end of the line.

I layed down on the small sofa next to the phone, exhausted from the stress and travel. How could Jo sound like she was on death's door but then be feeling good enough to be singing on stage the next day? How could she leave me hanging here without notice after traveling for twenty-six hours? I was concerned but furious at the same time. Jo could occasionally be a little self centered, but she would never be so rude as to totally disregard me. She must have been so out of it when she called that she didn't even remember our conversation. I couldn't help but wonder if Jo had a visit from that terrible doctor.

I closed my eyes for what felt like a minute and was woken up by the phone. I picked up in a groggy state, and heard Jo's voice. "Sarah, what are you doing in New York? Shouldn't you be in school?"

"Jo, do you *not* recall being so ill that you begged me to come? I told you I'd be here today. I just spent a lot of money and time to get here. And now you're acting like everything's just fine?"

"Honestly, no. I don't remember calling. I'm so sorry. Listen, I can't talk long but Eddie Fisher, our headliner, had a death in the family so Monte called and pleaded with me to come in. He knew I was sick but sent Doctor Max up to see me. I felt so much better within an hour or two. I'll come straight home after the two o'clock show and we'll talk in the morning."

"I'm worried for you, Jo. You promised you wouldn't let that doctor in. Get back here as soon as you can."

The next morning, I woke to Jo sleeping soundly next to me in her double bed. I squinted at my watch. It was already ten. I was shocked I'd slept so late. Shaking her shoulder, I whispered in her ear, "Rise and shine big sister. It's coffee time."

She grudgingly rolled over, pulled at my wrist to check the time and groaned. "I never get up until noon. Buzz off."

"Not today. We have things to sort out." I got up and pulled on her arms, dragging her out of bed. "Come on, take a quick bath. You'll feel better." She sat on the floor staring up at me with messed hair and black smudges of makeup under her eyes. "I'll make it nice and hot and wash your hair just like Mom used to do for us."

She was still sitting on the floor with her eyes closed, already asleep when I came back and pulled her up. "Come on, get in there."

Jo gingerly climbed in, at first sensitive to the hot temperature but she gradually acclimated and sank in. She heaved a sigh of contentment, held her nose and slipped under the water and came up again with her hair drenched. Then I began a soft, head-massaging shampoo.

"Sarah, that feels so good. Thanks. Please keep going... So, have you forgiven me for being so forgetful?"

"Let's be honest, Jo. You aren't forgetful. You were feverish, hallucinating, and going through withdrawal from what I think are amphetamines, which are probably the major ingredient of your so-called vitamin shots. I'm going to the New York library and doing a little research on this stuff, but in the meantime you *must* stay off the wine and shots. And I don't care if God himself is giving the shots or pouring the wine. You say no! It's so obvious both are affecting you terribly. So, unless you want to live the life of a daily drunk or drug addict, we're working together to get it all out of your system."

"Sarah, I don't think I can go through another one of those painful nights again. You have no idea."

I shook her shoulders and she felt like a wet rag doll. "Yes, you can, Jo. You can do it all. You never shied away from anything in your life. Well, except perhaps a few math exams. I'll be here with you every step of the way."

"But what about work? I can't go on stage having hallucinations with my stomach cramping up."

"Jo, if it means that you can't work for a few days or a week, that is what needs to happen. We'll call your agent and have her explain everything to your boss. That's her job; she needs to represent your needs."

I dunked her one more time and pulled her up, wrapping a towel around her body and another one on her head. "You're all clean now. Let's keep it that way."

Jo reached her arms around me and offered a hug. "I love you little sis."

"Good, remember that a few days from now."

CHAPTER 44
THE MOUSE AND THE FOX
JO-JO

I stared into the small bathroom mirror looking at myself in disgust, knowing Sarah was right. My wet hair hung limply down from my gaunt face, with the dark circles around my eyes looking more prominent. Soon, even the makeup and white powder wouldn't be able to erase them. Hadn't Jeanne Templeton warned me? I'd been at the Copa for four months and I'd slowly let myself slide into a dangerous form of dependence. When Doctor Max showed up yesterday, I should have kicked him out, told him I didn't need his stupid shot, but instead, I was honestly relieved. When Jeanne explained that the Vin Mariani was no good for me, had I listened? No. I continued to drink the vile red wine night after night with some of the band. I now recognized I had cravings that I couldn't walk away from. It was not only difficult to perform without them, it was the reason I was going in to perform.

The drugs were right there, ready to be consumed within the back hallways and alleys behind the Copa, and nobody took a second look. It was the way of the world in this darker side of the business. Most every evening, during the band breaks, some of the musicians and kitchen help gathered in the back and shared hand-rolled cigarettes the guys called muggles. The distinctive sweet smell of the smoke would mix with all the cooking scents as I passed by.

Although I'd been offered muggles frequently, I had yet to partake. I thought the smoke might damage my voice because it was inhaled so deeply. I'd also noticed a few top headliners heading to the bathrooms with little rolled packs of their own injection kits. I had accidentally walked into a few unlocked doors and witnessed needles being used. And now I was ashamed of myself for becoming one of them. The only difference was that someone was injecting me. Nobody coerced me; nobody forced me. I had nobody to blame but myself.

I turned to look at Sarah hanging up two damp towels. Would she be strong enough to guide me back to the normalcy I needed? Would I let her keep me from what I knew I would want so badly in only a few hours. I had my last shot from the doc around four yesterday afternoon. I was afraid of the symptoms that were about to kick in.

Sarah was talking. I turned to listen as she draped a light print kimono over

my shoulders. "So, Jo, pick up your phone and call Nanette, or Fran, or whatever her name is. Tell her that you won't be able to work today or possibly next week. If you can't talk to her, I will."

I nodded and said in a tired voice, "I think she's been stealing from me. For a while now. I'm hungry. Let's go down and get food."

Sarah looked upset at me and said, "Not like this, Jo. Some photographer might spot you looking like hell and you'll end up in one of those newspapers with all the photos. Let's get you dressed. But first, call your agent... and what do you mean...She's stealing from you?"

I sighed. Each thought and full sentence took so much concentration, forcing me to speak slowly. "I found out... a while back. Not positive, but she's probably stealing from my earnings. Fifty or a-hundred dollars a week. Just haven't found the time to ask her."

Sarah shook her head and turned to me and stared. "That is ridiculous! How could you *not* address this? That's a lot of cash, Jo. Call her *right* now. I need to meet this person. Why are you still doing business with her?"

"I signed some sort of contract…last November." I shrugged. "Maybe I'm mistaken about the theft, but I'll make the call."

Walking to the sofa, I tried to knock the cobwebs out of my brain. I sat down, asked for an outside line, and called Fran.

"Fran?…Jo-Jo. Really need to speak with you. It's important. Can we meet at Rise and Shine?"

"Hmm, I've got a new client. I'm lining him up with some burlesque joints. I could meet you soon at the cafe for a few minutes. Yeah, you don't sound so good. Let's meet in ten minutes."

"Thanks, I'll be downstairs." I clicked off and looked up at Sarah. "She'll be here soon." I remained seated and felt like all energy had drained from my body. "Can you help me get dressed?"

Sarah pulled a simple, print dress down from the closet. I pushed myself to stand. I stepped into it and she buttoned up the back. Then she brushed my hair into a short ponytail and put it all under a beret. I put on some lipstick and rouge to make my pallor look less grey. Even Sarah confirmed that I didn't look good but I might pass for simply tired.

In the elevator, Sarah explained she was coming along for moral support but wouldn't be afraid to speak up if necessary. I loved my sister; Sarah could be tough and obstinate when she needed to be. I glanced over at her for the first time since she'd dragged me from bed. Somehow she looked different. She was wearing an especially loose sweater and skirt, which was frumpy looking. That wasn't unusual, but then I noticed her side view.

"Sarah, don't take this the wrong way, but I've never seen you like this. Have you been eating a lot lately?"

She turned and stared at me, hesitating. "You might say that. Eating for two, I guess."

"What!" You're pulling my leg, right?"

As the elevator doors opened, she looked straight ahead. "I wish."

We continued walking to the hotel cafe as I whispered to her, "Sarah, I can't believe you haven't told me about this. So the baby is yours and the professor's?"

"Well, the baby is mine and was a parting gift from the professor.

I'll make sure he has *nothing* to do with this baby. He is deceitful; a most terrible person, really. Just so you know, I haven't told anybody else." At this point, Sarah broke down in tears. I pulled her toward the lobby restroom so that she could calm down. We were quite a pair.

I got her some tissues and hugged her closely while patting her back. "There, there, sweetie. It's going to be OK. I bet you'll be a wonderful mother." That comment made the tears come even harder. "Sarah, I'm just so surprised. I wished you'd told me earlier."

She blew her nose and patted her eyes dry. "Jo, you've been so preoccupied. How could I bother you?" Sarah glanced at herself in the mirror, splashed water on her face, and ran her fingers through her long hair, sucking in a few jagged breaths to stop the tears. "Anyway, that's enough about me. It's time to go and confront the enemy."

"I call her the Whiplash Witch." We both giggled a little, releasing some tension. "Sarah, honestly, I can't believe you've come all this way and I'm so glad you're here." I grabbed her hand. "Let's go little sis."

As we walked into the Rise and Shine, I saw Fran already seated at a table, clicking her glossy red nails on the table. We walked up and pulled out our chairs.

"Fran, my sister, Sarah. She's come for a visit and wanted to meet you."

"Sister? Ah yes, the twin." She glanced for a second in Sarah's direction. "Hello. Sorry I don't have time to chat, but like I said, I've got meetings lined up. What's wrong, Jo-Jo."

I tried my hardest to keep my voice firm and confident, but my insides were starting to feel like jelly. "Uh…two issues, Fran. A little birdie let me know that my Copa contract was for at least two-hundred a week. Whereas, you told me it was for one-fifty, which is the amount that's been going into my account. I need that rectified and reimbursed."

She lit a cigarette, turned her head away, and blew out a plume of smoke. "Not sure where you're getting this *wrong* information, but I'll look into it."

"Monte Proser told me, and I need a refund."

"Jo-Jo, you know how he is. I'm sure he was confused. But like I said, I'll look into it." She looked away from us as she spoke and began tapping her nails again. "So, the second issue?"

I hesitated for a brief moment and then came straight out with it. "I have a problem Fran, and as my agent, I expect you to support my needs. I'm not proud of it, but I'm attempting to wean myself off B12 shots that everybody at the Copa seems to be taking. Only problem is, after a day or two, when I don't take them, my body begins twitching, I get feverish, and start hallucinating. It's absolutely terrible. I need a week off to let these drugs work through my body."

Fran's face was blank, without emotion, as she took another drag. "Why in God's name did you get involved with that crap. Methedrine...great at first, but then later, it's hell."

"A doctor was giving the shots; I thought they'd be good for me."

"Yeah, that old Doctor Feel-Good hooks his patients every time. Look, Jo-Jo, you have a contract to fulfill. Tough it out, or take the shots for another two months. Tell the doc to give you a lower dose. Just something to take the edge off."

Fran began to gather her bag and cigarettes, as Sarah grabbed her wrist and pulled her back to her seat. "Excuse me, Miss Jordan. What my sister wants is a week or two off. She is ill and *desperately* needs recovery time."

Fran pulled her hand away. "Do not touch me."

"Jo is your client and you need to make her wishes known to her boss right away. That's *your* responsibility. I am forbidding any more dangerous chemicals be put in my sister's body. If you won't talk to Monte Proser, then I will."

Fran laughed and then sneered at Sarah. "And who the hell are you? Some little Green Tree country mouse telling me what I need to do."

Sarah amazed me as she went nose to nose with Fran and

brought her voice to a low simmering boil. "For one, we'll file a lawsuit for breach of contract. Two, we'll talk to Monte personally about you not paying Jo her full salary, and I would suspect he would never hire any of your other clients again. Three, we expect to have Jo's additional funds brought in cash to her room tonight by eight o'clock. *Now*, you may leave."

Fran must have been in shock having someone stand up to her as forcefully as Sarah had just done. I wanted to stand and cheer, but my body would only cower and shake in my chair. Fran then stood up and bent down towards me, whispering, "I'll make the call to Proser and give him some excuse. But Jo-Jo, there's no way you can pull this other crap off. You're weak and pathetic."

My body was now shaking from the inside out, but I steeled my mind, looked directly up at her, and said in a raspy voice, "Just watch me."

CHAPTER 45
NO EASY FIXES
SARAH

*W*hile Jo went upstairs to rest, I shopped at a corner market and bought fresh fruit and vegetables, along with aspirin. Back in the room, I peeled oranges, apples, and tangerines for vitamin C and cut up some fresh broccoli and carrots to munch on.

Within a few hours, Jo had gone from slightly shaking to writhing in pain on her bed, begging me to call the doctor who had administered the vitamin shots. I pulled up a small chair and sat next to her. "Jo, I'm your doctor now. I'm not leaving you until you're yourself again." I grabbed her hand and held it tight, as she squirmed and thrashed. "Look at me, Jo. Look me in the eyes. Have I always told you the truth?" She stared at me with a wild, distant look but eventually nodded. "We will come out on the other side of this. It may take a few painful days or maybe even weeks, but we're going to walk out of this room together. You'll be singing and dancing again. I know it." She gripped my hand tighter in acknowledgement, hopefully meaning she believed me.

I'd noticed an ice-making machine down the hall which was free to guests. I'd never seen such a contraption before but thought the small cubes would feel good on Jo's feverish forehead. As I filled a bucket, I heard knocking and a man's voice in the direction of Jo's room. I hurried back and saw a man wearing a suit, dark glasses, carrying a small black bag. He was rapping again on Jo's door more forcefully. "Jo-Jo Anderson, Doctor Max here, open the door please."

I approached him quickly. "Excuse me, sir. I'm her sister. Jo-Jo's not feeling well and won't be having visitors."

He knocked again, ignoring me, and then turned and said, "I got a call. I have medicine to help bring Jo-Jo's energy levels up. It'll only take a few minutes. Open the door please. It's crucial we don't let any negative symptoms linger too long."

I cleared my throat, speaking louder. "Doctor Max, step away from the door. You've done quite enough with your cocktail of amphetamines. Tell whoever sent you that we appreciate their concern but Jo will get through this without your tainted medicine."

He shook his head and gave me the edge of a cynical smile. "Suit yourself. It's ridiculous to put her through this downward spiral."

"Well, it appears you were the one that put her…"

Jo-Jo interrupted us, opening the door, looking like death. She grabbed the door frame and leaned toward him, grabbing his wrist. "Doc, I thought I heard your voice. Please come in…"

I stepped between the doctor and Jo, pushing her back into the room, while slamming the door in his smug face. I yelled through the door, "Go away! Do not come back." Jo collapsed on the floor crying, seeing the opportunity of receiving the drug she craved disappear before her darkened eyes. I pulled her back up and slung Jo's arm

around my shoulder but she pushed me away and stumbled to the floor again.

"He was here to see me. Not you! And now he's gone." She began crying and whining. "He had my medicine. You're no doctor, Sarah. He knows best."

I pulled up on her arms again, dragging her back into her bedroom as she continued to moan and cry. "You said you were going to make me feel better, but it's worse, Sarah! It's so much worse."

"Jo, it's gonna be alright. Please believe me. He's pushing poison." I helped her back into the bed. "Try to sit up for a minute. I have some fresh orange slices. I just had one. They taste so good. I'm going to bring you a plate."

Jo had purchased a few plates, cups, goblets, and napkins to eat occasional meals in her suite. I put a spread of orange and tangerine slices on a plate and placed one in her mouth. "Just suck the juice out before you chew. Isn't that good?" I popped one in my mouth too. "Probably the best orange I've had this year."

Jo continued to chew and I wiped the dribble from her mouth. "Ready for another one?" She nodded and put her head on my shoulder, sucking on that orange slice like a little kid. Eventually we both finished everything on the plate. "Good. At least you have an appetite. Now, take this aspirin for me and a big drink of water. Jo continued to be compliant as I layed a cool compress on her forehead and fed her occasional ice chips until she fell asleep.

I fed myself more of the chopped, raw vegetables knowing I had to eat healthy for the baby. I put my feet up on the small sofa and laid back, closing my tired eyes, feeling exhausted. Just as I began to doze off, I heard knocking at the door again. I jumped up immediately, not wanting the knocking to disturb Jo's sleep, and opened the door.

I stared at a pretty woman with short, dark hair, a heart-shaped face, and twinkling blue eyes that turned up at the corners. She held out her hand to shake. "Hi there, I'm Jeanne Templeton from the Copa. I'm a good friend of Jo-Jo's."

I immediately felt wary, thinking Proser may have sent one of his lackeys to get Jo back to work. "I'm Sarah, Jo's sister. She's asleep right now. Sorry, but I don't think I should disturb her. She's going through a rough patch."

"I understand, trust me. I just wanted to see if she needed my help. Monte asked me to come and check on her, but I can see she's in capable hands."

I got a good feeling from this woman and relaxed a bit. "Thanks. Please come in and sit down for a minute. All I have to offer you is ice water and chopped vegetables."

"A glass of water would be great."

I filled a goblet and handed it to her as she sat next to me on the sofa. "So, Jeanne, I threw that Doctor Max out of here. He said he was sent to give Jo-Jo more of that horrible vitamin shot. Can you believe it?"

"You did the right thing, Sarah. Keep her here if you can for at least four or five days. It'll probably take at least that long. Hopefully, the drugs will be out of her system by then. It's a tragedy, really. She's such a sweet and talented girl. But I hope she'll come out stronger. I've met a lot of addicted people in the last few years. Jo-Jo may be naive but she seems resilient."

"Thanks. Honestly, she and I are both new to this stuff. But I'm here to support her however long it takes. I took a leave of absence from school. We're sticking it out together."

"Bless you. She's lucky to have you. I'll tell Monte that she's working on getting off the methedrine. Monte's not a bad man. He just doesn't understand the side effects. He seems to truly believe the shots are some kind of miracle drug. I'm trying to get the Copa cleared out of this stuff...but you know how show people are."

"No, I really don't. But I'm beginning to see the darker side for sure. Leave me your number and I'll call if I have some good news or setbacks."

"Sure thing, sweetie. That would be great. Call me anytime."

The next day, I felt exhausted having little sleep while trying to adjust to the small sofa and my growing belly. By late afternoon, Jo was awake and she offered me her bed. She moved to the couch in the front room and asked me to turn the radio on to some music. A few hours later, I was awakened by what I thought were voices. They were muffled by the song on the radio and the closed door. I sat up and listened more intently. I definitely heard a man's voice, although he was speaking softly. I jumped up, opened the door and saw Jo-Jo, bent over, exposing her bruised thigh to that same doctor, who was pulling a needle from his bag.

In that second, I grabbed a glass goblet from the night stand and screamed while throwing it at the doctor's head, surprising them both. It smashed against his forehead and blood immediately began trickling down his ruddy face. "I told you already! Stay the hell out of here. I'm calling hotel security now."

He pulled out a hankerchief and began wiping blood from his eyes. "I came on behalf of your sister's begging, not you." With the needle still in his hand, Jo pulled at his arm trying to force him to give her the shot. "Do it Doc. Now."

I lunged forward, grabbed the syringe and smashed it against the coffee table, while Jo collapsed back on the couch, crying as she watched the broken glass and its contents trickle onto the carpet. "Get out now, Doctor. If you don't, somebody will be looking into whatever this junk is that you're selling."

He grabbed his bag, seeming to not want the extra attention. I truly doubted he was ever an MD. I held the door, and for the second time, slammed it in his face. Jo-Jo fell from the couch to the floor and lay there having what looked like a toddler tantrum, mumbling and shrieking about what a terrible person I had become.

From that day forward, I remained in the front room, manning the door like a jailer. Jo and I went through four more days of hell. She had crying jags and shakes, followed by long hours of sleep. When she eventually awoke, Jo acted like a ghost of herself. She was despondent, lethargic, and didn't seem to care about anything. She refused to bathe, get dressed, and barely ate or spoke. During those dark days, I truly wondered if I would ever get my sister back. After the fifth day of my arrival, we had a slight breakthrough.

Jo asked me to give her a bath and wash her hair. My sister had always prided herself on her appearance. I knew if she recognized her need to get clean, she was back on her way to more self aware-ness. She walked like an invalid, slow and bent as I helped her into a warm tub. It was hard to imagine this was the same person my mother and I had watched on the Copa stage, singing and dancing with such enthusiasm only last December. I was angry at what the club's environment was doing to her.

A day later, with a little convincing, she found the energy to get dressed. We finally walked out of the depressing hotel room and took a short walk around the block. Breathing in a little outside air was wonderful medicine for both Jo-Jo and myself. I had only left the room for a second quick trip to the corner market, only after Jo fell asleep. The dark rooms had not done a lot for my mental health either.

The following two days, I noticed marked improvement. She was beginning to carry on coherent conversations. She even laughed a few times. I think Jo was searching for her old tenacity, her joy of life and discovery. It was all slowly coming back.

On Sunday morning, sharing a small breakfast at the Rise and Shine, she began eating her food with an intensity that she'd always shown in the past. "Sarah, I think we should order more eggs, don't you?"

I placed my hand on hers, and nodded. "Yes! Let's make it a gooey cheese omelet."

CHAPTER 46
A WALK IN THE PARK
JO-JO

I was beginning to feel stronger and had moved beyond the see-saw of clawing pain to the depths of lethargy. My estimated one week off from the Copa had now gone beyond two weeks. I knew I was not one-hundred-percent, but I felt strong enough to make two important calls. The first was to Monte, to make an appointment with him the following afternoon. The second was to Justin Winkleman, attorney at law, and the guy who had sent me roses at the Copa months ago.

Inspired by Fran's attire, I had earlier asked Angie Chin to make me a smart, snug-fitting suit in a powder blue with black trim. It had been hanging in my closet for over two months, but I had yet to wear it. I knew I needed that special suit of armor today. It was important that I felt and looked powerful, even though I was far from it. I also insisted Sarah attend both appointments with me. She had become my right arm and half of my brain for the last several days. I wanted and needed her strength right now while mine was still shaky.

I powdered the dark circles still lingering around my eyes, and put on extra makeup to cover the dry flakey patches that had erupted on my cheeks where I had continued to scratch them. I donned the fitted jacket which featured a thin black belt at the waist and a matching skirt with a kick pleat at the back. I topped it off with a hat that rolled up over my left ear and curved down over my eye to the right side of my face. I walked into the living room wearing my suit and wobbling in tall black heels and asked "What do you think?"

Sarah's jaw dropped after having just nursed me through the bleakest days of my life. "Movie-star swanky. But we need to work on that balance."

I looked at my sister and really laughed. It felt good to laugh again. "Sarah, let's head downtown and find you something at Macy's. Most of your things are probably getting too tight. Is there such a thing as maternity chic?"

"Doubtful. Chic is the opposite of how I feel and look."

After a thorough search of Macy's maternity wear, I purchased Sarah a loose polka-dot blouse with a bow at the neck and a skirt with a stretch waistband. Sarah looked at herself in the dressing room mirror, frowned and folded her arms across her chest. "It's comfortable." But that's all she would say about it.

The two of us walked into the Copa at three o'clock. Monte was at his usual table working on an employee schedule while looking up occasionally to chuckle at a comedian who was in the middle of his nervous audition. Sarah and I walked down the stairs to Monte's table. When he saw us, he stopped the comic and said, "Nice act kid. I'll be in touch if something opens up." That was a line Monte used when he meant no.

He nodded at me and said, "Well look at this… my little song bird is finally coming back to the nest. Ladies, have a seat. Jo-Jo, you're looking top-hat. Sure you've been sick?"

We both pulled out chairs at Monte's table and sat down. "Very sure, just ask my nursemaid and sister, Sarah. Sarah, meet Monte Proser, owner of the Copacabana."

They both shook hands and Monte asked her, "So, you've been taking care of our girl?"

Sarah nodded. "Yes sir. We've had a few tough weeks but I think we're over the most difficult part."

"Sorry you had to kick that on your own, Jo-Jo. Didn't realize you were having such a tough time. It's not easy. But honestly, ladies, the hardest part was *not* last week. The difficult part is what comes next. Because the temptation is always going to be around the next corner, the next bathroom, or the next frigging broom closet. Someone will always be out there tempting your fate if you truly want it badly enough. You have to decide what's more important to you-- a good career, true friends, a family that loves you, or if you want the rush and the high. A lot of people choose the high every time."

His words rang true. "I'm ready, Mr. Proser. If you still want me back to fulfill my contract, I'd like to rehearse with the band for a day or two. I've lost some of my endurance but I feel sure I'll get it back."

Before he could answer, Sarah said, "Mr. Proser, you may know how to run a beautiful club, but I have to ask." Proser looked at her with irritation and impatience but said nothing. "Do you honestly think it's wise to have a doctor peddling amphetamines near the premises? It obviously affects people in different ways, but I would have to say in Jo's case, it's highly addictive. It's a bad business move."

"Yeah, I'm looking into that. The Doc isn't as careful and knowledgeable as I initially thought. I believed the shots would help give people a boost with all the late hours, but it's come to my attention that it's not working for everyone."

I nodded and asked, "So, Monte, are you still interested in having me come back?"

"Absolutely. The band and I have missed our little canary. We made do. I called in a few backup singers to cover, but they weren't Jo-Jo. You're our girl. We just need you to remain healthy."

I smiled and thanked him. "Monte, we spoke a while back and you were going to check on my weekly rate. You said you thought it was two-hundred. Was that correct?"

"Yeah, two-hundred...but I gotta come clean with you. I budgeted you for two-fifty a week but told your agent I'd give her fifty a week out of that if she'd convince you to stick around for a while. She said you had your heart set on auditions for MGM and wanted to take off for Hollywood."

I was now seething. Nanette not only was stealing from me, but also took a bribe regarding my career. This was worse than I thought. I realized now that she had probably never attempted to call MGM, or worse, had lied and told them I no longer had interest in auditioning.

"I must tell you, Monte, I'm disappointed that she was paid a portion of what you intended to pay me, but maybe this type of agreement is commonplace. Seems like a bad idea though. But I do know this; Fran is also taking *another* fifty dollars from me each week, on top of what she's getting from you. She is a thief, and I plan on getting out of my contract with her. If I stay on, I'd expect you to pay me my full salary of two-fifty a week. Would we be in agreement on that?"

Monte nodded. "I have no issue with that. Fran's a tough bitch and I can't abide by crooks."

"Good. Then I'm your girl, Monte, but I'd like that contract all in writing today, please. In addition, could you please write up a statement that you were paying her an extra fifty dollars out of my budgeted salary. I have an appointment with my attorney and need him to take a look at everything."

My directness seemed to shake Monte up a bit. "Attorney, huh? Looks like you're definitely back in the saddle. Uh, I suppose, as long as all this is just between us. Paperwork and details aren't my real strong suit. Hand me one of those cocktail napkins."

Sarah leaned over and opened her satchel. "Mr. Proser, you're welcome to use my extra paper and I suggest you make a copy. I have carbon paper handy. I use them for my classwork all the time."

Proser shook his head and laughed. "I see why you brought the little mamma along. She's a great asset, this one."

I smiled and put my arm around Sarah's shoulder. "You got that right, Monte."

After we had my contract in hand, Sarah and I stood up and walked proudly out of the Copa, assuring Monte I'd be back in fine form for rehearsals tomorrow. As we exited the place, I collapsed on

Sarah's shoulder as my strength and false confidence evaporated. "My goodness, Sarah. I never could have spoken to him like that without you next to me. That was exhausting."

"I'm so proud of you, Jo. You did great in there."

"I can't walk in these heels any more. We're taking a cab to our second appointment. We need to conserve our strength for round two."

Winkleman's law office was in an area near Battery Park, which I was unfamiliar with. Heading south in the cab, I asked Sarah, "So, what did you think of Monte?"

Without hesitation, she said, "Mixed feelings. Seems to be a knowledgeable and friendly enough guy but, Jo, I don't really trust him to put your best interests first. He will always put his and the club's needs above yours. That's probably normal in business, and I know we've both been sheltered from a lot of these things, but something about him just doesn't square. I say use your Copa connections and then move on."

"I agree. It honestly makes me nervous being around the drug use. I still feel the draw and craving and I'm kidding myself if I think I'm fully recovered. Sarah, you are my strength and I can't thank you enough for sticking by me."

Sarah patted her stomach and said, "Don't worry, your time will be coming for payback. Jo, can you believe I'm having a child!" Pointing to her stomach, she said, "I still can't believe all this is happening."

"I know. I almost split a gut when Monte called you *little momma.*"

"Well, I can hardly hide it now that you've dressed me in this matronly maternity garb. I haven't worn a big bow around my neck since I was six."

The cabby pulled up to a brick building with a discreet gold metal sign reading: *Winkleman, Crookshank, and Smigel.* Sarah and I got out and she stared at the sign for a moment. "I don't know Jo...It's as if the three people with the oddest sounding names in law school banded together to start a firm."

"Well, Justin Winkleman is the only lawyer I know in Manhattan, so let's hope he's a good one. How do I look?"

"Better than me, but you could use a little lipstick. Let's get this over with."

A receptionist welcomed us into a pleasant space, offered us coffee and then walked us to Justin's office. He stood up from behind a large, dark wooden desk and came over and offered me a quick hug and Sarah a handshake.

"Jo-Jo, your call was a pleasant surprise. Still at the Copa?"

"Yes, I took some time off but I'm starting back tomorrow."

"Great. Have a seat. Tell me, what can I help you with?"

We both sat down across from his massive desk. "Justin, I have a contract with a bad talent agent that I need to get out of, and I have proof that she's been stealing from me. I'd like to sue her to get back the money that is owed to me. She's already been confronted once about it and ignored my request."

"Interesting. I'm sorry to say, I'm a tax attorney, Jo-Jo, but for you, I'm happy to help out if I can. Let's see your original contract and then you can tell me about the theft." He read through everything, laughing occasionally at the wording Fran had put into her draconian agency contract and then I explained the fifty-dollar-a-week theft which could now be proved by Monte's paperwork.

"Yeah, Jo-Jo, we should be able to do something using this stuff from Copa management. You probably have two options. We can either sue Miss Jordan for breach of contract for not following the best interests of her client, or I can send her a simple letter threatening her of the same and see if she runs scared and returns the money to you. We can handle this on a contingency basis of which we usually take forty percent of anything we recoup for you, or you can let me take you out to dinner on your next night off and there will be no charge."

Sarah raised her hand and said, "She'll take that second offer. Jo, just get your money back, cut ties with the Whiplash Witch, and get a pleasant dinner out of the deal."

Winkleman smiled and said, "Your sister, Sarah, is quite clever. I suggest you follow her advice."

"So, you really think Fran Jordan will release me from my contract?"

"She'll have to, Jo-Jo. We have proof right here that Proser agreed to pay you two hundred a week and give her fifty as long as she convinced you to stay at the Copa. If she was paying you only one-fifty, she was clearly embezzling from you. She either accepts the offer of reimbursement and release of contract or we sue and threaten to ruin her credentials as a talent agent. She'd be a fool not to accept, and in the scheme of things, there's not that much money involved, eight or nine hundred dollars."

"Well, it's a lot of money to me. I only wish I could see the look on Fran's cold, indignant face when your letter is delivered."

"I'll do you one better. I'll attempt to personally deliver the letter and report her reaction back to you."

"Fantastic, I love that idea! In that case, I certainly accept your offer, Mr. Winkleman and look forward to our dinner. Any Monday evening works best for me. I recently lost my appetite for a while, but I'll work on having it back by then."

"Excellent. I'll start work on this soon. You two ladies have a lovely day."

When we stepped outside, the wind had picked up and the sky had turned dark, but I suddenly felt that a large black cloud that had been hovering over me for weeks had suddenly lifted. I felt lighter, stood taller, and joined arms with my sister. "Sarah, I've never been to Battery Park. Let's just keep walking south and soak in this magnificent day, shall we?"

Sarah pulled out a colorful walking map from her satchel and studied it. "Oh yes! There's a view of the Statue of Liberty there. Considering that you've hopefully been released from the tyranny of Fran Jordan, I think that's totally appropriate."

CHAPTER 47

CONNECTING TO THE MOTHERSHIP

SARAH

*R*eturning from Battery Park, Jo-Jo was tired and collapsed on the bed while I answered the ringing phone.

"Is this Jo-Jo Anderson's room?"

"Yes, but this is her sister, Sarah."

"Sarah! Good to talk to you. It's Wilhelmina, the hotel operator. We spoke months ago, remember?"

"Yes, that's right. What a memory you have. How are you?"

"Very well. Still stuck in the basement but I'm getting out a little more. I may be promoted and moved to reservations soon."

"Moving up in the world. That certainly sounds exciting." Poor Willie, she really needed to be released from the operator's dungeon.

"Anyway, Sarah, a Mrs. Mariah Anderson is on the line and she doesn't seem too happy. Should I tell her Jo-Jo's not available?"

"No, put her through." Jo and I had purposely not been writing or speaking to Mom, not wanting to worry her, especially during the last months of her pregnancy. I was girding myself for a difficult conversation when Wilhelmina came back on and said Mrs. Anderson had disconnected. As I hung up, someone began knocking on the door.

I opened, seeing the surprise of my life, staring out at Mother, who was sweating profusely, and David with a rare scowl on his face.

I stepped aside to let them in and asked. "Mom, Dad? This is a *huge* surprise. How...how are you?"

As usual, Mother spoke first. "Well to be quite honest, I'm exhausted, angry, and upset. I've been trying to reach both of you girls. Nobody's been answering my letters or phone calls. And, Sarah, what on God's green earth are you doing in New York? Don't you have exams coming up?"

As Mom's voice picked up volume, Jo wandered out from the bedroom in her wrinkled suit. "Mom...David? What's going on?"

This time David spoke up in his low but firm voice. "What's going on is that your poor, pregnant mother has been worried sick about both of you and neither of you have taken the time or consideration to call or write to her. Girls! She's seven months pregnant! I took Mariah to this God forsaken city so that the two of you could hopefully rest her concerns. Now that I see you are both alive and well, I'm going to our room to rest while the three of you hash things out. In two hours we're all meeting for dinner whether you like it or not!"

David's temper was rare and it took us all by surprise. With wide eyes we simply nodded as he left, slamming the door.

Mom glanced at Jo with concern. "Jo-Jo, darling, you're so incredibly thin and pale. What happened?"

Before Jo answered, I suggested quietly, "Let's all just sit down and let me get everyone some ice water." I filled water glasses and added ice from the bucket and contemplated on how to start. "Mom, you asked me about my exams. I have been studying and preparing for the last few weeks, but I took a leave of absence. Jo was really ill and needed my help."

She looked at both of us with concern and anger. "Why have I not been contacted? Sarah, I finally found out from your roommate, Barbara, that you'd left for New York over *three* weeks ago. You shouldn't be interrupting your school. It's everything you've been working toward. I really don't understand you two sometimes!"

I took a deep breath, trying to slow my heart rate. How to explain both Jo's recovery and my situation would take delicate work. "Mom, please calm down. Remember, at this stage of your pregnancy, you shouldn't be making trips. We didn't want to worry you. There were quick decisions that had to be made."

"Well, Jo? Have you recovered? I have to say, you're not looking your best."

"Honestly Mom, Jo's doing much better. We went out today. It was beautiful in Battery Park, and we took a ferry around the Statue of Liberty."

"Sarah, Quit trying to change the subject. Let Jo speak for herself."

Jo looked down, twisting her knotted hands together. "Mom, I didn't want to trouble you, but I've had a real tough time. Through no fault but my own." Jo took a deep breath and then let the details spill. "Let me get all this out before you start yelling. I began taking B-12 shots a doctor was giving--supposedly energy boosters. It sounded like a good idea with all the late nights I worked--but my reaction to them was a euphoria I've never felt before. I soon found myself wanting and needing them almost every day, and when I couldn't get a shot, I quickly spiraled down."

Jo finally looked up and gave us both eye contact. "Mom, turns out they were highly addictive, something called amphetamines. Sarah has studied up and knows more about them than I do. But I've been through several days of agony trying to get off the stuff. Hallucinations, stomach cramps, vomiting. I think I'm on the other side, but Sarah has been an immense help."

"Oh my, Jo! I can't imagine. My daughter... injecting narcotics?" She reached across the sofa and grabbed Jo's hands. "Darling, please come home. Please! This city and that club--it's just too dangerous. Remember, that terrible woman who took you from me, the woman I refuse to speak of. I heard she ended up here, amongst all her unsavory show-biz friends. That's the kind of people living here."

Oh Mother, if you only knew, I thought, as Jo continued to explain. "Mom, I know you have a right to be concerned, but please trust me. I've learned so much through this process. I'm starting over with a clean slate. I'll be at the Copa for two more months of my contract and then, hopefully, I'll find new work. The money is too good to

turn down right now and I'm meeting a lot of people with connections. So tell me, how are you, David, and Sammy?"

"Fine, fine. Don't change the subject on me, Josephine! Money
isn't everything; remember that. And you better be wary of these so-
called people with connections. And what about you, Sarah? How
will you get school back on track? How much have you missed?"

After hearing what Jo revealed, I decided a full confession was in
order. Apparently, she hadn't noticed yet that as Jo had shrunk in
size, I had grown. Poor Mom. I took a deep breath. "I took a leave
of absence, but if I can finish all my remaining work and exams
within ten weeks of leaving, I'll receive full credit for the semester. I
plan to stay here through some of the summer and help Jo. But
she's so much better, Mom. Almost back to normal. I'm proud of
her."

Mother shook her head, pulling a hankerchief out of her bag
and touching her tearing eyes. "I'm leery of this talk of addiction,
but knowing the two of you are both working at it together, well,
that comforts me. So Sarah, you'll be studying hard this summer,
then. Correct?"

"Yes, among other things."

"Other things? What other things?"

Baby announcements were supposed to be a time of joy and
celebration. But I felt ashamed and had wanted to hide this admission for as long as possible. This was going to be one of the most
difficult statements in my life. "Mother...uh, you're not the only
person having a baby this summer."

"What? What are you saying?"

Emotions flooded through me. This was not the way it was
supposed to go. How to say this without destroying her confidence
in my judgment? I felt I was nothing, if not strong in my ability to
make good decisions. Now all that had been blown to bits. I hesitated a few more seconds. "I'm pregnant, Mother. Finishing my fifth
month. Probably due in August."

"You, Oh my God... Sarah? Of all people. I *never* expected this!
Who's the father? You never even mentioned a boyfriend."

"There will be no father, and I have no desire to speak of him.

I'm sorry I can't tell you more but he absolutely will not be allowed to be a part of this family."

"I see. I'm sorry...I'm... having trouble taking all this in...ex... excuse me." Mom stood up with difficulty, hankerchief to her face, wailing away as she walked into the bedroom. We both just sat there listening to her cry, unable to do anything about it. It was the lowest I could recall feeling in my relationship with my parents. It was always so important for me to make them proud of us. Jo and I had gone way beyond simple disappointment.

Later, with a shaky voice and wet eyes, she returned to the room, continuing to stand. "My darlings...*please* listen to me. Life is always about making the right decisions and sometimes it's just easier taking the wrong path. But we are extremely fortunate. We have each other. *We are each other's best resource.* Don't ever forget that, girls."

Jo and I began to sniffle too as Mother continued, only stopping occasionally to blow her wet nose. "Sarah, you may stay in New York for now, but I want you home by early July. We have to make plans and I'll need your help when I'm due. You'll get some good practice time with your new brother or sister. Jo, you have a valuable resource staying with you right now. Your precious sister, who dropped everything that was important to her at a moment's notice and came to you. Use her wisely and kindly. I don't know much about the way this addiction works, but you have always been strong. You need to find your inner strength and resolve. I know you, Jo; you must fight this with everything you have or it will *dog you* the rest of your life."

Then her large dark eyes burrowed into me. "And Sarah, you have the most life-changing event you can ever imagine coming soon. Use your time well in preparing for it. I'm certainly not happy about hearing any of this. Raising a child is difficult enough for two parents. But for one, almost impossible...trust me, I know! We'll have to come together as a family to reconcile with this. David and I will do some talking tonight. In the end though, Sarah, you'll have a child to raise which will be more challenging than you ever imagined, but that baby will make you stronger and smarter as well. And, one more thing, if the two of you *ever* again ignore my calls or letters, I'll be showing up in person--all two of me, huffing and puffing through that lobby."

Jo-Jo stood up and grasped onto Mother, hugging her to the point that I thought she'd hurt the baby. I glommed onto the wet, sobbing hug, whispering, "We love you Mom and we're so, so sorry. Please forgive us."

Jo nodded and said, "I promise to keep you up on all decisions going forward. Mom, you need to rest. You've had an emotional and exhausting last few days. I can't believe you're still standing. Please, join David and call us when you're both ready for dinner. I'm sure you have a lot to talk about."

After Mom left, we just sat and stared at each other, drying our tears, realizing we probably had the best and brightest mother in the world. Jo shook her head and held up her thumb and forefinger. "I almost came this close to admitting I was suing Nanette for theft and looking for a new agent."

I shook my head vehemently. "No! Way too much right now. I think hearing one of her daughters is a recovering addict, and the other, currently a college dropout and a husbandless mother-to-be, is quite enough for one conversation. Best wait until there's more positive news on that front...or better yet, let's just keep the subject of Nanette Jorgenson between us forever."

CHAPTER 48

TO CATCH A THIEF

JO-JO

*B*y the following week, I'd had a few Copa performances under my belt and was feeling stronger and more confident *without* the amphetamine enhancements. Both Jeanne Templeton and Shep Fields had also helped convince Monte to ban the Vin Mariani and Doctor Max and his brew of bad medicine from the premises. Multiple absences and erratic temperaments had made it difficult for Jeanne and Shep to keep cohesion within the band and dance troupe.

As a way of ensuring my sobriety, Sarah insisted on staying with me throughout each day, including my rehearsal time at the Copa. Once it was showtime, Jeanne took over the vigil of watching me during the pre and post performances. I didn't like the feeling of being treated like a child, but it was the care they knew I needed.

Just like Dottie at the Ebb Tide lounge, Monte also heard something special in my voice that reminded him of Doris Day, the singer for Les Brown's Band. Monte arranged for me to do a medley of a few of Miss Day's current hits with Shep's band. My set was placed before a new duo act, Martin and Lewis.

Lewis was a comedian I found kind of annoying, but Dean Martin was a charming man I developed a big crush on. He had a casual, easy singing tone that I could listen to all day. And handsome too, but Jeanne already had her eye on him.

By the following Monday, Martin and Lewis moved on to the 500 Club and I looked forward to my dinner with Justin Winkleman. I was curious what had happened regarding legal actions with Fran. He picked me up at The Dixie, while Sarah stayed home and studied for finals. Justin took me to a candle-lit, small Italian restaurant called Puglia in Little Italy and introduced me to delicious pasta with mussels and cannoli for dessert.

He sat and stared at me for a minute, as I hoped the dim candle-light was hiding my skin imperfections. Then I dove into the food with relish. "I love the way you attack a meal. Looks like you have your appetite back again. You're not as sick as you were at my office."

I looked up in surprise. "I never mentioned I'd been sick, did I?"

"I could tell. You were not well that day. Something was off."

I was amazed at his intuition and attention to detail. I tucked this thought away and was happy to be sitting across from Justin's calming presence.

"So...I assume you're interested in hearing what happened to dear Fran Jordan."

"Oh yes! Tell me all the details. But please, eat some dinner first. Join me. Everything is delicious."

He took a swipe of linguine, managing to artfully roll it around his fork and snap it up in small quick bites. Then he put his fork down. "So...I had the pleasure of speaking with Fran this morning. I bought a bouquet of flowers at the corner market and then pretended I was there to deliver them. The door man called her and she insisted I bring them up."

"Aren't you clever?"

"Well, you said you wanted to know her reaction when she heard about the lawsuit. I figured getting into her apartment would be the best way to get the total picture."

"I appreciate your ingenuity!"

"Anyway, she looked excited when she opened the door. Nice looking lady by the way, but not my type. She asked me to wait in the foyer while she got money for a tip. Inside the bouquet, I'd put an envelope with my letter requesting your repayment and the threat of a lawsuit. When she came out of her bedroom, she handed me a two-dollar tip. I explained that my client had sent a message with the flowers and had requested that I personally read it to her. She seemed quite pleased, with her eyes lighting up, perhaps thinking I was doing some type of singing telegram."

"I love this! So far so good."

Justin nodded and continued. "I pulled out the letter and started reading the accusations and monetary requests. When I read the portion regarding immediate repayments to client Jo-Jo Anderson, she snatched the legal letter out of my hand, grabbed back her two-dollar tip, and told me she'd heard quite enough."

"DId she try to throw you out?"

"No, because I explained forcefully that she needed to know the full consequences of not taking immediate action. She continued to stand there with her arms crossed, breathing heavily. I think if she could have forced smoke through her nostrils, she would have."

"Yes, she's quite the dragon lady." I slipped another bite in, and asked, "Then what?"

"She turned and stared out at her Central Park view and picked up a cup of coffee she'd been drinking. I could tell her hand was shaking with either fear or anger as she attempted to take a few sips. Then I asked if I should finish reading the document and she said, 'I can't hear any more of these ridiculous accusations.' I explained to her that we could do this one of two ways. With the easy way being immediate back payment of all money owed to you. I said that if she did that, then the incident would remain between the three of us and would go no further. But if she didn't, her name and agency would be dragged through the mud with all the talent bookers."

"I'm surprised she didn't toss the coffee at you."

"She's a bully and preys on the weak. With people like that, you have to act as tough as they are. I could immediately tell, she's the type that is always sizing up her opponent to figure out how to take them down."

I slapped my hand on the table. "Yes! That's exactly right. How did you know that?"

"Well, as a tax attorney I run into a lot of liars and thieves always looking for the quick way out. So anyway, Fran first insisted she'd mail me a check. I refused but insisted, instead, that we take a walk to her bank for a quick withdrawal. We walked the few blocks together without communicating, and Fran always stayed a few steps ahead."

I laughed trying to visualize this. "Yeah, knowing her, she was hoping for a quick get-away down a dark alley."

"Nothing that dramatic, thank goodness. Once at the bank, she handed over the cash. I thanked her for her time, and asked her to never contact you again."

Justin then reached inside his suit pocket and pulled out a roll of one-hundred dollar bills. I believe this is all yours, Jo-Jo."

I counted it and smiled. Fran had not only paid me the extra fifty dollars a week she had deliberately stolen; she also paid me the weekly fifty dollars that Monte had given her for keeping me working at the Copa. "Mr. Winkleman, I believe this dinner will be on me. I must add that although you're my first, you're by far the best attorney I've ever hired."

"Well thank you. And you are the most charming and unique client I've ever had."

"I'm honestly surprised to hear that. I have to ask, after sending me roses and taking me out for dinner months ago, why didn't you ever call me back?"

Justin took another tidy bite and considered the question before he spoke. "I could tell on opening night you were going places. Jo-Jo, you were fantastic! Confident, looked sensational, and a great voice to boot. You're going to be a big star. I can sense these things. I just didn't want to get involved with someone that already had one foot out the door."

"I'm flattered you think that, but please give me a little credit. For the time being, my feet are firmly planted. And at present, I'm free most Monday and Tuesday nights if you'd like to examine my feet more closely."

He considered the idea for a moment. "I can work with that." Then he forked in another perfect bite of linguine.

"Also, if you don't mind, I can tell I'm going to need a few lessons in pasta swirling. I can see that my technique needs help."

"I've been working on this for a while. It may take several lessons. I suggest we celebrate today's success with a bottle of cold, dry Champagne? It'll be marvelous with this dinner."

Here it was. My first real challenge with sobriety. I was on my own and so tempted. Just a few glasses would be fun. I was with a great guy I trusted. Why not? It was simple, plain Champagne. Then, in my mind, I saw Sarah's face and heard Mother's voice.

"Justin, thanks, but how about a ginger ale?"

"Excellent choice. I'll join you."

CHAPTER 49
GOODBYES
SARAH

I'd been in New York for almost six weeks and Jo had not relapsed once while on my watch. The changes made at the club definitely helped. But I wasn't so naive as to think that an addict simply needed easy access to find their favorite drug. Jo had bitten from the apple and definitely enjoyed the high, but not the side effects from withdrawal. If Jo really sought out cocaine or amphetamines she could find them among band members, wait staff, or even customers. Coming to the club daily with Jo, and studying for exams while she rehearsed, I'd witnessed narcotics being openly abused. But thankfully, not by Jo.

Her growing relationship with Justin and friendship with Jeanne were a big help in keeping her clean, and she truly loved her work and spent most of her time focused on improving her act. It was fun to watch her grow as a performer. Because she was currently without an agent, Monte put up with me hanging about the club serving as Jo's assistant and manager, although he continued to call me *little momma*, to the point that I grew to like it. It was now quite obvious that I was expecting and I decided to embrace it rather than hide from it.

By the week of finals at Iowa State, I felt I was ready to take my exams. I contacted the dean and asked if I could possibly take them here in New York and have them mailed back within a few days. He agreed to that arrangement and sent me the name of a professor he knew in the city to proctor the taking of my exams, along with the dates and times. Once I completed those, it was time for baby preparation. By mid-July, my new little sister or brother would be here. And in August my own baby was due. It was a lot to take in.

Although I had dreaded it when I arrived, the city of New York continued to surprise me. Once Jo was on the mend, I found I truly enjoyed my time. The variety of food was endless, the main library was magnificent, and just as Jo had done, I began to make a few friends at The Dixie. In fact, Willie, the operator, and I had become close friends and went out together on her days off. I'd also received letters from Barbara and Lester, both checking up on me and my sister's health status. Lester was proud to let me know that ramp number two was now firmly in place at the student library. It made me happy to hear that.

I still wasn't quite ready to admit my pregnancy to friends from school, afraid that if word got out, it might affect my scholarship, but I knew, eventually, I would have to. I planned on doing that on my terms.

Towards the end of June, my stepfather sent me one of his rare letters:

> *Dearest Sarah,*
>
> *Just wanted to emphasize that Mariah is sure looking forward to your support and help with your new brother who will be arriving soon. We actually don't know if our baby is a boy or a girl but I'm quite convinced it will be a new little brother for Sammy. Although a baby girl will be just as welcome.*
>
> *I've been busy anticipating our bumper crop of corn. Our acreage is high with bright green field corn as far as the eye can see. I am predicting that our hundreds of acres will far surpass the knee-hi-by-July saying that is always bandied around town.*
>
> *Perhaps we haven't told you enough that we are proud of the sacrifices you made to help Jo in her time of need. And we plan on doing the same for you when your little one comes along. I'm sure you have fears and doubts,*

and we certainly don't condone how all this came about, but you will have our support and help. We already have the wife of one of our farm hands hired to help us with the two little ones, and we have redone my parents' old bedroom as the new nursery.

Mariah and I look forward to seeing you soon. That about sums it up.
Your loving father,
David

I THINK David's letter was my parents' way of reminding me to come home soon, before I became as entranced by the pull of Manhattan as Jo was. I said my goodbyes to friends at the Copa and The Dixie, leaving with mixed emotions. Although I doubted I could ever live in a big city long term, it was an experience I would never forget. Jo-Jo and Jeanne accompanied me to Penn Station and Jo took care of all my transportation costs. It was so hard saying goodbye to both. Jo-Jo and I had become so close. Probably even more so than we were children. Our eyes were wet with tears before I climbed the steps of the train.

Jo hugged me tight and whispered, "I'll never forget the strength you have given me. You are truly my heart and soul and best friend."

"Thanks, Jo. I feel the same." I grasped her wrists before climbing on board. "Now remember, your next step is finding a good, fair agent and then start looking for a good opportunity."

She laughed, tapping my belly. "I know... *little momma* is still keeping me on track, and I'll be there when your little one decides to arrive."

We kissed each other one last time on the cheek and I gave Jeanne a big hug and thanked her again. I slept for a good portion of the ride to Chicago, and then set my mind to upcoming tasks at home for the remainder of the trip.

David and Sammy were waiting for me at the station. David was wearing his familiar denim overalls and a light-weight shirt underneath and Sammy was dressed much the same. I was definitely back in Green Tree. I had to laugh realizing I hadn't seen a single man dressed in overalls while I'd been in New York, yet here, almost every man in town wore them daily, except perhaps on Sunday.

As we got into the truck, David explained, "Mariah wanted to be here but she's feeling a bit out of sorts today. These last few weeks seem to be wearing on her."

"That's certainly understandable. I'm glad I'm here to help. So, have you two decided if you're having the baby in the Albert Lea hospital, or having a home birth?"

"Well, we're kind of split on that decision. Mariah is opting for a home birth, but she wants Doc Greenly present, along with her mother. Now, I think we should take the more modern approach, with the birth in the hospital. But you know your mother. Stubborn as a mule once she decides on something."

"Yes I do. But maybe I can convince her otherwise. Although, I have to say that Jo and I came out pretty good with only Grandma and Aunt Elizabeth at home for our momentous arrival."

"True, but your mom isn't nineteen years old anymore either. Although she acts like it. Just yesterday, she was down on her knees scrubbing floors when I came in for dinner. And that was after she'd driven to Blue Earth and back to show one of Billy-Boy's houses. The woman never stops."

"You're right about that."

Walking into the kitchen, I noticed Mother wasn't at her usual spot next to the stove. In fact, I was disappointed not to have the scent of fresh baked bread wafting through the back door. Sammy called out, "Mommie, Sarah's home. I'm bringing her my new kitten." Then he slammed the kitchen door, running to the barn.

I heard a slight whimper upstairs. Assuming it might be Mom, I yelled for David to come quickly. He dropped my bag on the kitchen floor and we both ran up the stairs, David following two steps behind me.

I bent down next to her bed. "Mom, I'm here. What can I get you?"

She had put on an old nightgown and appeared to be sweating heavily. "My Sarah! I'm so thankful you're here." She looked up at David with fear in her beautiful eyes and said, "Something's wrong,

David. I called the doctor, but he's apparently in Minneapolis. I called my Mother... She'll know what to do."

"What is it, Mom? How does it feel different?"

"A lot of pressure in my lower abdomen, quite a bit of pain. I think this baby is coming early."

David just stared blankly for a few seconds and then stepped into action. "I'll try to contact Doc Greenly and get him back here. Guess he could make it in three hours if he left soon. Mariah, maybe we should think about heading to the hospital?"

Mother shook her head. "I honestly don't think I can move now. The pain is so severe. Please, call Mother again. Make sure she's on her way."

I heard Sammy coming in yelling for me to come down and see his new kitten, but all I could do was hold Mom's hand tight and reassure her. "Grandma's on her way. Don't worry."

Mother was beginning to sound more delirious, speaking in short, breathy words. "I don't know...Something's wrong. Need a cool cloth...Water please? Sarah...I'm sorry."

"Mom, that's the whole reason I'm here. You're going to be fine. I'll be right back."

I went to the kitchen to retrieve a cold cloth and glass of water while David was yelling at Sammy to go outside with the cat. Sammy began crying because he was being yelled at, and David kept attempting to reach the operator to connect with my Grandmother. He was so upset that the operator had to ask him to repeat himself three times. No one answered at my grandparent's house, so we assumed she was on her way. As he hung up the phone, he looked at me and repeated, "We should go to the hospital." Then he went outside to wait, while I went back upstairs with the water and a cold compress.

Upstairs, I kept glancing from the window, watching for Grandma, counting the minutes. I saw David pacing the front yard until he heard the rumble of my uncle's truck heading up our drive. My grandmother stepped out with her bundle of midwife medical tools. Lucky for us, she had helped deliver countless babies throughout the community for years. I ran downstairs again to greet and update Grandma, while my uncle and David stayed out in the yard. Upstairs, Grandma took over while I assumed the assistant's position.

She slipped on her glasses and quickly lifted Mom's nightgown up to her breasts and began feeling her stomach, retouching tender areas and feeling for the shape of the baby in the womb. "Mariah, unfortunately, your child has turned. When did Doc Greenly last examine you?"

Mother shook her head. "Not sure…Don't know… two weeks?"

Grumbling under her breath, Grandma said, "Doesn't matter. He's never around when you need him. Right now the baby is breech, feet first; a precarious position. Mariah, this may hurt some. It's very late in the process but I'm going to try to turn your baby around." I helped Mother drink some water and placed another cold compress against her forehead. I watched my Grandmother's strong gnarled fingers feeling her way, slowly attempting to turn the shape of the baby's head from Mom's upper rib cage toward the bottom of her pelvis. This was followed by loud groans from my Mother.

Grandmother was sweating as much as my mother. She continued to try but then exclaimed, "Damn it! It's no good. The baby's not allowing me to move the head. I'm afraid it's the umbilical cord. The baby is stuck, Mariah. I'm so sorry. A Cesarean birth is the best option."

Mom yelled out in agony and frustration. "Do it Mom. You have to do it."

"Mariah, I don't have the knowledge or the equipment. You know I can't do that. Sarah, we have to move her to a hospital! I just hope there's time."

I ran down the stairs and yelled at David to get Mom into her Ford quickly, explaining what Grandma had said. My uncle and stepfather raced up the stairs and carried Mom down to the sedan which had a reclining front seat. Sammy and I jumped in the back, while Grandma and Uncle Clem followed in his truck to Albert Lea. Mother was screaming out in anguish most of the thirty-five miles, as David raced to the hospital.

Once Mom was on a gurney and whisked to a room, the mood became silent and somber in the waiting room as the minutes ticked away. Finally, an obstetrician came out. His mouth was set firm, unsmiling, a mature man who looked like he had delivered both good and bad news to hopeful parents for years. Introductions were made and he said in a deep, gravelly voice, "Well folks, we performed the emergency C-section. Looks like Mariah is going to make it through. She's weak, lost a lot of blood, but I would imagine she'll be strong enough to come home in a few weeks." We all gave a sigh of relief. "Unfortunately, your baby girl didn't make it. Looks like there was a complication with the umbilical cord collapsing, preventing blood flow and oxygen to the baby. Could have happened when the attempt was made to turn her, but we'll never really know."

At this point Grandmother burst into tears, crying and moaning, saying, "My fault, we should have come straight here, it's all my fault."

The doctor put his arm around her for comfort. "No ma'am. You can't blame yourself, and you probably saved your daughter's life. There's no way to know. We can only do the best we know how."

He shook my father's hand while patting his back and said he could go in now to see his baby girl before the mortuary was contacted for the body. A visit with Mariah would need to wait until she awoke.

We sat quietly in the waiting room while David slowly walked into the room where the baby lay. Later, he shuffled out as if in a trance, and then looked at me. "Sarah, take your brother home. Clem, Mother Sarah, thank you for all you have done. I need to be alone. I'll stay the night here with Mariah and call when I'm ready to be picked up." Then he looked at Sammy who was beginning to whine and ask for Mom. David knelt down to his son's height and explained, "Your mother is very weak right now. She can't come home. I have to stay with her. We lost your little sister tonight. You and Sarah go home and pray for her soul. Will you do that son?"

Sammy nodded his head, looking up at his father. David took

out a handkerchief and wiped Sammy's nose gently. He hugged us both as tears ran down his face, and we left him in his solitary grief. He had always been a man best left alone when he needed to sort through his thoughts.

That was a heartbreaking night for all of us.

Every inch of my body felt exhausted. But I was unable to sleep. So many thoughts about family and connections kept flowing through my mind. I couldn't help but think how truly tenuous and fragile life was. Somehow, the lucky ones made it safely from birth to death--but all the wonderful, difficult, joyful, and pitiful times we shared in between were truly miracles--a chain of inexplicable events which we had the privilege of passing through. I softly patted my protruding belly. I now wanted this baby, my precious baby, more than ever before. This would be a child for all of us.

CHAPTER 50

AN AGENT OF CHANGE

JO-JO

*F*rom the letters I received from home, I could tell that July had been a month of misery and regret for my family. I personally felt terrible for not being there for support. Before the funeral, David and Mom had named their baby Mariah Arlene Williams. From the tone of everyone's letters, it seemed that Mom felt guilty for hesitating, believing her mother could save the child. Grandma believed she had harmed baby Mariah when trying to help turn her. David wished he'd insisted they go directly to the hospital, and Sarah put pressure on herself, believing her baby's birth would be a form of salvation for the family.

In a private call, Sarah said, "There's one thing I know, Jo. This family cannot go through another month like the one that just passed. I've done the research. Almost sixty percent of women in the country are opting for hospital births, although I know it's difficult in some rural areas."

"Knowing you Sarah, you'll make sure yours is a perfect hospital birth. And this time around, I'm taking time off for this baby's arrival. You and the family deserve my full support."

On August twentieth, on a hot, sunny afternoon, David Billy-Boy Anderson was born to my beaming sister who could not have loved her ginger-haired, green-eyed baby more. The lucky boy was surrounded by two very happy and relieved grandparents, an elated seven-year-old uncle, tearful great-grandparents and me, the doting aunt. Baby David was absolutely beautiful. We all remarked on how he had the coloring of his namesake, David, and Sarah never mentioned to anyone but me, that her baby's features actually resembled those of the man she refused to speak about.

Once at home, Sarah looked to be immediately comfortable in her nursing and mothering duties. Although she had promised Mother she would return to school, Sarah was having her doubts and spoke to me upstairs about them. "Jo, leaving Davey will be impossible. We're just now getting to know each other. I would feel so guilty. It's not right."

"Certainly understandable, Sarah, but you have to know in your heart that your baby will be cared for with great love by his grandparents. David dotes on him as much as Mother, and the new caretaker, Maria, is wonderful. Trust me, David Billy-Boy Anderson is going to be one fortunate baby surrounded by so many caring people. And remember, by continuing with school, you'll help ensure his future. You have to look at the big picture."

In the end, it took Mother, me, and David to convince Sarah to return to school. She insisted she'd come home for weekend visits at least once a month and I promised to make it home much more often than I had this past year. I knew I needed that strong family bond and my sister's nagging to help keep me on the straight and narrow.

The day before I returned to New York, Sarah received a call from Lester. He asked if he could offer her a ride back to school to start the new semester. She agreed and thanked him. I couldn't help but notice the small little grin she carried around with her the rest of the day. That night, in bed, I asked, "So how do you feel about Lester? He seems like a really nice guy from what you've told me about him."

"Lester *is* nice. But right now all the love I can possibly give is wrapped up in that little bundle sleeping in the nursery. With school and everything else, I can't see giving anyone more of myself right now. But you never know, perhaps in time…"

And then I heard snoring from the exhausted little momma.

~

BACK IN NEW YORK, my relationship with Justin continued to grow. I adored his sense of humor, admired his knowledge and education, and loved the way he made me feel safe. I was lucky to know him.

After my debacle with Fran Jordan as my agent, I had been dragging my feet on finding another one; and had made no progress towards finding a new job. Things were going well at the Copa, but I knew I was ready to move on. It was Justin who pushed me toward a new agent. Saul Zims was an old college pal of his who'd recently moved from the William Morris offices of Hollywood to those in New York. He was open to signing new entertainment clients, trying to make his mark with the top talent agency in the country. As a relatively unknown, I was nervous about going in. But all Zims could tell me was no, and I'd be no worse off.

I wore the same blue suit I'd worn a few months before. My suit of power. I'd gained a few pounds since then and felt like I looked and sounded better, although occasionally my confidence still felt unsteady. I took a cab over to Madison Avenue and took the elevator up to Mr. Zims office. Once inside the grand offices of the William Morris Agency, I was impressed and worried. Was I worthy of being a client? A pair of attractive receptionists greeted me behind a glossy front desk. One asked my name, stood up, and said, "Welcome. Follow me, Miss Anderson. Mr. Zims is expecting you. Tell me your preference, coffee or tea?"

I had to laugh to myself, thinking of my first meeting with Fran, when she had greeted me wearing a flimsy robe with her hair in rollers. Once I signed with her, I foolishly thought I was in the big leagues. The William Morris Agency was most definitely on a different level.

With coffee in hand, I entered the office of junior associate, Saul Zims. A short, robust young man in a gray three-piece suit who greeted me with a winning smile. "Miss Jo-Jo Anderson, the sweetheart of the Copacabana." He stepped over and shook my hand.

"Didn't think I'd ever see you coming to see me. Before Justin told me, I assumed you'd already been snapped up by another sharp agent. Please, sit down."

We spoke briefly about Justin and their friendship and then he got down to brass tacks. "So Jo-Jo, let's hear all about it. Your hopes and dreams, where you see yourself in the next few years, what other aspects of the industry are you interested in pursuing?"

I was pleased with his question. Nobody had really asked me this before. "Honestly Saul, as much as I've enjoyed performing at the Copa, I've thought a lot about getting into the movie business. I enjoy acting. I was approached several months ago by James Appleton, one of Mr. Mayer's representatives at MGM. I'm think-ing--some colorful, new musical? But I'm sure that would take a while, working myself up through the studio system."

Zims nodded his head and looked thoughtful. "Yes. I can see that. You certainly have the face for it. Perhaps a more updated and current Ginger Rodgers type? But from the rumblings I hear, Mayer might be forced out at MGM, and a lot of actors are jumping out of the studio system. But let's keep that little tidbit between us."

"Really?" I was surprised. "I thought LB Mayer ruled the movie world."

Zims shrugged his shoulders and said, " For now maybe, but I just moved here from Hollywood and you hear things. It's a small town. But let me make a left-turn suggestion, especially if you like the idea of staying in New York. Have you considered television? It's certainly the wave of the future."

"Television? That little box in the hardware store window? Seems like it only shows the news and game shows? And it's always fuzzy. Do many people really watch it?"

"Yes! My prediction, within the next few years, is that the movie business is gonna take a tumble. The improvement of television reception is getting better all the time and families around the country will start tuning into all kinds of TV shows. Variety enter-tainment, dramas, soap operas, comedies. And why? Because after they buy their TV, all the shows are free to watch in the comfort of their own home. It's like a radio with moving pictures. What could be better?"

I was still surprised Zims considered this a better opportunity over films. "So television? You really think that would be a good move for an actor?"

"I'll bet my bottom dollar. Jo-Jo, I've been looking at the numbers. Last year, in '46, about twenty-thousand Americans owned television sets. By the end of this year, it'll be about three-hundred-and-fifty-thousand. Next year projections are over a million. Each year the number of TV sets sold will skyrocket! And why is that important? Because all four TV networks are going to need hours of entertainment to fill the airwaves. Jo-Jo, you need to get in early and become *America's* sweetheart. Mark my words, once we get you on the right show, everybody in the U.S. will know your name within a few years. I know it in my bones."

"Well, you certainly present a promising case. It sounds quite exciting. What do you think about the recording industry? I'd love to make a record."

"Yes, works hand in hand with the acting. Records can introduce you to entirely different audiences, who then might decide to tune into a program you're a regular on. This is what I suggest we do. We'll take a multi-pronged approach. I'll shop you around to a few recording studios, and take a look at proposed programming on the networks and see what kind of shows we can send you out on auditions for. On your end, keep performing at the Copa for now and I'll grab you more publicity everytime you perform with a big name. That way, the network head honchos will be more familiar with you."

"I like that idea. I think you're on to something, Saul."

"So...we got a deal then? You're interested in signing with me?"

A big time agent really wanted me and had a plan. Yes, I wanted to sign with him! "Absolutely. If you promote me with the same enthusiasm you showed today, I think we'll make a wonderful team."

"I agree. Oh, one thing to keep in mind with TV; it adds about ten pounds to everyone on the screen. So actors really have to watch their weight."

"Hmm, I have to say, I have a healthy appetite. Justin will attest to that."

"Oh, I wouldn't worry. They have pills for that. Look at Judy Garland now; stays real thin. Anyway, this is gonna be great, Jo-Jo. Can't wait to start working together."

Leaving the William Morris Agency, I was over the moon. I loved the spunky energy of my new agent, his vision, his creativity. And Saul was an associate of the top agency in the world. It had clout and they were now working for me! I hadn't felt this good since the night I won Talent Jackpot.

It was a warm fall day. I took off my suit jacket and decided to walk, maybe I'd walk all the way to the Stage Deli, work up an appetite, and order lunch. I decided it was a perfect way to celebrate signing with Saul. To get there quicker, I circumvented the center of Times Square and walked past the seedier side, ignoring the peep show barkers attempting to lure customers inside. I approached a burlesque theater with posters featuring Lili St. Cire, an apparently famous dancer in the art of strip tease. As I walked past, I heard a familiar voice behind me.

"Well lookie here. It's The Deli Girl slumming around the strip joints. Thought you'd moved on up."

It was an annoying, high pitched man's voice that I recognized only too well. I turned to see Billy the Wonderkid, sporting a goatee, dressed in a dapper suit, with a fedora pulled down over his bangs. And instead of his mother/wife hanging on him, it was none other than Fran Jordan. I could only assume Billy was her new client.

I had to hold back my laughter and spite. "Billy, good to see you. Fran, you as well. Where's your *mother* these days, Billy?"

"Uh, there's been a parting of the ways with our business ventures. But I'm going gangbusters. Fran's got me singing at some top joints. I got a whole new act. I go by William K now."

I looked back at the burlesque theater they'd come out of. It had definitely seen better days. "Yeah, I can see that. Sharing the marquee with no less than Lillie St. Cire. Congratulations! Well, I'm off to grab lunch. Good luck to you both."

I walked on with an even bigger grin across my face. Fran had not said a word, purposely ignoring me, and looking clearly embarrassed to be handling a client like Billy the Wonderkid. But after I thought about it, they were actually perfect for each other. They'd spend most of their time checking to see whose hands were in each other's pockets.

When I walked into the deli, Max Asnas was at the register, Chuckles was banging on the grill frying up eggs and hash browns, and a new, young waitress was taking orders. When she made it over to my table, she asked, "Hey there, ma'am, how's everything going today?"

I chuckled at her deep southern accent and said, "You must be new."

"Yes ma'am, been here about a month, straight out of Biloxi and just getting the hang of things." Then she lowered her voice, admitting, "I'm really a dancer. Hoping this is temporary."

"Great. I think I'll take a skyhigh pastrami on a kaiser roll with a dill pickle on the side. And how about a cup of coffee, black."

Then from the back of the counter I heard, "Well, you're a sight for sore eyes." It was Chuckles who was setting up his eggs order. "Max, look who's here."

Max and Chuckles walked around the counter, saying hello, as the Biloxi beauty stopped in her tracks and said, "Wait a minute. Are you The Deli Girl? Oh my goodness…You're the reason I'm here! I listened to you on Talent Jackpot back home and I thought, if you could make it, maybe I could too. Are you still at the Copacabana? I'd give my right arm to be dancing there."

By then Max was standing behind Biloxie and shooed her away. "Hey, Betty Belle, back to work. Table three is waiting on their drinks. Miss Anderson's a busy woman." I was amused that Asnas was now calling me *Miss Anderson* and considered me a busy *woman*. Chuckles gave me an onion scented hug and Max honored me with a sit-down visit.

He bent my ear with all his glorious street gossip for the next forty-five minutes. He seemed to know every problem and issue each club and shop owner within a two-mile range was in the midst of. The two of us carried on like old friends, and as I took a giant bite of New York's best pastrami sandwich, I could not have been happier.

Before leaving, I invited Betty Belle to the Copa to watch a rehearsal with the dancers. She was so excited that she collapsed on a chair and began crying. It was pretty funny, but I could honestly relate to her emotional excitement.

As I walked home, I was already thinking about my next letter to Sarah, telling her about my new agent and the possibilities of television. I couldn't wait to get her take on everything.

CHAPTER 51
OH, BABY!
SARAH

*I*t was early September and classes were starting next week. I'd put off leaving baby David until the last possible day. I'd been nursing him and was surprised at how much I enjoyed every minute of it. I'd expressed several bottles to put in the deep freeze but it wouldn't be long before he'd be fed an evaporated milk formula. I hated leaving Davey, but I'd been convinced he'd receive ample love and attention. I was shocked at how attached I'd already become to this tiny, gurgling, happy baby.

Lester pulled up into our drive on the Sunday before classes began. It was close to lunch time and Mother had pulled out all the stops to welcome Lester. After he had called, offering to drive me to school, she continued to describe him as a *promising young man*, even though I said I wasn't interested in Lester in that way.

Mother, David, and I came outside to greet him and I handed him his crutches from the back of the truck. After meeting Lester, Mother had remained quiet but finally spoke to him after he came inside. "Lester, I have to tell you something. I swear, you are so like my first husband, Sarah's father, it's uncanny. David, you remember Sam. Am I right?" David nodded in agreement.

"Lester laughed a little nervously and asked, "So did he have one leg too?"

Everyone laughed, but Mom said, "No, but he had your same smile, the fly-away light hair, the tall, lanky body. I'm sorry. I know this all sounds quite odd, but the likeness is uncanny."

I changed the conversation and brought it back to the lunch she and I had prepared and we all sat down for a friendly Sunday dinner. The conversation flowed and everything felt comfortable as we finished with a dessert of apple crumble and ice cream. Then baby David started crying upstairs. Before Lester's arrival, I'd told my parents I wasn't sure if I was ready to tell my friends about my baby yet. When the crying commenced, Mother stood up and said, "Sounds like Davey is hungry. Excuse me for a few moments, everyone."

I immediately felt the denial of something so important to me was ridiculous. I stood up and said, "I'll take care of him, Mom. Lester, in a few minutes, will you join me in the living room? There's someone I'd like you to meet."

"Sure thing."

I took a bottle of breast milk out of the refrigerator and went upstairs, then picked up Davey from the crib and came down to sit in a rocking chair. Lester came over looking a little confused and asked, "So, who's this little guy?"

"Les, I'd like to introduce you to my son. He was born three weeks ago. Davey, meet Lester Adams. He's a wonderful friend of mine."

I glanced at Lester's face. There was a look of total surprise. "Really? Damn!" But then I watched the curve of a smile as he took a close look. "Now that's a darn good looking boy. Well done, Sarah! Somebody's been busy this summer."

"Oh Lester, you have no idea."

"Well good, then we'll have something to talk about on that four-hour drive, 'cause I got nothing."

I teared up while feeding Davey, knowing it would be a month until I would do this again. Eventually, I handed him off to Mom, who was always eager to coo over her grandson. David helped me load my suitcases in the back of Lester's truck. We all said our good-byes and Lester was wholeheartedly welcomed back. As we drove down the long gravel drive, he asked, "So, how do you feel about starting a new semester?"

"Gosh, I don't know…excited, sad, eager, overwhelmed. But yes, I'm ready."

A few minutes passed in silence as Lester turned onto the main road. "Well, Sarah… I'm all ears. Let's hear about it."

Oh gosh, where do I start?"

"Remember, that day you called and I took you to the train station. Before leaving you seemed upset and kissed me goodbye on the cheek."

"Of course, I remember that day."

"Start there."

ABOUT THIS NOVEL

FALLING FROM THE NEST--The Sisters Of Green Tree is a stand-alone historical fiction novel which also serves as a sequel to my earlier novel, *The Lost and Found of Green Tree*. After completing the first one, I never considered writing a follow-up book. But the suggestion for a sequel was mentioned often in readers' comments. About a year later, I decided to give it a go and I'm so excited that I did. So, whether this is a sequel for you as a reader, or a first time read of the two novels, I hope you enjoy jumping into the world of 1946 and into the lively lives of sisters, Jo-Jo and Sarah Anderson. This was an absolute joy to write.

Bobbie Candas lives in Dallas, Texas with her husband, Mehmet. She has written five novels and is always on the hunt for new ideas for her next writing project.

SO, WHAT IS FICTION AND WHAT WAS HISTORICALLY TRUE

Jo-Jo, Sarah, and all the secondary characters from the fictional town of Green Tree were pulled from my imagination. Regarding Jo-Jo's world in Manhattan, there was an actual Stage Deli which opened in 1937, located on 834 7th Avenue in Midtown which was owned by Max Asnas, a businessman in the area known for his sense of humor, hard work ethic, and as someone who seemed to have an ear for all the gossip in the surrounding theater district. Later, under different management, it remained open until 2012.

Also, a bonafide real-life character was Monte Proser, the original designer and partial owner of the famous Copacabana Night Club, which opened in 1940 at 10 East 60th Street, between Fifth and Madison Avenues. Proser led an extremely colorful life within the saloon business and the entertainment industry, and had an eye for selecting young talent. Also, the mafia run side of the Copa was financed by mobster Frank Costello who handpicked Jules Podell to control the receipts. Also real are the top entertainers of the era mentioned in the book as performing at the Copa, including comedian Joe E. Lewis, who was attacked by gangsters in Chicago and hospitalized for months.

Club 21 was also a top restaurant and bar of the era, and served as a destination where top entertainment figures commingled with economic leaders. After a long run under different owners, it closed in 2021.

The famed LB Mayer of MGM studios presided over the Hollywood film company successfully from the twenties until 1951 when he was finally forced out when the studio saw big declines in profits, partially due to the growing popularity of television. In the novel, the character James Appleton, Mayer's fixer, is fictional.

And there was, indeed, a popular radio show called Talent Jackpot broadcast on the Mutual Broadcast Network and hosted by the mentioned, John Reed King. The prizes awarded in the story, the applause-o-meter, and voting from the live studio audience were all based on the actual Talent Jackpot radio show. The show later moved to television for a brief time.

Jo-Jo's Manhattan home, The Dixie, was an actual seven-hundred room hotel in Times Square which advertised rooms with a bed, bath, and radio for twenty dollars a week in the mid-1940's. The hotel had a few nightclubs within it, several restaurants, and a city bus depot in the basement. The hotel exists to this day under another name but is very run down and certainly not the tourist draw it was in Jo-Jo's era.

Within Sarah's world, all the students, teachers, and the administration mentioned are fictional characters. The University of Iowa in Iowa City was a well established co-ed college offering a variety of degrees which opened in 1847. Sarah's dorm, Currier Hall, was the oldest female dorm opening in 1917.

There is currently a Young Republicans organization on this campus, but I'm not sure if there was one established at the University of Iowa in 1946. Nationally, the organization was created in 1931 as a political and social group for young men and women between the ages of 18 to 40 to draw support for candidates within the Republican party.

The volunteer group, Help for Heroes, was a fictional organization, although there was certainly a need for assistance for the many disabled vets returning to school under the GI Bill. During this time, there were many efforts made by some of the larger corporations to train injured vets for the workplace. But most needs for the disabled were not fully embraced by state governments until the passage of the 1973 Rehabilitation Act, when many needed building reforms and designs became mandatory.

All films, radio programs, music, and recordings mentioned were all part of the popular cultural influences of the era and I attempted to keep the economic and political events referred to by characters as accurate as possible.

Although illegal drugs were not as prevalent in the US in 1946 as they are today, there was certainly drug usage found within the entertainment, nightclub, and film communities, along with other groups throughout society. The B-12 vitamin shots administered and the Vin Mariani mentioned in the novel were popular drugs used and discussed in a biography written about Monte Proser, *King of the Nightclubs*, written by Jim Proser.

Another excellent entertainment source was the biography, *Lion of Hollywood: the Life and Legend of Louis B Mayer*, written by Scott Eyman.

CREDITS ON MUSIC MENTIONED:

Much of the music written during this era of big bands, jump blues, and swing was really fun to listen to, with entertaining lyrics and arrangements. Many of the songs mentioned are still available to hear online.

Chattanooga Choo-Choo: lyrics by Mack Gordon, composed by Harry Warren, and originally recorded by Glen Miller and his Orchestra, vocals by Tex Beneke and the Four Modernaires, used in the film Sun Valley Serenade, 1941

Boogie Woogie Bugle Boy: written by Hughie Prince and Don Raye, originally performed by the Andrew Sisters, 1941

Choo Choo Ch'boogie: written by Vaughn Horton, Denver Darling, and Milt Gabler, recorded by Lois Jordan, 1946

In The Mood: (originally called the Tar Paper Stomp), written by Wingy Manoney and Joe Garland, most popular recording was by Glen Miller and His Orchestra, 1939

Sentimental Journey: written by Les Brown and Ben Homer, lyrics by Bud Green, recorded originally by Les Brown and His Orchestra, vocals by Doris Day, 1944

Give Me Five Minutes More: written by Sammy Cahn and recorded by Frank Sinatra, 1946

The musical--Oklahoma: music and lyrics by Richard

Rodgers and Oscar Hammerstein II, songs mentioned: Surrey With the Fringe On Top, first performed by Alfred Drake, I Cain't Say No, first performed by Celeste Holm, Oh What a Beautiful Morning, first performed by Alfred Drake, 1943

The musical--Annie Get Your Gun: lyrics and music by Irving Berlin, songs mentioned: There's No Business Like Show Business, I Got the Sun in the Mornin', both first performed by Ethel Merman, 1946

The Trolley Song and **The Boy Next Door:** from the film, Meet Me in St. Louis, music and lyrics by Ralph Blane and Hugh Martin, originally performed by actress Judy Garland, 1944

Sunday, Monday and Always: music by Jimmy Van Huesn, lyrics by Johnny Burke, most popular recording by Bing Crosby, 1943

OTHER NOVELS BY BOBBIE CANDAS:

Welcome to Wonderland: A Dramedy

https://tinyurl.com/36d5vzfv

The Lost and Found of Green Tree

https://tinyurl.com/57kcxzvb

Imperfect Timing

https://tinyurl.com/2nttb8x4

Luck, Love, and a Lifeline

https://tinyurl.com/ycy39rc8

FOLLOW BOBBIE CANDAS ON SOCIAL MEDIA

INSTAGRAM
https://www.instagram.com/bobbiecandas/?hl=en

GOODREADS
https://www.goodreads.com/author/list/
8292457.Bobbie_Candas

FACEBOOK
https://www.facebook.com/bobbiecandasauthor/

AMAZON AUTHOR PAGE
https://www.amazon.com/stores/author/B00MNS6KV0?
ingress=0&visitId=687c10aa-aa95-4d14-8a1b-71fce6b815c7&ref_=
ap_rdr

 facebook.com/bobbiecandasauthor

ACKNOWLEDGMENTS

Special thanks to my early first-time readers on this novel: Jeanne McCaffrey and Susie Criswell. You are the greatest sounding boards, and always keep me pushing forward!

I have the absolute best beta readers! Many thanks for plowing through a draft of *Falling From the Nest*. It's so refreshing to get another person's point of view. Your comments and suggestions were greatly appreciated and well utilized: Liz Brammer, Vicki Brumby, Katy Clayton, Susie Criswell, Julie Flo, Beth Lonergan, Jeanne McCaffrey, Michael Pole, Nancy Putnam, Bird Thomas, and Tia Tomlin.

I can't say enough good things about my online pals at Creative Writers of Dallas--the ability to give weekly postings of new material and gather excellent feedback was invaluable to me. In addition, I treasure all the varied conversations we have over so many topics and writing challenges. Special thanks to group regulars: John Archer, Tom Terrific, Kelley Shaw, Ray Wood, and Jacob Meadors. My best rewrites came from your valuable suggestions.

My cover and interior book designer, Betty Martinez, is the best! Thanks for being so easy to work with and having such wonderful, creative skills. I appreciate your work in making all the words on the page look beautiful.

Special thanks to Dr. Cari Candas and PA Demir Candas for medical advice needed in a few scenes; it's always good to check in with the doctors!

And, of course, a big thank you to my husband, Mehmet Candas for his patience and tech advice. Wherever we traveled, he always allowed me time with my other constant companion, my sweet laptop, Hi-Ho-Silver!

I have a really deep and special appreciation to all the readers of my earlier novel, ***The Lost and Found of Green Tree.*** I hope this sequel lives up to your expectations, gives you pleasure, tickles your emotions, and allows you to travel back to another time and place.

AN EXCERPT FROM THE LOST AND FOUND OF GREEN TREE

BOBBIE CANDAS

PROLOGUE

*M*y latest issue of Silver Screen calls this decade a time of great progress for the modern woman. They even gave it a name, 'The Roaring Twenties.' Well, I can assure you, the only roaring going on in Green Tree, Iowa, is the occasional motorized tractor chugging down Main Street.

The name of Green Tree probably has you conjuring up images of a lovely hamlet, with winding hilly streets, surrounded by a thick forest of evergreens, populated by lots of interesting people. No. There's just the one tree. A big, unshapely elm, growing off to the side of the brick county court house which is the center of a grid of straight, organized streets servicing the surrounding farming community, populated by, well...mostly farmers.

Of course, there's a few of us town-folk too, running the integral businesses supporting the area. But there's no movie theater, or community stage. No elegant restaurants, and only the one clothing store. There's a popular hardware store—for my needs, useless. And I'd have to say the same for the Farm and Implement Store. Although, I should add that we do have a coffee shop which sells cherry-flavored soda-pop, a personal favorite, a pool hall selling ice cream, and the drug store which just added a modern pay phone to the wall.

Also, I'd be remiss not to mention a fabric store run by my grim auntie who is assisted, under forced labor, by me, Nanette Jorgenson.

Amongst all this, I can absolutely assure you that in Green Tree I saw no possible future employment for dynamically inspired women, such as myself. By my teen years I already knew I was meant for bigger things.

NANETTE JORGESON

$\mathcal{I}$ stood confidently on the makeshift plywood stage in front of the courthouse, lined up next to nine other hopeful girls, each of us praying to hear our name called. It was August, a warm late afternoon. My face muscles were beginning to ache after showing off my glistening smile for at least forty-five minutes. The Green Tree judges of the 1927 Harvest Celebration were about to decide the winning candidates for the Corn Queen's Court. Whoever was selected as queen would be the envy of every girl in town and had the honor of presiding over the Harvest Celebration parade, the corn-eating contest, the fall fruit-pie competition, and the Harvest Celebration dance.

We were judged on poise, beauty, ability to communicate, posture, and popularity; all attributes many friends have told me I excel at.

Our Green Tree mayor, dressed in a dark plaid suit, bow tie and straw boater, was droning on about all the upcoming festivities which were essentially the same ones we had every year. Just get on with it...announce my name. I was born for this. If my name wasn't announced as queen, I might not accept the role of princess or duchess. I didn't like playing second fiddle and certainly hated third.

With a crowd of next year's potential voters in front of him, the mayor couldn't simply get to the point, feeling compelled to remind us of all the good things the funds generated by the festival would do for the village. While he talked, I looked about, nodding to a few friends standing in the crowd. I saw my best friend, Catherine Anderson, and her cute younger brother, Sam, with that girlfriend of his, Mariah. What did he see in her? I then waved at Melinda Perkins. She wasn't really a friend, but was strong competition and I was happy she'd decided not to run for queen this year, so I was being nicer to her.

Then finally… "Alright. So now folks, here's what we all came to see. Our beautiful line-up of Corn Harvest Court hopefuls. Gosh, I wish we had room for all of them in the parade. Have you ever seen such a lovely group of young women?"

The mayor's pandering was followed by a light smattering of applause and a few whistles. The sun was about to set, the mayor was losing his audience, and my feet were beginning to hurt standing tall in Auntie's borrowed high heels with my hands on my hips, continuing to flash my broadest smile. The mayor raised his hands as if he was stopping a tidal wave of applause. "OK… Alright. Let's quiet down. The judges have given me their decisions. Ladies, if I call your name, just step over here next to me. So— without further ado—for our Corn Harvest Duchess, we have… Miss Amy Shulwater."

Amy Shulwater? With the chipped tooth and frizzy hair? I guess there were perks when your father owned the implement dealership. Light applause rose from the crowd, as a young boy rushed over from the side of the makeshift stage with a dozen ears of corn tied together with a green ribbon, handing them to the new duchess. Some towns offered rose bouquets, but in Green Tree, you got corn.

The mayor jumped in with a handshake and then read from his card, "Congratulations Amy! Next, for the title of Princess, we have another town-beauty… Miss Miranda Plum." Miranda stepped forward, gushing, accepting her gift of corn.

This was it; my big moment, or utter defeat.

"And now… good people of Green Tree, the recipient of our

tiara, the satin banner, and *two* dozen ears of corn goes to our 1927 Queen of Corn... the lovely Miss Nanette Jorgenson."

Was it my imagination, or had the crowd erupted in massive applause? Forget the produce, just put that crown on my head and pin the banner across my chest. I stepped over to receive my handshake and congratulatory hug. Queen Nanette was crowned!

That week was magical for me and transformative. I cut my long blonde hair into a permed and crimped bob, almost giving Auntie a heart attack when she saw my thick eight-inch braid cut off and sitting on my vanity. I led the parade while waving from the back of a decorated, spanking-new red truck, borrowed from a dealership in Clear Lake. Auntie provided me with a silver sparkling fabric which I sewed into a draping drop-waist dress, hemming it rakishly short, exposing my knees. I felt special; little girls pointed at me when I walked down Main Street, while friends from school would stop and congratulate me. Topping that, I danced with every young man in town at the festival celebration. But most importantly, at the dance I met James Iverson.

He was from neighboring East Point. Four years older, and the most handsome man I'd ever seen; a tall, strapping guy with a manicured dark mustache, whose father happened to own a bank. I'd given him a wink on the dance floor and he'd eventually made his way over to me. When he asked me to dance, that was it. I'd found my man.

AT THE HOT CUP, sitting next to a table of grizzled farmers, I was gossiping with my friend, Catherine Anderson. We both took long sips of our colas, gearing up for our weekly gab exchange. "So, how are all your brothers doing, Catherine? I still think young Sam is the cutest."

"Forget it Nanette, you're too old for him. Besides, he's crazy about Mariah. They've been dating over a year now."

"Don't be silly. He's cute but not my type. I'm ready for someone more mature in the business field. Speaking of which, at the dance, did you notice a tall handsome gentleman? Mustache, suspenders? We danced together at least five times."

"Gosh, yes… I think every girl at the dance was ogling him."

I lowered my voice, saying, "Name is James Iverson. Son of a banker, great dancer, and even better *kisser*."

"You've kissed him already! Nanette, be careful."

"Oh, don't be such a bluenose. It was only a little kiss. He drove me home from the dance, and guess what?" I pounded my hand lightly on the café table. "We have a date for next weekend. I'm over the moon! *Never* felt this way about a guy before."

"Nanette, you're so lucky. Why can't I ever meet someone like him?"

"You will, Catherine. Just get your brothers to introduce you to their friends. You're bound to meet a great guy."

She nodded, playing with the straw in her drink. "I suppose, but all their friends are farmers too."

I glanced around, making sure nobody was eavesdropping. "True. James seems different, not like all these boys we grew up with. A college man…. and a banker."

"Yes, you mentioned that."

I checked my watch; I was running late as usual. "Darn. Auntie is watching the clock; I'm supposed to be getting the groceries. I'll let you know how the date goes."

"OK. Please keep me posted, Nanette. I'm dying to hear how it goes." As I walked out, two more girls from school walked into the Hot Cup, waving at Catherine. I knew she'd spread the gossip about my date with James.

James Iverson. I couldn't get his face out of my mind. When I told Auntie about him, she approved of my Saturday night date. Although, at eighteen, I was officially an adult. No permission should have been necessary. But when I was twelve, my dad passed away, and his Aunt Edwina had been clucking over me like her prized hen ever since.

I checked my *Silver Screen* and *Photoplay* magazines religiously and had cut out photos of several styles of dresses I wanted to copy and sew for myself. Auntie owned a small fabric and yarn store in Green Tree, so I'd always had access to my own creations. That week, I made a light green cotton dress with white piping, with the green fabric perfectly matching my eyes, and I accessorized it with a long string of pearls. Fake ones, but who could really tell?

Now that I had the crimped hair, the dress, and the right makeup, I found it hard to tell the difference between myself and motion picture star, Marion Davies. I wanted to stun James Iverson. I stared at my reflection and then back again at the magazine photos of Marion. The comparison was pretty darn close. If Marion could attract the attention of publishing tycoon William Randolph Hearst, I could certainly hold the eye of James Iverson from No-Where, Iowa.

Peeking out the window, I watched James drive up in his shiny dark-blue Chrysler Roadster. So stylish, I had to pinch myself. I took a minute to ask him into our small home and introduce him to Auntie. She'd made me promise to do this and immediately began grilling him. "So, James, Nanette tells me you're an East Point resident. Have a cousin still living there. Would you know Bonnie and Steven Billows?"

"Why, yes ma'am. The Billows… a fine family. I believe they've held accounts with our family for years. Miss Jorgenson, if it's alright with you, I'd like to take Nanette to see a new film in Clear Lake. It starts at eight-thirty, so we'll need to head out."

"Certainly, of course. You two enjoy this lovely evening." I could tell Auntie approved. She wasn't giving him her usual squint-eye.

He'd decided that we should see *Phantom of the Opera,* starring Lon Chaney. Clear Lake was a thirty-minute drive from Green Tree, allowing us a little time to get to know each other better. When we sat down near the back of the dark theater, he immediately put his arm around me, and the movie became so scary I had to hide my eyes against his jacket a few times. Before the film was over, we'd kissed twice and my heart was almost jumping outside my chest. Leaving the theater, James placed his hand around mine and I felt like we melted together.

He suggested we take a drive by the lake. "It's beautiful this time of year, Nanette. Only us, the water, stars, and the moon. You'll love it."

"Sure, sounds magical. Just as long as I'm home around midnight." Auntie was a stickler on the curfew, but perhaps tonight she'd allow me a little leniency with James being such a promising beau.

We drove past some cottages built along the water and cruised a bit further, parking in a grove of overhanging willows near the lake's edge. It was dark, with a background sound of frogs croaking melodically. We drove across freshly cropped grass which invaded my senses, a salute to summer's final hurrah. And as promised, a big bright moon danced across ripples on the black lake. I felt like I was on a film set. He pulled a silver flask from his inside jacket pocket, took a long swig and handed it to me.

"Maybe I'll try a sip. I really don't drink." It was strong whiskey, too bitter for me. I handed it back quickly. "It's gorgeous here, let's walk a bit."

"In a little while." He stretched out his arms above his head. "I'm feeling really comfortable, but it's even better in the back seat. Let me show you." Always the gentleman, he got out, opened my door and let me slide across the spacious, padded back seat. It was lovely. He leaned over and kissed me, but this time he inserted his tongue. It was one of those French kisses the girls at school were always giggling about.

He looked down at me. "You're so beautiful, but you know that, don't you?" His hands moved slowly lower to my breasts, gently rubbing them, as he groaned in anticipation. I pushed his hands away, surprised he'd try such liberties already.

Nervously, I asked, "Maybe we should get out and walk? It's so nice by the lake."

"It's nicer here." He pushed me back, pressing my head down on the arm rest. "You're going to love this. Pretend you're my very own little movie star."

Before I could sit up, his weight was on top of me and his hand was pushing up my dress and snaking into my panties. I wedged my elbow out on the open side and tried to stop him, but his right hand knocked my arm away and then jerked more aggressively on my panties, ripping one side as he yanked them down. "Come on Nanette, you want this as much as I do." I heard his belt unbuckle and the sound of his zipper.

"No, I'm not ready. It's too soon. Not like this." I struggled to keep my legs together, grasping the skirt of my dress tightly.

But he roughly batted my hand away again, then thrusted his fist between my thighs, pushing my legs apart. He began pushing hard, but nothing was happening. James asked me hoarsely, "Your first time?"

I nodded, repeating myself, "James, no! Get off. I'm not ready." This was all going terribly wrong.

He ignored my pleas, continuing to ram his penis into me, eventually sliding inside, as he grunted on top in jerking motions for what seemed agonizingly long. He finally stopped, got off, went out to his trunk, and handed me a small white towel. "Here, you might need this," and then he walked over to the lake's edge, turning his back to the car.

I quickly removed the remains of my panties, putting them in my handbag and then wiped the blood and wet stickiness from the seat and between my legs. I was in shock as I watched James outside the car. I was so afraid he'd come back and want to do it again. As the shock began to wear off and the reality of what had just happened hit me, I began to cry. I felt dirty and disgusted with myself.

James was now leaning against the hood of the car, puffing on a lit cigar and continuing to take leisurely swigs from his flask. He eventually came back, opened the door, then looked at his watch. "Well, it's getting late. Probably don't have time for that walk. Guess I better get you back home."

"I'm staying back here," I said in a defiant voice.

"Suit yourself."

There was no discussion of what had just happened. I no longer cared about James Iverson. I hated James Iverson. I sat next to the window and stared out at the dark farm roads, and rode home in silence. Could I have kicked him, bucked him off, screamed?

Nothing about what had happened was how I'd dreamed it would be; it was dirty, painful and felt all wrong. How did he go from fairy-tale prince to, to... that? Arriving at my house, I opened the car door myself, slamming it abruptly on James and never heard from him again. That, at least, was a relief.

Although my thoughts and nightmares often trailed back to that terrible night, I put on a show to others, pretending my life was absolutely normal. All that continued until October, when I realized I'd missed my period--twice. How could that be possible? Some of the girls at school who'd whispered about 'doing it,' said you never got pregnant on your first time. I couldn't tell anybody. Like I'd tried to tell James, I wasn't ready for any of this. This could not be how my life was supposed to play out. I became sick to my stomach. Often.

Then, I quickly developed a plan.

MARIAH ANDERSON

$\mathcal{I}$'d never forget that day back in September 1924. Gosh, that seems so long ago. I'd been at Green Tree High School for only a few days, coming from a country school with a total of twelve students, grades first through eighth. Now at Green Tree High, there were thirty-two students in just my freshman class. One of my first assignments was an oral presentation on Germany for world geography class.

The night before, upstairs in our small crowded bedroom, I practiced my report out loud so many times that my two sisters, Arlene and Janeen, were throwing their shoes at me to make me stop.

"Mariah, if we have to hear about that darn Danube River one more time, Arlene and I will beat you with these shoes instead of just throwing them. We have studies of our own. Shut up, please!"

"Sorry, I'm so nervous. Imagine, standing in front of over thirty students. I want everything perfect."

In preparation for the task, I'd done three days of library research and created a poster from butcher paper. The morning of my big report, I'd borrowed my older sister's new light-pink lipstick and curled my shoulder-length dark hair. I wore a knitted pull-over sweater over a starched white collared blouse, and a pleated skirt

Mother had recently sewn for me. All of this preparation, just to give a five-minute report.

Standing in front of the class, most kids looked back at me with bored expressions. I cleared my throat, nervously pulling on my sweater, and began, attempting to exude a sense of confidence.

At lunch, I joined a table of girls I'd recently met at band practice. While unwrapping my cheese sandwich, I watched a handsome blonde boy, dressed in overalls and plaid shirt, walk over to our table. Sitting down next to me, he introduced himself and offered me his hand to shake, as my new girlfriends giggled and rolled their eyes. I grasped his rough calloused hand and shook it while he announced, "Mariah, I'm Samuel Anderson. Don't know if you've noticed me, but I'm in your geography class. Four rows over, two chairs back. Just wanted to stop by and say I liked your report. Seems like you really did your homework."

I was suspect that any boy from Green Tree would really be interested in a report on Germany. I nervously strung a few random sentences together. "Uh… thanks? I enjoy reading about new places. I plan on traveling a lot someday."

"Why?" He blinked, looking suddenly surprised.

"Why not? There's certainly something more interesting in this life besides cows and corn. That's about all I ever see around here." I took a few bites of my sandwich, and watched all the girls at my table turning their curious heads toward us.

"Nothing wrong with cows and corn. Kept my family fed for years. And I tell you, Mariah, farming's changing."

"Maybe… Send me a letter all about it when I'm up in New York working in a skyscraper office."

"And of all places, why would you want to go there?"

"Because it's not here." Our banter had the girls' heads switching back and forth, not wanting to miss whatever was about to happen.

"Just so you know… there are so many new planting techniques coming out. I been reading up on it. Farming's exciting." Sam slapped his hand on the lunch table, signifying he'd won the discussion.

I shook my head and laughed. "Challenging maybe, but I don't know about exciting. My parents have farmed for years." I shrugged my shoulders, looking around the table. "I just know I want more. Someplace where I'm not always side-stepping cow-pies, or worrying about rain and drought. But I like your passion about farming, Sam." I started wrapping up the remainder of my lunch. "I guess we all need to be inspired by something."

Sally Neilson, sitting on my other side, nudged my elbow. "Seems like farming isn't the only thing Sam's excited about."

Ignoring her comment, he lowered his voice and said, "Mariah, I'd like to buy you a slice of cake at the Hot Cup this Saturday. Let's talk more about this."

"This may sound strange but I really don't like cake." I picked up my books for class and stood up. "But I do love pie."

"They got that too."

"All right, farmer Sam. I'll meet you for pie, but don't plan on changing my mind about farming."

INITIALLY, I was a little leery of this over-confident, tall, fair-haired boy. He seemed too sure of himself, to the point of being cocky. But honestly, I was flattered that Sam seemed to like me, a little nobody farm-girl with straight brown hair and hand-made clothes. But eventually his steady persistence and laughing blue eyes won me over and we began seeing each other regularly outside of school a few times a week.

I told my two sisters that I'd never met a boy my age who already knew what he wanted and was hell-bent on getting it. Those plans included having his own farm, marriage, and a family. In his mind, everything was all laid out. But I knew there was plenty of time for things to change; we were young, with years ahead of us, and that first love was so intoxicating.

At fourteen, with Sam in my life, the simplest of things felt fresh and new; the thrill of holding hands walking down Main Street, or sitting on a blanket together at outdoor movies on the courthouse lawn. We'd share a bag of popcorn, and watch the silent movies of my favorite actress, Mary Pickford, while Sam loved laughing through the Buster Keaton and Chaplin films.

There was one early date I'd never forget. A company passing through town set up a temporary roller-rink in our village park, and all our gang from school decided to give it a try. Sam sprung for the forty cents on our rentals as we both clamped the metal skates onto our shoes and had them keyed tightly to the soles. I'd only tried skating once before and Sam was a total novice, so we gingerly clung to the rails spaced around the rink which was set up on a plat-form. A large amplified Victrola played all the popular songs from the radio. When they put on my favorite, *Five-Foot-Two, Eyes-of-Blue*, I forced myself to push off from the sides and courageously skate to the tune of the music. As I gained more confidence, I pulled Sam along and soon we found ourselves skating hand in hand. We went round and round the platform, gaining in speed. It was exhilarating. When the song ended, everyone else dashed to the sides, waiting for the next record. But Sam pulled me to him and in the middle of the rink, wrapped his arms around me, and gave me a long kiss. I knew people were watching, but I had to kiss him back. If I'd been alone, I would have kissed him all night. I adored feeling Sam's strength wrapping around me and his hot breath in my ear, whispering, "You're the one."

I felt a deep shudder go through me as we broke apart, and then began skating to the next tune. That first passionate kiss resonated, making me realize Sam might be more than a passing romance.

NANETTE

I'd always wanted to get out of Green Tree, move to a larger town, and find an exciting job. With a possible pregnancy, there was now more urgency for my move. Nobody I knew could find out about this. I looked at a map and chose Mankato, Minnesota, about eighty miles north of Green Tree; not too far, but large enough to allow me some anonymity for a while. I wasn't sure what I was going to do *if* I was pregnant, but at least I could figure it out privately, on my own.

Aunt Edwina had one part-time assistant at the fabric store and me; but she could easily run it without my help. Besides, she'd never paid me for working there, but instead, gave me a meager weekly allowance. After dinner, I announced we needed to have an important conversation.

I started by serving tea and her favorite dessert, pineapple-upside-down cake. I'd actually paid a neighbor down the street to bake it. Sitting across from her at our dining table, I moved aside the bowl of waxed fruit and picked nervously at our lacy white table cloth.

"I've been contemplating this for a while now, Auntie. You know I've always wanted to get out on my own eventually." She raised her eyebrows and stared at me, saying nothing. "Well, I think it's time.

Ever since graduation I've been thinking about it....time for me to fly my wings and try new things." *Exceptionally good title for a future movie; I should write that down later.* I took a deep breath, and just told her. "I've decided I'm applying for jobs in Mankato."

"Mankato? That's Minnesota!" She said it as if I'd just announced I was moving to the North Pole. She shook her head, looking resolute. "No, Nanette. And besides, what if that nice gentleman, Mr. Iverson, comes round again."

"I told you already, he wasn't the man I thought he was. I have *no* interest in dating him... ever."

"You were always too picky. He was a good catch."

I rolled my eyes and ignored her comment and put a large slice of cake in front of her. "Take a bite, you'll love it. Besides, Auntie, a girl needs to see a few places before she settles down. I have skills. I type, good at selling, and I sew. I'm certain I'll find a good job there. There's just the issue of some seed money to find myself a little place to get settled. Will you help me, Auntie? Please?"

She took a big fork full of cake with sweet pineapple, laced with brown sugar crumbles. She savored it, took a sip of tea, and licked her lips. "I don't think so. Here's an idea. What if I start paying you at the store? I hate the idea of you being out there in the world all alone. There's too many unscrupulous people out and about these days. It's wild in the cities and Mankato's just too far."

Her comment immediately had me thinking of the predatory James Iverson. "Auntie, danger can lurk anywhere, but we can't let it consume us. And I've already checked. Mankato's only a two-hour train ride." It was actually closer to three hours, but who was counting? "And I could come back to visit some weekends." Auntie took another bite, listening and nodding. "This is actually a perfect time to apply. Most businesses are going gangbusters right now. If I hate it there, I can always come back, run your store and let you retire."

"Retire? Me? I don't know what I'd do with myself if I wasn't working. I don't need to retire!"

"How's the cake? I know it's your favorite."

"Delicious; your best yet, Nanette."

"You think so? Thanks. So then... if you're fine without me at the store, and based on your advice and business savvy, how much money do you think I'll need to find an apartment and maybe get a proper working wardrobe?"

"Hmm. Let me think on that. Oh, speaking of work clothes, we received the most adorable patterns for suits today. You'll need a smart suit, perhaps in a tweed."

"I agree. Let's discuss the money later. First, we'll need to pull a new wardrobe together. I appreciate your advice and style tips, Auntie, and I'll make you proud. There're so many details we need to consider." I jumped up, leaned over, and gave her a big hug. "Thanks so much. You're the berries! Got to go; I'm meeting Catherine."

As I walked out the door, she suddenly got up and yelled after me, "I didn't say yes. You're not going anywhere. There's more to talk about... Nanette?"

I squeezed an official 'yes' out of her within two days. Phase one of my evolving plan was coming together.

During my final week in Green Tree, my morning sickness began in earnest, confirming my pregnancy fears. I wasn't showing at all but I was having trouble hiding my nausea, making quick runs to the outhouse throughout the day.

By early November, I was on a train to Mankato with three suitcases of clothing, shoes, and hats. Auntie had given me enough cash to cover a few nights in a hotel and two months' funds for food and rent for a small apartment. If I didn't find a job during that time, I had promised to return home. In addition, she'd given me strict instructions to write her one letter every week, or she threatened to come there herself and drag me home.

The train trip to Mankato was a nightmare, with the rocking car motion making my vomiting bouts even more intense. I arrived green and exhausted; my face covered in a sheen of nervous sweat. Standing on the depot platform in my new travel suit with three large suitcases, I had no idea on how to get to the Front Street Hotel, where I'd reserved my first two-night's stay. The town looked larger and busier than I'd imagined, but apparently not large enough to have taxis.

In front of me, I watched a workman unloading wooden crates of produce from a freight car onto his dray wagon. Perhaps he could help. Dragging my three suitcases over one at a time, I walked up to the tired looking man. "Hello sir, any chance I could get directions for the Front Street Hotel? Would it be far?"

He stacked another wooden crate of cabbage in the wagon, while glancing up at me. "Nope, not too far. A little less than a mile west." He jerked his thumb in the hotel's direction.

"I see." I looked to my left, sighed, and stood there staring despondently, considering my options.

"Is all them cases yours?"

"All mine."

He stepped over, put them in the back with the cabbage crates and said, "OK, then. We best go now. I've got a delivery to make. You can get up front." He settled on the springy front bench and grabbed my hand, helping me step up.

"Why, thank you. My goodness, is everyone in Mankato as nice as you?"

"Nope, I just have a weakness for pretty girls with lots of suitcases."

"Well, you're very sweet. I'm Nanette Jorgensen and you're the first person I've met in Mankato."

The man nodded, touching the bill of his ragged cap. "Pleasure to meet you, Miss Jorgensen. I'm Obidiah Dawson, lived here all my life, and know lots of people. So, Front Street Hotel?" He snapped the reins on his two broad-backed black horses, turning them around. " What brings you to town?"

"Work. Just moved here from Green Tree, Iowa and decided to branch out a bit." The breeze picked up as I held on to my cloche hat with my hand. "Actually, I'm looking for a job and an apartment."

"A lady on a mission. I like that. This here is Front Street, main business street of Mankato. Not a bad spot to start your job search." Obidiah pointed out local landmarks as we made our way down to my hotel. Along with horses and wagons, there were numerous cars zipping up and down the asphalt road and several two, three, and four-level red-brick buildings on both sides of the street. It was impressive. We passed all of the larger buildings and eventually arrived at a dreary looking two-story wooden establishment with peeling paint and a sagging front porch. A creaking sign swung from the top level, *Front Street Hotel*. The place looked run-down and far from exclusive.

Noticing my unenthusiastic expression, Obidiah said, "Yeah, not exactly what you kids would call the bees' knees. You sure this is where you're staying?"

I took a deep breath and smiled. "I'm sure it'll be just fine. Wish me luck, Mr. Dawson." I climbed down, thanked him, shook his hand, and yanked my bags out of the back. "Do you suppose they'll come out to get my bags?"

He laughed at me as he began moving his horses. "No, Miss Nanette. I doubt any bellhops will come scampering out here. Good luck to you."

Here I was, arriving at a flea-bag hotel in a horse-drawn cabbage wagon. Not an auspicious beginning to my new life and definitely *not* movie star material.

MARIAH

$\mathcal{B}$y the middle of my junior year in high school, Sam was still the only boy I'd ever dated. Everyone knew we were a couple. Forgoing all his extra-curricular activities, including basketball and track, Sam began attending only a half-day of school. Instead, he focused his efforts on farming a new piece of land his father had rented from a retiring farmer, Lars Stevenson.

One late afternoon, after band practice, I walked out the school's side door and was surprised to see Sam sitting on the hood of his dad's old Model A.

He opened the door for me and we both got in. "Thought I'd give you a ride home today, but I've got a few things I need to get off my chest." He turned away from me and stared out the front window. "Been thinking about it a lot. There's something I need to say. Something important."

"You seem nervous. What's wrong?"

Clearing his throat and still looking straight ahead, he said, "Mariah, I love you more than I can express. You told me a long time ago you wanted to move to a big city, experience the world, travel to far-flung places. But I can't give you that. I'm committing full-out on this new land Dad's rented. I promised my father I'd give it everything I had. It's a chance to be on my own and try out all the new methods I been researching. Dad believes I'm ready."

I nodded and smiled. "I know. You told me already. And you're lucky to get the opportunity, especially at your age. He must really believe in you."

"He does. But I can't do it alone. I don't want to do it alone. It has to be with you. That's the only way I can see it. The two of us together, Mariah. A partnership. Maybe down the line, some years from now, I'll take you to Paris or that Germany you know so much about." He turned to look at me and took both of my hands. "What I'm trying to say is…will you marry me, Mariah? I love you so much and I'll do my darndest to make you happy."

I sat quiet for a moment, thinking, then looked down at the school books on my lap. I did want more from life than living out on an isolated Iowa farm. What about a career of my own in New York or Chicago, or taking a trip to Europe? But, if I was honest with myself, could I imagine a life without Sam? My days began and ended with me thinking about him, imagining his grinning face, entwining our arms around each other, passionately kissing him. If I left Green Tree, wherever I traveled or worked, I'd be thinking about him, longing to be with Sam. So, what was the point of moving elsewhere? As much as I hated to admit it, he'd changed my mind about being part of a farming family. If Sam was with me, I was on board.

I looked up, smiled, and threw my arms around his neck and kissed him hard, not caring who noticed. "Yes....yes! I'll definitely marry you. I love you so much. But not until I graduate. I must graduate high school."

"Whatever you want. I'll wait. But I've decided this is my last year. Work on the property is nonstop. I can't spend any more time doing class work. Several of the guys are dropping out after this year."

"I hate to hear that, but I understand. My Dad never went beyond eighth grade and did fine."

"You're going to love the house, Maraih. In the evenings, I'm going to work on fixing it up, just for you. It's old and needs updates, but I'll make us a good home. Can you see it…a place of our own?"

"Yes. It may be rented but we'll make it ours, a special place."

That afternoon, the drive back to my house was a turning point. I'd committed to a new life, separate from my parents, older brothers, and sisters. It was scary but also thrilling to think about. As long as I had Sam, I knew I'd be fine. He made me feel safe, beautiful, and desired; important requirements for a sixteen-year-old girl. I convinced myself I was ready to make this journey with him as Mrs. Mariah Anderson, while my dreams of travel and a life off the farm became a wistful memory.

NANETTE

$\mathcal{D}$ragging my first two bags to the hotel's porch, I critically eyed the worn and cracked leather armchairs spaced across the front, under a torn awning. I retrieved my third bag from the street, and held one of the large double doors open with my foot, while grabbing my other two bags and dumping everything inside. Checking out the interior, a damp musty smell mixed with the scent of tobacco greeted me and then gnawed at the yellow bile bubbling up again in my stomach.

I was nervous, having never stayed in a hotel, and unsure of the protocol. Auntie had insisted I stay at an all-women's place, but actually this was the only hotel the phone operator could locate for me when I called to make an inquiry. And anyway, what difference did it make? In the small lobby, there were two men in suits and bowler hats, both reading newspapers. As I walked in, feeling queasy, one of them glanced up, folded his paper, and left it on the arm of the lobby chair.

Walking out the door, he smiled at me. "Good day, miss. You look a little lost, may I help?"

I took out my embroidered handkerchief and wiped my brow. "Thank you. Just a little overheated. Uh, registration?"

He pointed to a small counter in the corner. "You have a lovely day."

While walking to the registration counter, I grabbed his abandoned newspaper, and stepped up to the counter. A balding man with glasses looked up from his desk.

"Yes, madam?"

"Hello, you're holding a room for *N. Jorgenson* for two nights."

He paged through a ledger. "Hmm, I see that, but is the room for you?"

"Yes."

"Well, if that's the case, it's quite impossible."

I was nauseous and agitated. I needed a room immediately. "Impossible? Why, for heaven's sake?"

"Because you're a woman. A lovely woman, no doubt. But... we do not allow unescorted women here. It's simply not proper."

I was surprised and confused, but tried my best to remain calm. "So... you do take women, just not unescorted women?"

"We take *married* women who are traveling with their husbands or families."

"Oh, I see. Yes, of course. Understandable. My husband, uh... Nathan Jorgenson, will be along. He's coming from Chicago and meeting me here. We have business in Mankato--real estate. I'll need to check in now though, freshen up and meet him at the station later. Let me get the room prepared for him. He likes things just so; you know how husbands can be. What room are we in?"

The clerk looked uncertain. "Well... if you're sure he'll be here later, I suppose you can register for the two of you; sign here, names and address please." He handed me a large metal key. "Room 2 F, upstairs, to the left. Bathroom's at the end of the hall."

"And I'll need someone to bring my bags to the room please." Ridiculous... needing to have a man tag along merely to rent a dive hotel room. I was fuming, although I kept my face calm and my smile glued. "Thank you, and what's your name, sir."

"Harold White, hotel manager."

"Well, Mr. White, I appreciate your understanding." It looked like Nathan Jorgenson's train would be running very late today or might not arrive at all. I quickly walked upstairs, then dashed to the communal bathroom, as a bout of morning sickness erupted. I dry heaved into the toilet. By now, there was little left to throw up except a disgusting yellow liquid. I wet my handkerchief in the sink, located my room, and fell across the squeaking narrow bed, placing the wet cloth over my forehead. I suddenly missed the comfort of my own familiar room, the stocked kitchen, the path leading up to our flower-laden front porch, even Auntie's nosey and concerned questions seemed endearing at the moment. I closed my eyes, dying for a nap, but was interrupted by a voice and rapping on the door. "Your bags, Mrs. Jorgenson."

I jumped off the bed and opened the door. "Oh, thank you, Mr. White. Very kind of you." Placing the three cases on the printed linoleum floor, he smiled and stood there, waiting.

"I guess I better get to unpacking a few things."

"Yes, lots to unpack. Would you like me to open the window?"

"Certainly, thanks."

"Will that be it, madam?"

"Yes, thanks again."

What was he waiting for? Money, a tip? I'd never tipped before. What was appropriate? I fumbled for my pocketbook. "Here you go." I handed him a quarter, which he looked at with disdain. I anxiously searched through my coin purse, handing him another coin, plastering on my best smile. "Mr. White, your service is simply impeccable. Good day."

Back on the bed, I leaned against the rickety headboard, put my damp handkerchief

across my forehead, sighed and decided to open the newspaper I'd swiped downstairs. Hmm, where to look for a job? Flipping through the pages, I was distracted as my eye spotted an ad for a movie playing downtown: *The Gold Rush*, starring Charles Chaplin. Well, why not? For an aspiring actress needing to study acting skills, a movie theater might be the ideal place to apply for work; something to tide me over until I was discovered. Job-search completed, it was time for my nap.

MARIAH

$\mathcal{U}$nlike his brothers, Sam's love of farming was more than a job; it was all he ever wanted to do. From an early age, he'd always been curious about crop rotations, more effective seed hybrids, and unique plowing techniques. He'd told me about experimenting on his dad's farm, and tinkering with machinery was his child's play. In this regard, he and his father, Alfred Anderson, shared a common passion.

With three-hundred and twenty acres, my future father-in-law owned one of the largest farms in the county, managing it with the help of Sam's three older brothers, all still living at home with their mother, Gerta, and sister, Catherine. Although he was the youngest, Sam was eager to be independent and strike out on his own. With the aid of his father, they convinced a retiring farmer to lease his farm to Sam. Once settling into it, he had managed two successful harvests, and now he only needed his recently graduated wife to join him. Together, we convinced ourselves we'd make a formidable team.

It was late May, 1928. Our wedding was a small, modest affair. For something old, I wore an antique gold locket my mother gave me. For something new, I purchased an impractical but beautiful pair of white satin pumps. For the borrowed, I wore my older sister's wedding dress; the price was right and I loved the simple bias-cut style. And for something blue, I selected a simple blue ribbon to wear around my neck adorned with the gold locket. I thought the bride's good-luck mantra was silly but I wasn't willing to test my luck on this marriage.

I walked down the aisle beaming, staring ahead to Samuel who stood confidently at the altar. I was proud of him looking so handsome in his new and only suit. As I stepped across from him, Sam, in silence, mouthed, "I love you." At that point, any nerves or doubts I was holding on to flew out the church doors. I knew I was making the right choice.

My family attended a country church surrounded by rich green fields of knee-hi corn stalks and the gravestones of family and friends who had passed. We were blessed with a dazzling, crisp, blue-skied day with a slight breeze. Between my family, the Anderson crew, a few of our closest school friends, and essential relatives, our wedding guests filled most of the pews in our Lutheran church.

After the service, everyone filled their stomachs with plates of food contributed by many of those attending, while my uncle took a few photographs of Sam and me, and our families. These formal family photos were rare, and weddings often provided the few times everybody could gather together in front of someone who owned a camera. Sam's parents, Alfred and Gerta, seemed a bit in shock after the ceremony, keeping to themselves. Their youngest and seemingly favorite son was flying from their tightly woven nest.

His mother, Gerta, gathered her brood. "Sam, get your brothers. Alfred, gather round. You too, Catherine. Let's get a family photo." She pulled her husband, crew of four sons and daughter together, but seemed to purposely exclude the new bride, while I stood off to the side waiting.

After my uncle shot the picture, his parents began walking away, as Sam spoke up. "Ma, Dad...we didn't get one including Mariah. Come on, let's do one more." Sam pulled me close; we were front and center. His mother, to our left, remained rigid and curt. Later,

Sam quietly said, "Sorry. Mother is kinda like our general; thinks she's the commanding officer. But, thank God, I've gone AWOL."

Luckily, the Anderson farm was eight miles away from our place, so I wouldn't have to look at her disappointed face daily.

As a wedding gift, Sam's parents gave us their old Model A, an exchange which seemed to miff his older brothers. My parents gave us a few dairy cows, not terribly exciting or romantic, but my dad was always the practical one. For our honeymoon, we drove the Ford thirty-five miles to the larger Minnesota town of Albert Lea where we checked into a downtown hotel for two days.

It was a weekend I'd never forget. It was the first time either of us had stayed at a hotel. It was just a simple room, with a springy double bed, a desk and chair, and a bathroom down the hall. But it was our room and our bed. We had made love before, a few rushed and secretive times in the backseat of the car, but it always felt off, like something special was missing. Now we had the luxury of lying in a comfortable double bed in private, exploring each other's bodies for hours.

As the sun came up through our hotel window, I looked over at Sam who was awake and smiling, his head propped up above two pillows. I asked, "So, after almost four years of waiting, was it worth it?"

He grabbed and kissed my hand, "So worth it. You're perfect. All I ever wanted." From my calendar calculations, our family was started that day, and the twins came tumbling out nine months later.

NANETTE

The sound of traffic woke me with a start. A breeze blew through the short dingy curtains hanging at my hotel window. I stretched, feeling exhausted, not wanting to move. Pushing myself out of bed, I stared through the window looking out onto Front Street. The commotion seemed to be caused by cars honking at an ice-delivery wagon blocking their way. I checked my watch; it was already three o'clock and my stomach was shooting out hunger pains.

I passed a tiny round mirror hung above the dresser, and my reflection caught me by surprise. Disaster; my hair and face looked terrible. Makeup smudged, with more lipstick on my pillow than lips, and my waved bob in disarray. I opened one of my bags, pulling out a hairbrush, lipstick, powder and rouge. I needed to impress for my first possible job interview. Having slept in it, my suit was wrinkled, but it would have to do.

Walking quickly down the stairs in my new heels, I saw Mr. White checking in another guest, and hoped to exit before he noticed me. As I grabbed the front door, I heard his annoying voice. "Mrs. Jorgenson, just *now* leaving to meet your husband?

"Yes, I fell asleep. He's going to be upset; need to hurry. Will we see you this evening?"

"No, I get off at five. Good day to you." That was convenient, no elaborate lie needed for Mr. White until tomorrow.

The honking cars were now slowly going around the large ice wagon, and I saw a young delivery man walking back carrying empty ice tongs. I scurried up the sidewalk to ask him directions. It had worked for me this morning, maybe I'd get lucky again.

"Sir… sir? Any chance you know how to get to the Mankato Movie House?"

Ignoring me, he climbed onto the bench of the wagon, then pulled off a kerchief tied around his neck and wiped his tanned face. I stepped directly across from him, and asked again more loudly. "Mankato Movie House? Do you know how far?"

He stared at my face, smiled and leaned over, reaching for my hand. In a strong accent, he said. "I take." Was that an Italian accent? Whatever it was, I liked the sound.

"Well, thank you. Is it close?"

He nodded, clicked his team of four horses forward and we continued down Front Street. One block down, he stopped in front of a restaurant. Smiling again, he said, "Ice."

He went to the back of the wagon and pulled out a massive block, carrying it through the back door of the restaurant. Then he climbed up again. This continued with three more stops as the ice-man made his deliveries. He said only "ice" as he got down, but then smiled at me each time he came back. I kept sneaking side glances at him as he managed the team of horses. Strong chiseled chin, long nose, with dark curling hair showing below his hat, and biceps that bulged under a rough and soiled cotton shirt. But at the rate of his deliveries, I figured I'd be better off walking to the theater than hitching a ride with my handsome ice-man. The view was good but the conversation was limited.

After his third delivery, I explained, "I'll walk to the theater. In a bit of a hurry." As I turned to step down from the bench, he reached for my arm and said, "I take." Attractive as he was, trying to explain my needs to someone with a vocabulary of 'ice' and 'I take' was frustrating. He continued, making two more stops, finally we arrived at a building with a marque and he said, "Movie" and then pointed at me saying, "Movie star," grinning with a broad smile, as if he'd made a joke. Well, maybe there was more to this delivery man than just big biceps. His vocabulary was expanding.

I looked bashful, casting my eyes down, then pointed to myself. "Me? No, not a movie star. But maybe someday. Thanks for the ride."

As I jumped off the step, I heard, "Tomorrow, I take?"

"Maybe?" I shrugged my shoulders demurely and said, "I'm Nanette. What's your name?"

He pointed to his chest. "Romero."

Romero… it did sound Italian. We didn't have any of those in Green Tree. Dark, mysterious, strong. Very Rudolf-Valentino-like, my favorite exotic movie star.

I waved goodbye and turned toward the glass cubicle in front of the theater. An older gentleman in a burgundy uniform with gold braid was sitting inside selling tickets. I leaned into the opening. "Hello sir. I'm Nanette Jorgenson and I'd like to speak with the manager, please."

"He's inside; but I can't let you inside unless you buy a ticket."

"But I'm here on business. I want to inquire about a position."

"Far as I know, there ain't no jobs here. If you wanna to go inside, you need to buy a ticket."

I was so hungry and I'd already wasted fifty-cents on my tip to Mr. White. I certainly didn't want to pay to see a man about the mere possibility of a job.

"What's the ticket cost?"

"Twenty-five cents, miss."

"So, if I pay twenty-five cents, will the manager see me?"

"Don't know. He might be busy."

"Oh, for heaven's sake. You're running quite a racket here, sir." I dug in my purse and gave him a quarter, and walked through the lobby. Seeing an usher, I used my most authoritative tone and said, "Sir, I need to speak with the manager. It's quite urgent."

"Sure, miss." He pointed to a hallway beyond the concession

stand. "Name's Mr. Grant. Just knock on the door. He should be in there."

I took a deep breath, knocked with exuberance, and heard a high-pitched nasal voice say, "What is it now, Daniel?" I opened the door a few inches, poking my head through.

"Hello, Mr. Grant, it's not Daniel. I'm Nanette Jorgenson. Do you have a couple minutes?"

He looked at his watch as if there was a massive line of people demanding his time. "I suppose. What can I do for you?"

I sat down on a small wooden chair in front of his desk. The office was tiny, not much more than a closet, with a few movie posters tacked on the walls. Grant was a small man with pale skin and reddish thinning hair. Someone who looked like he'd stayed in a dark theater too long.

I punched up my enthusiasm level and began. "My goodness, how lucky you are to work in this fine theater surrounded by all these movie memories."

He was now flipping through the newspaper. "Uh-huh… well, let's get to it. I've got a lot on my plate today."

"It's just that the movies…they're all I dream about, really. And that's why I'm here today, Mr. Grant. I wanted to inquire about a job. I'm new to the city and this was the first place I wanted to apply. Now, some of my best skills include handling money and giving change; I'm also trustworthy, prompt, and *excellent* with customers."

"Well, you're certainly not shy; I'll give you that. Unfortunately, I have no openings. All my staff have been here a while now."

"I see." I sat for a second gathering my thoughts. "But, Mr. Grant, are they *good* at their job? Really good?"

He closed his paper, and ran his hand through his thinning hair. "I believe so, my dear."

"Does your ticket seller get customers excited about the movies you're presenting? The man selling tickets today certainly didn't seem to do that. Does the person at your concession counter always sell a drink *with* your popcorn? Does your usher keep your lobby and theater sparkling clean? If you hire me, Mr. Grant, I promise I will increase your ticket and concession sales. I'm assuming your salary is based on overall business performance?"

"That's certainly none of your business. Anyway, it's *not possible* to hire you. All of our uniforms are designed for men."

I laughed at the minor obstacle. "That's no problem. I can easily make a skirt to go with your jackets. I suggest you try me out at least part-time; you'll be impressed. If you don't see improvements and increases on the days I work, I'll turn in my uniform."

He pulled a clipboard off the wall and studied it. "I do spread myself pretty thin during some of my employees' days off, and then again, people get sick, have emergencies."

"I'm your girl, Mr. Grant; you obviously need some help here with your spotty schedule. What does the position pay?"

He looked around his desk flustered, seemingly confused at the turn the conversation was taking. "Well, I don't rightly know. Let's see… the men make forty-five-cents an hour, so, as a part-time woman, I suppose thirty-five cents?"

"I'll take the job for forty-five cents an hour and not a penny less. Remember, Mr. Grant, that will still be a bargain because I'm going to make *you* more money. Now, let's discuss my schedule."

I left fifteen minutes later, with a burgundy and gold jacket tossed over my shoulder and a job paying a fiercely negotiated forty-cents an hour, which included all the movies I cared to watch and free popcorn. I'd allowed Mr. Grant to bargain me down a nickel just to let him keep his pride. The job started in two days.

Now, time to find some inexpensive food. I was so hungry, and pie sounded especially good if my unsettled stomach would allow me to hold it down. I noticed a small café across the street. Traffic was clear at the moment. I walked quickly across with my eyes on the prize—the café showcased three different pies on a stacked pedestal. With my hungry eyes glued to the window, I accidently stepped into a massive warm pile of horse shit. The nasty scent bloomed around me as I pulled my sticky brown foot and new shoe out of the mess. Continuing across the street, I tried to scrape the excrement off my shoe onto the curb before entering, but the smell grew only stronger. I attempted to step inside, but customers at the front tables turned suddenly towards me, wrinkling their noses, looking disgusted. Backing out, I decided to return to my hotel, clean my shoe and foot, and then try a restaurant closer to where I was staying.

By the time I arrived, it was well past five o'clock so I had no fear of Mr. White being there. The smell of the shoe wasn't as bad as it had been earlier but the scent still lingered. On the front porch, I wrapped the shoe in my handkerchief and hobbled in, walking up-stairs, ignoring the registration desk. A minute after I locked my door, there was loud knocking outside.

"Mrs. Jorgenson?"

Now what? I opened the door a crack. "Yes?"

A young man in white shirt sleeves stood there, clearing his throat, looking nervous. "Mrs. Jorgenson, Mr. White wanted to make sure I checked on you."

"I'm perfectly fine. Thank you for checking." I closed the door, but the knocking resumed. "What is it?" I asked through the closed door.

"Has Mr. Jorgenson arrived?" I opened the door again.

Putting on a sad face, I said, "He's been delayed, unfortunately. Long delays along the line from Chicago, apparently. Hopefully tomorrow. Thanks for asking, though." As I began to close the door, his foot crossed the threshold.

"Well, madam, in that case, I'm going to have to ask you to leave. Mr. White was quite explicit with me that you could only stay here *with* your husband."

Maybe tears? They were usually effective. "I can't believe this. It's just that I'm so exhausted, waiting at that train station for over two hours, and now you're throwing me out?" I collapsed on the bed starting to wail. "Sir, surely you can see this is not my fault and you're tossing me to the street?"

"Sorry ma'am. Rules is rules. Mr. White's the boss."

"This is absurd." I wiped my tears with my jacket sleeve. He wasn't budging, leaning against the door with his arms crossed.

"Alright, it's a tacky little room anyway. Excuse me while I visit the powder room; I expect a full refund and I'll need my bags carried downstairs."

I hobbled to the bathroom taking my shitty shoe with me. Where to now? I'd suddenly hit an impasse.

MARIAH

*T*hey arrived, almost together, in our small drafty farm house.

Jo's wail broke through the tension, quiet, and cold as I envisioned Sam downstairs nervously stubbing out a cigarette, with a long stem of ash clinging to it in the bowl. He only smoked when he was nervous and I could smell the smoke snaking up the stairs. I'm sure he was glancing up the narrow wooden staircase, pensive, waiting for confirmation. Then my baby's wails were replaced by my own as I screamed out in agony once again. The waiting had been going on for hours. Samuel had chores to finish and a barn to close up, but I knew he wouldn't leave while I was upstairs in our bedroom going through this agony.

Then the room turned silent, no shrieking from me for at least a few minutes. I heard his heavy boots climbing the steep stairway to the two bedrooms at the top. He softly rapped on the door and asked, "For God's sake, how are things going in there? I'm at my wit's end waiting."

His sister, Catherine, called out, "All Good. Very busy here. Go tend to your darn cows, why don't you? It may be a while."

After hitting the door in frustration, I heard him sigh and then trudge downstairs. As I counted breaths between the next contractions, I envisioned him in the mud room, putting on his heavy belted coat, wool cap, and thick work gloves. Our cows would be ornery tonight. They didn't like to be kept waiting.

Lying back against the black iron bed, I smiled for a few brief seconds of relief, but that was broken by several waves of excruciating pain. It was hard to focus. I was hot and sticky but the bedroom air was so cold I could see Catherine's and my mother's breath coming out in small puffs. I tried panting away the sharp pains of labor, as my mom instructed. My mother, Renalda, held her new granddaughter, Jo, in a corner wooden chair, while Catherine held my hand and whispered encouragement for one more hard push.

"You can do this, Mariah. You're almost there. Remember, the pain is temporary."

It may have been temporary, but so is life. "I don't know if I can do it again. I've pushed all I can. It's more than I can bear." In anguish I called out, "My God, Ma, how could you ever do this time and again? I never realized...." Then I grabbed a damp cloth on the nightstand, putting it in my mouth as I gritted my teeth. Holding fast to Catherine's hand, I pressed down with one final, excruciating shriek as my second baby, Sarah, made her delayed entrance into the world, joining her eager twin. Even in those first few minutes, Sarah was always a few steps behind Jo.

I shuddered in relief after hours of struggle. We were truly a family now, with two daughters, both perfect to my eye. Jo, towheaded with a light sprinkling of down-like hair, and Sarah, with a thick dark shock of hair. As my mother cut and tied Sarah's cord and then bundled her up, she said, "You rest now, Mariah. You'll soon have double the work, but twice as much to love."

At that moment, an overwhelming sense of maternal duty overruled the fear that had dogged me these last few months. I'd doubted I was up for this herculean task of nurturing and raising a family, but now I felt content, amazed, fatigued, but excited by the challenge. Mother laid the twins on my chest for a moment of exhausted bliss before their weak crying commenced.

Only after cows were milked, pigs fed, and tools put away, did

Sam return to the house. After removing rubber boots and washing in a pan of cold water in the kitchen sink, he walked into the small front parlor. I was lying on the short sofa, covered in a quilt, while my mother and Catherine talked softly, sitting in chairs across from the bright burning embers in the fireplace, each holding one of our beautiful daughters.

Seeing me on the sofa, Sam came directly over and knelt down. "What are you doing down here? Should you be moving so soon?"

"Shhh, you'll wake the babies. I'm fine. Catherine and Ma practically carried me down. It's just too cold upstairs. I was afraid for the babies."

"I'll bring our mattress downstairs."

"So go look!" I whispered. "Go see what we created. They're amazing."

My mother had suspected and suggested twins, but the actual confirmation was still remarkable to Sam.

He grinned widely, "So, two for the price of one! You were right, Renalda. And who do we have here?" Samuel peeked into the blanketed bundle she was holding and scooped up Sarah.

Catherine whispered, "That little dark beauty is Sarah, and I have Jo. Quiet now, Sam. They just went to sleep."

He gingerly picked up Jo as well, holding them both, and grinned down at their tiny sleeping faces. He softly spoke to us, saying, "I'm one lucky man with three beautiful girls to take care of now." It was a lot of responsibility for a young man of nineteen, but Samuel seemed to have been planning for this his entire life.

MARIAH

*I*n late-summer, with the stove heated up, the hot still air in the small kitchen made me yearn for cold winter days. I twisted my long dark hair up in a bun, pulling it off my neck, while sweat dripped down my back. Then I scoffed, knowing in the winter we had to layer up four garments thick just to keep warm inside. Now here I was, wishing for bone-chilling winds to come blowing through. I reminded myself, count your blessings and enjoy the moment.

I checked the clock. It was 2:30, which allowed me about an hour for dinner preparation before my napping twins would wake for their feeding. Because I was still nursing, all tasks needed checking off before Jo and Sarah woke with hungry cries. I quickly rolled out a mound of lefse dough; the potato flatbread helped fill Sam's stomach that was never quite satisfied. Samuel worked so physically hard that he burned through calories like a work-horse. Between meal preparation for him, breastfeeding two demanding babies, and keeping up with my large vegetable garden, I had to squeeze in chores of laundry, dish washing, collecting eggs, and keeping an ever-growing sounder of pigs satisfied. As a fine dust blew through my screens, sweeping often ended up last on my endless to-do list.

I slid my circle of flattened lefse onto a pan on the stove top, and glanced around at my simple life. As tough and demanding as some days were, I knew we were lucky. We had a solid non-leaking roof over our heads, a round pine table with four sturdy chairs surrounding it, and a linoleum floor in a pretty floral pattern which Sam had installed as an early wedding gift. As a young married couple, we understood there was time down the road to accumulate better furniture, maybe a heating system, and in time, hire some household help. Perhaps it wasn't the life I'd dreamed of, but I was with a man I loved fiercely. We had two thriving daughters, and a rented home we thought of as ours.

As the lefse baked, Samuel surprised me, poking his head in the window, as beads of sweat streaked through a layer of dust across his face. "Hey there, how you doing, beautiful?"

I smiled back, pushing strands of hair out of my face. "Not feeling very beautiful; just rushing to get some dinner started."

"Good, and set a few extra places. David and Billy-Boy, from the Thomas farm, are helping me with the pump. OK if I invited them?"

"Don't know what I have to feed the three of you, but I'll find something."

Then, from upstairs, the crying commenced.

THAT EVENING AROUND SEVEN, our neighbors had left and the twins' final feeding was done. Samuel was in his usual spot, sitting in the brown upholstered chair reading his newspaper from the light of an overhead oil lamp. I was bone-tired, sitting in my rocker, and leaned over to set Sarah down on a blanket.

"Well, that's done for the night. These two are wearing me out, Sam."

He looked at me, peeking over his paper. "Well, I hope you're eating enough. I honestly don't know how you do it."

I shrugged at his concern. "I'll be fine, but just look at these two. I sat back and watched, amazed at their eight-month growth. After a few minutes I announced, "Well, I'm putting these little ladies to bed. Want to say good night with me?" I glanced at Sam but his head was already beginning to nod, dozing off after his tiring day. "Never mind," I whispered to the girls, as I climbed up the steep stairway. "Your Daddy worked hard today. I'll say good night for both of us."

I would have to supplement their feeding soon. Like Sam said, I needed to keep up my strength to hold the house together. We were a two-person company, committed to keeping our fragile and fickle business functioning and profitable. Our farm was one-hundred-and-sixty acres of rich blue-black Iowa soil. Lars rented both the acreage and house to us. We planted and harvested the crops, with fifty percent of the profits going back to Lars. Any improvements we added to outlying buildings and livestock were our responsibility, but we also got to keep those profits. The few dollars our egg and dairy money earned each week was precious and used as credit toward other needed staples. The occasional slaughtered swine or cow was also a big boost to our monthly earnings, and kept us fed with a steady supply of smoked meat.

I assumed, one day, we'd buy the farm, but for now we scrimped by. Married for less than two years, Sam and I had already worked through several challenges. After learning how to balance our books, I'd learned so much about the perils and success of a farmer's tenuous budget.

Although we both had extended family throughout the county, there were some days I felt so alone, as if it were Sam and I against the world and all it could throw at us. With no phone and miles between family members, it could feel isolating. I still thought about what it might be like living in a bigger city, working independently, but I knew those thoughts were now only silly dreams. I was a fully committed wife and mother and there was no going back.

After putting the girls down for the night, I came downstairs and saw Sam awake again, checking the sports page. "They went right to sleep, thank goodness. Let's see if I can find some music."

Sam nodded. "Sounds good."

Like most farms in the area, we had no electricity, but Sam had recently purchased a large battery-operated radio for fifty-five dollars on credit. I admonished him for his reckless spending but reveled in this connection to the world. Both he and I would dial through the static most evenings, eventually tuning into programs broadcast primarily from Des Moines or Minneapolis. Our new prized possession was placed on a square table between my wooden rocker and the armchair. Samuel often dialed into baseball games and I loved listening to the comedy shows like *Fibber Magee and Molly*. In the evening, as the darkness of the surrounding acreage closed in around us, we'd put tasks to the side briefly, as we tuned in, imagining the faces of entertainers we listened to each night.

After an hour, Samuel stood up and stretched, picked up a lantern and said, "Well, that bathroom isn't going to build itself. I'll get a little more framing done before I go to bed." The indoor bathroom, a rarity among farms, was going to be another of his generous gifts for me. We were building it as an extension off the mud room in the back. I got up reluctantly and sighed. "I'll help. It'll be so worth it in the end." We joined in together for one more hour of labor.

By October, the last of the preserves had been squirreled away in the cellar, our corn harvest had been excellent, and my garden was sputtering out the last of the fall produce. Our newest joy was our completed bathroom, with water piped in from our windmill tank. The simple room, with tub and toilet, was glorious and the envy of most of our neighbors, still using outhouses. Sam had purchased the needed tools, lumber and supplies from his uncle's hardware store and was paying him back in small monthly installments. I allowed myself a weekly guilty pleasure, luxuriating in a hot Friday evening bath, as Samuel looked after the girls.

Tuesday evening, while I was shutting windows in the front room, Sam said, "Special news, Mariah. Best listen for a minute." A news report was interrupting the *Amos 'n Andy* show. Static crackled through the room, followed by beeps, then the deep and serious voice of a newscaster came through clearly.

"We interrupt this program to report today's dramatic market sell-off on Wall Street in New York, with stock prices tumbling to record lows after several years of unprecedented highs with frenzied trading. Thousands of Americans, from wealthy tycoons to poor widows, have lost their savings, and today, eleven high-flying financiers committed suicide, reacting to the downward spiral of the market." The announcer went on for several more minutes relaying the shocking news, calling it, 'Black Tuesday.'

"Oh my God, Sam. That's devastating. I had no idea the stock markets were so unstable. And those poor men…jumping out of windows. Can you imagine feeling so desperate? And to think, I used to dream about moving to Manhattan."

He shook his head, remaining silent for a few seconds. "Sounds terrible. Shocking news. But keep in mind, Mariah, we're in farming. It's necessary, steady work. Be thankful we'll be safe from all that big-city banking business."

I naively nodded my head in agreement.

Made in the USA
Monee, IL
30 September 2024

66850531R00226